AFTER HASTINGS

Steven H Silver

After Hastings Copyright © 2020 by Steven H Silver. All Rights Reserved.

All rights reserved. No part of this book may be reproduced in any form or by any electronic or mechanical means including information storage and retrieval systems, without permission in writing from the author. The only exception is by a reviewer, who may quote short excerpts in a review.
1632, Inc. and Eric Flint's Ring of Fire Press handle Digital Rights Management simply we trust the **Honor** of our readers.

Cover designed by Laura Givens

This book is a work of fiction. Names, characters, places, and incidents either are products of the author's imagination or are used fictitiously. Any resemblance to actual persons, living or dead, events, or locales is entirely coincidental.

Steven H Silver
Visit my website at https://www.sfsite.com/~silverag/

Printed in the United States of America

First Printing: July 2020
1632, Inc and Eric Flint's Ring of Fire Press

eBook ISBN-13 978-1-948818-93-3
Trade Paperback ISBN-13 978-1-948818-94-0

AFTER HASTINGS

CONTENTS

BOOK I: Grievances 1
   Chapter I 2
   Chapter II 8
   Chapter III 16
   Chapter IV 20
   Chapter V 21
   Chapter VI 23
   Chapter VII 27
   Chapter VIII 30
   Chapter IX 32
   Chapter X 33
   Chapter XI 36
   Chapter XII 40
   Chapter XIII 42
   Chapter XIV 44
   Chapter XV 46
   Chapter XVI 48
   Chapter XVII 51

BOOK II: Reactions 55
   Chapter I 55
   Chapter II 61
   Chapter III 65
   Chapter IV 68

Chapter V 70
Chapter VI 74
Chapter VII 77
Chapter VIII 79
Chapter IX 83
Chapter X 88
Chapter XI 91
Chapter XII 95

BOOK III: Alliances 101
Chapter I 101
Chapter II 112
Chapter III 118
Chapter IV 120
Chapter V 125
Chapter VI 128
Chapter VII 131
Chapter VIII 136
Chapter IX 140
Chapter X 149
Chapter XI 154

BOOK IV: Rebellion 163
Chapter I 164
Chapter II 167
Chapter III 174
Chapter IV 178
Chapter V 184
Chapter VI 190
Chapter VII 195
Chapter VIII 199
Chapter IX 201
Chapter X 203

Chapter XI 207
Chapter XII 209
Chapter XIII 210
Chapter XIV 210
Chapter XV 211
Chapter XVI 212
Chapter XVII 213
Chapter XVIII 215
Chapter XIX 216
Chapter XX 217
Chapter XXI 219

BOOK V: Interlude 221

Chapter I 221
Chapter II 224
Chapter III 225
Chapter IV 226
Chapter V 234
Chapter VI 237
Chapter VII 246
Chapter VIII 249
Chapter IX 253
Chapter X 256
Chapter XI 258
Chapter XII 261
Chapter XIII 266
Chapter XIV 267
Chapter XV 272
Chapter XVI 274

BOOK VI: War 281

Chapter I 282
Chapter II 284

Chapter III	292
Chapter IV	297
Chapter V	301
Chapter VI	302
Chapter VII	305
Chapter VIII	306
Chapter IX	306
Chapter X	307
Chapter XI	308
Chapters XII	308
Chapter XIII	309
Chapter XIV	310
Chapter XV	310
Chapter XVI	311
Chapter XVII	312
Chapter XVIII	312
Chapter XIX	313
Chapter XX	314
Chapter XXI	315
Chapter XXII	316
Chapter XXIII	318
Chapter XXIV	319
Chapter XXV	320
Chapter XXVI	321
Chapter XXVII	325
Chapter XXVIII	329
Chapter XXIX	333
Chapter XXX	335

AFTER HASTINGS

To Kate and Pat, who were there at the beginning
To Robin and Melanie, who weren't
And, as always, to Elaine, who was there throughout

Steven H Silver

Steven H Silver

AFTER HASTINGS

BOOK I: GRIEVANCES

1066 . . . Then came William, eorl of Normandy, into Pevensey on Michaelmas eve, and as soon as they were prepared, they built a stronghold at the town of Hastings. This was made known to king Harold; he gathered a great army and came against them at the ancient apple tree. William came upon them unawares, before they had gathered; the king, nevertheless, fought very hard against with those men who would stay with him, and there were many killed on both sides. The king put the invaders to rout, slaying many thousands of Franks. Eorl William's Bretons turned against their master and helped the king when they saw the battle turn. Although eorl William escaped the field, he was sorely defeated and many of his men lay now in six feet of English arable.

—THE ANGLO-SAXON CHRONICLE

CHAPTER I

Cold January winds whipped around the palace at Winchester, howling as they moved over and through holes and crevices in the massive structure. Inside, Harold relaxed in front of a blazing fire, listened to the otherworldly howls, and breathed a sigh of relief. He was finally putting his realm back into order after the invasions of the previous year. Hardraada lay in a mass grave with Harold's traitorous brother, Tostig, and the dead of his army, the only land which he was able to claim after his raid in the North. William the Bastard sat at his capital, Rouen, too weakened after his defeat at Hastings to pose any sort of threat to England for many years to come. Harold had already replaced the earls who had been killed at Stamford and Senlac Field in Hastings with his own men. Following his reconciliation with his final continental enemy, Harold and England could look forward to a time of peace which would be reminiscent of the reign of Cnut in the early years of the century.

A knock on the door interrupted Harold's thoughts. The king put his goblet of mead down on the table next to his chair and glanced at his friend, Aethelwine. Aethelwine motioned for a slave to open the door and shifted his leg closer to the fire. He had suffered a leg wound at Hastings, and although it had healed properly, the cold weather tended to exacerbate his condition.

The slave opened the door to reveal one of the palace pages. The young boy, it took Harold a few moments to come up with the name Eadwine, bowed quickly to the king and Aethelwine, before entering the room when Harold nodded in his direction.

"The papal legate, Hildebrand, has arrived in Winchester and requests an audience with you at your earliest convenience."

AFTER HASTINGS

"Already! Damn, he made good time from Dover." Harold scowled at Aethelwine before turning back to the messenger. "Has His Holiness finally agreed to recognize my right to rule the English?" Harold asked, perhaps a bit too sharply.

The page showed no reaction to the king's surliness. By now, most of the king's entourage knew that Harold had no love for the pope, who, three months after William was soundly defeated, still refused to drop his backing of the Frenchman.

"I could not say. The legate merely sent a message saying he was here and requested an audience with you."

Harold turned to Aethelwine, who had returned to his seat across the table. "Do we wish to have the papal legate interrupt our evening of relaxation?"

"I would imagine that this Hildebrand would wish to rest himself after the long journey from Rome. I hardly want to have some foreigner yammering at me in Italian or Latin tonight."

As Aethelwine finished speaking, the eerie howl of the wind dropped abruptly to punctuate his sentence with a sudden silence. Eadwine looked toward the room's windows and quickly crossed himself. Harold simply ignored the lack of wind and continued, filling the silence with his voice.

"Aethelwine, my friend, you have a good point. We've been relaxing here this evening. All Hildebrand is likely to do is take up some of our time to tell us that His Holiness has come to his senses and wishes to recognize my right to be king in the land which elected me and which I defended from not one, but two invasions. Since he will hardly be in an antagonistic mood, there is no reason we should hurry to see him." Harold turned to face the young page. "Tell the legate that we hope he had a safe and swift journey and we wish him a comfortable and relaxing stay in England. Extend my invitation to Hildebrand to attend my anniversary banquet tomorrow. He can help us revel and, at the same time, keep his priestly eye on us all to make sure we don't overindulge and go against the precepts of the Church." Harold's chuckle held just a touch of scorn. "After you deliver this message to the legate, find my brother and have him join us."

Eadwine quickly bowed his head to Harold and slipped out the door, carefully closing the stout portal behind him. As the iron latch fell into place, the slave lifted a pitcher to refill the king's now empty goblet.

The two men sipped at their drinks in silence for a few minutes as the howl of the wind picked up once again. Finally, Harold stood up and walked to the window. The wind blew his long hair around his face as it created knots which Harold knew would be painful to force out. The cold air caused the king to shiver, but it was also invigorating, and Harold stood by the window for a few more minutes before walking over to the fireplace. Cold and hot formed a nice contrast, he thought, as he warmed his hands and arms.

Turning his back to the fire, he faced Aethelwine, Harold's face betraying only business. "What do we know about this Hildebrand?"

"He is a trusted councilor to Pope Alexander. In some unclear way, Hildebrand was instrumental in Alexander's election. I also understand that he is reform minded and views the church in England and the empire as being horribly corrupt. I've heard rumors that he disagreed with Alexander when the pope sent the papal banner to William when the bastard rode against us last October, although I'm not entirely convinced of that."

At that mention of William's name, Harold felt his blood begin to rise. The Frenchman believed that two promises made to him, one by Edward and one by Harold, although under duress, constituted a rightful claim to the throne of England, despite that the *witanangemot*, the elective council, declared in favor of Harold. William, however, had dropped his claim, something the pope had so far refused to do. Harold calmed himself. With the pope's acquiescence, the last of Harold's foreign enemies will have accepted his claim to the English throne.

"Assuming we are correct and the pope has finally agreed to recognize us, how far do you think we'll be able to push Hildebrand?"

AFTER HASTINGS

"I didn't say he was favorable to you, merely that I had heard he disagreed with Alexander over sending the papal banner to William, not William's right to England. From everything I've heard, Hildebrand is canny and won't be willing to give you anything he can avoid."

"Will I be able to threaten Hildebrand into making concessions?"

"Again, what I know of the man is only through hearsay, but I don't think so. Alexander hasn't had a rival since Honorius was anathematized two years ago. Even the Germans dropped him after 1065. If you threaten to support him instead of Alexander, the only company you'll have is the archbishop of Canterbury, and I hardly think Hildebrand will take that threat seriously enough to make even a few small concessions."

Harold nodded, "You're right. I suppose the pope's recognition will be enough to content me this Twelfth Night."

As Harold and Aethelwine drank from their goblets, a sharp rapping on the door cut through the whistling howl of the wind. The slave opened the door to reveal Leofwine, Harold's brother.

Leofwine was a tall man for a Saxon, and let his hair grow long in the back. His chin was beardless, in the style currently worn by the English, but he sported a neatly trimmed moustache over his lip. His deep blue eyes tended to draw the attention of everyone, no matter where he went.

Leofwine took long strides across the room to help himself to some mead and pulled a chair close to the fire. He dropped into the chair, took a long drink of mead and turned to his brother. Despite sitting by the fire, Leofwine retained the cloak he wore over his regular clothing. "Damn this cold weather. It's bad enough with the cold and damp in the spring and autumn, but these English winters are made by the devil himself."

Unlike Harold, who loved the cold and damp of his kingdom, Leofwine longed for a warmth which never came to England. Already, the two brothers had discussed the possibility of Leofwine making a pilgrimage to Jerusalem once Harold was secure on the throne, possibly even stopping to visit the pope in Italy as Harold's representative. Harold knew that Leofwine was already making plans to leave in the late spring.

Although Leofwine had little, if any, call for religion, Harold knew his brother saw the pilgrimage as a means of escaping England's harsh environment for the warmer, drier climate of the Holy Land.

"Come, my brother, your blood is just thin." Although they hadn't been particularly close before Harold became king, they had learned to be friends in the aftermath of Hastings. At one time, they had only been two among six brothers. Now, three of their brothers lay dead and Wulfnoth, the remaining, youngest brother, was either dead or a prisoner of William of Normandy. Their ability to joke together had not come easily, but now that they had found it, they both relished having a surviving, and loyal, brother.

"My blood may be thin, but at least it is all still inside my body. To surviving!" Leofwine raised his goblet and emptied the golden mead into his throat. Instead of rising from his chair, Leofwine hooked his foot around the leg of the table and dragged it across to where he sat by the fire. When it was almost in his reach, Harold leapt up from his chair and grabbed the pitcher of mead from the tabletop to refill his own and Aethelwine's goblets. From the heft of the pitcher when Harold handed it to Leofwine, the earl could tell that he was left with only the dregs.

"BOY!" Leofwine's deep bass voice drowned out the howl of the wind and the slave jumped to his side. "Fetch us more mead."

The boy hurried from the room. Leofwine allowed a small smile to form on his mouth before he turned to Harold. "Now, what was so important you had to drag me away from my comfortable fire so I could be blessed by your comfortable fire? Aethelwine is here, so it isn't just a lack of company."

Harold walked back to where Leofwine sat and handed his brother his own filled goblet. "We've received word that the papal legate, Hildebrand, has arrived at Winchester this evening."

"Already! He only landed at Dover a few days ago. He must have had fast horses, and even then he couldn't have dawdled."

AFTER HASTINGS

"How he did it is immaterial. The point is, he is here already. I've sent word that he shall attend tomorrow's celebration."

"That will certainly put a cap on your anniversary. Having the pope, himself, recognize you as king, as he should have done last Epiphany." Leofwine's smile suddenly flagged. "Who else knows Hildebrand is here?"

"As far as I know, just the three of us, Hildebrand and his retinue, any of the servants who have taken care of the legate's baggage, the townspeople who are billeting the group, anyone the servants have gossiped with, and anyone else in Winchester I imagine. Leofwine, this isn't exactly the sort of thing we can keep secret."

"No, I suppose not, but I would prefer not to advertise anything until after the legate has announced the pope's recognition."

Aethelwine spoke for the first time since Leofwine had entered the room. "Perhaps we can arrange for Hildebrand and his retinue to be put in some empty apartments here in the castle. Although everyone will know they are here, they won't be parading around Winchester to remind everyone of the fact."

"An excellent suggestion!" Leofwine banged his goblet down on the table, splashing mead across the tabletop as well as his arm. "At the same time as it keeps Hildebrand from the public eye, it will demonstrate the proper honor to the legate and the pope."

"See that it is done."

Leofwine walked to the door and opened it to find the slave standing in front of it with a large pitcher of mead. While the slave placed the pitcher on the table, Harold bellowed for Eadwine to get his steward. When the man arrived, Harold told him to find Hildebrand a place within the castle and arrange to move the legate and his entourage into the keep immediately. Turning back to his brother and Aethelwine, Harold raised the pitcher in a toast. "And now to finalize tomorrow's celebrations."

CHAPTER II

Harold's banquet hall had been decked out in red and gold for the event. Large tapestries hung from the walls, depicting the three Magi presenting the gifts of gold, frankincense, and myrrh to the infant Christ. Interspersed with these were carved and painted wooden images of the great English saints: Edmund the Martyr, his body pierced with innumerable arrows; Alban, whose head lay on the ground while his executioner's eyes fell from his head; and Oswald of Northumbria, raising his ever-youthful hand against the pagan forces of Paenda.

The sounds of conversation mixed with music and song as small bands of minstrels made their way around the vast hall. Men and women in colorful robes also wandered around the tables, trying to find others who could be of some service to them. The king sat at his table, raised on a dais above the rest of the hall, permitting his guests to come and congratulate him on the end of his troublesome first year as monarch of England. Every now and again, Harold caught sight of the queen, Edith, circulating among the crowd, not seeming to care for her husband's party. The queen seemed to spend most of her time on the arm of Earl Morkere, her brother. Harold didn't mind the queen's inattentiveness. She had served her purpose in bringing about secure relations with Morkere and the North. Besides, Harold still had his mistress, Ealdgytha Svannehals, when he required a more amorous relationship.

One long table sat empty, awaiting the arrival of Hildebrand and his entourage. The legate had responded to his invitation by indicating he desired to arrive after the banquet had started. Harold had thought it odd, but figured Hildebrand wanted to make a big entrance. No matter how much the Church preached humility, its prelates always wanted more aggrandizement.

When the steward rang a bell, the nobles and clergymen moved to find their way back to their seats. Before the last of them sat down, servers were already entering the Great Hall, bearing huge platters of roast meats, pies, and vegetables. The smell of fennel and aniseed filled the hall, mixed with the ever-present smell of the noblemen. Before the trays were brought to the tables, the servants paraded them past first the steward and then the king, to gain approval.

As the guests were served, they fell on their meals, without waiting for anyone else to have food before they began eating. Although conversation had practically ceased with the arrival of the food, it was replaced by the din of the assembled noblemen cutting and chewing their food. At one end of the hall, all the minstrels had assembled and began to work together fill the hall with music. In this they were aided by the shape of the stone walls and ceiling, the hanging tapestries only slightly damping the music.

At the head table, the king carefully carved strips of meat and, spearing them with the tip of his knife, fastidiously raised them to his lips. To his right, Leofwine had cut his meat into cubes and was busy popping them into his mouth with greasy fingers, subsequently wiped on his tunic. Occasionally one of the brothers would mutter something to the other, frequently a snide comment about one of Harold's guests. Their conversation was trivial in all matters, never once touching on Harold's forthcoming meeting with the papal emissary.

The banquet had been underway just long enough for the main course to be served when the massive doors to the hall were opened. Following a herald's cry, Alexander's ambassador, Hildebrand, entered the hall. The slight man, along with his well dressed entourage, walked directly from the door to Harold's place at the table, positioning themselves in front of the sovereign.

"Milord, permit me to present myself to you. I am Archdeacon Hildebrand, in service to His Holiness Pope Alexander. His Holiness has sent me from Rome to take care of business which has grown out of the unpleasantness with which you were involved a few months ago." The pope's ambassador was a swarthy man with a large nose and dark eyes. His countenance reminded Harold that only a few generations earlier this man's ancestors were said to have been Jews. Since that time, one of his cousins had sat on the seat of Saint Peter and this man was considered by many to be the power behind Alexander. Some even were speaking of him as the next pope.

Harold leaned back in his chair and flashed a smile at Leofwine. The king's brother returned the smile with a quick wink.

Hildebrand paused and waited for the king's permission to continue. Sensing the upcoming victory, Harold waited a few moments before granting the papal legate approval. When Hildebrand seemed on the verge of fidgeting, the king nodded his acquiescence. As the emissary began to speak, his retainers moved closer to him, as if preparing to fend off an attack.

"Pope Alexander wishes it to be known that the person who refers to himself as Harold Godwinsson, sometime known as King Harold of England, second of that name, sits upon the throne which, by right and God's will, belongs to Duke William of Normandy."

With this opening speech, all other sounds in the room ceased. The constant noise of conversation vanished. The sounds of knives cutting and teeth rending halted as every ear tried to hear the words that Hildebrand had uttered. As if realizing he now had the entire room as an audience, Hildebrand continued his message in a quieter voice.

"Said Harold's crimes are numerous. He has conspired to keep the throne from its rightful owner. He has broken his oath to support William of Normandy's claim to the throne of England. He has rejected the arbitration of Pope Alexander. He has supported the irregular appointment of Stigand to the see of Canterbury. Furthermore, until such time as the aforesaid Harold relinquishes any and all claim to the throne of England he shall remain under the ban of excommunication.

"His Holiness also takes this opportunity to reinforce the ban of excommunication which has been pronounced on the person of Stigand, who calls himself archbishop of Canterbury against the wishes of the Holy See, Saint Peter, and Jesus Christ.

AFTER HASTINGS

"Finally, should any person in the realm of England or abroad lay finger on the emissaries of the most holy Pope Alexander, said person shall also be placed under the ban of excommunication, neither able to receive the confession or holy unction, their prayers to God unheard.

"In nomine Patris, Filii, et Spiriti Sanctus."

When the echoes of the archdeacon's voice died away, silence reigned in the banquet hall. Harold, his jaw slack, stared at the cleric. Around the king, his brother and advisors stood agape, wondering what Harold's response to his humiliation might be. The papal party, however, simply turned its back and began to walk from the room. When they had crossed halfway to the large, double oaken doors, Harold regained his composure.

"I am the rightful king of England," his light baritone voice called after the retreating group. "Tell your master that England belongs in Saxon hands, not the grip of the continental bastard. Harold Godwinsson is the rightful king of England. I was crowned by the witanangemot, not the Bastard. I never swore any allegiance to him."

The majority of Harold's speech fell only on the ears of his subjects, for Hildebrand and his entourage had already left the hall to make their way back to the guest quarters which had been set aside for them. On the dais, Leofwine rested a hand on Harold's shoulder and stooped to whisper into his brother's ear.

"Be calm, Harold. The pope just wants to be able to negotiate from a position of power. This excommunication means nothing. Once you make a few concessions to the papacy, Hildebrand will retract the ban and announce Alexander's support of your claim to England instead of the bastard's. You would do the same thing if you were in his position."

Harold rubbed the back of his neck and rose from his chair. He motioned to his brother and Leofwine turned to the stilled crowd. "I apologize, but other business calls my brother's attention. Please, continue your revelry. Harold, the rightful King of England, crowned by Archbishop Ealdred of York, asks that you make merry in his absence."

Leofwine followed the king from the banquet hall and the two men walked from the building which housed the public rooms to Harold's private apartment. Overhead, a half moon lit the night sky. For some reason, it reminded Harold of the star which had appeared in the heavens to presage good fortune for the Saxons and the defeat of their enemies less than a year earlier. The king pulled his cloak tighter around his shoulders in an attempt to ward off the cold as the two brothers hurried in silence the short distance to the private residence.

Inside the main room, a large fire was burning, casting an orange glow around the room. Leofwine stood close to the hearth, extending his hands to the flames. Harold merely shrugged out of his cloak and took a goblet of ale from the slave who poured it. When Leofwine rejected Harold's offer of a drink for himself, the king turned the conversation to his humiliation.

"I had expected, when we defeated the bastard, that the pope would accept my right to the crown as elected by the witanangemot. Instead, he continues to support the foreigner on the basis of Edward's promise, which should carry little weight according to our traditions.

"We have been fighting the French menace ever since Edward started to bring his foreigners here more than fifteen years ago. Before we fought these Frenchmen, we fought their Danish forefathers. For the first time since Aethelred fled the country in front of Svegn, England can be ruled by the Saxons. His Holiness, however, sees us as children who can not rule ourselves but must be looked after by some nanny whose ancestors were no more than bandits when our own predecessors were kings nearly to rival Charlemagne."

Leofwine played with the ends of his moustache as his brother bellowed in his anger. Harold had focused entirely on the pope's attack on the monarchy and failed to think about the other, lesser attack. Leofwine allowed his brother to continue his tirade for a while longer before he tried to calm his brother down.

AFTER HASTINGS

"Harold, put down your drink. It's time for us to talk productively, instead of cursing the pope." Leofwine forced a goblet of mead from the king's hands and continued. "In there, I told you that this is just the pope's bargaining position. He'll make concessions, I assure you. Despite his attack on you, his real concern is the state of the Church in England, which he sees as being different from the Church on the continent, and Stigand. Last year, you demonstrated that you did not particularly like the archbishop of Canterbury when you were crowned by Ealdred.

"I'll send a letter to the pope for you. We'll explain that the Church in England has been following continental practices since the time of the blessed Dunstan, nearly a century past. We can also offer Stigand as a sacrifice."

Harold stared into the half-empty wine goblet. "And after we rid ourselves of Stigand, who will the pope replace him with? I refuse to permit that Frenchman from Auxerre to try to take the seat at Canterbury."

"We can ask that His Holiness find a Saxon to represent him as primate of England. Surely there must be one Saxon cleric who Alexander will trust."

"See to it then." Harold strode through the door to his apartment leaving his brother alone in the room. Leofwine pulled on his cloak and went out into the wintery night to find a clerk who would be able to write the letter to the pope.

Leofwine and the clerk worked on the epistle until the candles had burned low in their holders. Frequently, Leofwine would halt in his dictation to have the clerk read back a portion of the missive. When at last the ink had been sanded dry and the letter could safely be rolled, Leofwine excused the exhausted cleric. With letter in hand, Leofwine went to the apartments of the papal legate.

Hildebrand only kept him waiting a few moments before he agreed to see the earl.

"It is good of you to see me so late. I have brought a letter from my brother to His Holiness. We offer a compromise in hopes that the pope will see fit to lift his ban against my brother." Leofwine handed the vellum to Hildebrand. With a raise of his eyebrow, the legate unrolled the sheet and began to read in a deep voice.

> "From Harold, by grace of God and the consent of the witanangemot of England king of the English, to His Holiness, Lord Alexander, by divine permission Pope, second of that name since Saint Peter, we give greetings and hope all is well.
>
> "For as long as memory serves, the king of the English has been selected by the noblemen of England acting with the guidance of Supreme Counsel. In the present time, these men form the witanangemot, in the past they formed the bretwalda. Such an arrangement has functioned since before the time when your most holy and revered predecessor Gregory sent the saintly Augustine to convert our forefathers from their heathen errors. This saintly Augustine and the holy Gregory blessed the manner in which the Saxons selected our monarch and promised not to interfere, for as the historian Bede tells us, Pope Gregory saw that the Angles had good customs which should be used by Augustine.
>
> "While in recent times, King Edward, who departed this world one year ago, selected a man to succeed him to the crown, such a practice has never been used by the English and goes against all our custom. We beseech you, therefore, to accept the judgment of Pope Gregory and the apostle to the Angles and accept Harold as the rightfully appointed and anointed king of the English.
>
> "Your accusation that the English have turned from the proper path of God is also untrue. Although we followed strange custom when Augustine arrived on our shore, he and his men taught us the proper way of worship. The old ways were put to rest after a meeting held at the monastery of Whitby, and although the English may have lapsed since that time, the holy Dunstan, formerly archbishop of the see of Canterbury, moved to correct the English in all ways and reformed the wayward Church in England.
>
> "To one of your demands, we do acquiesce. We submit that the removal of the irregularly elected archbishop of Canterbury, Stigand, shall occur at such time as a replacement shall be appointed. Since the current difficulties stem from the appointment of a

AFTER HASTINGS

French foreigner to the see of Saint Augustine, we would ask that a native of English soil be nominated and submit these names which we are sure will meet with the approval of the canons of Canterbury. First our cousin Æthelric, who was once before nominated for the archbishopric and whose declension set off the current troubles or second Sihtric, who is currently the abbot of the monastery at Tavistock.
"*We commend this letter to your courier the archdeacon Hildebrand, along with a gift of Peter's pence to demonstrate our desire to remain within the good graces of Your Holiness.*
"† *Haroldus, rex Angliae*"

Hildebrand rolled the letter carefully, wrapping the scroll with a strip of vellum and placing his seal over the seam. One of his attendants carried the vellum to Leofwine to have him add the royal seal next to the papal signature.

"I will see that your offer is made to His Holiness, although I can not promise, or predict, what his words will be."

"Thank you." Leofwine fiddled with his moustache to hide his nervousness. "We can only hope that the pope will agree with our pleas. Now, I bid you good night." Leofwine turned quickly and exited into the chill January air. A light snow had begun to fall and he hurried back to his rooms where, he hoped, a roaring fire would already be waiting for him.

When Leofwine appeared in the banquet hall the next morning, Harold informed him that the papal party had already left for the continent, under royal protection. Leofwine related to Harold the contents of his letter and the two men arranged for the names of Æthelric and Sihtric to be officially sent to Canterbury. Both men knew that Stigand would raise a fuss and that Æthelric was too old to finally assume the duties which had first been offered him fifteen years earlier. Sihtric would be the next archbishop of Canterbury.

CHAPTER III

Harold reached out his hand to touch the peasant's head. Thin wisps of gray hair tickled the palm of the king's hand as a shower of disturbed hair fell to mix in with the general dirt and mud on the floor in front of the king's throne. Harold quietly commanded *"Sana hic homo."* Having received the king's touch and blessing, the man shuffled, with the aid of a royal servant, toward the audience chamber's door.

Aethelwine stood next to Harold for support as the king performed the single duty of kingship he found most disagreeable. King Edward had been able to cure certain diseases with just a touch of his hand and a blessing. According to Leofwine, some of the kings of the French had claimed the same power. Aethelwine had suggested that Harold continue the ritual healing which Edward had started in England. Although Harold had originally balked at the suggestion, he eventually agreed. However, he forced Aethelwine's presence whenever the diseased masses were brought into his proximity.

Each time one of the dirty peasants left, having felt the light touch of Harold's hand on his brow, another, equally filthy, replaced him to receive blessing. Harold found himself thinking that he must rule over the most diseased kingdom in all of Christendom.

"How many more of these wretches must I touch," Harold murmured to Aethelwine in Latin.

"You are past the majority of them. Perhaps another dozen or so."

"Have you been able to ascertain whether this is doing any good. Have any of the blisters and boils vanished since I've been touching the awful things?"

"Just this morning, I received word from a small town in the Danelaw, called Wilavustone, or some such, that a smith who received your touch at Nottingham six months ago was fully recovered and once again as healthy as if he had never been ill. The locals are praising your name for your intervention."

AFTER HASTINGS

"Well, then, all is not lost."

As they spoke, Harold continued to touch the supplicants who took his foreign conversation with Aethelwine to be the blessing they believed he was offering to God and Saint Edward the Martyr. Harold was suddenly jolted back to reality when the last person in line replied to his Latin with a Latin comment of his own.

"*Omnia est perit, meus rex.*"

Harold looked down from the throne and found Stigand standing on the floor before the dais. The archbishop's anger painted his face a crimson red from the base of his neck to the back of his tonsure. The blond fringe of hair which encircled his head stood out, practically white against the deep hue of his skin. Harold shifted on his throne, restlessly, hoping that his page would have enough sense to find Leofwine, who could handle the angry archbishop.

"I have heard vicious rumors that you intend to remove me from the archiepiscopate which I have held for fifteen years. I was canonically elected during the reign of your holy predecessor to my position to replace Robert of Jumièges. He was the criminal and should not have been made the archbishop. The pope, himself, Benedict, the tenth to bear that that name, sent me the *pallium*, which I wear to this day. There is no reason to try to find somebody to replace me, God's representative to England."

Before Harold could say anything, Aethelwine interrupted. "Pope Benedict. I understand he finds his seclusion at Sant'Agnese in Rome to be very quiet. My lord Archbishop, it has been eight years since Benedict renounced the Roman see, and seven years since he was deposed and degraded by a papal synod."

"A mock court led by Pope Benedict's accuser, this very same Hildebrand who is now trying to remove another duly elected and consecrated archbishop. As well as the rightful king of this island."

"The issue here is not the propriety of the king's position, rather the position you are in."

Stigand addressed his response to Harold. "The bishop of Rome does not care for the propriety of things in England. Even your twin defeats over Hardraada and the Bastard could not convince this so-called pope of your right to rule. He only cares that he control everything. He is no more God's representative on Earth than your father was, despite your father's name."

Leofwine appeared, much to Harold's relief. Although the king did not have a problem running the day to day affairs of the kingdom, or even the occasional crisis, Harold found it more and more difficult to stand up to the archbishop. Stigand always knew how to put Harold on the defensive. Whatever could Godwin have seen in the man to place him in the most powerful ecclesiastical position in the kingdom? Of course, Stigand had given Edward many of the same problems that Harold was having with him. The king couldn't help but think that if he had let Stigand crown him instead of breaking tradition to be crowned by the archbishop of York, his relationship with Stigand might be more smooth. Nevertheless, Stigand would be offered to Alexander as the sacrificial lamb so Harold could retain his throne, solving two problems at once.

"Those are harsh words. Do you perhaps have some anti-pope you would like to see on Saint Peter's Throne? I understand Honorius, living in Parma, still entertains the desire to sit in the Vatican. Or perhaps you would like to see your older friend, Benedict, return to his see. How does it feel to know that two of the popes who recognized you are still alive? To which one do you give precedence?" Leofwine smiled a wolf's grin at the archbishop. The king's brother stood, smiling, hoping, and waiting for Stigand to give him the arrow to fire his last shot at the archbishop.

"There is nothing wrong with Honorius's claim to Rome. He was elected and then ousted after a proper election. If any should be called an anti-pope it should be the vulture who had to be installed by the same French troops who tried to invade our country but six months ago."

Leofwine turned his smile, now victorious, toward the assembled earls. "Of course, Stigand champions the cause of the anti-pope of Parma.

AFTER HASTINGS

Was it not by the hands of a previous anti-pope that this 'archbishop' of Canterbury received his own *pallium*?"

"All accepted Benedict as pope until the very same Hildebrand, who declared our king an excommunicate, placed Benedict in prison."

Harold sat back on his throne. Although he couldn't be said to enjoy the wordplay between his brother and the archbishop, he was pleased that his younger brother was strong enough to attack the obstinate primate.

Leofwine turned to glare at the irate churchman. "Benedict's election was as legal as William's claim to the English throne. Furthermore, Alexander's excommunication of you is only the last in a line of five popes who have called a ban upon you," Leofwine smirked maliciously at the archbishop, "or is he the sixth? Once the pope responds to our letter, my brother will be confirmed as the rightful king of England and England will finally be under the guidance of a properly elected archbishop." Leofwine spun away from the now speechless archbishop, in effect dismissing him as finished business and not worthy of Leofwine's continuing attention.

The archbishop's face was a deeper hue of red than Harold had thought possible. The king imagined that he could see the blood throbbing in the primate's temples, his veins a dark purple against the archbishop's vermilion countenance. Two of Stigand's retainers rushed forward to guide the archbishop from the room. Once they passed outside the hall, Harold heard loud shouts from the hall. The king turned to Leofwine and raised an eyebrow in query.

"I took the liberty of arranging for the detainment of the archbishop once I was informed that he had received word of our offer to the pope. I thought that he might cause a problem for you."

Harold paused for a second. Leofwine's actions seemed to push the king past some undefined point, like Caesar crossing the Rubicon on his push to Rome, Harold could no longer turn back. Stigand had been sacrificed to the Papacy and would have to be dealt with. Leofwine's comment comparing Benedict to William worried the king. If Stigand should get free and form an alliance with William. . . . Harold shook the thought from his head. William was a pious enough bastard that he would not wish to endanger his eternal soul by forming an alliance with the outcast clergyman. Still, Stigand would simply have to spend the rest of his life in prison.

CHAPTER IV

Hildebrand sat at the side of the longboat which would ferry him across the channel, watching as the last of his entourage's luggage was loaded by the stevedores. Behind him lay Rome and the Lenten synod called by the Pope. Hildebrand had expected to speak on behalf of the Vallombrosan monks, but Alexander decided his presence was more urgently required in England at Harold's court. Hildebrand didn't like the English king, hadn't liked him when he was an earl, either. The entire Godwin clan struck the archdeacon as being a little too rough, a little too eager to spill blood. Hildebrand had no doubt that the English would never try to institute the Peace of God or the Truce of God, one of the reasons Hildebrand had pressed Alexander to support Duke William.

Duke William had already begun to try to reform the Church in Normandy. The various bishoprics, which had been acting independently of Rouen, were now firmly yoked to the archiepiscopal see, although Hildebrand feared that this new centralization would fracture with William's power broken. Not only was William's political power destroyed, but the man himself seemed to have been broken by the defeat on the field at Hastings only five months earlier. The Duke's fabled ruddy complexion was a wan, pasty white, making his flaming red hair seem even more like fire than Hildebrand presumed it normally would. William's court had done an admirable job in keeping the duke's condition from becoming a well-known fact, but it couldn't stay secret much longer. Hastings had left William a broken man. His wife, Matilda, had confessed to Hildebrand that she didn't expect him to survive for long. His defeat had filled him with anger, at both Harold and his English as well as the Bretons who had committed treason and joined Harold when the French army broke.

As a sudden breeze sprayed a mist of the salty water on Hildebrand, one of his companions, Abbot Lanfranc, approached him. Lanfranc leaned against the side of the longboat and looked down into the blue waters of the channel.

"What are the chances Harold will be willing to accept me as his archbishop?"

Hildebrand turned to look at the abbot. "In all honesty, very little. If you were the only issue at stake, I think there would be a good chance Harold would oust Stigand. There is no love lost between the two men. Stigand particularly dislikes Harold since Canterbury was not given the honor of crowning Harold king. However, His Holiness has made it clear that Harold can not be permitted to remain on the English throne. His Holiness supported William against the English, and as long as England is ruled by Harold, the papacy is weakened. Harold's acceptance of you would only come with his abdication of the monarchy. He won't do that."

CHAPTER V

The light from torches set into the walls mixed with the clear sunlight which streamed through the windows, giving a strange coloration to the room. Edith sat next to a window, allowing the purest sunlight to fall on the embroidery she was doing. Morkere, earl of Northumbria, had commissioned an embroidery to commemorate Harold's accession and his two great victories of the previous year. The queen had agreed to help in the manufacture and was working on a scene which depicted Harold's breakneck ride from Stamford to Hastings. Surrounding the queen were other noblewomen who had agreed to complete the lengthy and intricate design.

Edith only listened to the gossip with half an ear, refrained from taking part in the chatter of her women-in-waiting. Mostly they talked about matters which even they realized were insignificant. Lately, however, much of their talk revolved around the political fate of the kingdom. The pope's demands on King Harold were widely known, and although few knew the actual fate of Stigand, speculation was rife among all levels of the nobility, regardless of gender.

Edith, though, worried about her own problems. Married just over a year, Harold was her second husband, and she loved him no more than the first. In fact, every time she looked at him, the king reminded her of Gruffydd, who had been slain when Harold had tried to invade Wales while Edward was still king. Edith could still remember Harold's face when she first saw him. He had appeared triumphant, standing amid the carnage of the battlefield, a huge smile across his blood-spattered face, as if he took strength from the wounds of the dead and dying. In that moment, even as her ladies-in-waiting commented on the Saxon's bravery, Edith was repulsed by him.

Without a protector since Gruffydd's death, she couldn't stand against Harold when he married her shortly after becoming king in order to strengthen the loyalty of the North. Now Edith found herself working on a gift from her only surviving brother to the man who called himself her husband. The queen couldn't even be proud of her position as the royal consort. For years Harold had been going to the bed of Ealdgytha Svannehals and had not shown any inclination to visit the queen's bed in the future. The queen looked over to where Edward's queen sat, stitching another portion of the fabric. "How alike are we, who were called queen but never had the chance to give our husbands children," she thought.

Suddenly, her reverie was broken by something one of the women, Aelfgyfu, said. Edith listened more closely, trying to find the thread of the discussion.

". . . erheard my husband say they should be arriving any day."

"I wonder what word they bring?"

"I've heard that although that Hildebrand comes, he is not the leader of the group this time. Instead some Italian, Lanfranc, is in charge."

"Hildebrand, Lanfranc. . . . Why do these foreigners give their children such strange names?"

Edith knew that her husband would be aware of the truth behind the rumors which the women were circulating. She found it slightly odd that although her husband was the king, she had to get all her news from her ladies-in-waiting who actually knew their husbands. Looking once again at the queen dowager, Edith wondered about the relationship she had enjoyed with King Edward. He had only been dead for twenty months and already people were talking about him as if he were a saint. Did she see her husband as a saint, or did she agree with her brother, the current king, that Edward was a strange man who had invited the foreign invaders into the kingdom? Edith shook the thought from her head and turned her attention back to the needlework image of her husband, pricking out the thin line of his moustache.

CHAPTER VI

While Edith stitched, Harold sat reading a dispatch from an agent who had seen the papal party at an inn just outside Dover. The agent had ridden nonstop until he reached the king's castle at Winchester to deliver the message. Upon discovering the court had moved to Oxford, the agent had dictated his message to a clerk and arranged for another man to carry the letter to Oxford.

Oxford was a small town of no particular distinction, although its position was central to the southern portion of the kingdom which formed the power base for the Godwinsson clan. A wall surrounded the town, but there was no castle and the royal party was forced to find lodgings at inns and with private citizens. Harold was not happy that he and his advisors were forced to take over a large house near the center of the town. On the second day the royal court was in Oxford, Harold announced that a royal keep would be built on a small hillock overlooking the western edge of the village.

Back inside after surveying the newly selected site, Harold and his closest advisors considered the news brought to them by the messenger. None of the men were happy about being in Oxford. Combined with the dreary weather and the upsetting tone of the letter, the city was almost unbearable. A fact that actually made Harold even more desirous of his new building project since it gave him something to think about besides his difficulties with the Church.

"The pope is holding firm to his position." Morkere sounded resigned to the situation. Even before the messenger had arrived, the northern earl favored settlement with the Church and spoke to that end. Despite the magnificent tapestry Morkere had ordered, Harold knew that the earl held him responsible for the death of his brother. Rather than drawing the two men closer together, Harold's marriage to Edith served to further wedge them apart as the earl viewed the royal marriage more as an ownership proposition than a partnership.

Harold chose to ignore Morkere's pronouncements of doom and turned instead to Leofwine. Harold knew that Leofwine didn't always agree with him, but also that his brother would work for Harold's, and therefore England's, best interest.

"I know what the letter says, but I think it would be the most prudent to wait until we actually have spoken to Hildebrand and Lanfranc before we settle on a course of action." Leofwine rubbed his finger across his moustache. "Your agent may have been mistaken about what he heard. After all, didn't you say that he was in a tavern at the time he came across the papal legate? Seems to me that he might have tipped back a few ales too many before he tried his hand as a spy."

AFTER HASTINGS

Harold shook his head slowly. "No, this is a good man. If he says that he heard Hildebrand invite Lanfranc to see Canterbury before coming to see me, that's what he heard."

"Didn't the report say that they were speaking in a foreign tongue? Couldn't Hildebrand have said something about Canterbury and your fellow only misunderstood him?"

Leofwine was beginning to annoy Harold. The king wished that his younger brother would give him some credit. After all, Harold was elected by the *witanangemot* to lead the country after Edward's death. Surely that should count for something, especially since Leofwine had been a member of the council and championed Harold's cause. Harold turned on his brother, his eyes a smoldering black beneath his light brows. "Do you think me a fool?" The outburst was more an accusation than a question. "My man has a fine education and understands the Latin tongue in which the two clergymen were speaking. Hildebrand is coming with the pope's hand-picked candidate to fill Stigand's position. Granted, that is all we know for sure. We do not know whether he accepted the proposal we placed to him, or if he intends to make good his original threat." At this last, Harold turned to face Morkere who wore an expression of studied indifference. Harold suspected that Morkere would be just as happy with Harold removed, although there was no hard evidence to support this contention.

"The pope is a reasonable man," Leofwine interjected, "We offered him a way out which would allow both parties to save face. There is no reason not to assume that he will accept you offer."

"What you say may have some merit, but the candidate he is bringing with him is either French or Italian, which does not bode well for his acquiescence."

Despite Leofwine's assurances, Harold was still troubled. He had been receiving messages about the pope which he had not been sharing with his brother. However much he tried to ignore the implications of those messages, he was worried by them. According to some merchants living in the English Quarter of Rome, the pope was a harsh man who did not like to be trifled with and was not quick to forgive. According to some of the Saxons, Alexander viewed the removal of Harold as something of a personal vendetta. In fact, the only part of the situation which could be seen as a bonus for Harold was the fact that the pope used Hildebrand as an emissary.

By all accounts, Hildebrand was a fair man, although perhaps occasionally too zealous in his piety. At the same time, an innermost dread seemed to fill Hildebrand, as though he saw an unspeakable horror in the events which had caused the rift between the island and the Apostolic See. Whatever the reason, Harold was now aware that he could use Hildebrand, who would try his hardest to make sure that nothing happened to destroy England's already strained relationship with the papacy.

"I fear that Alexander is not as 'reasonable' as my brother suspects. Very likely, Morkere is correct and His Holiness has elected to make further attempts against this island. However, I also consider that my brother is unerring in his suggestion to wait for Hildebrand's report before confining ourselves to a specific course of action which may prove faulty when the full situation becomes known to us." Harold looked at the faces of his advisors. Leofwine had a smug expression, demonstrating his feeling that he had achieved an important victory over the Northern earl. The expression of resignation on Morkere's face indicated that the Northerner agreed with Leofwine's assessment of the situation between the two men as victor and vanquished.

Desiring to keep some peace between the two men, Harold dismissed his brother, but asked Morkere to remain. Once the echo of Leofwine's footsteps on the wooden floor of the inn had faded into the distance, Harold turned to Morkere.

"The agent who forwarded today's missive is not, of course, the only agent I have in the field. Other servants have sent me notices which lead me to believe that you are correct and Alexander has no desire to reach an accord with me, despite my brother's optimistic desires. I have, therefore, been working on alternative courses of action. To this end, I have sent messengers to the land of the Scots. Although I have arranged for them to send me an emissary, he requires an escort. I would like you to take men to meet with him at Edinburgh and bring him safely to me at Westminster."

Morkere finished off the goblet of ale he held in his hand and stared into the empty chalice before replying to the king. "Of course, milord. Will this man be among the court of King Malcolm, and if not, how am I to recognize him?"

"We have arranged for him to look for a band of Englishmen on the banks of the Forth, just downriver from Arthur's Seat. In order to keep total anonymity, even from you, he will be dressed as a holy man. If you check the banks of the river shortly after noon on any given day, you should recognize him." Harold turned his back on Morkere, dismissing the earl. As the Northerner reached the door, Harold's voice once again filled the room, "Morkere, take enough men to bring this ambassador back safely, but not enough to rile the Scots. I shall see you in Westminster in one month's time." With this, Morkere firmly closed the door behind him.

CHAPTER VII

Although Harold had at first considered making himself difficult for Hildebrand to find, upon later reflection he decided to remain at Oxford until the papal party managed to arrive. Whichever way the negotiations went, he desired to have them finished before he moved on to Westminster to meet once again with Morkere and the representative of the Scots group.

Harold was now sitting on a makeshift throne in the public room of a tavern in Oxford, a haughty Leofwine, who, with Morkere's abrupt disappearance was even more confident of his victory, standing behind the chair. Ten feet in front of the chair, Hildebrand stood, slightly in front of the other Italian, Lanfranc of Pavia. While Hildebrand wore the simple robes of a monk, he was upstaged by Lanfranc, who dressed almost as if he were a member of the fractious Italian nobility.

This meeting had begun poorly when Hildebrand made reference to the missing archbishop. Harold managed to turn the conversation by claiming that Stigand was meeting with Archbishop Ealdred at the latter's see. Although Hildebrand and Lanfranc obviously did not believe Harold's explanation, and may even have heard the truth during their journey from the coast, the men at least chose to pretend to accept Harold's accounting of Stigand's whereabouts.

Unfortunately, the meeting did not improve after this beginning. Hildebrand, continuing to be the spokesman for the party, quickly came to the papal point. Lanfranc was to assume the duties of archbishop of Canterbury immediately. Once in office, his first job would be to see to the reform of the divergent Church in England. Finally, Harold was to relinquish the throne of England to William of Normandy.

As soon as he had finished announcing his terms, which were no different from those which Hildebrand had earlier offered at Winchester, one of the papal servants reached into a bag and pulled out an archbishop's *pallium*, which he promptly placed over Lanfranc's shoulders. Harold now found himself facing this pretender archbishop amid a room of silence. After donning the *pallium*, Lanfranc was obviously waiting for Harold to make some sort of announcement.

"What would I receive if I submit to the pope's demands?" Harold asked Lanfranc, more to gain time than out of any real interest. Harold doubted he could believe anything either Italian said from this point onward.

Lanfranc's English was not as good as Hildebrand's, and his Italian accent was very thick, making many of his words practically unidentifiable. "After your excommunication is lifted and William is crowned at Westminster, His Holiness has agreed to permit you to retain your title as the Earl of Wessex. His Holiness feels he is being particularly lenient in

AFTER HASTINGS

not punishing you for the usurper you are. Furthermore, it is my recommendation that you agree to these terms with the greatest expedience."

Harold sat back on his throne, realizing for the first time that he had been leaning forward, like an over-eager child, hanging on the Italian's every word. Pursing his lips, Harold glanced at his brother, standing next to him. Although Leofwine's face did not betray the anxiety he was feeling, his body practically shouted to Harold. Instead of attacking the papacy and Alexander's ambassadors, as he was about to do, Harold simply requested the opportunity to speak with his advisors.

Lanfranc was pleased with the conciliatory tone in the English king's voice. Hildebrand had reported that Harold would be unmovable. Instead, the king appeared to be ready to give in after a short interview. In this light, the archbishop-elect saw no danger in permitting Harold the interview he had so humbly requested.

Lanfranc and Hildebrand left the throne room, permitting Harold and Leofwine to discuss the issue in private. Aethelwine also moved closer to the throne to offer his own view of the proceedings. Before either of his advisors could say anything to him, the king held up his hand. "I have arranged a meeting to take place in Westminster," Harold announced. "I will not give an answer to these men until after that meeting has taken place."

Both Leofwine and Aethelwine had surprised looks on their faces. Harold was startled that neither had heard anything about his plans, but not particularly displeased. Leofwine recovered from his shock first and asked the obvious question. Harold brushed him off, explaining that there was, as yet, no reason to identify the man with whom he would meet. "Aethelwine, please make it known that the court will leave Oxford the day after tomorrow. That will give us enough time to get to Westminster for my meeting." Harold dismissed the two advisors and lifted a large goblet filled with ale to his lips.

CHAPTER VIII

The next day, the town of Oxford was in an uproar. Servants and courtiers were running all over town, taking care of business which would have to be resolved before they left, provisioning for the journey and packing. Men were finding their mistresses to make last minute farewells. Nevertheless, the hustle and bustle which surrounded Harold's orders did not affect the king himself.

Two other men who were relatively unaffected by the decision to leave, Lanfranc and Hildebrand, sat calmly in a tavern while their servants repacked everything they had brought. Lanfranc took a drink of the English wine which sat before him and made a face. "Barbarians!" he muttered softly so only Hildebrand could hear. "I almost wish Harold does throw me out so I'll be able to live in a place where the wine tastes like wine instead of their colored filth."

Hildebrand had grown accustomed to Lanfranc's outbursts since Hildebrand had met the archbishop at his abbey at Caen. Nothing about this country pleased the archbishop. The wine was undrinkable, the climate too damp and cold, the people surly, the food fatty and inedible. Although Hildebrand regarded himself a patient man, he looked forward to the end of this assignment when he could leave Lanfranc behind. Hildebrand believed that he knew what his next assignment would be. Rumors had filtered down to him that the pope would be sending him back to Constantinople. Alexander knew that Hildebrand had spent time there in the past, however no amount of explanation would make the pontiff believe he had not managed to acquire the language of the Greek world. Hildebrand was not looking forward to being sent to the East. Although warmer than England, the food and language were strange and the people even more aloof. Hildebrand wished that he could just settle in Rome, or even better, in Cluny, where he had once tried to enter the monastery.

AFTER HASTINGS

Hildebrand suddenly realized that in his musing and remembrances he had missed something Lanfranc had said, something more important than a complaint about the food.

"You've had more dealings with this Harold and his family," Lanfranc repeated, "what do you think his position will be, now that we've explained the pope's requirements?"

"Harold is proud, as was his father, Godwin. He'll believe that the pope's demands are open to negotiation and try to reason with us. I would guess that his first gambit will be to offer Stigand as a sacrificial lamb. Stigand seems to have vanished, but I have sources which have described a break between the usurper of the land and the usurper of the see. Harold will also ask that a suitable candidate, other than yourself, fill Stigand's place. Harold will attempt to place his own man in the position, but eventually will realize that you are the only man the pope will accept.

"Harold will eventually accept you and the changes you'll make to the Church in England, although he will not do so with good grace. The only reason he will permit you to become archbishop is that he will believe it is the only way to save his position on the throne. Of course, he is mistaken in this. The pope feels that Harold's victory over William was a personal affront after Alexander blessed the Normans. He feels that Harold has made the papacy appear foolish and will never acquiesce to his monarchy."

Lanfranc was listening carefully to what Hildebrand said. He had no doubt the archdeacon was correct in his interpretation of the king. Once Lanfranc was in control of the Church in England, Hildebrand would begin his work to undermine the monarchy so that Harold would have no choice but to relinquish the throne. Lanfranc, in truth, cared nothing for the secular politics of the situation, but only aimed to reform the Church. If Harold permitted him latitude to bring England's Church in line with the continent, he had no qualms about serving the Anglo-Saxon monarch.

CHAPTER IX

The court had been in Westminster for three days when Morkere came to see Harold. The earl was still dusty from the ride from the North when he walked into the recently finished palace built by Harold's predecessor, Edward. Harold received Morkere in a small antechamber off the king's private sleeping chamber. The small room was decorated with thick tapestries covered in needlework depicting scenes from the early years of Saint Augustine's mission to convert Harold's heathen Anglo-Saxon forebears. Apart from four wooden chairs and a large round table, the room lacked furnishings. In the center of the table sat a decanter of wine and three goblets.

After the servant who had shown Morkere into the room departed, the earl motioned at the table. "Three?" he asked, in a voice still dry from the road, "Are we to be joined by someone?"

Harold shook his head. "Help yourself," the king invited as Morkere lifted the bottle of Italian wine Lanfranc had given him. "There are usually four goblets in here, but the other one is sitting in the other room." Harold sat in a chair next to the narrow window and waited for Morkere to finish his drink.

Morkere gently placed his goblet back on the table and turned to Harold. "I've brought your monk from the Scots." Harold did not detect any irony in the earl's voice. Despite being in the man's company for nearly a week, Morkere still had no idea who his charge was, a situation which suited Harold perfectly.

"I trust that you have made my guest comfortable." The question hardly needed to be asked. Morkere knew the importance Harold placed in this guest and had seen to it that he was provided with a set of luxurious rooms. Even as this meeting was taking place, the mysterious Scot had the chance to clean the dust of the road off his body and replenish himself with a large, private banquet provided by the king's kitchen.

The king already knew about the accommodations which the Scot was enjoying, for he had instructed his steward on the treatment of his guest before Morkere had even neared London. However, Harold allowed Morkere to think that the treatment of his charge was due to his own authority. Nevertheless, Harold would need to see his visitor quickly. "Arrange for our guest to be brought to me sometime before dinner. I would like to discuss some matters with him before I next see Lanfranc and Hildebrand." The king spat out the two foreign names as if he had taken a bite of poisonous food. Morkere realized that the pope must have had Harold up against the wall until the delivery of the silent "monk" who had just ridden down from Edinburgh, although Morkere was unimpressed by the man and had no understanding of how he could effect such a change in the monarch.

CHAPTER X

The dinner which was served that evening was one of the most elaborate feasts Leofwine ever remembered seeing his brother host. It came close to, although it didn't quite surpass, the repast which Harold had held following his defeat of the French at Hastings. Despite the late time the dinner had begun, the hall was illuminated as if it were the middle of a field at noon on Midsummer's Day. Bards and musicians wandered between the long tables, playing their music for all to hear while jugglers and clowns followed, offering a mute accompaniment to the loud revelry which Harold had ensured would echo throughout the hall. Although the party was traditional in many ways, Leofwine couldn't help but think that Harold had broken with the style he had established during the first twenty-one months of his reign.

Harold's guest list also differed from those in the past. In addition to the vast array of courtiers and noblemen who would normally be at one of the king's feasts, Leofwine noted the presence of a large number of clergymen, from nearly all levels of the Church hierarchy and representing all regions of the kingdom. Although Leofwine only knew a few of them, he realized that the clerics he did know, while unfriendly toward Stigand, had no great love for the idea of a foreigner sitting at Canterbury.

Another innovation which Harold had introduced was a small head table. Edith, Morkere, Leofwine, and Harold's other advisors were relegated to the long wooden tables set up throughout the hall. At the head table was room enough only for the king, the two foreign dignitaries, and an empty chair. Before the banquet, Harold had offered no explanation for the extra setting except saying, "Hildebrand's people have a tradition about the sudden arrival of a guest at a banquet. Perhaps their messenger will arrive this night."

Leofwine had been watching Harold closely throughout the evening and realized that the king was more animated and gleeful than he had appeared since his first meeting with Hildebrand when he thought the pope would capitulate. It was obvious to Leofwine that Harold had some sort of plan which he felt would end the stand-off between himself and Rome. Since Morkere had only returned to the king's side this afternoon, he must have something to do with it. Leofwine casually moved from his place to Morkere's table and sat down next to his rival earl.

"I take it your journey to the North was a success," Leofwine said, implying a knowledge which he didn't have. "How are things in your earldom?"

Morkere studied Leofwine's face. Although the Northern earl viewed Harold as his main enemy, he had come to do so in an almost dispassionate manner. The king's brother, however, always seemed to rub Morkere the wrong way and Morkere had taken an instant dislike to him from their first meeting, a dislike which had in no way lessened during their many encounters over the years. "Northumbria is quiet and productive, as it always is. My people have their lands and peace, there is not much else they can desire," Morkere responded warily. Northerners had an implicit distrust of the Southerners who had usurped the powers of the bretwalda and caused most of the political power of England to be focussed in the lands below the Humber.

"I'm sure Harold was glad to hear that you Northerners are not restive but rather accept him. I'm sure that he would hate to think you were allying yourself with the pope against the king's rule."

"Your brother has no question concerning the loyalty of my subjects," Morkere replied in a petulant voice. The Northern earl resolved to spend less time at court. Although he enjoyed being near his sister, the men surrounding Harold were not to his liking, and he didn't enjoy playing their Southern games. He decided to end his conversation with Leofwine and get back to the important business of eating and drinking. "I really am not at liberty to reveal any more of my mission in the North. When your brother wants you to know why I was sent to Northumbria, I'm sure he'll let you know." Morkere turned his back on Leofwine and resumed eating the magnificent feast Harold had arranged for his court.

Spurned, Leofwine chose not to continue his interrogation. Morkere had made it obvious that he was unwilling to tell Leofwine the purpose of his mission in the North. Rather than push for an explanation which would not be forthcoming, Leofwine simply noted Morkere's response for future retribution and moved back to his own table. At his table, a monk, the abbot of Athelney, was presenting his views of the compromise Pope Alexander would offer Harold. The abbot was very careful in his phrasing, as if the pope could hear every word he said. Nevertheless, he was certain that Harold would remain on the throne and Alexander would, with all respect, give way before the English sovereign.

Leofwine chose to ignore the loquacious abbot. The man's ramblings were based on no hard information, but were merely an attempt to ingratiate himself to the nearby king who could, conceivably, overhear the monk's words and give the monastery a rather large gift during the upcoming Easter season. Instead, Leofwine ruminated on the tantalizing clues Morkere had given him. Leofwine quickly realized that Morkere had not said anything, but rather simply agreed with everything.

This realization caused Leofwine to become even more angry with the Northern earl. Morkere had never shown any signs of being devious. In fact, Leofwine often thought Morkere to be the less intelligent of the queen's two brothers. Morkere was demonstrating a wiliness which Leofwine could not believe the earl possessed, or else the earl was simply following the orders of somebody else, perhaps Harold, to keep Leofwine in the dark.

Leofwine stared at his brother, wondering what was happening that was so important that he wouldn't even trust his brother with the information, although he could confide in his Northern brother-in-law. Leofwine glanced quickly at Morkere, seeing him as a traitor who would sell Harold to the pope as easily as he had commissioned the magnificent tapestry celebrating Harold's victory.

CHAPTER XI

Harold sat at the head table watching the colorful pageant which swayed in front of him, lapping at his feet as the waves had dampened the feet of his father's patron, King Cnut, earlier in the century. Harold found himself enjoying his lofty position for the first time in many months. He had the feeling that he finally had his argument with the pope under control and, even if he didn't win his battle tonight, he would at least bring about a climax which would pave the way for a resolution to his dilemma.

Harold looked out at the diners and saw each as a player in some sort of elaborate play he was staging. Morkere sat at his table, practically oblivious to any underlying tension in the room. The earl seemed aware only that he had played a major part in whatever was going to happen, not knowing or caring what purpose his role may have had. Leofwine, running around, trying to discover how the drama ends, seeing plots within plots in even the most innocent of lines. Harold, himself, played the lead, commanding the other characters and ensuring they perform as they ought. Waiting in the wings were Hildebrand, Lanfranc, and the Scottish monk.

Harold was brought from his reverie by a serving steward who whispered in his ear. The two foreigners were waiting outside the door. Harold asked the steward to tell Hildebrand and Lanfranc that they would be admitted shortly. As the steward retreated, Harold crooked his finger at Leofwine.

The royal earl was out of his seat and moving toward the king's table in an instant. Harold knew that Leofwine was driven to distraction by the suspense and had decided to let his brother know that the final act was about to begin. As Leofwine approached, Harold motioned the courtiers around him to give them some privacy and the two men were suddenly surrounded by a circle of calm amidst the turbulent ocean most of the banquet hall resembled.

Harold pulled Leofwine's head so close that the king's moustache tickled the earl's ear as Harold whispered in his ear. A large grin spread across Leofwine's face as Harold told him that the two Italians were about to enter.

As soon as Leofwine arose from next to his brother, the large wooden doors at the end of the hall opened and a papal herald announced Archdeacon Hildebrand and Archbishop Lanfranc. Leofwine glanced down at his brother and noticed that Harold, typically pale, had lost even more color upon the use of Lanfranc's title. At the distance Harold was from the door, the papal emissaries would have been unable to detect the color change. Harold's face resumed its normally grey complexion before the clergymen had walked even halfway to the king's table.

Harold arose and extended a hand to the two men. "Deacon, Abbot, would you join me for dinner. I'm sorry to have begun without you, but I was just told you had arrived." Harold motioned for two places to be set near him at the high table. While the stewards brought out food, Hildebrand and Lanfranc inclined their heads to Harold.

"We thank you for your hospitality." Hildebrand again bowed his head to the king. "May I present the Abbot Lanfranc of Caen, His Holiness's choice to replace the pretender Stigand on the seat of Canterbury."

Harold saw no reason to drag out the exhibition any more than necessary. "You offer to trade an English Stigand for an Italian Lanfranc. If I accept these terms, will His Holiness accept an English king for an English land?"

Hildebrand dissembled, "His Holiness believes that by accepting Lanfranc as archbishop instead of Stigand, you are showing your willingness to permit the reforms the Church is undergoing throughout the rest of Christendom to take place in England. The pope sees Stigand as a barrier to this reform taking place in England."

"England has long been known for the propriety of its Church. Did not the blessed Dunstan and Oswald and the holy Aethelwold take care to write guidance for the English Church?"

"Of course they did, and ever since the Holy Gregory first sent Augustine to these shores, the English Church has had a special place in the heart of the popes. His Holiness wishes for this bond to continue, yet sees a hinderance in the person of Stigand and prays that you will eradicate this barrier and permit Lanfranc to take his rightful place as the head of the English Church."

"If I divorce myself from Stigand, would His Holiness insist on this foreigner, or would he consider a native son of English soil to sit on the *cathedra* at Canterbury?"

"I am afraid that the pope is settled on Lanfranc. In the first place, Lanfranc was Pope Alexander's teacher when His Holiness was at Bec. Furthermore, as you can see by his dress, Lanfranc already wears the *pallium*, indicating his right to hold the position of head of the English Church. As much as you claim your right as head of the English country, so too must Lanfranc be accorded the title of the head of the English Church."

Harold looked at the greying clergyman. Lanfranc had lived many years in Italy and France. He wouldn't live much longer. If Harold accepted him, a new archbishop of Canterbury would soon follow and the whole business, Stigand and Lanfranc, would be ended. Particularly if Alexander would give in on the other issue. Yet all hinged on Harold's remaining King of England. "Very well. It shall be done. Tomorrow I will announce that Lanfranc is the rightful archbishop of Canterbury. He will be invested in his see and, as soon as he renews my coronation, he will be permitted to start on his reformation of the English Church."

Lanfranc and Hildebrand exchanged a satisfied look as Harold ordered food to be placed before the two men. There was no reason they shouldn't allow Harold his perceived victory and neither man really desired the confrontation they knew would erupt the next day. Harold had agreed to the two issues which were necessary, Stigand would be replaced and the English Church would be brought into step with the Roman Church. Lanfranc knew that Hildebrand could accept these two victories and allow Harold his throne. However, Hildebrand had some strange vendetta against the English ruler which Lanfranc did not, and could not, understand. Furthermore, Lanfranc did not believe that Hildebrand's position on the issue was worthy of a Churchman of the legate's stature. Lanfranc kept these thoughts to himself, partly ashamed, but in the knowledge that he needed Hildebrand and the support of Anselm, now Pope Alexander II, who had fallen nearly completely under the control of Hildebrand.

With Harold believing himself victorious and everything under control, the evening continued without incident and Hildebrand and Harold even seemed to get along well together, talking over trivial matters until the torches had burned low in their wall sconces.

CHAPTER XII

Leofwine arrived at Harold's door shortly after the sun came up. Whatever plot Harold had been hatching with Morkere seemed to have been effectively ended by the agreement of the previous evening, but Leofwine still wanted to talk to his brother before the announcement was to be made shortly before midday. A quick, double rap on Harold's door alerted the king that his brother was about to enter, and Leofwine did not wait for an acknowledgement.

Harold sat in his large bed, looking rather wan, the effects of drinking too much the night before. Although Harold didn't suffer from headaches, the morning after frequently left him dry-throated and sounding like a bullfrog with laryngitis. His rasping, croaking voice was difficult to listen to, but Leofwine knew he was working against a time limit.

"Good morning, my royal brother. I would like to have a word with you before Hildebrand gives you your thirty pieces of silver in return for Stigand." Although the words were taunting, Leofwine's tone demonstrated that he was gently ribbing his brother.

Before Leofwine could continue or Harold could formulate a response, a loud knock came on the door. Responding to Harold's motion, Leofwine bade the guest to enter. A moment later, Aethelwine opened the door and approached the king with a large mug of warm, honeyed water. Harold gratefully took the mug from his friend and drank its contents in only a few quick swallows. He cleared his throat and gestured for Leofwine to continue.

"My brother, I would prefer to speak to you alone." Leofwine gestured at Aethelwine. "What I have to say is for your ears alone."

Aethelwine began to turn from the door, but a word from Harold made him stop. "Leofwine, my brother, you are getting to be too suspicious. I know what you came here to say, as does Aethelwine and any other man who knows you. You have come to warn me that Hildebrand is not going to give in as easily as I would like to believe. Instead, he intends to betray me as soon as I make Lanfranc the archbishop of Canterbury."

Leofwine could only nod his head in agreement. Harold was no fool, but rather an able ruler and ept at playing the game of politics, perhaps moreso than Leofwine. In the past year, however, Leofwine had become used to playing the role of chief advisor to his brother and speaking the obvious was a large part of that role. The one time he failed to bring the obvious to Harold's attention would be the one time Harold was blinded by appearances.

"If Hildebrand should try to play me for the fool I think he believes me to be, I have a plan which will make him think again and recognize me as the rightful king of the Angles."

"Hildebrand will never do that. We've been wrong about the situation. Alexander doesn't have particularly strong opinions about who sits on the throne in England as long as reform is made to the Church. Hildebrand is the one who turned the pope against you. He takes your defeat of William personally and will never agree to your right as the monarch of England unless Christ himself came down from Heaven to place the crown on your head. Even then, I'm not sure Hildebrand would accept your rule."

"He will accept my rule." Harold's tone indicated that he was sure of his position. In fact, Leofwine could not remember hearing Harold so sure of himself since late October when William had fled to Normandy and rumor had reached to England that he was too ill and too weakened by internal strife to attempt another crossing of the Channel.

The king turned to Aethelwine. "I think it is time to let my brother in on my plans. Will you please bring Father Colum-cille in? I know that my brother has been wondering about his presence ever since he arrived with Earl Morkere from Scotland."

Leofwine sat in a large wooden chair next to Harold's window to wait for Harold to reveal his plan. However, Harold simply rose from his bed and began to dress while waiting for Aethelwine to escort the Scottish monk into the royal bed chamber.

CHAPTER XIII

Although Lanfranc and Hildebrand were ready long before the midday hour appointed for Lanfranc's recognition as the archbishop of Canterbury, the two men couldn't enter the throne room until they were called for. Lanfranc accepted the delay stoically and merely sat reading a treatise he was writing about the evils of Nicolaitism. Occasionally, his quill would move from inkwell to parchment to cross out a word or phrase and replace it with a better one. Hildebrand, however, reacted as if the delay were a personal affront. He paced across the room from the window to the door and back. His route took him close to Lanfranc's arm and he even jostled the abbot on one pass. Lanfranc finished writing the word "*tolerantiam*" and put his quill aside.

"Hildebrand, Harold isn't keeping us waiting out of spite. We're waiting because we began to prepare too early. He has agreed to make me archbishop of Canterbury and accept the reform of the English Church. It is just a matter of time. Here, let me read some of my treatise to you. Perhaps you'll be able to spot flaws in my logic where I am too close to the issue."

Hildebrand thought for a moment and sat across the table from Lanfranc. "As it will help pass the time and perhaps help you get past a moment of difficulty, read on."

Lanfranc lifted the parchment to catch the light better, and was about to start when a knock sounded on the heavy oaken door. Hildebrand instantly sprang across the room to open the door. A young Anglo-Saxon page stood in front of the portal, his fist raised to knock again. Hildebrand had swung the door open so quickly that the lad didn't have time to arrest his hand's motion before he had rapped on the legate's chest.

Lanfranc let out a small laugh as he told the youth to enter. Awkwardly squeezing between Hildebrand and the door jamb, the boy moved into the room and bowed to both clergymen.

AFTER HASTINGS

"I'm sorry, milord," he said quietly to Hildebrand before he began to recite his message. "I bear a message from the king, Harold. Although he had originally promised your graces an audience at midday, he requests that you have patience. Some important business has arisen with which he must deal before he can speak to you and he begs your tolerance until he has taken care of this concern."

Hildebrand was about to shout at the young boy when Lanfranc cut him off. "If your ruler must attend to other affairs, we understand. Please let us know when we should expect to be ready."

The door was hardly closed behind the boy when Hildebrand let loose a yell for one of his servants from the other room. "Something has gone wrong," the legate said to Lanfranc. "Harold has figured out what I plan to do and he's found a way to circumvent the pope's plans.

"Giovanni, go and try to find out what has happened that this Anglo-Saxon warlord feels he must make us wait." The short Tuscan turned and quickly left the room.

"Hildebrand, of course Harold knows what you plan to do. He probably figured it out before we had even arrived in England. And if he did not figure it out for himself, his brother Leofwine figured it out for him. It doesn't take a genius, or an Italian, to understand politics. I really don't see what Harold can do to thwart you and the pope. He is merely making us wait to take out some of his anger at being impotent against the Holy See."

Hildebrand dropped heavily into his chair. "I suppose you are probably right, but I still think Harold has found some sort of stunt to pull."

A sharp rap sounded on the door. On Lanfranc's admission, the Tuscan, Giovanni, entered and spoke rapidly in Italian, "The English king is meeting with a messenger who just arrived from York. It appears that Ealdred, the archbishop of York, has died."

CHAPTER XIV

Even as Hildebrand and Lanfranc were receiving the news of Ealdred's death, Harold, Leofwine, Aethelwine, and Colum-cille sat in conference in the king's library. Harold had already dismissed the messenger from York who had thanked the king and made his way to the kitchen where royal servants would see that he was fed all he could eat.

"All of you know what I plan to do when Hildebrand deposes me, or excommunicates me, or whatever it is he plans to do. I still want to keep that secret. Especially from the Northerner, Morkere. Despite my marriage to his atrocious sister, Morkere still doesn't entirely trust me, nor I him. Despite his proximity to the Scottish border, he'll balk at the step I intend to take.

"However, I've decided to change my plans slightly. Archbishop Ealdred's death changes the circumstances and we must take that into effect. Father Colum-cille, who has made the long journey down from Scotland, has been helping me by looking into the early days of the Church in England. Father, will you read what you told me earlier?"

Father Colum-cille walked to the only shelf in the king's library and took down one of the twelve books which sat upon the shelf. Carrying the large tome to the table near the window, he placed it carefully on the table and opened the bejeweled cover. Quickly moving through the parchment pages, Colum-cille found his place.

"What I am about to read comes from the historian, the Venerable Bede. He lived in the North when the Heptarchy still ruled England, before Alfred's grandfather united the seven kingdoms. Bede has included a letter from the holy Pope Gregory with instructions to Augustine, who was sent to teach the Kentishmen."

Colum-cille had a good, deep reading voice. Despite his thick Northern accent, the Southern men had little difficulty following what he read.

AFTER HASTINGS

"'The bishop of the town of London must be ever hereafter consecrated of his own synod, and receive the pall of honor of this holy and apostolic see wherein I. . . .' That is Gregory. 'wherein I by the authority of God do now serve. Moreover, we will that you send a bishop unto the city of York, whom you yourself shall think worthy to be appointed; on such condition only that, if the said town with the country about receive the word of God, he himself be authorized to make twelve bishops more and enjoy the honor of metropolitan.'"

Harold interrupted. "What Gregory is saying is that the two archbishoprics in England should be at London and York, not at Canterbury. When Lanfranc is established at Canterbury, I can simply move the archbishopric to London."

"And Alexander will either deny you permission to make the move or he'll arrange to have Lanfranc made archbishop of London instead. Besides, they'll have deposed you long before you can do so," Leofwine looked worried, possibly for the first time Harold could remember since they had faced the Bastard across the now forever bloodied Senlac field at Hastings.

"There's more, my brother. Father, please continue from the next paragraph."

Colum-cille took a few moments to find his place before he could continue. "'Betwixt the bishops of the towns of London and York, let this be the difference hereafter, that he be held highest that is first ordained.'"

Colum-cille closed the tome. "What the Blessed Gregory has said is that Canterbury, or rather London, is not primary to York. Rather the two archbishops should alternate in primacy based upon the seniority of the office holder."

Aethelwine spoke for the first time since the meeting started. "That's all very well, but I fail to see how that helps us."

"It's actually quite simple." Harold put an almost paternal arm around his friend's shoulders. "I'll simply arrange to have Father Colum-cille named archbishop of York before I recognize Lanfranc in his capacity of bishop of Canterbury."

Father Collum-cille turned from the book to the king, "With all due respect, my Church, brought to these islands by the Blessed Columba before Gregory sent Augustine does not recognize bishops and archbishops."

"But the Saxons do recognize these positions as authoritative. If it becomes necessary to revert the English Church back to the way it was before the Synod at Whitby, the only way to do it will be for you to start as an archbishop. Later we can eradicate these Roman offices."

Collum-cille's manner demonstrated even more humility than normal as he quietly muttered, "As you wish."

CHAPTER XV

Nearly three hours had passed since servants brought their midday meal to the two Italian clergymen and their retainers. Lanfranc had spent the time rewriting a treatise on clerical marriage while Hildebrand alternately raged and stewed. Clerical servants were sent on missions throughout the castle and Westminster in attempts to discover what the death of Ealdred would mean to Hildebrand's plans and when Harold would deign to meet with the papal legate and the new archbishop of Canterbury.

The cause of the delay, which none of the Italian spies could ascertain, was the hastily arranged raising of Colum-cille to the vacant archbishopric of York. Harold had summoned all the nobles available to Edward's cathedral at Westminster without giving an explanation. Only after all had assembled and the housecarls had bolted the doors was the congregation informed of the reason for the ceremony.

AFTER HASTINGS

With Harold sitting in the front row of the cathedral, the bishop of London, unaware of how his life would shortly be changed, raised Columcille to the archbishopric.

As the ceremony began, one of Harold's messengers, leading a honor guard of eight housecarls, knocked on the door to the Italian emissaries' chambers and requested that the two Italians accompany them to a meeting with the king.

Lanfranc dropped the stylus he was using and straightened the stack of paper he was working on. Carefully placing them into a leather pouch, he made sure that all his luggage was together. "Alfred, please see to moving my belongings to my new quarters, wherever they might be."

Following the messenger, the two men were led through the dark corridors of the castle and out through a small side door. Horses were being held by a small group of Saxons wearing the king's livery. The messenger motioned for Hildebrand and Lanfranc to mount the provided steeds and the party began to ride through the streets of Westminster to Edward's cathedral.

The journey from Edward's palace in Westminster to the abbey he had built was not far, but the day was warmer than expected for April in England and by the time the party arrived, the Lanfranc and Hildebrand had both drenched their robes in sweat. The party was met by Harold just inside the cathedral doors and offered a change of clothing, provided by the abbot of Westminster.

"We'd be delighted," Lanfranc said before Hildebrand could complain about the austerity of the dress Harold proffered, "These are the proper raiments for a man of the cloth to wear." He took the two plain, reddish-brown robes and grabbed Hildebrand's hand as the abbot led the two men to a room where they could change.

"After the ceremony, I would like to speak to you in private," Harold's words were obviously directed to the papal legate.

Hildebrand raised his free hand in an indication of agreement and continued to allow Lanfranc to drag him after the abbot. Harold watched until the men had vanished and then turned to re-enter the chapel where the waiting assemblage of nobles would witness their second archiepiscopal consecration of the day.

CHAPTER XVI

On one side of a small table in a small antechamber near the Westminster's main chapel, Harold stared at his adversary's dark brown eyes and large nose, and reflected on the fact that they had only met four and a half months earlier. During those brief months, Harold had come to abhor the legate's face. Hildebrand's lower lip stuck out and his upper lip twisted in a perpetual sneer. It reminded Harold of a man who had taken a big bite of a pastry and was rewarded with a bitter juice rather than a sweet filling. Sometime before their first meeting, Hildebrand had taken an intense dislike, not only to Harold, but all of Harold's kinfolk, and quite possibly the entire race of Saxons. Harold could see no other reason why Hildebrand would choose to remain so steadfastly behind William the Bastard and his failed cause.

On the opposite side of the table, Hildebrand maintained the composure of a man who knows that he fights with Christ at his back. Harold was not only an usurper, but also an oathbreaker. Harold had demonstrated his respect for the Church only grudgingly, and had to be made to see, along with Heinrich in the Empire and Philippe in France, that the Church must reign supreme throughout Christendom. If the monarchs felt that they could flaunt the power of the Church, and therefore God, there was no knowing how far they might try to extend their power.

Both men knew that this small, conventional room would see the end of their dispute. When Hildebrand reached for one of the chalices filled with mead which had been left on the table, Harold elected to take the initiative.

"I presume that you will be returning to Rome now that archbishop Lanfranc has replaced Brother Stigand. Please give His Holiness my best regards and my personal assurance that reform of the Church will begin as soon as possible. I will have a scribe write out an epistle for you to carry back to Rome."

Hildebrand placed the goblet down hard, causing some of the golden liquid to run down the side of the gilded cup. "I'm afraid we have some other matters to discuss before I take ship back to the continent." Harold's body tensed as the king wished he could have the support of his brother or Aethelwine in the room, but he and Hildebrand had agreed to a private meeting between just the two of them. "First of all, I understand that Archbishop Ealdred of York has passed to the Lord, *requiescet in pace*." Hildebrand made the sign of a cross, almost as an afterthought. "When I travel to Rome, I would like to bear the name of a candidate whom the monks of York would like to succeed their former master."

"If that is all, I believe that we can call this meeting to an end." Harold felt a sense of relief. It would be no problem to make Hildebrand believe that the monks of Yorkminster had elected Collum-cille to be their new leader. As the king began to rise, however, Hildebrand cleared his throat, freezing Harold in his awkward, half-bent position.

"There is still the matter of the rightful ruler of England." Hildebrand's voice was no colder than at any previous time during their relationship. The lack of any warmth, whatsoever, vitalized Harold and gave him strength.

"The rightful ruler of England sits across this table from you!"

"The rightful ruler of England sits across the Channel from me. The man who sits across the table is an oathbreaker and usurper."

"I was elected by the witanangemot, which is more than can be said for the bastard you support who made me take an oath under duress," Harold calmed himself without giving Hildebrand time to interrupt,

"However, we have gone over all this before and I doubt that I can make you see reason. Therefore, let me give you some further messages to take back to your master in Rome.

"The new archbishop of York is a Scottish priest named Collum-cille." When Hildebrand started to interrupt, Harold waved him aside, "He was consecrated to this position earlier in the day, before Lanfranc. According to the letters sent to England by the holy Pope Gregory, this means that York takes precedence over Canterbury for as long as Collum-cille shall live.

"Collum-cille, rather than Lanfranc, will be in charge of conducting the reform movement in England, although I must tell you that Archbishop Collum-cille leans more toward the Irish form of Christianity and monasticism than the Roman form."

Hildebrand sat back, having decided to let Harold finish his speech before interrupting. Half-listening to Harold, Hildebrand used the opportunity to study the way the Saxon's mind worked for future reference.

"Furthermore, also following the instructions of Pope Gregory, the bishopric of Canterbury will be subservient to the archbishopric of London. As such, Lanfranc won't even have as much power as he would if he were merely the subordinate archbishop." Harold picked up his goblet of wine and raised it in a toast to the papal ambassador.

"From this time forward, the pope and his legates will be regarded in England as would ambassadors from France or the Empire."

Hildebrand waited a few moments to ensure that Harold had finished speaking. When the silence made the case clear, Hildebrand began to speak in a low voice, "I had been warned that you were intelligent and ruthless before I first came to these shores, both by English merchants in Rome and by William at Rouen. Our meetings in January and now in April had led me to much the same conclusion. Now, however, I see that you had fooled all of Christendom. Your words here demonstrate clearly that rather than intelligent, you are a fool. Your own people will never support this last folly you indulge in. With England laid under an Interdict, they will quickly overthrow you in order to save their immortal souls. You have brought about your own defeat, 'king' Harold."

"I don't think you understand the nature of the Saxon people. Nearly one hundred years ago, as the world was nearing the end of the first millennium since the death of the Christ, an Anglo-Saxon abbot, named Aelfric, wrote about the Saxon perception of a king. I would read it to you, but I fear you don't speak Anglo-Saxon. Aelfric said, '. . . after he is consecrated as king, he then has the power over the people, and they are not able to shake his yoke from their necks. . . .'

"Furthermore, since Aelfric wrote those words, England has been ruled by the Danes and then by my brother-in-law, Edward, who tried to inflict French ways on us. The Saxons are tired of rule by outsiders and want an Anglo-Saxon king. I am that king, and they will accept me rather than invite more foreign influence. As for your Interdict, all the sacraments will still be observed in England no matter what the pope, or his emissary, might say. We have Celtic priests from Wales, Scotland, Cornwall, and Ireland to help us revert to the older practices.

"I thank you for this meeting. A safe conduct will be arranged to see you to the coast."

With these words, Harold rose and walked from the room. As he exited the doorway, four housecarls entered to escort Hildebrand back to his chambers, now emptied of Bishop Lanfranc's effects.

CHAPTER XVII

Hildebrand stood in the middle of his room, overseeing the servants who were packing for his return to Rome. Harold had managed to outmaneuver him, causing him to return to Rome and Alexander with less than even the partial victory he held in his grasp only hours earlier.

Alexander would naturally call for a war against the heretical English. Harold could hardly stand up to the might of the Empire and France. Nevertheless, future centuries would always remember Hildebrand as the man who lost England to the heretics. If posterity remembered him at all.

Hildebrand couldn't guess whether Harold was right in his assertion that the English would follow their king. Certainly, the Saxons were a strange people, quite different from the Franks or Italians, and even from the people who lived in their native Saxony. But would they really follow a heretical king against the papacy and the Roman Church?

Hildebrand could only think about the recent break the Byzantine Church had made with the Apostolic See of Rome. Although both sides said they wanted a reconciliation, there was little evidence that such would take place. Of course, the Greek departure from the True Faith was based on strong, but erroneous, beliefs in the nature of the Trinity and other doctrinal issues. The Saxons would be separating from the Church for mere political reasons.

Hildebrand's depressing musings were disrupted by a quiet knocking on the door. A servant who was folding one of Hildebrand's robes draped the fabric over his arm and opened the door. A small, pale-skinned woman entered the room and quickly knelt before Hildebrand, stretching to kiss the legate's ring.

"Your Grace," she began, in a Latin even more strangely accented than that of most of the English, "I've just heard what my husband did." Only with these words did Hildebrand finally placed her as Harold's queen. "I would have you know that many in this land will disapprove of my husband's actions. When the time comes, my brother and I will help you rally these forces against the heresy which threatens to tear this island away from the mother Church."

Bending to kiss Hildebrand's ring once more, Queen Edith quickly rose and left the room before the papal legate had time to say anything more than a quick "thank you."

AFTER HASTINGS

Hildebrand stood for a few moments, staring at the door the queen had just closed. Her words had given him a sudden insight into the events. Harold's apostasy was a test from God, both for the Church and Hildebrand personally. But God had ensured that Hildebrand had the weapons to win this battle. It might take a little time, but in the end, England would return to the safe folds of the Mother Church. Satisfied, Hildebrand turned back to overseeing his servants and preparing to return to the continent and the pleasant surroundings of Rome.

AFTER HASTINGS

BOOK II: REACTIONS

The king summoned a magician from the land of the Scots who arrived and claimed the guise of a Christian monk. Falling under this magus's spell, the king turned his back on the Holy Church in Rome and returned England to the pagan religion of our forebears, although he claimed to be still a Christian. Throughout the land, decent men cursed the king's name for removing the True God from their country. Although many monks remained in England, more followed Hildebrand across the Channel into France, as the Israelites followed Moses from the land of Pharaoh.
—HISTORIA NOVORUM, EADMER OF SENS

CHAPTER I

Lanfranc's arrival at Canterbury was largely unheralded. He wondered if he could be of more service to the pope and the Church by remaining with Harold and trying to stabilize both the religious and political situation, but Hildebrand advised Lanfranc to get to Canterbury as quickly as possible. Even then, Lanfranc had given consideration to staying with the king, but, in a private interview with Harold shortly after Hildebrand's escorted departure, the newly consecrated bishop was practically exiled from the royal court and ordered to attend to his see.

Lanfranc's guide to Canterbury was a Saxon monk named Beornred. Brother Beornred was a burly man with more hair on his arms than most untonsured men had on their heads. Throughout the trip from London to Canterbury, Lanfranc wondered about Beornred, whose body seemed to shout nobleman, aetheling in this island's barbarous tongue, but whose demeanor was peaceful and introverted as befit a monk. More than once, Lanfranc found himself wondering if God had made a mistake and placed a warrior in the body of a monk to balance out Brother Beornred.

Lanfranc was broken out of his reverie by a quiet comment from Brother Beornred, the content of which Lanfranc had completely missed. Looking around, the bishop realized they had topped a hill and could see the city of Canterbury spread out in the distance. The town looked like the normal squalor Lanfranc associated with Saxon villages, but rising above was Christchurch, the traditional home of the archbishops of Canterbury, now demoted to mere bishops.

The architecture of the vast church was strange to Lanfranc's eyes, trained, as they were, on the recent alterations made in France. The stocky towers which formed the transept seemed to be set into the foreshortened nave of the building. They altered the normal cruciform in which churches throughout Christendom were built in a manner which Lanfranc found unpleasant and rather distressing. He reflected that the current schism begun by Harold was long presaged by the strange alterations the English made whenever they had a chance, as evidenced by their churches.

In almost no time, Lanfranc and Beornred had progressed from the small Church of Saint Dunstan at the top of the hill to the road leading to the archbishop's manor of Estursete, perhaps now just a bishop's manor, just across the Stour River from the walls of Canterbury proper.

The manor was a large building dating back nearly two hundred years, set among the open fields which belonged to whomever sat in the episcopal seat of Canterbury. As Lanfranc and Beornred rode along the road, Lanfranc noted that Stigand's steward seemed to take good care of the lands, as was to be expected since they formed a portion of the archbish ... no, the bishop's income. He resolved to keep as much of Stigand's staff as proved feasible.

The two men were met at the door by one of Stigand's slaves. Lanfranc made a mental note to discover whether such men actually were Stigand's or if they belonged to the bishopric.

"Welcome to the Estursete, the home of his lordship, archbishop Stigand. I'm afraid the archbishop is at court with the king, but I see you are a Churchman, and therefore welcome to enjoy the hospitality of this house."

Beornred took it upon himself to act as servant for Lanfranc and spoke to the slave, "We come directly from the court of King Harold with news important to this house and the city of Canterbury. In negotiations with the pope of Rome, Stigand has been removed from his office as archbishop of Canterbury. In his place, Pope Alexander has appointed Lanfranc, formerly of Caen."

The slave blanched upon hearing these words and seemed about to respond. Something about Beornred, whether the authority of his voice or his size, convinced the slave to accept what he had just heard.

"If your lordship will follow me, I will show you to the archbishop's chambers where you can refresh yourself from your long journey."

Stigand's rooms were small and dark, the narrow windows letting in only the minimum amount of light. In order to see the clothing in the archbishop's wardrobe, Lanfranc had to light one of the large candles which were kept in a box near the door.

Stigand's clothing was in keeping with Lanfranc's image of the former, and possibly last, archbishop of Canterbury. Bright colors of imported cloth formed the basis of his wardrobe. Eventually, Lanfranc found a robe which he felt was more suited to the dignity of his office and put it on, slightly surprised to discover how well it fit.

Leaving his room, he found a newly washed Beornred waiting for him. The two men set off for the entry of the manor, en route finding the slave who had let them in.

"I go to convoke the brothers of Christ Church. I have important news for them. I know not when I'll return, but at that time, I will call together all the household of Estursete."

The slave acknowledged these words as he let the bishop and monk out through the front door.

Westgate was located only one hundred paces from the end of the lane leading from the archbishop's manor. When they arrived, they were halted by a city guard, and Lanfranc remained silent while Brother Beornred spoke softly with the watchman. After a few moments, the two clerics were admitted to the city.

The streets of Canterbury confirmed Lanfranc's first impression of the city. The streets were paved in mud, interrupted occasionally by piles of horse excrement and large puddles where the dirt road was too saturated with water to absorb anything more. Garbage was heaped where the natural movement through the streets pushed it against all the buildings. The streets seemed practically lined with horrid beggars who had assumed that they would find more charity in a cathedral town than anywhere else in the kingdom. Lanfranc reflected that if nothing else good came of Harold's rash decision, the beggars would remove themselves from Canterbury.

As Brother Beornred led him through the crowded streets, Lanfranc turned his thoughts inward. He realized that since Harold's announcement at London a few days earlier his own thoughts had turned needlessly cynical and, worse yet, pessimistic. He had a major task ahead of him in trying to return England to the ways of the True Church and he couldn't let his attitude get in the way. He vowed to himself and God not to let the situation depress him.

". . . would like to step inside and refresh himself, I will call the brothers to convocation." Brother Beornred's soft, yet deep voice interrupted Lanfranc's thoughts. Lanfranc looked around, startled to discover that they were in the churchyard, standing in front of a reasonably small building. Lanfranc nodded his head and stepped into the small townhouse which Stigand had kept on the cathedral grounds.

Before Lanfranc closed the door, Beornred spoke again, "I will return for you when they have assembled in the church."

"Very good, Brother Beornred, but do not tell the monks any of what transpired in London. There is much good and more evil in Harold's actions. I wish to tell the brothers in my own way."

Closing the door behind him, Lanfranc was plunged into near darkness, relieved only by the thin rays of light coming through cracks in the shutters which covered over the windows. He moved to open one of the shutters and stumbled over a chair, bruising his calf in the process.

Unlike at Estursete, with the window open, the room was reasonably well lit, and Lanfranc was able to see that it was even more oppressively cramped than he had surmised. Among the clutter, Lanfranc saw few manuscripts or clerical trappings, instead finding himself looking at a room which would not be out of place in a hunting lodge.

While waiting for Beornred to return, Lanfranc began to pick through Stigand's belongings, trying to move everything he wished to be rid of to one side of the room. He had hardly begun to make headway when there was a knock on the door. Lanfranc opened the door to find his companion standing there.

"They await you in the church, my lord."

"And they know it is not Stigand who will be addressing them?"

"Yes, I told them they would be addressed by Lanfranc of Caen. Many of the brothers of Christ Church have heard your name and expressed some excitement that you would be giving them a sermon this day, for so they surmise is the purpose of your visit."

Lanfranc was filled with foreboding. "I fear they will not be nearly so happy to discover why I am really here."

Lanfranc entered the vast, hulking emptiness of the cathedral and began the slow walk to the front. He could practically feel the eyes of the assembled brothers of Canterbury staring at him, but he tried to ignore them all, keeping his eyes focused on the enormous rood-cross which hung in divine splendor over the altar. Upon reaching the pulpit, Lanfranc brushed aside assistance from the abbot to mount the steps and turned to face the convocation.

"My brothers in Christ, I greet you on this glorious day of the Martyrdom of Archbishop Alphege, who walked these very halls in the years following the millennium until he was struck dead by the invading Danes.

"Six months ago, the king of England, Harold, averted another invasion, which might give the blessed Alphege cause to smile. However, the appearance of the Normans on these shores was ordained by God and sanctioned by his emissary Pope Alexander of Rome. William of Normandy was to have brought to these shores a reform of the Church greater than the reform carried out by the blessed Dunstan two centuries ago.

"Yet King Harold thwarted this reform when, through the aid of the treacherous Bretons, he defeated the Normans at Senlac. I tell you that God's will is not so easily thwarted, and today I appear before you to announce that I am the newly appointed archbishop of Canterbury, by the Grace of God, the Order of Pope Alexander, and the agreement of King Harold. Stigand, one-time called archbishop of Canterbury, has been removed from this see."

Despite their discipline, a murmur worked its way through the assembled monks and priests. Lanfranc gave the congregation a few moments to settle before he continued.

"The enemies of God are strong, however, and seek to stop any reform of the Church in this island. Even as I was proclaimed to sit in the ecclesiastical throne of Canterbury, Harold brought in a Scottish monk to sit in the newly vacated seat of York and proclaimed that the archbishopric of York would take the primacy which has always belonged to Canterbury."

Even before the words were out of his mouth, the voices of the monks could be heard, this time not the mere curious murmur which had filled the cavernous cathedral, but an angry buzz. Lanfranc knew that the anger would grow greater as he continued to explain the new ecclesiastical situation in England. Eventually, Lanfranc continued, raising his voice to be heard above the angry grumbling of the monks as he explained first how Harold demoted Canterbury from an archbishopric to a bishopric and finally his break from the Church in Rome entirely.

This last piece of information had the effect of quieting the congregation entirely. Gone from their faces was the anger which had permeated the monks' features. It had been replaced by expressions of fear. Here in their own cathedral, the place they felt most secure from the world, these monks had been told that their very land had been taken from Christ by an agent of the devil himself.

Lanfranc realized that having first antagonized the monks by his very appearance, he would now have to give succor and comfort to men who had just been told that their world was turned upside down.

CHAPTER II

Aethelwine stood on the dock of Dover next to Hildebrand. At the end of the quay, Hildebrand's Italian escort was busy loading the entourage's baggage aboard the ship which would return the papal legate to the continent. Turning to look at the deacon, Aethelwine saw that Hildebrand was gazing intently on the distant shore of France.

"I imagine that you will return to Italy and Alexander to report on the king's conduct."

Hildebrand jerked, torn from his reverie by the sound of Aethelwine's guttural voice. "Yes," he replied, "After a fashion. I intend to visit the court of William in Normandy first. Possibly stop in Paris to see King Philippe before I continue south to Rome. I'll send a messenger on ahead, of course. Alexander must know of Harold's recalcitrance as soon as possible."

"I understand."

Both men lapsed into silence, Hildebrand returning his gaze toward the French coast and Aethelwine looking toward the bustling port of Dover. His attention was drawn to a small, white tavern located about twenty yards away. The sounds of Frankish boatmen singing could be heard coming from the common room.

"May I ask you a personal question?"

Aethelwine was startled by Hildebrand's question. On the entire ride from Westminster, where Harold had appointed Aethelwine to escort the Italians from England, Hildebrand had never initiated a conversation. Turning to look at Hildebrand, Aethelwine slowly nodded his head.

Hildebrand took a few moments to formulate his question to Aethelwine. Aethelwine had almost begun to think there was no question forthcoming when Hildebrand began to speak.

"You've known Harold for many years. What is your opinion of this apostasy into which he intends to lead your entire people?"

Although the inquiry caught Aethelwine off guard, it was not a question which he had completely ignored since Harold announced his intention of returning to the path of Celtic Christianity. Nevertheless, he was loyal to his old friend and didn't wish to betray that trust to the emissary of Harold's enemy.

"Under Harold's Church, the Saxons will still worship Jesus Christ as the savior even if the rites we practice differ from those espoused by the Church in Rome. As our writer, Bede, has told us, this was done in the past. As we can see now, the Church in Constantinople worships Christ in a different manner as well and God has not yet visited his wrath down on that ancient city. As long as we persevere in the worship of the one true

AFTER HASTINGS

God, I believe we'll be all right." Aethelwine hoped that his voice didn't betray the nervousness he was feeling in saying these things to Hildebrand. Although a portion of Aethelwine believed the argument, put forward to him by Harold the night before this journey began, another, more emotional part of him worried that by turning their backs on the Roman Church, Saint Peter would deny the Saxons access into the heavenly realm.

"That is a dangerous argument to advance. For although God has as yet shown little worldly retribution against the schismatic Byzantines, He has not permitted them entry into His Realm since they began their pagan ways.

"I have been to Constantinople and have seen with my own eyes the heathen practices which occur in the city founded by one of the great saints of the Christian faith. It is terribly sad to see them fall into error. Soon, I am sure, we will be able to show them the path of righteousness. Even as we speak, Alexander prepares to send an ambassador to visit the bishop of Constantinople. I only wish we could turn Harold from this heretical path before it is too far begun."

Aethelwine looked at Hildebrand and then turned his attention to the sea. "It is your own fault, really. You backed Harold against the wall. He was willing to give you almost everything: Stigand, Church Reform . . . anything. But you refused to accept, demanding the one thing he could not give up. If you had only agreed to let him remain on his throne and wear the crown of the Saxons, England would not be on this course."

"I'm afraid I could not have done that. William is the one who should sit as king of the Saxons. That is the will of God. We are but men and cannot stand in God's way." Without a further word, or permitting Aethelwine a chance of rebuttal, Hildebrand began to walk down the quay to board his ship to France.

Aethelwine wanted to yell after Hildebrand, but knew that he didn't have the right to call the cleric back. Within moments of his boarding the ship, the vessel put out from the pier and headed toward the channel which separated England from the rest of the world. Aethelwine reflected on how symbolic that narrow strip of water would become once Harold had fully broken England away from the Roman Church.

With a tear in his eye, Aethelwine watched as Hildebrand's boat slowly shrank to nothing as it moved toward the distant French shoreline. When the small white speck of sail finally vanished, Aethelwine dismissed his carls and turned to wander alone.

Although the streets of Dover were relatively straight near the docks, once they moved out of sight from the water they became progressively more circuitous. Aethelwine headed into this maze of streets, passing the whitewashed buildings of the city until he came to an inn which showed no signs of housing any singing Frenchmen. A small placard hanging next to the door proclaimed the tavern to be the White Cliffs, although the chalk cliffs were nowhere to be seen from the establishment.

Inside, the tavern was filled with succulent smoke from the pig which was being rotated on a spit over the central fire pit by a young boy, most likely the son of the innkeep. The pig itself was hardly cooked, since Hildebrand had left early in the day to catch a favorable tide and the pig would not be finished until the innkeep was ready to serve dinner. Aethelwine had no trouble finding an isolated table in the near empty room and was quickly joined by the boy, who had quit turning the pig. Aethelwine placed his order for a mug of mead and sat back to wait.

Although he had not wanted to show his feelings to Hildebrand, Aethelwine felt sure that the papal legate had discerned the true turmoil which was erupting constantly inside Aethelwine's mind. Harold was a good friend, practically a kinsman for all their closeness, but Aethelwine couldn't find it within himself to fully support the bold, and perhaps destructive, move Harold was taking by turning his back on the Church. No matter how good a friend Harold was, nor how loyal Aethelwine wanted to be to his comrade and king, this issue was bigger than life itself. If Aethelwine supported Harold, he could lose his immortal soul.

Although Aethelwine didn't really consider himself a devout, or even a particularly religious, man, there were eternal aspects to be considered concerning Harold's move. The millennium had changed more than two-thirds of a century earlier, yet the occasional monks and preachers were still declaring the world would end soon. Aethelwine had never put much stock in their decrees, but the apparent disintegration of the Church, first via the rift with Constantinople, and now Harold's proposed break, did make him wonder if these events were heralding the appearance of the Antichrist.

Aethelwine dropped his empty mead mug to the table and tossed a coin down next to it. Rising quickly, he strode past the young boy at the firepit and went in search of his men, still plagued by thoughts of friendship and damnation.

CHAPTER III

Leofwine relaxed under a large shade tree on the bank of the river Thames. He frequently came to this spot when he had some free time in London and watched the river rushing passed. Somewhere under those waters, the monks claimed, were the great iron tipped stakes the ancient Celts had used to keep Julius Caesar's armies from conquering London. Today, however, such thoughts led Leofwine to some confusion. Yes, the Celts had thrown back the Romans, but they were eventually conquered, just as the Romans were replaced by the Saxons in later years. Were the French simply latter day Romans with William their Julius Caesar? Would some grandchild of William one day play Claudius and lead his successful legions across the conquered lands of England? Such thoughts made Leofwine think of the priestly admonition, "For everything there is a season and a time for every purpose under heaven."

Leofwine tried to calm these thoughts with reflection. The Saxons were not the Celts, and they had managed to hold off invading Danes since before the time of Alfred. They could do the same against these Normans who, although they called themselves French, were just more Danes.

Few people who were acquainted with Earl Leofwine would have given credence to a calm and contemplative, much less educated, side of the fiery earl. He had gained his reputation on the battlefields, frequently commanding troops under his father against the late King Edward. His brusque and warlike mien, in fact, were all that had existed until recently, but at Senlac, when Harold had fought William, Leofwine had narrowly escaped taking an arrow through the throat. He had actually seen the arrow flying at him and managed to move slightly out of the way, although he could feel the fletchings fly past his neck and even draw a thin line of blood. In a more religious man, such a close call would have created another monk, a warrior for God instead of a warrior for the king. But Leofwine, who had little use for God, let alone Jesus Christ, had begun to look inward for guidance and to seek natural calm for his contemplation. In his few spare moments since the battle, Leofwine had begun to practice his reading as much as his war-making, expanding his horizons from the Roman military historians he had read to include some philosophers. He was beginning to open himself up to a larger world and was becoming a stronger man for his effort, particularly in his ability to advise his brother, the king. Unfortunately, Harold still acted on his own and without fully trusting Leofwine, as he had done in his asinine decision to break England from Rome.

Leofwine knew that Harold's decision would cause great consternation throughout the entire kingdom. Already both regular and secular clergy were speaking of leaving the island. The reaction of the clergy was no surprise to Leofwine. If anything, he was surprised by the number of clergymen who had agreed to remain in England, although many of them seem to have elected to do so with their eyes on the huge benefices which would become available with the disappearance of so many office-holders.

AFTER HASTINGS

What Leofwine found difficult to understand was the reaction of the nobility to the king's announcement. Leofwine always assumed that the world was divided into two types of people. A few believed strongly in God and they entered the Church. The rest knew that God existed but didn't really care much about Him one way or the other as long as He did His job and more or less ignored the day-to-day activities on Earth. Leofwine always assumed that this latter group formed the bulk of humanity. However, the reactions of many people in the past few weeks could only lead him to the conclusion that the vast majority of people were afraid that God would descend upon England and smite Harold and his supporters as He had done to the Egyptians who tried to keep the Israelites in slavery.

While Harold was busy worrying about the actions which the Pope would take now that England had broken her ties to Rome, Leofwine turned his attention to the discontented noblemen within England. Harold may have been right, in general terms, when he told Hildebrand that the Saxons were tired of foreigners interfering in their business, but too many of them felt blind devotion to the Church in Rome. A dangerous attack on Harold's throne could just as easily come from an unhappy Saxon as from the hordes of the French and Imperial armies which would soon be massing on the other side of the Channel.

The nobleman Leofwine believed to be most likely to rebel was Harold's long-time friend, Aethelwine. The earl had returned from his trip to Dover in a quiet mood and Leofwine at first assumed that Hildebrand had turned the earl. Speaking to members of Aethelwine's entourage, however, indicated that Hildebrand and Aethelwine exchanged only a minimum of words during the course of the journey. Nevertheless, Leofwine was still concerned about his loyalty to Harold, although the king refused to discuss the idea.

When Aethelwine uncharacteristically left Westminster within two days of his return from Dover, his personal guard included three agents who had sworn their devotion to Leofwine, each believing he was the great earl's only spy in Aethelwine's household.

Leofwine was startled from his reverie by a large buck coming out of the trees to drink in a small tidal basin of the Thames. Putting thoughts of kingdom and religion behind him, the earl reached for his longbow and quickly nocked an arrow, aiming to bring down the magnificent beast.

CHAPTER IV

Morkere sat in his Northumbrian keep far away from Harold and the dangerous game the distant king played with the even more distant pope. A Saxon like Harold on the throne was preferable to the foreigner the pope wanted, but Harold's current course of action seemed particularly perilous to the Northern earl. Morkere was in the middle of his great hall, surrounded only by the memories which this room retained for him. He had already listened to the advice of his regular counselors concerning the king's actions. Now he waited to hear the advice of his special advisors, for Morkere knew that the souls of his brother, Edwin, and father, Algar, still inhabited this hall. Morkere's father's link was obvious. It was from this high ceilinged, drafty hall that he had sat as earl over Northumbria during Edward's time. Morkere's brother's link was less obvious to people who weren't acquainted with him, for it was in this hall that his life, snuffed out at the Battle of Senlac by William the Bastard's troops, began.

Morkere knew that if he waited long enough, both of these advisors would give him the information he needed. While he waited for them to make their presence known, Morkere thought about Harold and the role Morkere had to play in the events of the Easter court. Had he known the use to which the Scottish monk would be put by the king, Morkere would never have agreed to fetch the old Celt from the borderlands for Harold. As far as religion was concerned, Morkere had no questions. He had been taught from his earliest days that only the pope in Rome had the right to permit a person into heaven. Nevertheless, Morkere had also sworn an oath to support Harold, both before and after the fateful battle at Senlac. If he broke that oath, even to support the Church, would he be allowed to gaze upon the visage of God after he died?

As if thinking about that hopefully distant time summoned them, Morkere suddenly felt the presence of his father and brother.

"My son," he could hear his father's deep, resonant voice, reverberating against the exposed ceiling beams. "I understand the difficulty you must feel, having to choose between your faith and your king. It is a tough decision."

"How can I decide which is the right course of action?" Morkere murmured to the physically empty room.

Edwin answered, "By what right does Harold rule? He is not descended from the house of Wessex. His claim is based on his sister's marriage to a king. Your sister is also married to a king, but you are descended from the royal house of Northumbria."

His brother's tenor dropped to the tones of father's bass, "Perhaps God has given you the chance to return that royal house of Northumbria to its rightful place on the wheel and return this land of Saxons to its rightful place in the eyes of God."

As suddenly as he had felt their presence, Morkere found himself alone in the quiet emptiness of his hall. A beam of the setting sunlight broke through the stained glass window at the west side of the hall, dyed blood red, and fell on a display of swords which hung from the Eastern wall of the hall.

CHAPTER V

Edith had remained at Harold's court from the beginning of December, through the Christmas court and the spring. Now that the Easter court was over, she decided to leave Harold and return to her estate at Gaddesby. The village had been a gift to her from her father, bestowed upon her in his will, just as his other lands and titles had been granted to Morkere and Edwin. Algar had provided the benefice to support her in case of the untimely death of her then husband, Gruffydd. Although Harold was more than able to take care of any of her needs, Edith retained Gaddesby as something of her own. She had even declined Morkere's offer to arrange an overseer for the estate in her absence.

Now, retaining Gaddesby would pay off. The village was centrally located, near to Nottingham, and could be easily reached by anyone who joined her against her husband.

Harold's idiocy in the matter with Hildebrand infuriated her. His blatant disregard for the ways of the Church could only lead to his own damnation. Edith was certain of Harold's damnation in any event, but his seeming single-mindedness to damnify the rest of the nation along with his soul was what she refused to permit. Nevertheless, she would have to be careful in her planning. If she were going to help Hildebrand and the Church regain England for God, she couldn't underestimate her husband, nor could she allow word of her plans to reach Harold's ears too early.

Edith had arrive at her estate shortly after noon and she spent the rest of the day making sure everything was in order. After a late supper, she planned to retire to her room and sleep while servants worked through the night to finish preparations which would make the estate inhabitable. Shortly after dinner, however, Edith had a surprise visitor.

"My lady," Edith's steward, Ordgar, entered the room with an apologetic, but urgent, air about him. "There is a rather important visitor who demands to see you."

AFTER HASTINGS

"If it is a messenger from my husband, you may tell him that I wish to see no one until tomorrow. Then, find an out of the way a place to let him wait until I'm ready to see him."

Ordgar paused, causing a slightly embarrassing silence between the two. After perhaps a moment too long, he explained, "Although your visitor may be from the king, I do not think your ordered course of action is wise. You see, your visitor is the king's sister."

The fact that Ealdgyth had followed her up from Westminster intrigued Edith. Not only was she the king's sister, but she was also the widow of the late King Edward. Never particularly close, Edith thought Ealdgyth's visit was linked, in some way, to Harold's recent bout with foolishness, but was at a loss for how it related. Harold viewed his sister as a political tool, nothing more but considerably less. Edith couldn't imagine a string of events which would cause Harold to send his sister as an emissary to see his wife. With this in mind, Edith gave Ordgar permission to see the former queen into the chapel, where the queen would arrive shortly.

After Ordgar left, Edith's servants began to make her presentable, fully aware that the woman she was about to meet would be covered in the sweat and dirt of the road to Gaddesby. She had never gotten along particularly well with Ealdgyth, which seemed strange considering how similar their situations were. When Edith finally finished straightening her hair, she left her private chambers and took a circuitous route through the garden on her way to the chapel, which was attached to the main house.

Ealdgyth sat in the front pew of the chapel looking up at the great rood which legend said had been placed in its position by Saint Sigebert. At the sound of the current queen's entrance, she quickly finished the prayer she had been saying and turned to face her hostess.

Edith walked slowly up the aisle, waiting for Ealdgyth to begin the conversation. The flickering torchlight caught the highlights of her golden hair, giving her a nearly otherworldly appearance. Nevertheless, Edith remained calm, reminding herself that this was the same woman she had known, if not liked, for several years. However, she had never had to ask the advice or generosity of Ealdgyth before.

Finally, when the queen was at the front of the aisle, Ealdgyth spoke, her voice soft in the stillness of the nearly empty chapel. "Greetings, sister. I have come to ask your advice and to discuss the recent actions of my brother with one I feel might be sympathetic to my position." It was clear that the former queen had practiced her speech throughout her journey to Gaddesby. Nevertheless, the tightness around her mouth as Ealdgyth spoke betrayed an uncomfortableness that Edith was surprised to see. Despite their differences, they had always maintained a level of cordiality.

In response, Edith bade her sister-in-law a curt welcome and motioned for her to continue. Ealdgyth moistened her lips and sat on the edge of the wooden pew. "I know that people spoke often of my relationship with the late king. I'm sure you know that no matter how much you distance yourself from court, you can never fully escape the gossip-mongers." When Edith nodded in agreement, Ealdgyth continued, "Although much of what was said had no bearing on the truth, there were some rumors which were nearly correct. Both Edward and I were highly religious, not just for show, but deep inside where Christ can see our motives. Although our marriage was a political matter and we never came to love each other, as sometimes happens, we did become friends. I would like to see Edward again after this life is over."

Edith noticed her visitor's hands fidgeted throughout her speech and her eyes kept flickering to the rood which hung over the altar. What Ealdgyth was about to say could amount to treason against her brother. Although Edith didn't really mind such talk, and Ealdgyth obviously had come to believe it was necessary, such things were best left unspoken. Edith decided to interrupt Ealdgyth's plea for help.

"You fear that Harold's actions may destroy all chances you have of attaining paradise," Edith finished.

Ealdgyth nodded her head vigorously in response to the queen's statement. The queen continued her observations with a question, "And you came to me because I have the king's ear?"

Ealdgyth shook her head, "No, I come to you because you, better than any other in this land, understand my situation. As a sister queen, I hoped that you, if nobody else, could help me from this difficulty."

Edith knew that her sister-in-law was no fool and probably had something in mind before she came to the queen for help. "What would you want me to do?"

Ealdgyth answered with a concise explanation, "I wish to travel to France and enter into a nunnery. It will permit me to remain under the true Church and strike a great blow at my brother, to have his sister so firmly in league with the Church."

"That would be a great blow to my husband, indeed. Are you so certain that I do not agree with Harold's course of action?"

Edith was gratified to see a look of surprise and consternation quickly cross over Ealdgyth's face, as if the thought that the queen and king actually agreed had never crossed her mind.

"I . . . that is to say," Ealdgyth began to dissemble, but Edith waved her aside.

"No, you are right. I disagree with my husband's plans and was just wondering how best I could serve to return England to the Church. When I heard you were here, I wondered if you were to join me in my endeavor or try to hinder me. In the future, this eleventh century since the birth of Our Lord will be heralded as a century when England saw strong queens, first Emma, your mother-in-law, then me, for obstructing my husband. Would you add your names to ours, or flee to join so many other queens in holy anonymity in a French monastery?"

"I may choose to seclude myself from the world, but in doing so I will serve God. Although these motives are noble in and of themselves, they will also serve as a sign to all who see them that Harold's own sister sees the evil he has wrought. I ask again, can you help me to flee this island?"

Edith sat on the edge of a pew and looked away from her sister-in-law, watching the candles burn on the altar until the rest of the room faded into a black blur.

"I suppose there are more ways to serve Our Lord and more ways to be a strong queen than the route I plan to take. I will aid you in your flight to France."

CHAPTER VI

Harold listened closely to the scraping noise of the whetstone on his sword. More than anything else, the harsh rasping tone of steel against stone told the king when his sword had a proper edge to it. When his ears told him he had finished the task, he carefully examined the edges and flat of his blade before turning to face Thurlkill. The lad was already standing with his war axe ready to either attack Harold or turn aside a sword thrust whenever the king made to attack him. The thane's chain armor bulged over the jacket of goosedown Thurlkill wore in order to blunt any successful attacks against him. Harold was almost ready to see the training jacket as an unnecessary addition to Thurlkill's attire. It had been many months since Harold had been able to break through the links of chain. Nevertheless, the jacket would decrease the amount of bruising on Thurlkill's ribs, even if it served no other purpose.

Harold tried maneuvering around Thurlkill to force the bright summer sun into the thane's eyes, but the boy had already learned to avoid facing south whenever possible. As Harold gave up trying to outmaneuver the boy, Thurlkill launched his first attack. Thurlkill's charge demonstrated the boy to have been trained by his father, Aethelwine, for it was typical of Harold's friend. Aethelwine had been working on a method of attacking with the great Anglo-Danish war axe which would not leave his entire body open to a sword or spear thrust. On the whole, he had been successful.

Now, his son emulated this method but gripping the axe higher up the haft than was typical. When Harold tried a low thrust, Thurlkill spun the axe, parrying the king's blow with the bottom of the shaft.

Soon, the sounds of king and thane exchanging attacks and parries filled the courtyard at Sarum Castle. Sweat poured off of Thurlkill. In addition to the physical exertion as he tried his hand against the English king, the combination of broiling sun beating down on his bulky attire of chain mail and goose down exhausted him. Along the courtyard walls, Harold's bodyguard had halted their own practice and preparation in order to watch their monarch battle a fourteen-year-old boy. Although Thurlkill was not yet experienced enough to tell, the house carls could easily see that Harold was restraining his attacks against the boy. Nevertheless, the warriors were betting trifling amounts on the outcome of the bout.

At the very instant the mood of the battle changed, the melee was over. Somehow, Thurlkill had managed to disarm Harold and the king signaled a rather surprised surrender to the youngster.

As the two began to strip off some of the armor they wore, a messenger arrived at the entrance to the courtyard. He muttered a few words to the guard who greeted him and was quickly led to the king, who sat on a low bench and poured an urn of water over his head.

"My lord, I bring news from the North," the messenger began without preamble. "Your brother-in-law, Earl Morkere, has summoned his fyrd as you commanded."

Harold nodded and motioned for the messenger to continue.

"The earl has also summoned the other Northern earls, including my lord, Arnketil, to meet with him at his holding in Morpeth to discuss your recent actions and the upcoming campaign."

"This is all as it should be. I don't see why Earl Arnketil saw the need to send you from the distant North to tell me that my brother-in-law was following my orders."

The messenger now appeared to be apologetic. "My lord, Earl Arnketil wishes to remind you that Earl Morkere became Earl of

Northumbria two years ago when he ousted your brother, Tostig, from that position. My earl now fears that Morkere desires to set himself up as king of all the Saxons in your place rather than aid you in fending off attacks from the French."

"And my subject, Arnketil, hopes to take in hand all the power Morkere will lose when I defeat him." Harold decided to be blunt with the messenger. After losing to a child, he was in no mood to have his rule threatened.

"Of course, my earl would stand to gain from Morkere's loss. But I must also say that Arnketil would prefer to have the power of the king in the far South than in the near North."

"Will Arnketil give me a guarantee that next year or the following year he will not attempt to become what my brother-in-law is? A usurper to my throne?" The Northern messenger could begin to detect a trace of redness welling up deep below Harold's features.

"My lord Arnketil has proposed that he will send his eldest son, and heir, Ranulf, to train and study with Your Majesty until such a time as Your Majesty sees fit to release Ranulf from your service."

Harold shifted on the bench and looked at the messenger's beardless face. Arnketil was offering his heir as a hostage. However, Harold knew that such a hostage only offered slight security. After all, his own brother was hostage to William the Bastard. Nevertheless, Harold would launch an offensive against William in an instant if cause and opportunity presented itself. Despite his experience with hostage-giving, Harold began to see something in Arnketil's offer.

"Arnketil has two sons younger than Ranulf as well." When the messenger nodded in agreement with Harold's statement, the king continued. "Does the earl have any daughters?"

"Just one. His sons, Wulfhelm and Coelnoth are eight and ten, while Ranulf is nearing fourteen summers. His daughter, Arnegifu, is but five years."

"Very well. Return to your master with my thanks for his timely warning. I desire that he send all three of his sons to attend my court at Petersborough in one month's time. Further, I will send my squire, Thurlkill, back to Deira with you to arrange for a marriage between Arnketil's daughter and my son. You both will leave for Arnketil's lands on the morrow."

The king stood and turned his back to the messenger. He walked slowly to where Thurlkill was sharpening his axe-head. Harold pounded the boy on the back, nearly causing the axe to fly from his hands.

"Congratulations, you fought that well. Your father will be proud of you when I recount today's bout to him. In the meanwhile, I have a mission for you of the utmost import. Tomorrow, you are to travel to the North to arrange the marriage between my son and Arnegifu, daughter of Arnketil. Just make sure its for Edmund, not Godwin. Also, drop hints to Arnketil that my children by Svannehals will become my heirs and Edith put aside once Morkere's rebellion is quashed."

Thurlkill nodded, his eyes gleaming with the twin excitements of being entrusted with such an important mission so shortly after disarming the king in practice combat. Enclosing his axe-head in a leather case, Thurlkill hurried from the courtyard to his rooms in order to make arrangements for the next day's journey.

CHAPTER VII

"My son has proven himself to be the worst kind of arrogant ass!" Gytha stormed around her room at Winchester.

Across the room, near an open window where he could take advantage of the cool breeze, a priest sat at a table, a tablet of wax in front of him and a stylus in his hand. He had been summoned by Lady Gytha and been listening to her rant while he waited for her to actually begin to dictate the letter she had summoned him to write for her.

Gytha finally sat in a large, stuffed chair next to the dormant fireplace and looked at the priest. "What is your opinion of my son's actions?"

Her bluntness surprised the priest. He moistened the end of the stylus between his lips while he tried to formulate an answer which was neither treasonous or heretical. Gytha had made her opinions clear during her rave, but that didn't mean that she necessarily wanted to hear criticism of her son from a third party. The priest eventually decided to try a fatalistic sortie. "Your son is simply doing his part in the great scheme which Our Lord, Jesus Christ, has laid out for all mankind."

"Bullshit!" Gytha's years with Godwin tended to show themselves most clearly in the soldiers' language she had picked up from her husband. "My son is simply trying to hold the power he has finally managed to get. He is as unscrupulous and irreligious as my husband was. Hell, Harold is probably worse than Godwin was. At least Godwin paid some lip service to the papacy. He never tried to take on the whole of Christendom, merely to keep the damn Normans from getting too strong a foothold in England."

The priest listened to Gytha and tried not to show any expression on his face. He firmly believed that there was no proper opinion for him to voice and so chose to keep all his opinions—of the pope, Harold, and Gytha herself—to himself.

When Gytha next began to speak, it took the priest a few moments to realize that her dictation had begun.

"To my son, finally in his rightful place as king of England, from your mother, Gytha Godwin's Widow. Fill in any extra titles for both of us which you think are appropriate."

The priest nodded as his stylus scratched letters into the soft wax of the tablet. He continued as Gytha poured forth the worst sort of invective against her son, insulting him personally, as well has his father and the upbringing which his mother had attempted to give to him. When Gytha was finished, the priest would copy his shorthand version of the letter onto a piece of vellum and send it off to the king, wherever he was at this time of the year for one of his priests to read to him.

CHAPTER VIII

Hildebrand was not happy. His mission to Harold had fallen apart on all fronts, although he still hoped to be able to salvage something. Now, his visit to William had helped to destroy the feeling of hope his interviews with Queen Edith and Earl Aethelwine had engendered. Although Aethelwine's words were phrases of conviction, Hildebrand sensed the unease which lay just beneath the surface. Such unease in one so highly ranked gave Hildebrand cause to hope that the majority of Harold's countrymen would hesitate to support their king's cause.

Upon arriving in Rouen, however, Hildebrand discovered that William's illness had taken a turn for the worse. The papal legate hurried to the duke's bed chamber as soon as he arrived in the city. William lay on his bed, his once robust body forming a practically skeletal outline on the sheets which blanketed the man. William, who only six months earlier had led a massive army against the English, now could scarcely raise his head from his pillow.

"I've returned from England. Although Harold refused to abdicate his throne and threatens to take England away from the light of the Church, the pope will always support your claim."

William's voice was barely a whisper and Hildebrand had to strain to hear him say, "It's over. Let Harold rule."

Hildebrand reached over to pat William on the hand. "That's the illness speaking. With the Lord's help, you'll recover and one day take your rightful place as king of England, just as Christ sits in his rightful place on the right hand of God, the Father. Get some sleep."

William closed his eyes and within moments his regular breathing told Hildebrand he had fallen asleep. Leaving the duke asleep, Hildebrand left the chamber to speak with the Duchess Matilda. As he passed through the antechamber of the duke's room, he passed four boys sitting in silence. A quick glance at them showed that three were brothers and, by the strong resemblance, sons of William. Although the fourth boy also looked vaguely familiar, Hildebrand couldn't place him. William's three sons frightened the legate. Robert, the heir apparent at fourteen, had an almost lupine appearance and seemed to await his father's imminent death with anticipation based on his assumption of the ducal power. William, only eight years old, already showed signs of looking the most like his warrior father in the days prior to Hastings. No doubt he would be called the most handsome nobleman in all of Christendom when he came of marriageable age. Nevertheless, there was something caustic and rapacious in his eyes. Richard, although only ten, was nearly as large as his older brother and offered the most hope for Hildebrand of all William's children.

As Hildebrand hurried along the corridors of the ducal palace, his mind formulated a number of different plans before finally settling on the one he would present to the duchess when he arrived at her rooms.

Matilda invited Hildebrand in with a courtly formality that lacked all of the warmth she had extended to the archdeacon on her earlier visit. Hildebrand sat down, putting his eyes on a level with those of the standing, diminutive duchess. She began to speak before Hildebrand could begin to outline his new plan.

"They say he doesn't have long to live." Despite the number of conversations they had had, Hildebrand never expected such an authoritative voice to issue from her small body. However, if the duchess wanted to begin with sentimental small talk, Hildebrand could reply in kind.

"No. He seems much worse than when I saw him a few months ago."

AFTER HASTINGS

"I'm worried. Robert is only a young boy. It isn't so long since William tamed his noblemen that they couldn't rise up against his son if William dies too soon."

Hildebrand realized he had misinterpreted Matilda's pragmatism for sentimentality and immediately revised his mode of thought. Matilda, like Harold, was one of the few people Hildebrand could never seem to get a firm grip on, much like a Saxon sniggler trying to bring in an eel with his bare hands.

"Was not your husband merely seven when he became duke? That's a year younger than your other William."

"Times, and people, are different. Robert is not his father. He lacks something, perhaps fortitude, to protect what is his. Yes, he will take the duchy and try to hold it, but a strong contest by one of his many cousins could cause him to lose everything my husband has worked to create, causing this duchy to break into tens of small counties and revert to that weak, pompous child who pretends to rule from Paris."

"Surely with good advisors, his uncles Odo of Bayeux and Robert of Mortain, to aid him, Robert will be able to retain his hold on the duchy."

"If Robert and Odo help my son, he will be able to exert his power, it is true, although it will be less power than his father holds. My husband lays dying yet his nobles have such great fear of his power that they still do not rebel as they did when William first became duke. However, what if Robert of Mortain chooses to lay claim to Normandy himself?"

"Robert's claim to Normandy is weak. Weaker than Guy of Burgundy's was when he rebelled in 1047. I wouldn't fear Robert of Mortain. The papacy will support your son's claim. . . ."

"Yes, papal support. It is such a wonderful thing that it has practically killed my husband." Rage flared in Matilda's dark eyes, but following a couple of quick, noticeable breaths, the duchess was once again in control of herself.

"Despite the disaster at Hastings, your husband still has the right to rule England. Edward promised it to him and Harold promised it to him."

Hildebrand's tone suddenly changed from explanatory to conciliatory. "However, with William's failing health, I think it appropriate to alter the claim a little. I would suggest that when your husband dies, Robert should take over as Duke of Normandy . . ."

"How kind of you," Matilda muttered.

". . . and Richard will lay claim to the throne of England. I suggest that we begin pushing that claim right now."

A horrified expression crept over Matilda's face. "You want to have two children ruling with only one set of advisors and regents. Are you . . . NO! I won't allow you to do this thing. England has already destroyed one of my men, I won't permit it to steal all of my boys."

"To back down from the English now would be to admit that William's claim was faulty. His claim was correct in every way and once he dies will belong to his sons. Richard appears to be a competent lad. He should begin to lay claim to his rightful lands now, before Harold can strengthen his position."

"And what is wrong with recognizing Harold's right to rule on that miserable little island?"

"He promised the throne to your husband," Hildebrand replied, "but more importantly, now, he has turned his back on the Church and become an apostate."

Hildebrand's words stunned Matilda and she slowly sank onto a chair, both anger and sparkle vanishing from her eyes. As the silence filled the room, Hildebrand was struck by another idea. He spoke slowly to Matilda. "There were four boys sitting outside your husband's chamber. Who was the yellow-haired child who was the same size as Richard and Robert?"

Matilda's two-word answer confirmed Hildebrand's suspicion, "Wulfnoth Godwinsson."

CHAPTER IX

 The smell of cow manure permeated the air throughout the tiny pastoral village of Heorlafestoun. In the small church, Swaefred the priest sat in a pew looking up at the great rood which hung in splendor above the altar. Although Christ's eyes were pointed upwards to look at His Father in heaven, Swaefred couldn't help but think that the Lord was looking down on his humble form sitting in a deserted church. A letter had arrived earlier in the day bearing the seal of the archbishop of York, as well as the royal signet of King Harold. Although Swaefred did not know the contents of the letter, for he couldn't read, he had an awful feeling deep within that he would not find the archiepiscopal epistle to contain cheerful news. As he sat, waiting for Osric, whose cart would take him into nearby Grantham, Swaefred prayed that Christ would show him the strength and the guidance he would need for whatever the archbishop wanted of him.

 However, the giant wooden rood hung silently in front of the church's stained glass windows. On a clear day, the effect of the light streaming in from behind the Saviour's head was enough to make even the staunchest pagan believe in His divinity. Today the sky was overcast and the large wax candles burning around the church clearly illuminated His serene face as He anticipated His reunion with His Father. The artisan who had carved the rood was a master in showing the expressions playing themselves across Christ's face. Swaefred only realized he had switched from prayer to artistic contemplation of the curves of the wooden messiah when his reverie was broken by a soft tapping on the frame of the church's wooden door.

 Young Osric, a carter who carried produce from Heorlafestoun to Grantham, stood just outside the church door. "I heard you needed a ride to Grantham." The boy almost seemed afraid to enter the church. Swaefred couldn't understand that reaction among the townspeople. All of them came to the church every Sunday, at the order of the Lord of Heorlafestoun, but they rarely appeared in the confines of the building during the rest of the week, as if they feared they would actually upset God by entering His house when the time wasn't right . . . as if He ever only wanted the invited to visit Him.

"Yes. I just need to close up the church. Could I prevail upon you to help me snuff out all these candles?"

Osric shyly shuffled into the church, his eyes wide with amazement at finding himself within the holy walls on a Tuesday. He took a candle snuffer in his hand with great reverence and slowly marched around the nave, carefully putting out one flame after another until the church was plunged into a murky darkness with little light coming through the small windows.

As Osric finished, Swaefred gathered up the letter from the archbishop and the two headed for the door. "I'll need to be dropped off in front of Saint Wulfram's," Swaefred said in a matter of fact way.

Osric only nodded in reply. His limited imagination couldn't really picture the priest anywhere except for a church or en route between churches. Swaefred had little call to be out and about Heorlafestoun, although he was frequently at sickbed whenever it seemed the intercession of a priest could do more good than surgery to help a stricken villager.

The trip to Grantham was mostly in silence, for Osric had no desire to speak to the priest and Swaefred was more concerned with the mystery contained in the note he bore. A strong wind blew from the north, blowing Swaefred's long red beard and the scarlet fringe around his tonsure. As he wondered about the letter, he gently smoothed his fiery whiskers. When Osric finally dropped him off in front of the great church in Grantham, Swaefred hurried inside to find a priest who would be able to read, and perhaps explain, the message from the archdiocese.

The inside of Saint Wulfram's was not much different from the church of Saint Andrew in Heorlafestoun, except in one important respect. Whereas the hundred villagers of Heorlafestoun could not fit into the church, and many had to stand outside for the Sunday Mass, they would practically be lost in the cavernous interior of Saint Wulfram's. The size of the church seemed to swallow up nearly all the glow from the tens of candles which were lit to give some faint illumination. Swaefred had to pause for a few minutes just inside the double wooden doors to permit his eyes to adjust from the grey gloom of the outside to the murky darkness inside the church.

"Welcome to Saint Wulfram's. May I help you, Father Swaefred?"

Swaefred jumped at the sound next to his ear. He turned to see that Father Maegleas, the chief priest of Saint Wulfram's, was standing next to him. In the dim light, Swaefred had not seen him approach from the shadows to one side of the nave.

"Yes, I think you can. Rather, I hope you can. I received a letter from the archbishop earlier today . . ."

Maegleas didn't allow the priest to finish. "Yes, we received one here, also. In the next few weeks, I'm sure that all parishes throughout England will receive this letter. But here, in the main church, is not the place to speak of it. Please, come with me into the gardens."

With his eyes hardly adjusted to the dark interior of Saint Wulfram's, Swaefred now found himself subjected to the brighter, although still dim, light outdoors. As the two men entered the gardens in front of Saint Wulfram's, the sun managed to find a hole in the cloud cover and shine down on them, bringing with it a hint of warmth which the overcast English sky had been hiding. The two men walked in silence, Swaefred realizing that Maegleas already had something to say, but was waiting until he was ready.

Eventually, when the two had left the churchyard and were walking through the narrow streets of Grantham toward the common green, Maegleas began to speak of the letters which they had both received.

"If you want me to read that letter, of course, I will, but I have a feeling it says exactly the same thing my letter said, so I can just give you a summary if you like."

Swaefred looked at the older cleric and simply nodded his head. At this urging, Maegleas related the contents of the letter, which opened up with a brief description of Harold's actions at Westminster with regard to Hildebrand, the Church and the archbishopric of Canterbury. This revelation stunned Swaefred and he had to sit down on a low fence they had come to in order to fully absorb the horrible things Maegleas was saying.

"However," Maegleas continued, once he had finished relating the first part of the letter, "that is not the only thing contained in the letter. Archbishop Colum-cille of York has stated that there will be a re-evaluation of all major clergy in England in an attempt to discover those with what he calls papist leanings. Any major clergyman who supports the pope and the Church in Rome will be stripped of his position and replaced with a clergyman who is more amenable to the new ways, although Colum-cille and Harold are both careful to refer to them as the ways of our Christian forebears."

"But surely the ways of the Church are eternal," Swaefred said.

"The ways of the True Church are eternal, but the adversary is always whispering in men's ears to lead them astray. King Harold and Colum-cille are trying to bring about a worship that has never found favor in His sight."

"The Celts calculated the date of Easter incorrectly leading to their correction many centuries ago, but Colum-cille is intent on introducing the old errors to this realm. I'm sure he will share other heresies as he gains power, whether the ancient heresy of Pelagius or Arius."

"I don't wish to become a heretic. What should I do?" Swaefred's voice held more than a touch of plaintive tone. He had been a priest all his life, perhaps not a particularly well-educated priest, but he knew the important offices and could give sustenance to his parish when they needed it.

"For you, I don't think it means anything, yet. There is no way for Colum-cille to test every member of the clergy. However, Saint Wulfram's is large enough that I'm sure I'll either receive a deputation from the archbishop or a summons to visit him at York sometime in the near future."

AFTER HASTINGS

"What will you say when you are tested?"

Maegleas looked weary. He had been born late in the first reign of Aethelred and was showing his age. At times like this, when he seemed resigned to an unhappy decision, all the sparkle went out of his eyes and his face seemed to sag along the lines which had crept into it over the years.

"I've spent my entire life following the teachings of the Church. I have always believed in Christ as our Saviour. I don't think I could possibly turn against more than five decades of belief just to stay in my position. If it comes to a test by the archbishop of York, I think I would rather leave Grantham and head to Flanders or somewhere else on the continent where I could still be a real priest. In any event, the time has nearly come for me to gaze my last on the green fields of Kesteven.

"But for you, Swaefred, the situation is different. If you don't make waves, stay unnoticed, I'm sure you'll be left alone. By staying in Heorlafestoun, you can try to remind people of the true teachings of the Church despite the devilish deeds of Harold and this Scottish mage."

Swaefred nodded his head, although only partly in agreement with the elder priest. Maegleas had been the village priest at Heorlafestoun many years earlier and had begun the training which allowed Swaefred to achieve that exulted position. Grantham and Heorlafestoun would be strange without the presence of his red-haired mentor.

"I fear that by staying I may endanger my immortal soul. Surely you can find a place for me in your entourage."

"Would you leave your village without the benefit of clergy? Or worse, with a heretical priest who teaches whatever that devil-worshiper Harold chooses to put into his mouth! If you help guide your parish in the ways of the True Church, Christ will be merciful and understanding and discount your remaining in a country of the damned."

Maegleas picked a flower from the vines which crawled up the garden wall and smelled it briefly. "I only leave because my task in England is complete. Even if I were to stay, Harold and his pet archbishops at York and Can . . . I mean London, would never let me remain at Grantham. To do so I would have to lie about my faith, which I would never do and never suggest doing."

"I see," Swaefred's features were twisted into the confused look he had always gotten when Maegleas had attempted to teach him his letters.

Maegleas put a comforting hand on the village priest's shoulder. "Yet something still troubles you. Do not worry, my friend. I would never lie to you about such an important topic as your faith. I know in my soul that although my role carries me far from these fields in which I grew old, Christ still has a job for you here in Heorlafestoun."

CHAPTER X

Pope Alexander paused in the middle of his preparations to leave the city of Rome. He had decided to move the entire papal court to the city of Venice during the course of papal negotiations with Byzantium. The Venetian doge, Domenico Contarini had extended an invitation to the papal court, although Alexander suspected it was based on Venetian fears of a Norman invasion from Robert Guiscard in Sicilia. Nevertheless, the invitation would also serve papal purposes. The papal court would be leaving Rome the next day to travel across the Apennine Mountains to Rimini on Italy's eastern coast for the first leg of the journey. A knock on the door sounded as Alexander returned to neatly packing away some documents he wanted to study on the course of his overland journey. At the pope's call, Lotario, Alexander's aide, entered the chamber.

"Your Holiness, a letter has just arrived for you from Archdeacon Hildebrand. The courier says it is of utmost importance."

Alexander took the scroll from Lotario and quickly scanned its contents. "Is the messenger still here?"

"I believe he is getting some food down in the kitchen."

AFTER HASTINGS

"After he has had a chance to clean up, send him here. There's no hurry, but don't let him dawdle."

With this dismissal, Lotario closed the door behind him. Once alone again, Alexander sat at his writing desk and reread the letter more thoroughly. When he was finished, he rang a small bell. Within moments, a page appeared and Alexander gave him orders to bring a select group of Alexander's advisors and the steward responsible for overseeing the travel arrangements. While he waited, he quickly wrote three letters. As he finished the third letter, the first of his advisors appeared at the door.

"Come in, Giorgio. Ask a page to step into the room as well."

Giorgio ducked his head back through the door and managed to grab a page who was running past with a large bundle of clothes. He brought the boy into the pope's room.

"Take these letters down to the chancery. They are to be copied at once. This letter is to be sent to Doge Domenico Contarini in Venice, apologizing that I will not be able to accept his hospitality after all. This second is a letter to my legate, Hildebrand, who I understand will be at either Rouen or Paris. The third is a letter which should find the Holy Roman emperor. I wish to have Heinrich meet me at Canossa." The boy took the three letters, tucking them into his shirt, and ran from the room in the direction of the papal chancery where copies of the letters would be made, notarized, and sent off to their recipients.

By this time, the rest of the men Alexander had sent for had arrived in the pope's antechamber and he was able to explain Hildebrand's letter.

"Welcome! We haven't much time, so I won't give you a long preamble. I have received a letter from Archdeacon Hildebrand, who was entrusted to deal with the mess in England. In very uncharacteristic fashion, he seems to have botched the entire problem. Harold now seems to sit firmly on the throne in England and William lies dying in Rouen. To make matters worse, the Saxon has announced his kingdom will return to paganism, although he calls it Pre-Whitby Christianity or some such nonsense."

At this pronouncement, the room was filled with gasps. It hadn't been too long since the Byzantines had also broken off from the Roman Church. Only recently a strong, monolithic institution, the Church now seemed to be crumbling before their eyes.

"How did this happen?" Poppo of Gaeta asked, speaking the question all were thinking.

"The details aren't important. What is important is that it has happened. Whereas before we could have lived with Harold as the English king, that situation is now completely untenable. Furthermore, Hildebrand tells me that William has renounced all claim to the throne of England for himself and all his progeny for all time."

As the advisors began to mutter amongst themselves, Alexander raised his hand, his ring of office glittering in the noontime sun. "Hildebrand has offered a suggestion for dealing with this mess already."

"Why should you still have faith in Hildebrand? He has so messed up this endeavor that it easily overshadows anything he has done for the good of the Church previously."

"Hildebrand has offered a suggestion which appeals to me. He is remaining in France where he will meet with King Philippe and Duke William's sons to plan an invasion of England. We will go to Canossa, where we will meet to bring the emperor, Heinrich, into the alliance as well. I would also like to send you, Giorgio, to Palermo to negotiate with Robert Guiscard. It will make the Venetians feel safer if Guiscard joins our alliance against England. Poppo, you will travel to see King Sancho of Navarre and Aragon to gain Spanish aid for this endeavor, although they may be too busy fighting the Moors in their own land to worry about the apostasy of the Saxons."

Poppo had been listening carefully to everything the pope had been saying and cleared his throat when the pontiff finished speaking. "Your Excellency, if William has renounced his claim for both himself and his sons, who will sit on the throne of England once Harold has been defeated?"

Alexander lifted the letter from his desk and glanced down the page until he found the name he was looking for. "William has been holding Harold's younger brother, Wulfnoth, hostage for some years now and raising him with his own sons. This Wulfnoth is untainted by the heretical turn of mind which plagues his brothers in England. He shall next sit on the Saxon throne."

CHAPTER XI

Dark storm clouds threatened from the west, moving ominously over the Welsh countryside as Aethelwine rode through the forests of Gloucester. To his right, the River Wye marked the erstwhile border between the lands which were nominally within the realm governed by Harold and those which existed amongst the anarchy of the Welsh princes. Aethelwine had come directly to his manor at Stauntun after he left Westminster. Harold's decision and Hildebrand's words made Aethelwine realize how much he had to think about the new situation in England. Ever since he was a boy growing up on the Welsh Marches, he found the best thinking place was between the giant stone monoliths of Buckstone and Suckstone just outside the village in which he was raised.

As a youth, the village priest, Father Streona, had tried to stop Aethelwine from playing around the twin monoliths. According to Streona, the stones were placed in their current positions by the druids, an ancient group of Celtic priests who worshiped the devil before the coming of the Romans. Streona further promised that the Lord Jesus Christ would visit all sorts of horrible punishments in the eternal afterlife to any who had dealings with the druids and their remnants. Although momentarily frightened after each of these lectures, Aethelwine would eventually return to the massive grey stones.

Stauntun was a small part of the holding which formed Aethelwine's property. His father had never paid any attention to the small village on the Wye, not even to visit his young son. Aethelwine realized how minor the estate was. He had other holdings the same size which he had never visited himself. Nevertheless, Stauntun had numerous memories for him. It was from the summit of the Buckstone that he first saw Harold when he was returning from one of his exiles in Ireland during the reign of King Edward.

It was to this same rock that he was riding now, ignoring the menacing thunderheads and Streona's predictions of damnation. His first glimpse of the enormous boulders came, as always, near a bend in the River Wye where a natural clearing pushed the trees back from the river banks. Sighting along the river, he could make out the side of the Suckstone peeking from around the forest, as if playing some sort of child's game while it tried, unsuccessfully, to stay hidden from Aethelwine. The earl tied his horse to one of the trees in the clearing, allowing enough slack in the lines for the animal to graze, or even drink from the river, and continued his journey on foot.

As Aethelwine worked his way through the forest, he focused all his consciousness on the task of climbing the hilly terrain, ignoring the more pressing reasons for his trip to Stauntun and the stones. There would be enough time for that when he reached his goal.

A rabbit shot out from behind a large oak tree, startling Aethelwine and nearly causing him to fall backwards down the hill. He laughed at himself and quickly worked his way through the dense foliage, jumping the numerous small brooks which trickled around the massive trees on their lazy route to join up with the Wye.

At length, Aethelwine entered the clearing which was home to the two massive stones, each easily twice the height of even a tall man such as William the Bastard. Slightly disturbed by thinking of Harold's enemy in this place which Aethelwine considered practically holy, he sat between the stones, allowing them to become two grey walls on either side of him while he gazed north, toward the land from which his ancestors had come centuries before.

The twin towers of stone had their normal effect on Aethelwine and quickly calmed him from the exertion of the ride and the climb through the forest. Once in a quiet mind set, he began to focus on the apparent idiocy which his friend, the king, was in the midst of accomplishing.

There was no doubt in Aethelwine's mind that all of Christendom would mass against Harold and England in an attempt to regain the island for the Church. Unlike Byzantium, which had also broken from Rome, England did not have a strong protector like Emperor Constantine Ducas. England would be crushed between the pincers of Christendom, including, perhaps, the Scots and the Irish, who usually ignored continental intrigues. If Harold could gain an alliance with the distant Constantine Ducas there would be some possibility that England would be able to survive the onslaught. Byzantium, however was a world away and Harold would need some allies even closer to England. Perhaps the Moors would be willing to join the English.

Aethelwine chuckled at the audacity of the thought, but then began to reflect on it. The Moors, who worshiped their false prophet Mahomet, might be willing to aid the English. They already had a strong hold in Iberia and had been trying for centuries to expand into Languedoc and Italy. The Normans of Sicilia were as much their enemies as the Normans of Normandy were Harold's enemies. The Moors might be able, for a price, to launch an attack on the French and the Italians to force the Roman forces to divide their armies against the attacking enemy and the English. Aethelwine would have to mention the possibility to Harold when he returned to court.

The thought of returning to Harold's court had a sobering effect on Aethelwine's mood. There was the question. Would he in fact return to the court of his friend? Streona had not been able to keep Aethelwine away from the ancient stones with his tales of damnation, but Aethelwine had not been worshipping the ancient gods of the druids. Harold was asking that Aethelwine abandon the religion which he had practiced his entire life, almost, it seemed, asking Aethelwine to return to worship of the gods Wodin, Tiw, and Balder. Such a course was a sure path for one's soul to eternal damnation.

Perhaps, Aethelwine thought, he should consult with old Streona. Although merely a village priest, he still was something of a scholar and might be able to shed some light on the situation. Even as he thought of consulting Father Streona, Aethelwine was able to hear the priest's voice ringing in his head. "Christ taught us to 'Render unto Caesar that which is Caesar's.' By extension, you should render unto Christ that which is His."

In theory, Aethelwine realized, this phantom advice was sound. In reality, the situation was more complex, complicated further by Aethelwine's relationship with King Harold. Streona was set in his ways. He wouldn't understand the intricacies of the situation, seeing it merely as a battle between the forces of God and the devil. Much as Aethelwine felt he needed advice, Streona was not the person to whom he could turn.

Once again, Aethelwine looked up to the tops of the twin stones. The first stars had begun to appear in the deepening blue sky. "God," he prayed, "both Harold and Hildebrand claim to speak in your name. Give me a sign, should I follow the pope or Harold. Does either really speak for you?"

Aethelwine lay on his back, the top of his head pressing against the slate-grey Suckstone, staring at the stars as they appeared in the quickly darkening sky. A breeze from the west mingled the sweet smell of the Wye with the aroma of the woodlands and helped cool the warm evening air. All around the clearing, the trees rustled in the gentle breeze, soothing the troubled thoughts from Aethelwine's disturbed mind.

Aethelwine awoke in nearly total blackness. High above, the night sky was studded with thousands of glittering specks of light—angels, according to Father Streona. In the darkness, Aethelwine could scarcely make out the massive shadows of the Buckstone and Suckstone. He stood slowly, using the Suckstone to help him balance himself and looked at the night sky to gain his bearings. High above, the plough wheeled around the polestar, allowing him to guide himself through the woods to where his horse would be waiting, grazing.

As Aethelwine stumbled through the woods, he checked the sky whenever a break appeared in the trees to make sure he was continuing on a northward course. Twice he had to make minor corrections. As he got to the clearing where he had left his mount, a brilliant light burst forth from the heavens as a star fell, flashing from the swan toward Dain. The brief flash brought his question back to mind. "Should I follow the pope or Harold?" The star burst toward the west, and England.

With conviction that he was on the right course, Aethelwine mounted his horse and rode back to the manor at Stauntun.

CHAPTER XII

London was the largest city Colum-cille had ever been in. The streets teemed with people, oxen, horses, and carts. The hustle and bustle of nearly fifteen thousand people amazed Colum-cille at the same time that it terrified him. He could scarcely walk into the street without thinking about how much he desired to return to the secluded monastic cell in Aberdeen. His self-imposed exile had lasted nearly thirty years, ever since he supported MacBeth against Duncan. Although Colum-cille supported the victorious faction, he had decided, following MacBeth's coronation, to eschew politics and live the life of a hermit. Such seclusion, Colum-cille reflected, had a tendency to make people forget the politics and see only the holiness. Duncan's son's rise over MacBeth's foster son, Lulach, helped shape Colum-cille's answer to Harold's request.

The question Colum-cille now found himself facing was whether Malcolm Canmore sitting on the Scottish throne was reason enough to live in the vastly over-populated city to help Harold before he moved to York, which was nearly as large as London. Surely London was fascinating, but there was nothing about the city that Colum-cille felt drawn to, with the possible exception of the new minster which had been built by the late King Edward.

The minster was vast, built in emulation of the style in vogue on the other side of the Channel. The newest, and most grand abbey in England, Westminster was suddenly a cathedral to match anything in Europe. Despite his knowledge that such grandeur was unseemly, Colum-cille could not help being in awe of such a massively incredible construction.

Edward had built a matching palace between the abbey and the Thames, but Harold had disavowed ownership of the palace and bequeathed it to the Church he had helped to reform. Colum-cille, however, agreed with Harold's estimation of Edward's palace and quietly moved into a small monastic cell built next to the massive cathedral, using Edward's palace only for official Church business when absolutely necessary.

Now, Colum-cille exited his austere cell and began to walk the short distance between the abbey and the Thames. Some day soon, Harold had promised, a second bridge would span the waters of the Thames near the archbishop's palace, in order to make Westminster as accessible as London proper. Until that time, Colum-cille would have to either walk through to London Bridge itself or hire one of the ferrymen to take him across to Southwark.

Southwark was important to London because of the vast gravel pits within the village's boundaries. To Colum-cille, however, the village proved to have another, more private, importance. Southwark was a place where the archbishop could escape from the office seekers who did not realize that many of the offices they sought had become extinct with the changes Harold had called for. In Southwark, nobody seemed to recognize the Scotsman, possibly because the citizenry of Southwark did not know what he looked like, but equally possibly because they did not expect one of the most important churchmen in England to visit such an area.

AFTER HASTINGS

On one of his first visits to Southwark, Colum-cille had discovered a small tavern called the Bard. He had begun to come regularly when he needed escape from the duties of archbishop and was known in the common room as Fleance of Caithness.

As Colum-cille sank onto a hard wooden chair at the back of the Bard, a shadow fell across the table. The archbishop looked up to see an elderly, stooped man standing next to his table.

"I have been trying to find you for quite some time." Colum-cille noticed that the man's grey hair was cut short, except where his head was bald, shaved in a continental tonsure.

"You obviously know who I am," Colum-cille replied calmly. "How did you find me here?"

"I followed you from the ferry. Despite your efforts, most of England's clergy still wear their hair in the traditional tonsure rather than the strange mode you wish us to effect. My name is Father Maegleas of Saint Wulfram's Grantham. I'm on my way to Ghent and wanted to meet you before I went."

Colum-cille felt relieved to hear why this stranger had approached him. Over the past several weeks, as many Roman priests had come to vilify him as had come to ask for advancement in the new Church. None on either side fully understood what the Celtic Church was and how it differed from the Roman Church. Not even King Harold, who had initiated the reform, seemed to fully understand the differences beyond knowing that he would no longer have to deal with the pope in Rome. Colum-cille gestured for the old priest to sit in the chair across from him. Maegleas slowly sat on the wooden chair and moved it so that he sat next to the archbishop.

"I won't patronize you. Surely you have been a priest as long as I have, and you understand what is happening. However, I imagine that I know something of how you feel. For years, I have been part of a minority . . . followers of the Celtic rite amidst a world of Romans. Even now, the Celtic Church will be but a single island amidst a Roman world. Nevertheless, within the shores of this island, the Celtic Church will reign supreme for the first time since the Synod of Streoneshalh. What one king set together, let another king tear asunder."

Maegleas sat quietly, his left hand resting on the table while his right fidgeted in his lap.

"May I ask, Father, if you understand the differences between the Church in Rome and the church which had its origin here in Britain?"

Maegleas looked closely at the archbishop, not fully sure of himself since the archbishop took the offensive in this conversation. "Bede teaches that the Celtic Church figures the date of Easter incorrectly."

"Yes, he does. But then, Bede was particularly interested in the matter of dates," Colum-cille replied calmly. "What else do you know of our practices?"

Maegleas had to think for a few moments. "I know that you place a greater importance on monasteries than the Church does."

"Yes. Although the Celts did not create monasticism, you'll find that we helped spread the practice, not only throughout the islands, but in France as well. There is more, of course, such as the role which the Celtic Church permits to women.

"Come, I must be getting back to Westminster. I would be happy to discuss the differences further as I walk back to the cathedral." Colum-cille rose and dropped a few pennies on the table. A moment later, Maegleas stood and followed the archbishop into the crowded streets of Southwark.

Colum-cille noted that Maegleas was as fascinated by the squalor and clamor of the city as he was himself. For a few moments, Colum-cille walked in silence, simply observing the nervousness the priest felt in being in such a crowded place. As they passed the "Bell," a few doors away from the Bard, Colum-cille spoke again.

"I trust that your home parish is a great deal smaller than London."

Maegleas noticeably jumped at the sound of Colum-cille's voice rising above the general murmur of the crowds. He took a few breaths before he answered the priest. "Yes, Grantham is a great deal smaller than London. But then again, so is every place in England."

Colum-cille smiled at Maegleas's observation.

"If I can return to our discussion from the tavern," Maegleas continued. "Although there may be much difference to your Church, the fact remains that Christ appointed Peter as his successor. As King Oswiu pointed out at the Synod of Whitby, only Peter could admit a soul to heaven." Colum-cille noticed Maegleas's use of the English name for the synod rather than its Celtic name.

"That is merely a claim that Rome has made to advance its power ahead of all its rivals."

"So you are positive that your soul will travel to heaven despite your Celtic ways?" Maegleas pushed.

"I did not say that. I hope that my soul will achieve heaven, but no one is assured a passage into heaven. All one can do is hope their good deeds will clear the way for their passage there in the . . ."

Colum-cille felt a sudden burning sensation in his side. He looked down to see a knife sticking out of his side, crimson blood running down the shaft and dripping to form a red pool on the street next to him. He saw the back of Father Maegleas's head vanishing into the crowded street and heard the priest shout, *"Sic semper hereticis!"* as pain overcame him and he fell to the ground.

AFTER HASTINGS

BOOK III: ALLIANCES

This country seem to support the insupportable actions of their king, which almost makes me glad that Duke William failed to annex this land of cutthroats and horse-thieves. Normans who have lived here for years have either fled or been attacked, in many cases both. Nevertheless, I have made my life in England since the days of good King Edward and do not intend to flee my adopted land if I can avoid the ignominy of such an action. Despite the king's support, there are rumors that he faces popular uprisings in many regions of the country from those who are loyal to the Roman religion. With the Lord's Grace, these uprisings will end Harold's insanity and make England safe for Normans and Christians. Written on the Feast of Saint Gregory the Great in the year of Our Lord one thousand sixty-seven.

—EUSTACE OF DOVER
LETTER TO HIS BROTHER, RICHARD OF RHEIMS

CHAPTER I

The salty tang of the ocean air permeated the small manor where Harold was staying during his visit to Bocheland. Harold did not particularly like the sea, an attitude which Leofwine always scorned in the king of an island nation. Harold generally replied that most of his time near or on the sea was associated with the various exiles which King Edward had forced upon the family. Worst of all, of course, had been the time Edward sent Harold to Normandy and he was captured by William the Bastard. However, Harold realized the importance of visiting all the important cities of his kingdom. If he declined to visit those which were too near the coast, he would alienate half the towns of England.

Frowning at the burning smell of the brine, Harold looked down at the piles of vellum spread out on the table in front of him. The kingdom was wracked by minor revolts and uprisings by peasants, clergy, and even some of the nobles. The various groups had been unable to link up, which meant that instead of fighting one massive battle against an organized opposition, Harold was forced to rely on the loyal nobility to put down uprisings in their own area.

So far, Harold's forces had been successful. The two biggest threats were Morkere's rebellion in the North, of which nothing had been heard since Arnketil's emissary spoke to Harold at Sarum, and Lanfranc at Canterbury. Harold had no doubt that Lanfranc and his monks wouldn't move against Harold directly, after all, they were monks and priests, forbidden to shed blood, but they could incite others against the king and prove a rallying point for all the minor rebellions which wracked the kingdom. Lanfranc and his monks made no secret that they were opposed to Harold's decision. They still considered Lanfranc an archbishop of the Roman Church and Primate of England.

The most pressing uprising at the moment was occurring near Colchester in East Anglia. Harold realized that he should probably attend to this particular revolt himself, but he couldn't quite bring himself to travel to East Anglia. Instead, he was sending instructions to a local baron, Thurstan of Gippeswic, who had been loyal to Godwin's family since before the exile of 1052.

AFTER HASTINGS

Harold's musing over the letters and maps in front of him was interrupted by a loud knock on the door. Still leaning over the wooden table, Harold motioned for a servant to let whoever was at the door enter. When the door opened, a small man, dressed for travel and covered in the dust of the road stood, framed by the door jamb.

He approached nervously and cleared his throat before speaking. "I bring an urgent message from London." He handed Harold a heavy brass scroll case.

Harold opened the end of the tube and worked the creamy vellum scroll out. He unrolled it and glanced at the seal on the bottom, indicating that the scroll had been sent by Aelfwulf, an ealdorman from London. He handed the scroll to a clerk, who read its contents out loud.

"To our lord, King Harold, son of Godwin, greetings.

"I take this opportunity to apprise you of a most sad undertaking which recently occurred in Southwark, just across the Thames from the City of London. Unbeknownst to all men, Archbishop Colum-cille of London has taken to Southwark in disguise in order to escape the crowds of London and the pressures of office-seekers and recalcitrant clerics at Westminster. On a recent journey to a tavern known as the Bard, the archbishop was followed by one of the aforementioned clerics who proposed to do injury to the prelate. This criminous clerk struck up a discussion with the archbishop which continued into the street as the two men prepared to return to London and Westminster. Shortly before reaching the Southwark end of London's bridge, the priest stabbed the archbishop in the side with a long knife and fled into the crowd.

"It is my pleasure to let you know that the priest, named Maegleas and absent from his church at Grantham, was quickly apprehended as he tried to take ship for the low countries and he is under the impression that his murder attempt was successful. I am also pleased to inform you that his impression is incorrect. Although Archbishop Colum-cille's wound was grievous, the archbishop is recovering quickly and is attended by the best surgeons available in London. He has asked that I send you this letter and that you not fret over his return to good health.

"The priest Maegleas has been sent under guard with this messenger to Bocheland in order for you to pass judgement on his evil deed. In the days since he was apprehended and imprisoned, he has shown no remorse over the heinous crime he has committed while holding the firm belief that the devil guided his knife true and he had killed the archbishop.

"Sent this twenty-second day of August in the second year of the reign of King Harold.

"Ealdorman Aelfwulf of London"

When the clerk finished reading the letter, Harold stood up from the table, walking to the large, open window and staring out at the sea. He stood there pensively for a few moments before turning back to the messenger.

"Have my brother Leofwine or Earl Aethelwine arrived in Bocheland?" He asked the exhausted messenger.

"I don't know, sire. I just arrived on the road from London. When I arrived, I made sure my soldiers would see to the priest's incarceration and I hurried to deliver my message to you."

"Go and find out. If either man is in Bocheland, I wish to see him immediately."

"Of course, your lordship."

The messenger hurried from the room as Harold sat down to the table, pushed the letter from Aelfwulf to one side from where his clerk had laid it and reached for the latest dispatch from Colchester.

The letter was from Thurstan of Gippeswic. Although a wonderfully loyal retainer and more than able warrior, Thurstan had difficulty in expressing the situation when he had to describe it. Unfortunately for Harold, Thurstan's scribe was not particularly capable of transforming the confused descriptions from his master into coherent thoughts on vellum. As far as Harold could tell from the letter, the revolt had begun in a small village known as Maldon, located on the estuary of the Blackwater River.

AFTER HASTINGS

Apparently it was a spontaneous uprising which had spread to a number of towns upriver before moving away from both banks. Thurstan's letter tried to persuade Harold that everything was under control, but its disjointed tone tended to make Harold more than a little nervous. Essex was too close to the continent for Harold to lose it to the Roman Church. It would provide too perfect a strategic site for a landing from France or the low countries.

Harold began to dictate a reply to Thurstan, which his clerk scratched into the wax tablet he used for composing letters. He hadn't gotten far when a knock once again sounded on his door. Harold, already standing near the door, opened it suddenly with a slight flourish. Aethelwine stood calmly on the other side of the door. Harold motioned for him to enter. When the king turned from closing the door, Aethelwine was seated in the chair next to the window, pouring himself a goblet of mead from the decanter which sat on the table.

"Welcome back to my court. Why haven't you been to see me yet?" Although Harold's words were harsh, his tone of voice was warm to his old friend.

"I only just arrived." Aethelwine indicated the dust and mud on his clothing. "This mead is just what I needed. Let me rest here for a few moments."

The two men sat in a silence, broken only by the crash of thunder indicating the start of a late summer storm. As Aethelwine nursed his drink, Harold listened to the desperate fall of rain on the roof above and street below. Finally, he resumed his conversation with Aethelwine.

"Are you familiar with the situation in East Anglia?"

"Not particularly. I've been ensconced in my manor on the Welsh Marches. Is it different than any place else? I understand there are plenty of petty revolts all across the country. The can't be particularly important, else you wouldn't be here in peaceful Bocheland."

"No, you're right, most can and are being put down by local loyalists. I'm more concerned about the North if and when Morkere decides to make his move, and what happens when Canterbury decides to become more active. But in East Anglia, there is a threat. The rebellion started small, but it has spread from the coast to the interior. I'm not entirely sure that Thurstan can handle it himself."

"What about your brother, Leofwine? Last I heard, he remains in London. I'm sure he could get to East Anglia fast enough, raising a *fyrd* along the way, and crush the revolt."

"If Leofwine is still in London, and a messenger can get to him before he leaves, that may be a good idea." Harold dictated a quick message for Leofwine, which the clerk dutifully scratched into a wax tablet and set aside until a copy could be made to send with a messenger to London.

"Speaking of London, there was a rather important incident there as well. A priest tried to murder Colum-cille."

Aethelwine's arched eyebrow indicated that although interested, he was not particularly surprised by this turn of events. As Harold continued the tale, Aethelwine sat back in his chair and poured himself another glass of mead. As the king finished, there was a knock on the door and the messenger who had brought news of Colum-cille entered.

"I'm afraid I could find neither your brother nor Lord Aethelwine, although the gatekeepers say that Lord Aethelwine has entered Bocheland."

Harold indicated Aethelwine seated in the room. "He has found his own way to me. I have another mission for you. You are to return to London immediately and deliver this message to my brother, should he still be in London. Keep alert on the road. If you should pass my brother on the way, see that he gets this message and that he turn back to East Anglia."

The messenger took the scroll and left. Without closing the door, Harold motioned to Aethelwine, "Come, it is time to visit our murderer."

The two men walked through the halls of the castle, occasionally nodding at an acquaintance. While walking, Aethelwine broached the idea of forming an alliance with the Byzantines or the Moors.

AFTER HASTINGS

Harold fingered his moustache while he listened to Aethelwine's proposal. "What you say makes sense. Despite our greatness as a people, our island is only a small outpost on the edge of the world. If the Moors and Byzantines join our cause, we will encircle the forces of Rome, whether they are in France, Italy, or the Empire. However, I'll need to send two parties who I can trust. Unfortunately, anyone I can send would be more useful in the short run to help fend off attacks from within the shores of the island."

"Harold, I have just returned from some of my holdings and I believe they are secure. I could travel to Spain or Constantinople and plead your case for you."

"It is very generous of you to offer yourself for this service which will take you far from your native land, but I think I'll need your advice here at home more urgently."

"Who else can you spare?"

"Nobody. That's where your plan falls apart."

"Is there anybody who can provide this service for you who wouldn't be necessary for the war you'll be fighting here?"

Harold considered, running his tongue along the bottom of his neatly trimmed moustache. Aethelwine's suggestion of someone who wouldn't be helping with the island situation had gotten Harold thinking. There were many exiles from England who were not able to return to England under Edward, yet hadn't returned since Harold had ascended the throne. Perhaps the most prominent of these was the Hungarian-born Edgar Aetheling, the great-grandson of Aethelred II.

Harold had already been in contact with Edgar's advisors and the prince had renounced his claim to the English throne as long as Harold's descendants lived. There was a possibility that Edgar would be willing to leave Hungary for the relatively short journey to the Byzantine court at Constantinople.

"Edgar Aetheling might be a good choice, although I wonder what influence his sister's recent marriage to Malcolm of Scotland might have on his decision regarding whether to help you. He may decide that he supports Rome and, as such, would consider himself a contender to your throne," Aethelwine pointed out when Harold suggested his distant countryman.

"Of course, you're right. It seems to be happening more and more lately, Aethelwine. I'm not entirely sure I like it." Aethelwine chuckled at Harold's left-handed complement. "Nevertheless, I still intend to see if Edgar is a possibility. Tonight I'll dictate what I want him and whoever I send to the King of the Moors to say."

"That still leaves the question of who you are planning to send to al-Mu'tadid," Aethelwine reminded the king.

"I know!" Harold responded, somewhat angrily. "I know that the number of men I can fully trust are few and needed here in my kingdom. I also know that the emissary I plan to send to Constantine in Byzantium is not entirely trustworthy and may not agree to the expedition in the first place. Furthermore," Harold continued, with a lessening of his anger, "I know who will be my representative to this Aelmutid of the Moors."

Aethelwine refrained from giving the Moorish prince's proper name and title while he waited expectantly for Harold's pronouncement. As Aethelwine's wait and Harold's smile continued to grow, the earl finally prompted his monarch. "And who will you send?"

"Why you, of course. With all your correct answers lately, I'm sure you'll find a way to convince the Moor that he should aid us. Perhaps you can point out that while the Romans are fighting against us and Constantinople, he can regain some of the land he lost to Ferdinand of Castile a few years ago."

Aethelwine was startled. "Are you suggesting that Christian lands be promised to the infidel Moor?"

Anger re-colored Harold's face, "Religion is not the issue! Politics is the issue. The Romans are no more co-religionists with the English than the Moors are. Just because the Romans accept Christ as the Christ doesn't mean they are truly Christian."

AFTER HASTINGS

Rather than assuage Aethelwine's shock, Harold's outburst made him wonder at his friend's sanity. Although Aethelwine realized the whole campaign against the Romans was political, he was amazed at how quickly Harold was able to form a concept of religion so different from any which had been viewed previously. As far as Aethelwine knew, even the Byzantines did not have such a radical view of their estrangement from Rome as Harold did. Certainly they would never suggest that the Moors were on the same level as the Romans. Of course, Aethelwine reflected, the Moors were an immediate danger to the Byzantines while they were rarely seen in England. Aethelwine realized that Harold's embrace of Colum-cille's Celtic Church was entirely political and had nothing to do with any religious beliefs the king may have held.

Harold's voice interrupted the thoughts which Aethelwine would have preferred not to have been having in the first place. "I anticipate that you and a messenger to Edgar will be prepared to leave by next Sunday."

"Mmmmm, yes that should be fine."

The two men paused as a gaoler opened the locked door in front of them. The manor in which Harold was living while resident at Bocheland was not large and a storage room had been hastily emptied and fitted with a heavy lock to house the criminous clerk who had attempted to murder Archbishop Colum-cille, a guard posted outside the door in order to ensure that Maegleas could neither escape nor be freed by his Roman co-religionists.

The door swung outward and Aethelwine had to take a quick step back to allow the door to pass through its swing. Inside, the room was dark but for the dim light which entered from the hall. For a moment, Harold though the room was empty, but then a small movement along one side of the small room's wall caught his eye and he could make out the huddled form of the priest.

"Let me light a lantern for you." The guard quickly applied flint to steel and lit a small lantern, which he respectfully handed to Aethelwine.

The earl lifted the small light and allowed them their first clear view of the cell.

Maegleas's grey hair was stringy and unwashed, sticking to his scalp, and a fine down had begun to appear on his traditionally tonsured head. He shielded his eyes from the light with a shaky hand, and his skin had gone a pasty white, in part from his captivity, but mostly from a breakdown in his health since he had attacked the archbishop. The crouched, palsied, broken creature which practically cringed before King Harold and Earl Aethelwine had clearly once stood tall and proud. His former parishoners would never recognize him.

"Rise to greet your king!" The guard's deep voice echoed throughout the small cell, causing Maegleas, Aethelwine, and Harold to start. With the help of the gaoler, Maegleas was able to attain his full height when Harold and Aethelwine entered the room.

Seeing the form before him, Harold turned to look at Aethelwine and nodded at his friend. Putting all thoughts of Moors, Romans, and Byzantines from his mind, Aethelwine confronted the man in front of him, prepared to interrogate him.

"I'm told you are, or rather were, a priest. Where was your parish and what are you called?"

Maegleas sniffled and let forth a low mewling sound which continued until the gaoler cuffed him. Following the sound of the blow, the whine was replaced by a whimpering sound from the cleric.

Aethelwine repeated his question and was rewarded with a low mutter from the cleric, "I am one without family."

Aethelwine glanced at Harold before continuing, "We know you have no family, for such happened when you became a priest. Even if you had family other than the Church, your attack on Archbishop Colum-cille has made you outlaw and outcast from all society, including any family you may have had." Aethelwine's response was punctuated by another strike from the gaoler, strong enough to knock the priest to the ground where he lay on the cold floor.

AFTER HASTINGS

Harold cleared his thought and Aethelwine moved closer to the king to hear what he had to say. Whispering into Aethelwine's ear, Harold explained, "We know his name and parish. He is called Maegleas and until a month ago he was the parish priest of Saint Wulfram's church in Grantham, up in Mercia."

Aethelwine nodded and turned back to the cowering form on the floor. Nodding at the gaoler, Maegleas's body was lifted to a standing position once again.

"Now, Maegleas of Grantham, no more of these games. We know that you are the one who attacked Archbishop Colum-cille in London for your Roman master. When did he send you orders to kill the archbishop?"

Maegleas let out a loud, wordless shriek which resolved itself into a flurry of words. "Southwark *ordine sancte* true Christians not archbishop *Haroldus qui regum sibi adrogat servus diabolici*." As the words tumbled from his lips, Maegleas's voice got progressively fainter and even the gaoler holding him had a hard time catching the last words of his rant.

The three sane men remained silent. None could ignore the ranting of the madman, yet none of the three knew precisely how to react to the lunatic's claim that Harold served the devil. Eventually, the firm voice with which Maegleas had delivered hundreds of sermons from the Saint Wulfram's pulpit cut through the silence.

"At least the Celt Colum-cille has been killed. My country will revert to the ways of the true Church once you are replaced by William of Normandy."

With the regaining of the priest's sanity, Harold knew how to react to Maegleas's speech.

"Maegleas of Grantham, I, Harold, by grace of God and election by the witanangemot of England, hereby declare your life forfeit for the crimes of treason and attempted murder of the archbishop of York." As he said these words, Harold saw a look of surprise cross the priest's face. "You are to die by hanging from a tree at the entrance of this estate on the morrow. May God have mercy on your soul." Aethelwine and the gaoler crossed themselves as Harold pronounced sentence.

As the gaoler closed the door behind them, Harold called his last words to Maegleas, "Archbishop Colum-cille is gaining his health back day by day and sends his absolution for your attempt. An English priest will be sent to prepare you for your passage into the next world before tomorrow."

CHAPTER II

Hildebrand looked across the room at the fourteen-year-old boy who had sat upon the French throne since he was only seven years old. Although Hildebrand could easily view this audience as a mere formality before seeking the approval of the boy's ministers, he instead chose to act as if the whim of the young king of the French was the linchpin which would hold the Church's alliance against Harold together.

Philippe wore robes which were only marginally finer than the travel clothes which Hildebrand had worn to journey from Normandy to Paris. Despite the boy's ancient title of King of the French which he had inherited from Hugh Capet, the French kings were weaker than the majority of their barons. Nevertheless, this monarch could be used to rally the various French dukes to the Church's cause against the schismatic English.

"Your majesty," Hildebrand began, dropping to one knee in front of the child's throne, "I come as a representative to you from the Court of Saint Peter to beg you grant a boon to God's representative on Earth." Hildebrand could as easily have demanded Philippe's aid, but after studying the situation decided to give the illusion that the French king had some power and was granting a favor to the pope. The first situation was laughable. The second was, unfortunately, all too real.

AFTER HASTINGS

Philippe sat quietly on his throne, looking down on the tonsured head of the papal representative, wondering how a grown man could possibly believe the flattery which Hildebrand was extending to him. Even if he was only fourteen, Philippe had been a king since he was seven and knew exactly where he stood in relation to his barons. If any of them, particularly the Norman duke who the Church had recently supported, ever decided that they could seize the French throne without being destroyed by the other dukes, Philippe would be the last French king of the Capetian line.

Philippe knew that if he pretended to believe the transparent praise which Hildebrand bestowed upon him, he might be able to strike some blow against the churchmen who supported one of his barons when they should have been trying to help support the French royal house against his rebellious nobility.

Looking down at the bowing prelate, Philippe realized he had kept Hildebrand waiting for several minutes without responding to the man's flattery.

"How may the house of Hugh Capet deliver aid to the see of Saint Peter?"

Remaining on his knee before the throne, Hildebrand looked up at the youthful face he was addressing. On the wall behind the king was a mosaic depicting the pagan king Merovech waging war against a Roman legion. Although Hildebrand disapproved of the mosaic for several reasons, he hid his annoyance and made a mental note to speak to Philippe's advisors about replacing the tiles with something more suitable for a Christian monarch.

"I have no doubt Your Majesty has heard of the recent events in England, where a pretender to the English throne has declared himself a schismatic. Such actions and decrees may not go unheeded by those who follow the true path as laid down by Saint Peter and the Church of Rome. To this end, the Holy Father, Pope Alexander, third of that name, has requested that Your Majesty arrange to aid the Christian cause by sending troops to fight against the English for the greater glory of God."

Philippe thought about Hildebrand's words for a few moments, then looked down at the cleric. As he motioned for Hildebrand to rise, he asked, "And when England is freed from these Arians who hold it, will you once again grant the kingdom to my vassal, the duke of Normandy?"

Hildebrand shook his head as he rose. "Duke William of Normandy has renounced all claim on England for both himself and his progeny. Instead, the pope has found another who will take the burden of the throne of England. The brother of the pretender Harold, Wulfnoth, who has been raised in a French court and taught the proper way to worship Jesus Christ."

"We have heard your request and would have time to consider it." Philippe turned sideways in his throne, indicating that Hildebrand's audience had come to an end. As Philippe's retainers cleared the chamber, the prelate couldn't help but reflect how imperious the fourteen-year-old was, as suited one who claimed to have inherited the throne of Charlemagne. At fourteen, Philippe could match the Holy Roman Emperor Heinrich IV, or even the Byzantine emperor in his haughty manner.

When the last of the retainers had left the room, Philippe looked over at Théobald, his senior advisor, and motioned for him to say what was on his mind.

"Your Majesty, we can only call up a handful of men to fight for the pope on our own, but we should be able to arrange for several hundred, perhaps even thousands, of men to serve from among the dukes and counts who owe vassalage to you."

Philippe did not reply to Théobald's estimate of the strength of arms with which France could supply the pope. Instead, he turned his gaze on the other advisors who had remained in the room with him. All had served his father, Henri. Old Guillaume, who had even served Philippe's grandfather, Robert, was said to have been born before Hugh Capet had died.

AFTER HASTINGS

It was Guillaume who next expressed his opinion concerning the papal request, his voice crackling with his advanced age.

"My young master. I have served your family for three generations. My father, too, served your great-grandfather before he was called upon to accept the throne of France from Bishops Adalberon and Gerbert. My fortunes have long been aligned with your house and as the Capetians have grown in power and prestige, I felt that I have done so, too."

Philippe tuned out the ramblings of his old retainer. Eventually, Guillaume would get to the point of his statement, but before that occurred he would recite his ancient links to the Capetian house with as much thoroughness as a priest reciting the lineages of the ancient Hebrews. In the meantime, Philippe examined the mosaic of Merovech on the wall behind him. Something about the picture formed by the tiny pieces of glass and tile pleased him more than the other mosaics which ornamented the floors and walls of his palace. The tie between himself and the early French king was something he found himself drawn to. Perhaps he would commission a painting or a tapestry for the opposite wall which depicted King Childeric defeating the Saxons on the Loire. Another pagan king would be a nice difference from all the post-Clovis monarchs who had embraced the ways of Jesus Christ. Somehow they all lacked romance in the mind of the young ruler.

Suddenly, Philippe heard the cough which generally signaled that Guillaume was finally ready to come to his point. Philippe hoped that whatever he had to say wasn't particularly obvious.

"Despite the great prestige which rests upon the house of Capet, it is a sad fact that those who have sworn service to you are not bound by your strength, but by the strength of their enemies. As long as I can remember, the popes have blessed the exalted position to which God has raised your ancestors, but never fully sanctioned the power which should, by rights, belong to your family. Support of Alexander in his mission against the English may well succeed in gaining the full papal support which is necessary for you to become as strong a monarch in your own lands as the emperor is within his far-flung lands. After all, both of you rule the realms of Charlemagne, why then has the emperor of the Germans so much more respect among his nobility than the king of the Franks?"

Philippe found himself pondering the old man's words. Normally, Guillaume only rambled and took up time better spent in other pursuits, yet this time he had put his finger on the problem.

Théobald recognized the strength of Guillaume's arguments and quickly spoke to fill the silence that followed the old man's comments. "What Guillaume has said is true and shows the wisdom of your father and your father's father in retaining his service. Advice like his is wise and should be heeded. We can bargain with this Hildebrand to gain the pope's favor and still give them what we will give in any event."

Philippe sat up on his throne and motioned for Théobald to be silent. "I wish to have some time in solitude. Send in my minstrel.

The group of advisors left the room and Philippe was only left alone for a few moments before he was joined by his minstrel. "Sing me a song of my ancestors while I think," Philippe commanded.

The minstrel strummed the lyre he held and spoke softly as he tuned the strings. "I shall sing the opening of a new song I am writing of your illustrious predecessor, Charles the Great."

With a quick strum on the strings, the minstrel began to sing.

"Carles li reis, nostre emperere magnes,
Set anz tuz pleins ad estéd en Espaigne.
Tresqu'en la mer cunquist la tere altaigne;
N'i ad castel ki devant lui remaigne,
Mur ne citét n'i est remés a fraindre,
Fors Sarraguce, ki est en une montaigne.
Li reis Marsilie la tient, ki Deu nen aimet;
Mahumet sert e Apollin recleimet.
Nes poet guarder que mals ne l'i ateignet."

AFTER HASTINGS

Philippe listened to the first stanza of the song and then turned his attention to the problem which he had faced since the arrival of Hildebrand at his court. Philippe knew what his advisors wanted, after all, they had said that he must support the pope against his fellow monarch. Nevertheless, Philippe chafed at having to listen to their advice.

While Philippe was a weak king, something he knew despite all the flattery of his courtiers, Harold had managed to claim the English throne and hold it against all challengers. Much as Charlemagne had done in Spain according to the song the minstrel was currently singing. Philippe could only dream of such power. If only Philippe could support the English, perhaps some of Harold's power and will could rub off on him.

"Guenes respunt: 'Pur mei n'iras tu mie;
Tu n'ies mes hom ne jo ne sui tis sire.
Carles comandet que face sun servise.
En Sarraguce en irai a Marsilie;
Einz i frai un poi de legerie
Que jo n'esclair ceste meie grant ire.'
Quant l'ot Rollant, si cumençat a rire."

Although Philippe was only half listening to the minstrel's words, something about this verse caught his attention. In the verse, Charles the Great had obviously ordered one of his knights, Guenes, to meet with a pagan monarch, perhaps to work out a truce of some sort. If it was something Charles could do, certainly treating with the semi-pagan Harold was something Philippe could do without losing respect. The questions of who should travel to England and how the negotiations could be carried out without being stopped by Théobald and the other advisors still remained. Philippe was sure he would be able to figure out an answer to those difficulties. Meanwhile, he listened as the minstrel sang of Charles's appointment of the mission to Guenes.

CHAPTER III

Neither of the women sitting in the dusty tavern felt entirely comfortable in their surroundings. The younger moved awkwardly in her seat, wishing she could have been almost anywhere else. The older woman did not allow her discomfort to show. Instead, she sat at the table, a mug of ale before her, as if she were the brewster herself.

Edith looked at her companion and felt envious at the older woman's ability to make herself comfortable in any surrounding. "I had a difficult time finding you. I never would have expected a noblewoman to be in such a common place, surrounded by all these thegns and ceorls." Edith paused to look around the crowded tavern. "Can we go somewhere more appropriate?"

"I see nothing wrong with this place. No matter what we believe, you and me, your husband and my dead husband, this is the real England. These are the true Angles and Saxons."

"These rabble? The real Anglo-Saxons? Your age certainly hasn't mellowed you. I imagine you'll next be telling me that any of these men could rule the country as well as my husband. Well, King Edward, at any rate."

"No. Most of these men would be incapable of ruling England. They haven't been trained to lead men and countries. They would do no better at ruling England than Harold would do if he were made a farmer or an artisan. Don't look so shocked. Has Harold ever ploughed a field or carved a statue? He would need to learn how. As a leader of men, he does a reasonable job. It is what he was trained for."

"Your support of my husband rather surprises me. You've always been one to make up your own mind and take whatever course of action you deem proper, no matter what anyone else thinks."

Godgyfu looked at the Queen for a moment and let out a snort. "I never said I supported what your Harold is doing. I've always believed in God and His Church."

"But if you don't agree with what Harold is doing, why didn't you fight him?"

"My days of fighting are long gone. If I were to ride naked through Coventry now, people wouldn't turn away from me in respect, they would run from me in terror." Godgyfu indicated her body, heavier now than when she made her infamous stand against her husband. She looked more like a crone than the angel she had been described as in her youth. "I've lived a good life, nearly at an end now. When I could help people, I did what I could, heedless of my own needs and humility. Now, my life is nearly at an end. God might excuse me for my desire to live my last few years in comfort."

Edith took a drink of ale. Godgyfu's frankness surprised her. Although there were more rebels and outlaws in England since Harold's momentous announcement, most people who had not openly declared against the king were circumspect in their criticism.

"If you disagree with my husband, do you not fear for your soul if you do not speak out against him?"

"You must think I am daft for speaking this plainly to you. I am an old woman who has many good deeds on my side of the balance. I have looked out for those whose care has been entrusted to me. I have stood up to my husband to relieve the burden he placed on our thegns and ceorls. The Church denounced me for that. Not because I rode through Coventry, although they have called me wanton and hussy as a result, but because I opposed my lord husband. The Church has decreed that, although absolved of the sin I committed, I will still spend time in hell before joining our Lord in heaven."

"But how can you support a Church which is so unforgiving? Surely Archbishop Colum-cille's Church would overlook any transgressions you might have committed."

"It doesn't matter what Colum-cille's Church might say. Colum-cille is not His vicar on Earth. That position was entrusted by Christ to Peter and his followers. The Saracen may say he can absolve you of sins, but he still worships Mammon. Colum-cille says the same thing, but he claims Mammon in Christ." As she spoke, Godgyfu summoned the brewster and arranged for two squabs to be brought to the table.

After the birds were brought, the elderly countess looked at Edith. "Tell me, truthfully, Granddaughter, do you support what Harold is doing? If you believe he is wrong, it is your duty, as it was mine, to stand against him for all the world to see. If you agree he is acting correctly, I grieve for you, for you have lost your soul."

CHAPTER IV

Hildebrand sat in his room, listening for the knock which he was sure would arrive when Théobald had finished pummeling reason into the dense head of the child who sat on the throne of Hugh Capet. The French kings had always been puppets of the papacy, ever since the day when Leo placed the crown on Charlemagne's head. Sometimes, the French kings needed to be reminded of Papal patronage, especially when a particularly stubborn man sat on the throne. Philippe had all the stubbornness of his father, Henri, as well as the truculence of a spoiled child. At fourteen, Philippe still seemed to believe that being called *rex francorum* actually implied having power. After dealing with Harold the usurper, Hildebrand was glad to be able to teach this child king what his rightful place really was.

AFTER HASTINGS

When the expected knock finally was heard, Hildebrand nearly jumped up from his chair. Feeling foolish at expressing such impatience, he took a moment to re-settle himself before calling for the visitor to enter.

Instead of the expected Théobald, a young page entered the room at Hildebrand's call. Apprehensively, the papal legate snapped at the child, asking what his message was.

Shifting his weight from foot to foot, the boy stammered out a reply, "The m-m-m-major domo re-re-respectfully re-re-requests your presence in his chambers." The boy quickly bowed and ducked out the door before Hildebrand had a chance to say anything.

As Hildebrand prepared himself for this second, and more important, interview, he reflected how tiresome these temporal monarchs and their servants could be. The Frank, however, could be kept waiting. He had no choice, or even desire, but to support the pope against the upstart islander. Keeping Théobald waiting would do no harm to the papal cause. The *major domo* was entirely a creature of Count Baldwin of Flanders. In the past, Hildebrand would merely have dealt with Baldwin and ignored the inefficient child-king. However, within a year or two Philippe would be old enough to attempt to break free of Baldwin's grasp. Hildebrand wanted to ensure that when Philippe did manage to exercise power in his own right he would be friendly to the papacy.

Eventually, Hildebrand deemed himself ready to set off in search of Théobald. His path took him past Philippe's audience chamber, from which the sounds of a song could be heard emanating.

"Jo vos ai fait alques de legerie,
Quant por ferir vus demustrai grant ire."

Hildebrand snorted in derision. Someday, Philippe would learn that to be a real king meant dealing with the issues at hand, not merely allowing his advisors to make all the decisions while he closeted himself with jongleurs and jugglers.

Théobald's chambers were at the end of a short hallway next to the king's audience chamber. Heavy tapestries, more appropriate to a Christian than those which adorned the audience chamber, muted the noises from outside the room, as well as ensured that words spoken within the chamber could not be heard by a passerby. Hildebrand knocked and waited for his admittance, which was spoken quickly and brusquely by the king's chief advisor.

"Please, have a seat." Théobald motioned Hildebrand to a large chair next to the fireplace. As the papal legate sat down, Théobald arose from his own seat and poured two cups of wine, presenting one of the goblets to Hildebrand before returning to his own seat. In the quiet the followed as Théobald drank his wine, Hildebrand examined the purplish-red liquid which filled his cup and the grainy sediment which sank to the bottom. The prelate took a sip of the thick, syrupy French wine and waited for Théobald to speak.

Eventually, after finishing and replenishing his own cup, Théobald began to speak, "The king is concerned about your proposed attack on a fellow monarch. He fears that it may set a precedent which would allow Rome to once again influence, even control, the events of foreign kingdoms, whether they are England, Germany, or France. For this reason alone, he is reticent about calling his barons to the support of the papacy. If, however, some assurance could be given that Alexander, and all future Popes, will not use this one instance as a precedent for intervention, I may be able to convince the king to support your cause and give up any idea of sending aid to Harold, whom Philippe sees as a beleaguered fellow monarch."

Hildebrand had to respect the forthright manner in which Théobald presented his case, although that same candid approach made the papal legate wonder what Théobald was hiding.

AFTER HASTINGS

"Might I ask what type of assurance the king would need in order to announce his intention to support the papacy? The pope is not entirely pleased with the king's previous decision not to aid his vassal William in his intentions."

"Surely you are aware, my lord, that the king must carefully balance the powers of his vassals. Had he been seen aiding the Norman against the Saxons, might not his other powerful lords think he favored William. They might rise against their king and commit a heinous sin. Further, Philippe's father, Henri, was a sworn enemy of William of Normandy, suffering him to retain his lands merely because they had been granted in God's name. The house of Capet surely has no desire to see a rise in the fortunes of their vassals.

"Furthermore, the king has noticed that although the papacy has blessed the house of Hugh Capet, none of Alexander's predecessors have really given their support to the Capetian monarchs. Philippe wants what is, by rights, his, the right to the power wielded by the Holy Roman emperor. In his own realm, Philippe would have the powers of an emperor. If the pope agreed to this statement, perhaps the barons of Aquitaine and Normandy and the other duchies which make up France would recognize Philippe the way Westphalia and Saxony recognize the superiority of Heinrich IV in Germany."

Hildebrand pursed his hands together and stared at his joined fingertips. His first reaction was to laugh out loud at Théobald's assertion that recognition by the papacy would change the political situation in France. A moment of reflection, however, stopped the words before they entered his mouth. Perhaps what Théobald was saying was something which merited deeper examination.

The papacy, just like the French monarchy, had experienced a long line of peaks and valleys over the years. In recent years, the papal office was practically a fief of the Holy Roman emperor. Only in the past few years, under Alexander, was the papacy truly free of the emperor's influence and able to even begin to confront Heinrich on his own level.

For this reason, Hildebrand was prepared to scorn Théobald's comments as idle flattery.

Hildebrand was stopped by the thought that Théobald might be right. What if a simple statement by the pope could alter political realities? Christ knew that had been the case in the past when Leo proclaimed Charles the Great the first Holy Roman emperor. It was the type of power wielded by Gregory the Great when England was first converted to the ways of Roman Christianity, which was even now threatening to revert to semi-pagan ideas.

For all the talk of the pope's power coming directly from Christ and Saint Peter, Hildebrand could not ignore the fact that true power and authority came from the willingness of others to accept that power and authority. If the pope acted as if his authority would be respected in the matter of the king of France, perhaps a day would come when the rebellious Frankish barons would listen when the pope made a declaration.

Across the room from the silent legate, Théobald sat on his own chair, sipping his goblet of wine and waiting for the cleric to respond to his proposal. Under normal circumstances, Théobald would never have thought of making such a claim on the pope, yet this was perhaps the one time in his life when he would have such an authority in such a position and Théobald couldn't squander the chance to advance his lord, and by so doing, advance himself.

Hildebrand separated his hands in a wide, expansive gesture and leaned back as far as he could in the chair. "I must admit that your request has caught me somewhat off guard. I need some time to consider your request and whether it will be acceptable to His Holiness, Alexander. I will let you know within a few days. Good day."

As he spoke, Hildebrand stood from the chair and began to move toward the door, his hand resting on the handle as he finished speaking. Théobald barely had time to nod his head before the papal legate had opened the door and left him alone in his private audience chamber.

CHAPTER V

Despite the cold weather, Lanfranc found himself breaking into a sweat. Around him on lawn surrounding the cathedral, other monks were toiling to clean up the debris deposited by the massive storm a few days before. A truly spectacular storm had interrupted Vespers service on Saint Nicholas's Day. The monks had stopped singing to rush to the doorways and watch as lightning illuminated the night sky brightly enough to read one of the hymnals. Crashing thunder was loud enough to drown out even the sound of all the monks chanting against the counterpoint of a steady drumming of rain on the leaden roof of the cathedral.

A loud scream echoed from the cathedral's nave where monks were busy cleaning up the shards of glass from the eight stained glass windows which were shattered by the storm. Lanfranc dropped the bundle of branches he had been carrying and started to run toward the massive stone edifice. As he ran, he half noticed the curl of smoke emanating from the roof of the cathedral.

As he approached the doors to the cathedral, he had to fight against a mass of monks who were trying to leave the confines of the building. Lanfranc pushed against the emerging mass of monks to force his way into the cavernous church.

Once inside, it only took a few moments for Lanfranc's eyes to adjust from the dreariness of the December afternoon to the darkness of the candle-lit cathedral. Halfway down the nave, he could see the shapes of three monks huddled around a large bulge on the floor. As Lanfranc moved closer, the shape on the floor resolved itself into the figure of a monk lying still on the ground.

Before Lanfranc could get to the kneeling figures, another monk grabbed his arm. "Your grace, a large lump of lead fell from the roof and struck Brother Faege." The monk crossed himself quickly as he looked toward the ceiling. Pushing the monk aside, Lanfranc ran toward the group gathered around the fallen form of Brother Faege.

One look at the crushed head of the monk was enough to tell Lanfranc that the monk had gone on to the next world. "Has anyone given Brother Faege his last rites?" Lanfranc's query was met with a nodding of heads by several of the monks. Looking toward the ceiling of the cathedral, Lanfranc could see other places where the leaden roof was beginning to melt. A flash of orange caught his attention and Lanfranc remembered the curl of smoke he has seen as he ran toward the cathedral.

"Hurry, everyone out!" He shouted at the monks who were still working in the cathedral. "The cathedral is on fire."

Within moments, the cry of "Fire" had begun to echo throughout the cathedral close and the city. A bucket brigade was organized with monks and townspeople forming a snaking line from the River Stour to the building. Despite their valiant effort, the fire continued to spread, and within hours the burning bulk of the cathedral illuminated the darkening December sky, visible for several miles into the countryside surrounding Canterbury.

While monks and townfolk milled around the brilliant cathedral, Lanfranc stood mutely watching his church go up in flames despite all he could do. His face was bathed with the light of the vermilion flames and seared by the heat, giving him a suggestion of hell fire which he would surely face if he could not bring the English church back into line with the correct practices which were enforced throughout the rest of Christendom.

Even as this thought passed through Lanfranc's mind, he knew that England, and perhaps the continent, would be full of people who were not able to interpret the fire as a warning from God that England had broken from the proper path. Around him, Lanfranc could hear murmers of the Cantabrigians, and even some monks, who claimed that the fire was a symbol of God's displeasure that Lanfranc and the Canterbury monks were trying to block Harold's attempts at "reforming" the Church to be "more in line with God's Will".

AFTER HASTINGS

Lanfranc calmly walked over to a group of men who were discussing what "God's Will" was. He listened quietly in the shadows for a few moments.

A large man with a florid face, partly from battling the blaze in the cathedral but mostly, Lanfranc guessed, a natural blush, was speaking loudly. "If that foreign priest were really serving God's Will, do you think He would have struck down the foreigner's cathedral? No! He would have set fire to the new archbishop's palace up in London."

It only took a few moments for Lanfranc to realize that the large man was preaching to the choir. All his comrades agreed with his basic assessment, yet each desired to make his opinion known.

"It needn't even have been London that was struck. Even Saint Mildred's or the Abbey of Saint Augustine where they are already following King Harold's Church would have shown His displeasure. I know that I'm going to start going to Saint Mildred's instead of Saint Mary's. This is surely a sign for all of us to stop going to churches where the Roman rite is still practiced," a mousy-looking man mumbled, twisting his fingers in his stringy, greasy moustache while making his proclamation.

Lanfranc listened for a few more moments before moving from the shadows toward the men. "I fear that you have misinterpreted God's purpose tonight. Although he may have struck the church with lightning, you'll note that all Christians have come together to save His Church. So, too, will all Christians arise to save the Roman Church which the king is trying to destroy."

The red faced man replied, "Sure, we all tried to save your church, but you'll notice that we couldn't. Christ Church is doomed to a burning demise. What does that say about your church and your Church?"

"It is not God who has failed in this instance, but we humans. He is merely telling us that in order to save the Church we must all work harder." Even as he spoke the words, Lanfranc knew that the illiterate townsmen's interpretation of events would be the view spread throughout the country. Many of the men didn't even stand to listen to his entire explanation but began to drift off, either to watch the fire rage on the cathedral green, to protect the houses surrounding the cathedral, or to make their way to a tavern to drink and discuss the import of the cathedral fire.

CHAPTER VI

Colum-cille stood behind the pulpit of Saint Paul's cathedral. The current bishop of London was William, who had been placed in the bishopric by Good King Edward as part of his campaign to introduce Normans into England. Although it was possible Harold would elevate William to the archbishopric, it was just as likely that he would choose someone who was loyal to him rather than a holdover from Edward's reign.

Colum-cille wasn't particularly interested in what Harold decided to do about London. His intention was to institute the changes he wanted to make in the Church and then step down as archbishop of York, since he felt that archbishops and bishops were as superfluous to the Church as the pope was. Priests would be tolerated and their influence would be limited to their local parishes. Holiness was to be found among those who pledged themselves to God with their entry into monasteries or nunneries to enter the contemplative life.

He looked out at his congregation, sitting in the pews arranged throughout the cathedral. To his right, King Aethelred Unraed remains were enshrined in an ornate tomb. The king's inability to rule his kingdom led to a half century of strife which Colum-cille hoped to help quell with the resurgence of the ancient rites. Colum-cille knew his reforms wouldn't be easy, but one of the most obvious differences was the date of Easter, and in the coming year, the Roman celebration would align with the Celtic calculation, so the transition would be eased. In fact, the difference in the date of the celebration of Easter would not be apparent for several years.

AFTER HASTINGS

He leaned against the pulpit and winced. The wound from the priest had closed up, but still caused him discomfort and occasionally pain. He had taken to walking with a staff that he found unpleasantly reminiscent of the shepherd's crook the Roman priests used. He would have to see about replacing it with something less ostentatious.

"In the name of the Father, the Son, and the Holy Spirit, welcome to this humble house." Colum-cille addressed the gathered. He could see Harold's brother, Leofwine, sitting almost regally in the front of the congregation.

"When the blessed Columba arrived on the shores of these islands, he was greeted by a people who held pagan beliefs and were ruled over by warlords from the channel to the highlands. Columba introduced the knowledge of Christ to these pagans, who embraced his teachings. More than that, they followed his example, and monasteries were founded throughout the land that the inhabitants could become closer to Christ and do deeds which reflected on his glory.

"These monasteries were not meant to set Christ's followers apart from the world, but to provide a place of temporary seclusion as well as community. Columba taught that the monks should move about the countryside, bringing the Gospel and their good deeds to all the people and letting them see what it meant to live a life devoted to the Father and the teachings of His Son that they may similarly lead such lives."

So far, he hadn't said anything the congregation would find particularly controversial. He knew that was about to change and he expected some uproar, although he had no idea where it would originate. He hoped it wouldn't come from Leofwine. He needed the king's brother's support and he also knew that Leofwine's men stood throughout the cathedral.

"Even as Columba's monks were teaching the true faith throughout this island, a foreigner came to our shores, not far from Senlac where good King Harold most recently turned away invaders. This man proclaimed that he also taught the ways of Christ, but he taught that no man could presume to know God's will or teachings unless he had the blessing of a foreign prince who styled himself 'pope.' This man taught that God would not hear the prayers of any man, be he humble ploughman to king upon a throne, unless those prayers were passed through an intermediary he called 'priest.' He claimed to preach the Gospel in order to separate man from God, not enjoin them together."

As expected, the congregation was getting restless. He was telling them that everything they had learned and practiced their entire lives was wrong.

"I have been asked by good King Harold to restore the old ways to this island, and so I shall. And surely, God will look at those who have been led astray by this distant pope and his priests and find mercy in His heart as they learn to worship Him correctly and do good deeds and none who followed the Roman ways in ignorance shall be denied their place in Heaven.

"From this time hence, monks will follow the rule laid forth by the holy Columbanus whether they are monastic or in peregrination throughout the land and they shall wear the tonsure you see I wear.

"Although priests are not necessary to make sure your prayers reach God in His heaven, they still have a place in the Church. While monks serve God in contemplation, priests serve God by helping their fellow man. Furthermore, while the foreigners teach that it is sinful for a priest to take a wife, Celtic priests, who offer succor to their parishes, have long taken wives to help perform the work of Christ on earth."

If anything, the announcement that priests could marry set off even more consternation among the congregation than the idea that priests could marry. While the first pronouncement only caused muttering and fidgeting, the idea that priests needn't be celibate caused people to jump from their seats.

Colum-cille found that he couldn't continue his sermon over the commotion of the congregation. A couple of King Harold's thegns jumped up to help Colum-cille from the pulpit while others worked to quell the increasing unrest that could well have resulted in a riot if they hadn't been in the cathedral.

CHAPTER VII

A freezing January rain, laced with sleet, fell from grey Northumbrian skies on the stone castle belonging to Morkere, Earl of Northumbria. The small stained glass windows of the great hall rattled where the sleet scratched against their smooth panes. The path leading to the castle, recently churned by horse hooves was quickly turning from a sticky morass into a frozen sea of mud.

Inside the great hall, eight men were assembled around a vast table. Empty except for a large, lit candelabra in the center, the table held promise of a tremendous repast after the men had concluded the business for which they had been summoned to the castle at Morpeth. Although many of the men lost no love between themselves, all were summoned because they had agreed, in some way, to support a revolt, led by Earl Morkere against King Harold of England.

While waiting for the earl to make his appearance, the men spoke quietly amongst themselves, sounding each other out to discover how far each man intended to commit himself to Morkere's plan and whether or not any plots were brewing which might be directed at himself. Sitting amidst this great storm of activity, his eyes closed as he listened to the scratching and rattling of the sleet on glass, sat Arnketil, perhaps the most powerful Saxon in the North with the exception of Morkere. As with the lesser men who surrounded Arnketil, he had his own agenda, but while they played for minor stakes, Arnketil's stratagem would possibly land him one of the biggest pots of all.

Arnketil did not approve of Morkere, a situation of which he was positive Morkere was aware. Nevertheless, Morkere believed that he needed Arnketil's support and Arnketil wished Morkere to believe that Arnketil would provide it. If everything worked according to plan, Morkere would soon be less powerful than Olaf of Pennistoke, who sat speaking to Uhtred of Tickhill. For Arnketil, the rewards could be nearly endless. The political structure of the North had been destroyed after the battle of Senlac when William's forces killed many of the North's most powerful lords before the Normans were routed. Harold had still not finished apportioning their lost land to the survivors. Once Morkere's Revolt fell, Arnketil stood to gain the lion's share of the lost lands. And, he well knew, with land came power.

As if thinking of the earl summoned him, Morkere strode, unannounced, through the large double doors at the far end of the great hall. The walk past the length of the table to his empty chair at its head, next to where Arnketil sat, was enough to command the attention, and silence, from all the assembled rebels.

Morkere didn't wait for any of the men to begin speaking again. Looking down the length of the table, he addressed the barons, "In the past, Northern England ruled all of this island. The king of Northumbria was the most powerful man in all England. Our ancestors were the undisputed lords of the island. It is only recently, within the past hundred years or so, that our great lands were subjected to the rule of the Southern weaklings from Wessex.

"Now my brother-in-law has embarked on a journey which will surely destroy all of England unless we separate ourselves from his folly. Soon, the combined might of Christendom will be brought to bear against our island.

"To avoid this disaster, I say the time has come to regain our ascendency over the Southerners."

Morkere's assessment of the situation was interrupted by Uhtred of Tickhill. "Our doom has been tied to the Southerners for too long as it is. I say we sever our connection to them and let the continentals do as they would like with the Wessexmen. We should look to the North!"

AFTER HASTINGS

Olaf of Pennistoke quickly leaped on Uhtred's words as if they were a battle cry. "Look to the North! Our brethren in Norway will come to our aid."

"No!" Uhtred's voice echoed throughout the hall. "There is no need to look to Magnus of Norway or Svein of Denmark for help. Our problems started when Svegn Forkbeard and his accursed son Cnut came to England fifty years ago. They tied us to the south more firmly then ever before and opened the doors for those French whom Edward brought over with him."

"Uhtred is right. I know Olaf's family maintains close ties to their clan in Norway, but an invitation to Magnus would only ensure a different overlord for the North once we threw off the shackles of Southern rule. What good is ridding ourselves of Harold and his idiocy if we merely replace it with the idiocy of other outsiders?"

"I'll tell you the good." Earmcearig's thick brogue stole all attention from Morkere's softly spoken words. "Harold has ruled for less then two years. He has already cost the North many of our best thegns. Were not my own father and brother killed when he led them against his own brother at Stamford Bridge just over a year ago?" As Earmcearig spoke, his accent became thicker as his agitation grew. By the time he was finished only Limhal and Gottcund could actually understand his words, although his meaning was discerned by all the assembled men. The border earl's hatred of Harold stemming from the battle at the Bridge was well known throughout the North, one of the reasons Morkere invited the man.

"Although I agree that ridding ourselves of Harold is important, even you, Earmcearig, must see that we should not replace him with another outlander."

Earmcearig slowly nodded his head and muttered a quiet "Aye" into his beard.

Arnketil allowed his attention to wander. Nearly all of the men at the meeting were sure to support Morkere in his attack on Harold. Only Sigeweard Bearn, sitting across from him showed the possibility of siding with Harold. As in Arnketil's own case, Sigeweard could see that the distant power of Harold was better for his own self interest than the immediate power of a King Morkere. Of the other men, Limhal and Heardcwide would fight anyone they were pointed at, in the latter case especially something which didn't have a Northern feel to it. Uhtred, Earmcearig, and Olaf were all known quantities.

At last coming to Gottcund, Arnketil began to wonder. The pious baron was nearly lost sitting between the enormous bulk of Heardcwide and the compact, but intense presence of Earmcearig. Gottcund could probably be counted on to side with Morkere as long as the Northumbrian earl agreed to allow England to return to the fold of the Catholic Church.

"Surely you see the importance of gaining the pope's blessing for an expedition of this magnitude," Gottcund said.

"And just how is the pope any different from any other foreign prince?" As soon as the words were out of Uhtred's mouth, Arnketil knew that they were the wrong ones to say to a man of Gottcund's faith.

"His Holiness, Pope Alexander II, is God's most direct and divine representative on Earth. If he does not transmit God's approval of our cause, our doom will be to fail."

"Yet we are going to war against God's own enemy, the worm Harold of Wessex. Surely, He will give his blessing against such a maggot whether we gain the pope's support or not," Earmcearig pointed out.

"Not necessarily. His arsenal is great and varied. If we displease Him by trying to do His work for the wrong reasons He will surely allow us to falter and then achieve His goal by other means. Even now, Alexander and Hildebrand work to unite the Christians on the continent in a holy war against Harold. If we have not His support, I can assure you that they will succeed where we fail." As Gottcund spoke, he fidgited with the small gilded wooden crucifix he had drawn from a fold in his tunic.

Arnketil looked down the table at the small wooden carving and could tell at a glance that it was probably the most valuable thing Gottcund was wearing. Something about the way Gottcund was looking around the table at men who he considered to be unbelievers made Arnketil realize that someone had to show support for his point of view.

"Earmcearig, you are a fool," Sigeweard Bearn said softly. Immediately all eyes were turned to where Sigeweard sat next to Morkere. "Just because we both fight the same enemy does not make us friends. Just an instance. Your father and brother fought against Hardraada and Tostig at Stamford Bridge," At their names, Earmcearig, Gottcund, and Sigeweard all crossed themselves, "and they fought alongside Harold Godwinson. That did not make them Harold's friends, but merely allies of convenience. Similarly, we can oppose this same Harold and yet remain un-friend with respect to the alliance Alexander is building on the continent. I agree with Gottcund that Alexander's blessing is necessary if we are to succeed, if for no other reason than to ensure that once we *déposâmes* Harold we do not have to fight off the rest of Christendom." Sigeweard's purposeful use of the Norman word for depose accented the foreigness of the concept to the barons. His point was taken by the majority of the men who were gathered around the table who fell silent upon his explanation.

The brief silence was interrupted by Uhtred whose desire for isolation from the rest of England bordered on a fanatical devotion to clan and hatred of outsiders. "How will these warriors for the pope come to fight us? We can easily hold the passes to the South!"

"And how did the Danes attack us fifty years ago?" Morkere answered, "The pope's army could just as easily land on the coast which lies near these lands." He gestured vaguely to the east.

"I think we can agree that requesting the pope's blessing can't harm our cause, but even as we send an emissary to request it, we should continue to plan our assault. I would like to aim for a time as early as possible. No later than the first of May. That will give us almost four months to prepare."

When everyone at the table had nodded their assent, Morkere began to outline his plans in detail. Slowly, through the night, a basic campaign plan was drawn up and each man learned the part he was to play in its organization and outcome.

CHAPTER VIII

Alexander stood next to the fireplace, staring out the window as snow fell lightly and silently on the already snow covered fields of Canossa Castle where Matilda of Tuscany played gracious hostess. Alexander had already waited through most of three days for Heinrich to arrive for the hastily arranged meeting between pontiff and emperor to discuss the threat of the English heretics. The pope could not help but feel that with every day the emperor delayed his arrival at Canossa, the English position would become that much more unassailable, for despite his knowledge that the Roman Church was the one true path of God, events in Spain and Byzantium had demonstrated that setbacks could occur against the Roman Church. Such events happening so close to the millenium seemed to hint that the Antichrist would soon appear.

Alexander turned his back toward the window and walked across the room. Matilda had turned over an entire floor of the castle to the papal party, yet because of the limited amount of time she had to prepare for the visit, many personal items had been left behind. Alexander picked up a small hand-mirror that either Matilda or one of her ladies-in-waiting had left sitting on the table. The pope examined his face in the small, polished metal of the mirror's surface.

The face that peered back at him was not the stern countenance of Pope Alexander II. Instead, he saw the kind, elderly face of Anselm of Baggio, the cardinal he had been before his elevation in September of 1061. Looking beyond the wrinkles and grey hairs, Alexander was able to make out the eyes and smile of the child Anselm who had once run across the family estates of Baggio in the summer. Continued gazing brought images of him as a student under Lanfranc at Bec. In those long lost days, did Lanfranc ever dream that this student would grant him the archepiscopal see of Canterbury? Somehow, Alexander doubted Lanfranc had ever entertained any greater hopes for young Anselm than a small parish church somewhere. As Alexander's reflection aged in the Pope's mind, if not the mirror, Alexander saw himself at the court of Heinrich III, speaking to Prince Heinrich, who was now on his way to meet with the Pope at Canossa.

No matter how hard Alexander looked at the image in the mirror, he could not see the regal pope who was the implacable enemy of Harold of England. Anselm agreed with everything that Alexander had done as pope, but there was still a barrier between the two men, separated by a mere vote of cardinals. To this day, more than six years into his papacy, Alexander still felt that Anselm was his real identity and Alexander was only a costume he put on when he had to give his attention to official business.

A knock on the door brought the pope out of his reverie and suddenly he found Alexander staring at him from the mirror. He hurriedly put the mirror back on the table and walked to the fireplace. It would not do to have people thinking him vain.

"Enter," Alexander called, when he was suitably positioned in front of the warm hearth.

The door opened just enough for Lotario to enter. He bowed his head to Alexander and spoke in his soft voice. "Your Holiness, I have just received word that Emperor Heinrich has been seen entering the village of Canossa. He should arrive within a half hour."

Alexander took one last glance at the mirror sitting on the table and promptly forgot the kindly image of Anselm he had admired in its shiny surface. Heinrich must only see the harsh, yet just, face of God's vicar. With January days so short, a halfhour did not give Alexander much time to prepare.

"Help me into my formal robes." Even before Alexander had given the order, Lotario had begun to move toward the cabinet which contained the pallium and staff which served as the regalia for the pope. He had worked for Alexander long enough that he could anticipate his master's requirements.

Within moments, Alexander was dressed and hurrying through the halls of the castle. Lotario ran ahead of the pope, pounding on doors and yelling to alert the members of the papal entourage that their presence would be required in the Great Hall.

By the time the last of the pope's company had arrived in the Great Hall, Alexander was firmly enthroned in the great chair which Matilda had provided for his visit. Standing to the pope's right, in a position of honor, stood Matilda of Tuscany, herself.

Despite her exalted rank as Countess of Canossa and hostess to the Pope and the Holy Roman emperor, Matilda's dress was reminiscent of the lowliest penitent. Her rough clothing was a perfect match for the harshness of her face. Although she seemed to dislike being in the presence of the pope, the same attitude existed no matter where she was nor whose company she shared.

It wasn't long after the last of the papal party arrived in the hall that a page announced the arrival of the emperor's entourage at the gates of Canossa. Glancing quickly at Matilda, the pope motioned for the page to admit the emperor.

While Alexander waited through the last moments calmly to all outward appearances, inward he seethed at the audacity of the Emperor to make him, the Pope, wait for nearly three days while Heinrich took his time in arriving at their meeting.

When Heinrich entered the Hall, he was still brushing freshly fallen snow from his shoulders and head. He walked briskly, the whole time, across the vast floor and past the courtiers and clerics until he stood at the base of the dais on which sat the great golden chair of the pontiff. Looking first at Matilda and then at Alexander, Heinrich nodded his head in the briefest movement.

AFTER HASTINGS

"We greet you Lady Matilda of Canossa and thank your for your hospitality in providing this location for a meeting between us and His Holiness. We also greet Your Holiness, Pope Alexander. As we have just arrived, we ask time to rest before our important meeting."

Alexander frowned at Heinrich as if he had tasted a particularly sour lemon. Before speaking, Alexander allowed a lengthy silence to build, almost to a crescendo. "You have kept us waiting for three days. A few moments more will not tax our patience much further."

Without flinching at the pope's remark, Heinrich merely nodded his head. "Until later then." He turned briefly toward Matilda, "Milady."

Within moments of beginning, the first audience between pope and emperor was over with the Holy Roman emperor and his company leaving the Great Hall. Alexander couldn't help but think that Heinrich was exiting the room with a minor victory over the Church.

Heinrich was shown to his rooms at Canossa by Matilda's major domo, a thin, dark-haired Italian with small, inset eyes peering from behind a large, aquiline nose. Although he spoke to the emperor in a deferential manner, the tone of his voice hinted at a certain amount of boredom.

"I am called Bernardo. If you have any questions, feel free to ask them of me. My mistress, Matilda, Countess of Tuscany, has released me to your service for the duration of your stay.

"While you are at Canossa, you will have total access to the northern tower, which we have cleared for your use. Your priest can celebrate mass in the private chapel in the tower, or His Holiness, Pope Alexander has agreed to say mass in the main chapel as long as he is in residence."

Bernardo fell quiet as the emperor's party entered the north tower behind him. Although one of the oldest parts of the castle, the tower had recently been redecorated. All the tapestries in the hallways depicted scenes from the life of Christ, beginning with Mary and Joseph's journey near the entry to the tower and culminating with Him seated on the throne of heaven following His resurrection next to the chambers which were given to the emperor for his residence.

"Our thanks, Bernardo." Heinrich put just the right amount of condescension into his voice. Bernardo's attitude had demonstrated to Heinrich that the major domo was already getting jaded after three days in the papal presence and Heinrich meant to instill in him the respect due to the Holy Roman emperor.

CHAPTER IX

Thurlkill found that he was enjoying spending February in the Northern castle of Arnketil. Within his first week at the baron's manor, the thegn had discovered a small cave overlooking a small mountain lake. Thurlkill found that the cave offered protection from the wind and snow and a small fire near the opening would keep him warm enough. Below the cave, the frozen surface of the tarn glittered, a natural mirror, whenever the sun was able to break through the heavy winter cloud cover.

Arnketil's frequent trips criss-crossing the English Northlands meant that there was little time for Thurlkill to take care of any negotiations involving the marriage between Arnketil's daughter and Harold's son. In fact, beyond a brief introduction to Arnketil when Thurlkill first arrived, the thegn had hardly seen or spoken to his erstwhile host. Nevertheless, Thurlkill had managed to strike up friendships with some of the other thegns and housecarls who served Arnketil. Through this informal network, he was able to learn something of the lord's activities.

It seemed that while Arnketil met with Morkere and other Northern barons, he also maintained a constant, if surreptitious, connection with Harold's brother, Leofwine, who had based himself in London. Through this clandestine message service, Arnketil was able to warn Leofwine that Morkere was behind an uprising about to erupt near Maldon in Essex. From what Thurlkill was able to gather, Leofwine's warning to the local baron had allowed him to avert the danger.

AFTER HASTINGS

To the south of the cave in which Thurlkill sat, a large group of men were riding up the road to Arnketil's castle. At first, Thurlkill dismissed the band as a bunch of merchants who were going to try to unload some of their wares, but he then recognized Arnketil's banner leading the assemblage. Slightly behind Arnketil's banner, in a position which denoted a honored guest, was a banner which took a few minutes for Thurlkill to recognise as belonging to Sigeweard Bearn, one of the wealthiest thegns in all of England.

Thurlkill was unsure where Sigeweard Bearn stood on the issues which were rending England, but had a sickening feeling that Arnketil had decided that supporting Harold had become undesirable. Although Sigeweard Bearn was powerful, he would not pose the same threat to Arnketil that Morkere engendered since he was merely a thegn, like Thurlkill, and not an earl or ealdorman.

Worried that this would mean an end to the marriage between Edmund and Arnegifu, Thurlkill hurried from the cave and ploughed through the snowy fields which separated him from the castle to which Arnketil and Sigeweard Bearn's procession was slowly proceeding. When the young thegn arrived at the gates, he saw that he had enough time to prepare for a formal audience and hurried to his rooms to change and warm up.

An hour, and a pitcher of warmed ale later, a warm, neat Thurlkill approached Arnketil's chamberlain, Neadhaes, and requested an audience with the returning earl.

"The master will be unavailable for some time, although I believe that he desires your company at dinner. He intends to eat immediately following Vespers."

"Thank you." Thurlkill found nothing strange in showing respect to the ceorl, despite Neadhaes's lower social rank. He needed the good graces of Arnketil's servant in order to salvage the mission which Harold had set for him. Turning from the chamberlain, Thurlkill wandered around the castle until he entered the practice yard. One of Arnketil's ceorls was busy clearing the snow from the courtyard with a heavy broom. Thurlkill relaxed in an alcove which had once held a statue and watched the man at his labor.

After watching for a few moments, Thurlkill left his hiding place and walked out to the center of the courtyard. Along the way, he grabbed a broom which was leaning, unused, against a snow-covered stone bench. As he walked, he began to brush the light powder from his path and joined in the general effort. Thurlkill worked without speaking, and it took the ceorl a little while to realize that he had gained some help. He looked over to the thegn and grinned a toothless smile, pausing only for the briefest of moments before continuing to clear the snow.

The clear, cold air had a crisp bite to it, but the manual labor Thurlkill did caused him to work up a sweat. Since the work to clear the large courtyard of snow was so tedious, Thurlkill permitted his mind to wander, reflecting back on the days only a year or two past when he would play in the snowdrifts at his father's manor at Staunton. It was while Thurlkill was thinking back to his irresponsible childhood, that the ceorl began to speak to him.

". . . talk to my lord Arnketil, aren't you? Won't you be happy now that his lordship has returned to Scinestorp. P'rhaps you'll have a chance to talk business with him finally."

Thurlkill was about to take umbrage at the ceorl's churlish words, but paused when he realized that there was no sarcasm in the man's voice, merely curiosity.

"Yes," he replied in a tentative voice. It wouldn't be appropriate to voice any of his concerns to a ceorl, especially one who worked in his host's manor and who was a total stranger.

While Thurlkill was trying to find something else to say, the ceorl began to look around the courtyard, as if to see if he had left anything out of place or missed any of the snow. When the man was satisfied that the job was completely finished, he motioned for Thurlkill to follow him.

"I imagine you'll be having an interest in what my lord Arnketil is saying to Sigeweard Bearn," the ceorl said *sotto voce*. If you'll follow me, I can show you a place where you can hear what passes in the lord's audience chamber."

Thurlkill realized what a huge risk the ceorl was taking in revealing his hidey hole to the thegn. "My name is Thurlkill, son of Aethelwine."

"Aye, I know. They call me Esnecund." Esnecund motioned for Thurlkill to follow him and keep quiet. As the two men left the courtyard, a light flurry of snow began to fall.

Esnecund led Thurlkill through a series of narrow passageways in the manor which were obviously the domain of the servants. Their walls were nearly bare, and where tapestries hung, they were old and threadworn or almost entirely without design, functional rather than decorative. Eventually, Esnecund pulled aside a grey tapestry to reveal a small hole in the wall. The ceorl pointed at the hole and Thurlkill bent close to the floor so he could see through the opening.

He found himself looking into Arnketil's audience chamber. Arnketil was sitting at a large table looking at a man who Thurlkill could not see through the small aperture. Thurlkill shifted to allow his ear to press up to the hole.

"Sigeweard is being settled into his apartments?" Although phrased as a question, Arnketil's tone made his words a statement to which there could only be one answer.

"Of course." The baron's companion's voice was muffled since he was facing away from the hole behind which Thurlkill crouched. Nevertheless, the thegn recognized the speaker as Neadhaes. "I've also had a request from the Southern boy to meet with you. He seems a bit, well, agitated."

"And you told him?"

"That you would see him at dinner. Following Vespers."

"Very good. That should give him enough time to wonder what my plans are." Arnketil paused to take a drink of wine, a habit which Harold had denounced as being tainted with a Frenchness. "I imagine that by now he has no idea what to expect when I finally do meet with him. Tell me again about this boy."

Thurlkill could hear Neadhaes shift in his chair before he answered his lord's order.

"The lad's name is Thurlkill. His father, Aethelwine, has long been a friend and advisor to Harold. Dating to even before the Godwin clan was banished briefly in 1052."

"Yes, I know this. Tell me about the boy, not history." Arnketil's voice seemed to betray irritation and impatience.

"Yes, then. Thurlkill exhibits many signs that he will be similar to Aethelwine when he grows up. He was born right around the time that Godwin died. The provisional deal that Harold worked out with our ambassador is for Thurlkill to arrange the marriage between Arnegifu and Harold's son. I imagine that your arrival with Sigeweard Bearn has thrown the boy somewhat. It might be exactly what you need to gain a stronger bargaining position."

Arnketil grunted in acknowledgement of Neadhaes's comment. "I really hadn't thought of it in those terms, but I suppose it's possible. I've merely been trying to persuade Sigeweard to get off the fence he's been straddling and stand firmly behind Harold against Morkere."

"Thurlkill seems to be intent on marrying Arnegifu to Edmund. Even after this Colum-cille recognises Harold's bastards, Edmund won't be in line to inherit his father's throne."

Esnecund tapped Thurlkill on the shoulder and pulled him away from the hole in the wall, allowing the tapestry to drop down over it.

"Someone is coming down the hall," the ceorl whispered into Thurlkill's ear.

The two men stood quickly and began to move down the corridor. Eventually, Esnecund led Thurlkill through a door into a smaller courtyard which, although recently swept, still had a light covering of snow on the cobblestones.

"I better keep you busy until dinner. Did you manage to learn anything?"

AFTER HASTINGS

"Why are you helping me this way? If your master finds out that you helped me to spy on him, I should think your life would be forfeit."

"My lord is not an evil man. I don't believe he would kill me that easily, although I would suffer for it. I like you. I've noticed how you've been neglected since you arrived. There are still some of us who believe in the king, for he was duly elected. The way Lord Arnketil was treating a representative of the king was simply wrong. Come help me."

Thurlkill spent the rest of the afternoon aiding Esnecund in the hundreds of little chores the ceorl was required to do each day. Mostly, the thegn aided in silence, trying to sort out the comments he had overheard Arnketil and Neadhaes make in confidence to each other, but also the words of loyalty Esnecund had spoken to a far distant monarch whom the ceorl would never see or meet.

Although not particularly religious, Thurlkill decided to go to Vespers before his meeting with Arnketil. He had gotten the impression that, rather than a great dinner to welcome Sigeweard Bearn to Scinestorp, Arnketil was planning on a private meal between himself and the Southern thegn he had not yet deigned to meet.

The services dragged on and Thurlkill found his mind continuously wandering to his upcoming meeting, the overheard discussion between Neadhaes and Arnketil, his conversation with Esnecund, and carefree times he had spent with his father and Harold's sons. Eventually, Vespers came to their conclusion and Thurlkill was free to meet with Arnketil for

The baron was seated at a small table in a small antechamber off the Great Hall. A goblet of a dark red wine sat on the table in front of him as he reclined in a relaxed position, for all the world like a man waiting for an old friend to join him.

"Have a seat. Neadhaes will be bringing in our dinner anon. Did you enjoy Vespers?"

Thurlkill was momentarily taken aback at Arnketil's knowledge of his movements and found himself wondering how much the baron knew. He quickly regained his composure and responded to Arnketil, "Your priest was very good. Was he trained in the South? I was able to understand him easily enough."

Arnketil laughed, "I can see that the king hasn't been teaching tact to his wards. I certainly hope he does a better job with my children. Would you like some wine? It comes from the vineyards of Burgundy."

Thurlkill looked at his host in astonishment. "I hardly think King Harold would approve of the location of your vintner."

"No, I don't suppose he would. But then, the king, for all his success in war must learn the importance of diplomacy and trade. In truth, I think you'll find this French wine superior to our English mead. If we can trade for a better product, why should we settle for less. It is hardly traitorous for me to desire the best I can afford."

Thurlkill conceded the point and reached for his goblet, which a servant promptly filled from the gold encrusted decanter which sat on the table. As the man finished pouring, Neadhaes entered bearing a plate of steaming meats, cheeses, and breads which he set on the table between the baron and the thegn before retiring wordlessly.

Arnketil piled some of the meat and cheese on a hunk of bread and began to eat, motioning for Thurlkill to follow suit. For long moments, the two men sat eating in a silence punctuated only by the sounds of chewing and drinking. Finally, Arnketil threw a bit of meat to the hound which was lying asleep in one corner of the room and spoke.

"I met your father once."

Thurlkill was surprised that Arnketil would begin with a reference to Aethelwine.

"I didn't know that."

"Yes. I met him once when I was at King Edward's court. I suppose it was a few years before Earl Godwin's death. Your father was a minor thegn from the Marches and I was a minor thegn from the North. We were seated at table together. Didn't have a whole lot to say as I recall. I thought he was a Southern prig and he probably thought I was an incomprehensible

AFTER HASTINGS

Northern barbarian. At the time, we were both probably right. I know I've changed since then and I imagine he has as well."

Thurlkill really wasn't sure how to respond to Arnketil's comments about his father. Although the Northerner's words were insulting, there seemed to be no intention of offense and Arnketil himself had admitted that his opinion of Aethelwine possibly no longer applied. Thurlkill decided to just sit quietly and wait for the baron to continue on his own.

"In any event, that was many years ago. Perhaps I'll meet your father again some day. The issue of the day is my daughter's marriage to the king's son. I am given to understand that King Harold has agreed to the marriage and it is simply a matter of deciding on the date and details."

Thurlkill nodded his head in agreement, "I believe that the king desires the marriage to take place in the South, probably in Wessex."

"That is fine with me. A royal wedding at Sarum Cathedral. Of course, my daughter is still a child. Merely five years old. Despite this, I presume King Harold will desire a wedding soon in order to cement our alliance."

"Harold hasn't specified when he sees the union taking place, but I believe it would not be out of order to plan an official ceremony for later in the year with a second ceremony once Arnegifu comes of age."

"How would Harold feel about a wedding in June, perhaps in the middle of the month?"

"It seems a reasonable request."

Arnketil shifted in his seat, "Fine, then Arnegifu and Godwin will be married on Saturday, June fourteen, Saint Dogmael's Day."

"Excuse me. I think you've been misinformed, my lord baron."

Arnketil raised an eyebrow.

"Your daughter Arnegifu is not to marry Godwin, but rather Edmund."

"But I thought Godwin was the king's eldest son."

"Godwin is, but Harold desires the marriage of your daughter to his second son, Edmund."

Arnketil lifted his goblet of Burgundian wine and sloshed the liquid around in the bowl. "Thurlkill, as I told you before, I want the best I can afford. In the case of liquids, I send to France for wine instead of English mead. In the case of sons-in-law, I look for future monarchs. Why should I permit my daughter to marry Harold's second son? Why, I might as well marry her off to Sigeweard Bearn's eldest son for all the good it will do her. Or perhaps I should marry her to one of Morkere's brats, they would be closer in age and who knows, perhaps Morkere will be the king some day. He certainly desires the throne."

Thurlkill paused, although he had expected Arnketil to use the suggestion of a marriage between Arnegifu and Sigeweard's son as an alternative to an alliance with Harold in an effort to promote a marriage with Godwin instead of Edmund. Thurlkill had no idea that Arnketil would be so blatant or go so far as to suggest alliance with Morkere. Thurlkill thought back to a conversation he had with Harold shortly before leaving for Scinestorp. Harold had suggested that Arnketil's greatest enemy in all England was Earl Morkere. Could Thurlkill trust Harold's impression of the situation and hold firm to Harold's wishes or take the chance that Harold had made a mistake?

"What would an alliance with Morkere gain you after he fell to Harold's forces?" Thurlkill asked without emotion. "My lord is being very careful. If the king were to get the impression that you are not completely loyal to him, I imagine that your lands would quickly become forfeit."

Thurlkill was pleased to see that his assessment of the situation had an effect on the northern baron. Arnketil leaned back in his chair and slowly took a sip of wine from the goblet he held in his hand. The baron, apparently rattled by the strength of Thurlkill's response, pulled the cup from his lips a little too quickly, spilling some of the crimson liquid on his tunic. The baron let out a howl as he jumped up from his chair. At the first sound of commotion, Neadhaes appeared at the doorway with three of Arnketil's ceorls, each armed with a short sword. When Neadhaes saw that

Arnketil was in no danger, he quickly waved the guards away from the doorway.

"Are you all right?" the steward asked his lord.

"I'm wet is what I am." Arnketil glared at Thurlkill. "This audience is at an end!"

Arnketil exited the room in a flurry of robes with Neadhaes dogging closely on his heels. Thurlkill helped himself to another goblet of the French wine and settled back into his chair, feeling confident that he had just won the first sortie in his battle with Arnketil.

CHAPTER X

Lotario and Johannes, advisors to Pope Alexander and Emperor Heinrich, had worked throughout the night to arrange the protocol which would attend the second meeting between the two princes. Their first agreement had been that the meeting would consist of as little pomp as possible and be closed to any observers. When the two men did enter the room, therefore, from opposite ends at the same time, they were accompanied only by Lotario and Johannes. The four men sat around a small, plain wooden table in unadorned chairs. The principals faced each other with their advisors on their right.

Alexander sat straight in his chair, looking down on Heinrich across the table from him. Although Heinrich stood taller than the pontiff, all of the emperor's height was in his legs while Alexander had a longer torso. "We have called you to Canossa to discuss a most urgent and serious matter on the western edge of the realms of Christendom. As you are no doubt aware, the English pretender has threatened to tear his domain from the loving arms of *Ecclesia*.

"Upon this man's call, the English people have become enamoured of his heretical views, making Harold Godwinson into a modern Pelagius.

While we did not agree to make this Harold king of England, we would have conceded his position, except for his determination to turn his back on the Mother Church."

Heinrich shifted in his seat, inhaling in an effort to bring his eyes level with the pontiff's. "You are afraid that Harold's actions will weaken the papacy throughout Christendom, especially coming so closely, as it does, on the heels of the schism with Constantinople," the emperor stated brazenly.

"This is not about the papacy. It is about the proper way to worship Our Lord Jesus Christ. There is only one right way to pay homage to Him. He said of Peter, 'You are Peter, the Rock; and on this rock I will build my Church.' After His crucifixion and resurrection, Peter came to Rome and converted the Romans to His way, becoming the first in the line of popes. Only the way descended from Peter is the proper way to worship Christ. All other ways, whether the Byzantine heresy, Arianism, or the Pelagian scourge which even now threatens the Saxons is wrong. Those who are led into temptation will suffer the eternal torments of hell."

Heinrich sat back in his chair as he listened to the pope continue his diatribe against Harold and the English. The emperor had spent the morning, and indeed the days leading up to this confrontation, discussing the problem with Johannes. On the one hand, if Harold successfully broke away from Rome, it would mean a weakening of papal power, something which Heinrich would be all too happy to see happen. On the other hand, Harold could be considered a pretender to the English throne and any pretender in Christendom was something to worry about. If it could happen in England, what was to keep such an event from occuring in the Empire?

Johannes's nudge under the table brought Heinrich back to Canossa. He ran his fingers through his beard while trying to remember what Alexander had been saying just before Johannes interrupted Heinrich's thoughts. Something about Harold as an usurper. Even if that wasn't what

Alexander was talking about, it was probably a safe bet that Heinrich could speak about that without giving away his wool-carding.

"*Sicherlich*, any kind of usurper is something to be concerned with. I will happily aid you against the usurper who has claimed the throne of England. Yet, it is my understanding that William has renounced any claim he, or his kin, have on the English throne. That sounds to me as if Harold can no longer be called a usurper or a pretender. If not Harold, then who shall be King of England?"

"Harold's youngest brother is still untainted by the Pelagian heresy which Harold had reintroduced into the kingdom of the Angles. Although he is also a son of Godwin, he has been raised under the reforming influence of the Norman court and will, we believe, make a suitable king of the English. It will be under his banner, as well as the papal banner, that the armies of Christendom will march to regain England for the Mother Church."

"By what right do you feel you may name kings at your leisure? If I agree to support you against the English, how do I know that you will support my son when the time comes for him to be elected my successor?"

"In the normal course of events, it is not the prerogative of the pope to name the rulers of Christendom. In this case, however, Harold has attempted to take his kingdom outside the bonds of Christendom and that gives me the right, the responsibility, actually, to step in and bind the English kingdom to the true way of God. If Harold is permitted to lead his land astray, he dooms thousands of souls to the eternal torments of hell."

Heinrich started to rise from his chair, but the steadying hand of Johannes on his wrist reminded the emperor that to stand without the pope's leave would go against the established protocol for the meeting. Heinrich would have to forego his nervous habit of pacing during this meeting. Although the emperor had no doubt that he would support the pope in this campaign, he wanted to make sure that Alexander knew that this was a war against a usurper, not against a heretic.

"As long as Harold remains king of England, he is a danger to myself and my fellow monarchs, including the kings of France, Aragon, and Sicilia. I am sure that they will aid in our cause to rid Christendom of this usurper. However, you must remember this, unfortunate as it is, not all of the kings of Christendom are as devout and pious and you or I. They may see this as simply a battle against an upstart. If you begin to try to point out the heretical nature of Harold's regime, they may believe that you are simply trying to gain power and advantage for the papacy at a fellow monarch's expense."

Alexander settled back in his chair, the hard wooden back pressing uncomfortably into his shoulders. The negotiations with the emperor were getting away from him somehow. It wasn't enough to just get Heinrich's support against Harold as a usurper. Heinrich would also have to support the papacy on the question of heresy. The pope leaned over to Lotario.

"I would speak with you in private."

"I believe that can be arranged." Lotario stood from his chair and looked across the table, addressing Johannes, "My lord, Pope Alexander, desires to take counsel."

Johannes glanced at Heinrich and then quickly nodded his head. While Alexander and Lotario retreated to one corner of the hall, the emperor and his advisor bent their heads close together.

"My lord," Lotario began when he and the Pope were as far as possible from the negotiation table, "may I be so bold as to point out that although Heinrich currently supports you for his own perverse reasons, he does support you. If you push any further, you risk alienating that support."

"What would you have me do?"

"Allow me to conclude the negotiations. You, and the emperor, can both attend to other affairs. I will work with Johannes to seal the alliance. We stand less chance of losing Heinrich's that support that way. I will still champion our cause in all its details."

Alexander turned away from Lotario and caught sight of Anselm's face reflecting in the glass. Alexander the politician would stay and see the negotiations through to the most minute details. Anselm just wanted to get away from the games he was being forced to take part in. It had been a long time since Alexander had allowed Anselm to have his way in matters of the Church. Perhaps now was the time to let Anselm speak.

With his back still toward Lotario, Anselm said, "Let it be so."

With Lotario and Johannes deep in negotiations, Alexander walked briskly through the halls of Canossa to his chambers. When he arrived there, he was startled to find a messenger waiting for him, the boy's clothing stained with the dust and mud of the roads he traveled. When the pope first entered, the boy was sitting in a chair by the fire with a goblet of mulled wine, but when he saw the pontiff, he rapidly jumped to his feet and then dropped to one knee.

"Your Holiness."

"Rise, my son."

The boy stood, trying to keep his eyes from Alexander's face. He reached into a pouch he carried and passed a scroll to the pope.

Alexander motioned for the boy to leave, which he did with gratitude, and then sat down in the chair recently vacated by the messenger. He unrolled the scroll and read it in the firelight.

"Lambert, legate in Constantinople, to Alexander, servant of those who serve God, greetings.

"I have heard of the difficulties which are transpiring at the other end of the world where the English have embraced the ways of Arian. Such news as this can only be bad, made worse by these troubled times and may signify the coming of the Enemy which will presage His Second Coming.

"In any event, I find that events in Constantinople have taken a turn about which I must inform you as they may have some bearing on your present difficulties with the Saxons and their heretic-usurper Harold.

"As you are aware from my previous epistle, the Byzantine emperor, Constantine, tenth of his name, died in May of last year. The government was officially given into the

hands of his empress, Eudocia, who was to serve as regent for their three sons with the able and wise advice of the late emperor's brother. Eudocia, however, has proven herself fickle, as is the way of all women, and has turned her back on her own children, much as Edward of England's mother turned from her children by her first marriage. Yesterday, the empress married a Cappadocian general, Romanus Diogenes. Romanus, with the support of his bride, declared himself emperor of the Byzantines, much to the horror of Constantine's brother.

"Within hours of his announcement, I found that an emissary from the English usurper had made his arrival in Constantinople known and was wooing the Byzantine emperor to his cause, as two heretics and usurpers will join against the pious and legal world in which we live under His gaze.

"I do not, as yet, know whether this Romanus will league himself with the English or fight Constantinople's own battles, of which plenty exist. In the past, Romanus, who is a skilled general, has focused his attention on the Seljuqs who threaten from the Eastern borders of the empire and who espouse the Islamic faith of the devil. Although it pains me to rely on the Moslems against Christian brothers, even misguided Christians such as the Byzantines, we can only hope that these heathens will continue to harass Constantinople and keep Romanus from allying himself with the English Arians.

"Written this feast day of the Saints Basil and Gregory Nazianzus, who fought against the original Arius in the fourth century after the incarnation of our Saviour, Jesus Christ."

CHAPTER XI

Nothing Aethelwine had ever heard or seen had prepared him for the utter strangeness of the Moorish court. The lands of Southern Spain and Northern Africa were sweltering ovens compared to the cool, moist climate of England. The people were strange in every way. Although not

AFTER HASTINGS

the black skinned monsters legend had painted them, their skin had a dark greyish quality to it. Their language and customs were like nothing Aethelwine had ever experienced.

For the first week after Aethelwine had arrived, he simply walked around the city staring at the strange architecture and trying to learn enough of the customs and language so he wouldn't embarrass himself and, by extension, Harold.

The royal city of Ishbiliya, Aethelwine had been informed, dated back to the time of the Romans, when it was called Hispalis. When the Visigoths had wrested the land from the Romans, they renamed the site Seville. Thus its name had remained until the Great Moslem expansion had gained control of the city and renamed it Ishbiliya. In the year's since al-Mu'tadid's father had established his capital at Ishbiliya, the city had continued to grow until it rivaled its nearest enemy, Cordoba.

Aethelwine was impressed with nearly every aspect of the strange city in which he found himself. The royal palace was the centerpiece of the city and Aethelwine always found himself catching his breath whenever he was permitted admittance to the palace grounds

As he wandered the city, he learned how outdated the news in England was. During the past few years, al-Mu'tadid had managed to extend his hold over Southern Iberia, creating a strong kingdom, which, if he could hold it together, would easily be able to rival the Christian kingdoms of the North. The process of accumulation which al-Mu'tadid used was reminiscent of those used by Angles and Saxons which Bede had described in his history of the English Church. Eventually, Aethelwine realized that he couldn't put off meeting with al-Mu'tadid any longer and approached the door to the *muluk*'s great palace. Gaining admittance to the monarch proved much more difficult than Aethelwine had imagined it would be, but eventually, after several days of trying, he made it into the al-Mu'tadid's audience chamber. In the month since then, negotiations between Aethelwine and al-Mu'tadid had gone slowly. The prince seemed more intent on prising any piece of information concerning Northern

Spain he could out of Aethelwine without even referring to Harold's problems in England. Although Aethelwine realized how important it was to Harold's cause to maintain good relations with al-Mu'tadid, he was at a point far past the time when he would have been shaking Harold physically to force him to see reason.

While waiting for the prince's daily summons, which might or might not come, Aethelwine sat in a small outdoor tavern. The tavern was housed in the side of a small building with lightweight tapestries extending from the room to poles which had been set up in the street. A few tables and stools had been placed under the covering. In accordance with the strange customs, Aethelwine was drinking a pulpy orange sherbet since the Moslems forbade alcohol in their cities.

While he ate, Aethelwine fanned himself with a small set of feathers he had bought in the bazaar to ward off the interminable heat of the morning sun. Although he still wore his good English clothing, he was almost to a point when he would have forsaken its familiarity for the outrageous garb the Moslems wore in the hopes that it would keep him cooler and more comfortable. The heat had served as the best medicine for Aethelwine's leg wound, though. The long, white scar from his thigh to his calf was not the only reminder of his injury at Hastings. Whenever the weather was cool and moist, nearly constantly in England, his leg throbbed. Although Ishbiliya was located in the verdant Guadalquivir River Valley, surrounded as it was by the dry Iberian plateaus, his injury nearly never bothered him and he could, at times, forget he had ever been wounded.

Aethelwine was just reaching into his mouth to retrieve one of the small white seeds which hid in the fruit when the messenger from the muluk appeared. The boy felt to his knees in the dusty road and bowed his head toward Aethelwine.

"Greetings, lord from the North. My lord, muluk al-Mu'tadid bi 'Illah, Abu 'Amr 'Abbad ibn Muhammad ibn 'Abbad, has requested your company." The boy prostrated himself again as Aethelwine rose from his seat to follow him back to the caliph's palace.

The streets were crowded with the mid-morning masses of Moslems, Christians, and Jews moving about their business. Aethelwine found the merger of the three religions extremely strange, especially in light of the homogeneity of Anglo-Saxon culture. Until Harold's argument with the pope, England had been a country of one religion. Now its people embraced two religions which were, however, different aspects of the same creed. In the Moslem lands, three completely different religions were practiced side-by-side, with Aethelwine's own religion in the minority.

As they walked through the streets of the *suq*, merchants of all three races called to them to buy, or at least examine, their wares. When Aethelwine had first arrived, he had explored the narrow, winding streets of the Moslem bazaar and bought several trinkets to take back to England. It wasn't long before he realized how badly he was overcharged by the local merchants of all three religions, all of whom expected him to haggle over their prices. Once he realized how badly he had been taken, Aethelwine resolved only to buy food for the remainder of his stay in the Islamic world.

As Aethelwine walked through the crowded, exotic streets, he found himself wondering whether the England he remembered really existed. The Moslem world through which he walked seemed so vivid and alive that it seemed impossible that such a grey, drab land as England could exist in the same world.

The audience room he was escorted into was one of the smallest he had seen so far in Ishbiliya. Even so, it would have dwarfed Harold's largest Great Hall at Westminster. Just the size alone impressed Aethelwine with the power of a people who could build such a palace and maintain it, even after a hundred years and a fragmenting of their kingdom, which was, no doubt, the effect al-Mu'tadid desired the building to have on Aethelwine.

The walls of the room were punctuated by large, arched windows, opening on courtyards and other audience chambers. Although Aethelwine tried to avoid gazing out through the windows, he could not help but see the tall, narrow palm trees which soared skywards in clusters from the courtyards, nor avoid hearing the trickling noise of water falling from the countless fountains which ringed the audience chamber he was in.

At one end of the hall, al-Mu'tadid sat on a large pile of cushions. Surrounding him was a group of five men, all dressed in the typical Moslem garb of long, billowing robes and turbans. Sitting directly next to al-Mu'tadid was a young boy, al-Mu'tadid's interpreter, Omar Yaziji.

Although Aethelwine never saw al-Mu'tadid in an upright position, the Moslem gave the impression of being short. He had a round face with a closely cropped greyish-black beard. When he spoke, always too quietly for Aethelwine to hear, his lip seems to twitch and sneer.

Mulak al-Mu'tadid conducted his entire negotiation with Aethelwine via Omar. Aethelwine still hadn't determined whether al-Mu'tadid did this because he did not share a language with Aethelwine, or because the Moslem felt it demeaned him to speak to a non-Mohammedan. After Aethelwine performed the proper obeisance, al-Mu'tadid's aide spoke, "His lordship, muluk al-Mu'tadid bi 'Illah, Abu 'Amr 'Abbad ibn Muhammad ibn 'Abbad welcomes you once again to his presence and hopes that your talks may bring both of you the happiness which is reserved for *Jannah*."

As Aethelwine sat on the cushions indicated to him by a wave of al-Mu'tadid's hand, an *'abd*, one of al-Mu'tadid's ceorls, entered and presented a tray to al-Mu'tadid. The Moslem prince indicated Aethelwine and the *'abd* turned to offer the platter of fruit juice and halvah to Aethelwine before returning to his master to have his offering accepted. al-Mu'tadid muttered to his interpreter and reclined on his cushions to eat while waiting for Aethelwine's response to make its circuitous way back to him.

"His lordship, muluk al-Mu'tadid bi 'Illah, Abu 'Amr 'Abbad ibn Muhammad ibn 'Abbad desires you to know that he is aware of the conditions in your distant land and has been apprised of the dispute between your *amir* Harold and the pope of Rome. His lordship wishes to know why you believe he should involve himself in this dispute between two *ahl al-dhimma* who live in such distant lands and who do not accept the *amir*'s judgment in matter of justice in any case?"

Aethelwine tried not to shift on the cushions. He had been expecting al-Mu'tadid to ask such a question but was surprised at how straightforward the *amir* had been. Even more surprising since Aethelwine had gathered that al-Mu'tadid's words were generally put into a more polite form by his interpreters. Aethelwine responded with the words he had practiced for this occasion, "Although it is true that my king, Harold, does not submit to your authority nor pay *jizya*," Aethelwine used the Moslem word for tax, "to Your Highness, he feels that this dispute between himself and the pope may prove either beneficial or detrimental to your realm in the long run, depending on which path you elect to take in the matter."

Aethelwine paused while Omar translated his words, making them more floral in accordance with Moslem custom, Aethelwine hoped. When the boy finished speaking, al-Mu'tadid nodded his round head and Aethelwine continued his speech.

"To work to your own disadvantage, all you need do is continue your actions as they have been, or to work with the pope against England. Either way will allow Rome to build in strength until eventually the Pope turns his attention to Spain and sees the non-Christians living here and calls for their destruction. If you aid my monarch in his quest for freedom from Rome, you will be helping to weaken the bonds Rome has with the rest of the world and the pope will not be able to call for your annihilation.

"To help King Harold, all you need to do is turn your attention north for a little while. Harrass the Christian Spaniards, the three kings, all called Sancho, who reign in Aragon, Leon and Castile and Navarre. By doing this, you will gain lands for yourself while keeping these rulers from joining in the alliance against my tiny kingdom.

"If you do this, King Harold pledges eternal friendship between England and the Taifa."

Aethelwine waited while Omar translated his request for al-Mu'tadid. Omar's translation took close to a quarter hour between his addition of flowery words and the interruption by al-Mu'tadid with questions for Omar which went unrepeated. Eventually, Omar turned back to Aethelwine.

"His lordship, *muluk* al-Mu'tadid bi 'Illah, Abu 'Amr 'Abbad ibn Muhammad ibn 'Abbad has said that he wishes to consider your proposal in solitude, surrounded only by his *'ulama'*." Omar motioned to the men who stood behind the muluk. "You will be sent for when his lordship has come to a decision concerning your supplication."

Omar bowed to al-Mu'tadid and began to back out of the audience chamber, Aethelwine following along with him. As the two men backed out the door, a Moslem was admitted to the audience chamber and Aethelwine could hear the formal words of annunciation being recited within.

Omar turned to Aethelwine after the chamber doors had been closed and motioned for him to follow along the open halls of the palace.

"Although the muluk has asked to be allowed to consider your request, he made his decision several days ago. Today was merely a formality. He wanted to see how flowery you could make your petition."

Aethelwine felt a sudden sense of trepidation. His comments to al-Mu'tadid were not couched in particularly eloquent terms. From everything he understood about the Moorish court at Ishbiliya, he may have doomed Harold's cause in the Iberian peninsula.

Omar, however, continued his explanation. "I think your king has good points and was careful to expand on your words. I know what you would say if you were a poet in your heart. I believe al-Mu'tadid will grant your request, although he will want some show of support from your Harold as well. My lord has long commented that the king of R . . . no, the pope of Rome, has been becoming too powerful of late and needed to be shown his rightful place as an unbeliever. Allah has granted that your strangely Christian king of the English may serve His purpose and who are we to question Allah's will?

"You may rest assured that when the time comes for al-Mu'tadid to distract the Roman Christians in the North, he will add large portions of Christian lands to his already substantial territories."

Two days later, Aethelwine sat down at a writing desk in his chambers and scribed a letter to Harold in Anglo-Saxon to let him know that al-Mu'tadid would serve his function in Iberia against the Spanish Christians when and if they joined Alexander's alliance.

Steven H Silver

AFTER HASTINGS

BOOK IV: REBELLION

1068. In this year King Harold first met eorl Morkere in battle at a field near Hrypadun to protect his crown.
—THE ANGLO-SAXON CHRONICLE

Earl Morkere and his northern barons faced the heretical king Harold in battle. In the early morning, Earl Morkere had a Roman priest say a Mass in the earl's tent. All the great Northern barons attended to be inspired by the words of Our Lord, Jesus Christ. When the Mass was over, Morkere took the field against the Pelagian followers of Harold. Morkere laid into the royal forces and managed to find Harold by his band of housecarls. In the thick of battle, Morkere and Harold exchanged blows. As Morkere was about to kill the usurper, baron Arnketil turned traitor against Morkere and through this treachery Morkere was forced to flee the field.
—VITA MORCARI, THOMAS OF BARTON
MONK OF CLUNY

CHAPTER I

The world outside Morkere's tent mirrored the feelings the earl was trying to contain within himself. After five days of avoiding Harold's army, Morkere's remaining forces had managed to make their way back to the North country they called home. They were now camped in a farmer's field, surrounded by the trampled mud which had recently been planted with the rye seed which would have provided the grain for the farmer's family.

Above, the sky was a sullen grey, hinting at a cold drizzle but so far the only moisture to actually dampen the day was the dew which formed in the early morning hours.

As Morkere picked at the breakfast which was in front of him, he began to examine the mistakes he had made at Hrypadun for the hundredth time in the past five days.

In retrospect, Morkere and his followers were not ready for the attack. Even attacking too early, as Morkere had done, was not his biggest mistake. That honor would have to belong to Morkere's trust of the untrustworthy. Morkere had never liked Arnketil, and knew from the beginning that the feeling was mutual. Nevertheless, he had put his trust in Arnketil because he believed the baron was an essential element in an attack on King Harold. Instead, Arnketil turned traitor at the worst possible time, taking Sigeweard Bearn with him and causing Harold's augmented forces to rout Morkere.

Morkere laid his head on the table next to the bowl which contained the thick porridge which formed his breakfast. The bowl swam out of focus as his eyes adjusted for the proximity of the wooden tureen. As he tried to focus, his attention was grabbed by a familiar, deep voice.

"Morkere, all is not lost."

The earl looked up at his empty tent. In a tremulous voice he responded, "Father?"

AFTER HASTINGS

"You still have the opportunity to defeat the Southern usurper and regain your honor."

"My forces are dead or in disarray, Harold is hunting for me countrywide, nearly a third of my men have turned traitor and joined Arnketil and Sigeweard Bearn in their flight to the king. By now, Harold has declared me to be outlaw. It is only a matter of time before my lands are given to Arnketil and Sigeweard Bearn."

"Although your cause may look hopeless, there remains the chance that you will rule all of England as king. You must remain aware and not despair."

Morkere suddenly felt alone. Without calling out, he knew that his father's shade had left him to the dejection of the late April day. Now that his father's spirit had left, Morkere felt a chill throughout his body. He rose from the chair and walked to the entrance to his tent. As he was about to stick his head out and call for some company, he heard a commotion from outside.

"Let me see Morkere."

"The earl is breaking his fast. He will not see you until after he has finished."

Morkere shouted through the tent's wall for the guard to send in the visitor.

Within moments, Gottcund had stuck his head into Morkere's tent. "You are not an easy man to find."

"I'm hoping Harold will find me only with difficulty as well," Morkere replied wryly.

"Our position would have been better had we waited for papal endorsement, you realize."

"We had a traitor in our midst. Waiting longer would have just given Harold more information than he already had. What do you know of the others?"

Gottcund sat across the table from Morkere. "I saw Earmcearig sliced down by a Southerner's battle axe. He was fighting bravely when it happened. According to one of my ceorls, Limhal was attacked from the back and fell through treachery when Sigeweard changed allegiances." Gottcund crossed himself at the mention of each of the dead men. After a moment, Morkere repeated the gesture half-heartedly.

"Treachery would be the only way Limhal would die in battle. He wouldn't allow it to happen any other way." Morkere allowed himself a small laugh at the thought of Limhal holding off one death in favor of a different one. "Have you heard anything of Heardcwide, Olaf, or Uhtred?"

"Nay, you ranked them on the other side of the battlefield from me. I haven't seen them since the Mass before the battle."

Morkere stood up from his chair and walked back and forth across the tent, mumbling to himself. Finally, he turned to Gottcund, who still sat at the table. "We can hold off the passes to the North and keep Harold at bay while we regroup. We can still reclaim England from the house of Wessex."

Gottcund looked at Morkere with sad eyes, "Yea, Harold won't retain his hold on England, but it won't be you who takes it from him. You and I are outlawed now, or if not now, soon will be. I'm off to the continent to join with Alexander's men. God is on that side and I mean to remain firm and steadfast in my faith. Goodbye, Morkere."

Morkere watched as Gottcund left his tent. Despite Gottcund's words, Morkere still felt elated that his father expressed the belief that Morkere could still defeat Harold. The past was full of stories of warriors who had been at their lowest only to rise above and defeat their enemies. Harold's predecessor, Alfred, dead for more than a century and a half, had sat in a peasant's house in the middle of a fen on the brink of defeat, full of despair, before he was able to snatch victory against the Danes.

Such thoughts as these flooded Morkere's head as he tried to devise a plan to marshall what remained of his forces and launch another, more successful attack against Harold.

CHAPTER II

Swaefred sat in the front pew of the church of Heorlafestoun and looked up at the stained glass over the altar. The overcast sky outside meant that only a small portion of light was coming through, dimming the brilliant colors of the portrayal of Christ raising Lazarus at Bethany. Although Swaefred knew the story came from the Gospel of John, such knowledge had very little meaning since Swaefred had never read, nor could he ever read, the Gospel, written in a language he hardly knew and in words he could not read or write. The village priest's sole acquaintance with the words of Matthew, Mark, Luke, and John came from lectures delivered by Father Maegleas before he had left for the continent.

Swaefred found his thoughts turning frequently to the old priest who had given him whatever education he could. Many of the things Maegleas's successor at Saint Wulfram's told Swaefred were in complete contradiction to the old priest's teachings. All his life, the Roman Church had discouraged priests from marrying, now he was being told that marriage was permited. Swaefred had no desire to marry, but he knew that the priest in Wyvill had taken a wife. Swaefred followed the advice Maegleas had given him on that long ago day in Grantham and tried to remain unseen by the Church. By the end of the first week after Father Egmund's arrival at Saint Wulfram's, Swaefred stopped questioning the doctrines and customs which the new priest espoused, giving in to the new religion which Archbishop Colum-cille would lead from his cathedral in York.

Swaefred's reverie was broken by the sound of rapid pounding on the church door. Although the door was unlocked, Swaefred rose from his pew and walked down the nave to the door. When he opened the door, a dirty, wet figure quickly ducked into the church and slammed the door shut behind him.

Swaefred turned to look at the figure who had run up toward the altar.

"Sanctuary! Sanctuary! I claim sanctuary in this house of worship," the man shouted at the top of his lungs. He was looking up to the stained glass

Swaefred had so recently been contemplating, as if Christ would be able to hear his cries.

The concept of Sanctuary was not new to Swaefred, although he had never actually witnessed anybody claiming Sanctuary. Now, this stranger was in his church claiming the protection of Christ against whoever was following him for whatever crime he had committed.

Swaefred walked back up the nave to where the man huddled behind the altar. For the first time, the village priest could see his suppliant. The man had a large, purple bruise over his left eye and the right side of his once long beard ended suddenly, as if a sword stroke had missed the skin but come close enough to shave off the beard. From the manner in which he held his left arm, Swaefred assumed it was broken.

"Welcome to the Church of Saint Andrew, my son. I am Swaefred."

"You must help me, Father. They'll kill me if they can get to me."

"You have Sanctuary here, but I must know your name and who is chasing you."

"I am called Heardcwide. King Harold's army is chasing after me." For the first time, Swaefred was aware that the man had a very thick Northern accent.

"Where are you from? Are you a Scot or an Englishman?"

The man grew belligerent and Swaefred realized that although hunched up he was facing an enormous man whose body was filled with muscle and no fat. "I am neither Scot nor English. I come from Bernicia in the North, near Lindesfarne."

Although Swaefred's grasp on geography was not wonderful, he knew that Lindesfarne, the holy island of blessed Saint Cuthbert, was claimed by the English kings. Nevertheless, the thought that he might be considered an Englishman seemed to infuriate this Heardcwide. Swaefred decided not to pursue the issue.

"You said the king's men were trying to capture you. What have you done to earn their ire?"

AFTER HASTINGS

"It was nothing I did. I came south with a great host, led by Jarl Morkere himself, in an attempt to convince Harold that there is but one true kirk and that Morkere was the rightful ruler of the North. When they defeated us at Hrypadun, I was forced to flee the field ahead of Harold's dogs."

The man got no further in his explanation when there was a slow, heavy pounding on the door. Swaefred opened the door a crack and saw a tall man with long blond hair and cold blue eyes staring at him. His clothing was among the best Swaefred had ever seen.

"We have come for the fleeing Northern dog Heardcwide of Elford. We demand his release to us in the name of King Harold Godwinson."

As the man spoke, he forced his way into the church and pointed at Heardcwide, who huddled his massive bulk behind the altar.

"My lord," Swaefred began, "This man has claimed the protection of the Church against you. I can not give him over to you, neither may you take him your captive until he has left this church or given up his claim of Sanctuary."

Heardcwide joined Swaefred in crying the word "Sanctuary!" again and again as if a warding against the king's men who stood in the church's doorway.

"Do you know who I am?" Their leader asked Swaefred, obviously not expecting an answer. When none was forthcoming, he continued, "I am Earl Leofwine, brother to our king, Harold."

Swaefred greeted this news by bowing low to the earl, but he then stood adamantly between the two large warriors who remained at opposite ends of the church from him. When Earl Leofwine motioned for two of his ceorls to take Heardcwide from the altar, Swaefred shouted at them, "STOP! If you break the Sanctuary of this church, your souls shall be damned forever in the fiery torments of hell."

The two men hesitated in their motion, eventually deciding to stop and remain safe from the village priest's threat.

Earl Leofwine peered down his nose at Swaefred. "Who do you answer to, Priest?"

"I answer to my lord, Jesus Christ."

"Do you answer to our king or the foreign bishop in Rome?" Earl Leofwine clarified.

Swaefred realized his danger and quickly responded, "I have always listened to the words of the priest of Saint Wulfram's Church in Grantham, now under the supervision of Father Egmund."

Earl Leofwine turned from the priest and strode from the church shouting, "Come, we ride to Grantham to get Father Egmund. Cuthred, remain in the churchyard. If the Northern pig puts so much as a toe outside the church, arrest him. In this case, I grant you the rights of immediate justice should the snake try to escape in any manner."

When Earl Leofwine and his men had cleared the church, Swaefred turned to Heardcwide. "You have at least half-an-hour before Earl Leofwine returns with Father Egmund. Can I get you anything to eat or drink?"

The Northerner nodded his head and Swaefred quickly ran to get a horn of mead and wheel of cheese. When Heardcwide received this bounty from the priest, he dug into the cheese like a man who had not eaten for several days, which, Swaefred reflected, may well have been true. Swaefred did not try to initiate any conversation with his charge, figuring that if Heardcwide wanted to tell Swaefred anything more, he would do so in his own time.

When Heardcwide finished eating, he asked Swaefred to hear his confession. The two men were huddled together when Swaefred heard the sound of horses outside the church and the sound of men's voices. He immediately recognized the light tenor of Father Egmund, as well as the more recently introduced voice of Earl Leofwine.

Rather than attempt to obstruct their entry into the church, Swaefred hurried to the door and threw it open to greet the nobleman's entourage.

AFTER HASTINGS

Earl Leofwine motioned for Father Egmund to enter the church first and followed quickly, motioning for his men to remain outside.

Once inside the church, Earl Leofwine leaned on the baptismal font, which stood next to the door so the entire village could witness the entry of another soul into Christ's brotherhood.

"I haven't the time to waste in a small Kesteven village. Father Egmund, please make this fast." An order, not a request.

"Swaefred, I understand you are protecting a traitor from the wrath of Earl Leofwine. Is this true?" Father Egmund fidgeted even more when he spoke than he usually did.

Swaefred indicated Heardcwide, who had resumed his position behind the altar, "This Northerner, Heardcwide, appeared at the door of my church asking for Sanctuary. Once he was admitted, he confessed his crimes to me. Despite the nature of these crimes, I have always understood that the grant of Sanctuary was inviolable." Something about Earl Leofwine's manner made Swaefred wonder if he understood the explanation of Sanctuary that Father Maegleas had taught him.

"Who was it who taught you about Sanctuary?"

"Your predecessor, Father Maegleas."

At the sound of the name, Earl Leofwine burst out into laughter. "I thought your town's name sounded familiar. You replaced the murderer." Bringing his face close to Swaefred, Earl Leofwine explained, "Your Father Maegleas was hanged for trying to murder Archbishop Colum-cille in London."

Swaefred sat down, stunned. He hardly heard Father Egmund's explanation of Sanctuary.

"What Father Maegleas failed to tell you, probably because it seemed self-evident and perpetual to him, was that the idea of Sanctuary was supported by the Roman bishop. It only has power where he could enforce it by his threats of eternal damnation. Although I'm sure King Harold supports the continuation of Sanctuary in certain cases, I don't think we can count on his generosity when the criminal is one who tried to take his throne away."

While Father Egmund spoke, Earl Leofwine regained his composure and moved to the door. At his call, four large ceorls entered and began moving up the nave to where Heardcwide huddled. When they reached the renegade, the Northerner began to flail about with his good arm until he was subdued by a mace applied to the back of his head.

Once Heardcwide went limp, the ceorls trussed him with ropes they had on their horses and hauled him from the church. Leofwine walked over the still form lying amid the gravestones in the Heorlafestoun churchyard.

Earl Leofwine called for Swaefred to bring any relics the church had. When Swaefred brought out a small crucifix and chalice, Earl Leofwine took them and looked down at Heardcwide, now beginning to regain consciousness.

"I, Earl Leofwine, brother to our king, Harold Godwinsson, who has been granted the rights of *sac* and *soc*, *toll* and *team*, *infangenethoef*, *blodwite*, *weardwite*, *hamsocn*, *forsteall*, *grythbryce* and *mundbryce* by my lord, by the Lord before whom this cross and chalice are holy, bring my charge with full folkright, without deceit and without malice, and without guile whatsoever, that this Heardcwide has broken the king's peace, and is guilty of the crime of *grythbryce*. Heardcwide, too, has assaulted myself and my king from ambush and is thus guilty of *forsteall*."

When Earl Leofwine finished his customary oath as an accuser, one of the ceorls spoke up, "By the Lord before whom this cross and chalice are holy, I Cuthred, ceorl of Earl Leofwine, declare the oath which Earl Leofwine has sworn is clean and without falsehood."

Earl Leofwine looked around at the crowd of villagers who had gathered around the churchyard to witness a case of the king's justice. "Is there any here who can truthfully speak on behalf of the accused, Heardcwide?"

AFTER HASTINGS

When none of the villagers deigned to speak in favor of the stranger from the North for fear of incurring the wrath of the most powerful earl in England, Earl Leofwine continued, "I sentence this traitor to death by hanging from the neck."

With a quick motion, the earl sent two of his men off to erect a gallows in the center of the village, across from the smithy.

By the time this trial was over, Heardcwide had regained enough of himself to let force a long stream of deprecation against Earl Leofwine and King Harold. The earl listened for mere moments before ordering one of his remaining ceorls to gag the condemned man.

When the gibbet had been erected, with more than passing help from the villagers, Earl Leofwine himself marched Heardcwide to the platform and placed a noose around the man's neck. Looking down at the crowd, Leofwine spoke for the first time since the trial, "This man has been condemned for turning traitor against his rightful king, Harold of England. He has been confessed by your village priest and may stand a chance of receiving God's mercy once he has shaken loose the shackles of this world."

As Earl Leofwine finished speaking, he motioned for Heardcwide to be raised off the ground. The Northerner's body twisted and jerked as he struggled against his bonds and the noose tightening against his gullet and cutting off his air. The body continued to writhe and jerk for nearly a quarter hour before it hung limp, dangling from the noose.

When Earl Leofwine was certain that the rebel was dead, he motioned for Father Egmund to come closer.

"Leave the body to hang in this village for a single day, then I want it cut down and beheaded. Let them bury the traitor's body in unconsecrated ground here. I expect the head to be exhibited at the gates of Grantham as a warning. My brother, the king, has had enough trouble from this area between the murderer Maegleas and now this traitor Heardcwide."

While speaking, one of the ceorls had brought Earl Leofwine's horse to him and the great earl mounted. With a last look at the dangling corpse, Earl Leofwine and his men rode off toward Melton Mowbray.

As the dust from their passing began to settle, Father Egmund called for Osric to arrange for the carter to return the priest to Grantham. Although loyal to Archbishop Colum-cille and the king, Father Egmund could not but help feel sorry to see the passing of the ancient tradition of Sanctuary.

CHAPTER III

While Morkere and his men moved through the English countryside, trying to make their way back North, avoiding bands of Harold's men, and sleeping in muddy fields, Harold lay on a large, soft bed in sumptuous quarters in the city of Ligoraceaster. Harold's legs were tangled in a mass of sheets as well as the long, thin legs of his concubine, Ealdgytha Svannehals.

Throughout England, Harold's mistress was known as being amongst the most beautiful women ever to grace the earth. Her sobriquet, "Svannehals," referred to her long, ivory neck which grew out of her creamy white breasts and was topped by a perfect heart-shaped face. Her coppery red hair dangled in long, thick braids to her waist, which was thin enough for a large man to surround with his hands. One look at Svannehals was enough to inform even the most casual observer that this woman had never found it necessary to do anything more strenuous than open her mouth or wave her hand.

Harold lay with his arm around Svannehals's long, thin neck and cupped one of her naked breasts in his large, calloused, warrior's hand. Occasionally, he would absent-mindedly play with her nipple, but the majority of his attention was focussed on the words coming from her full lips. Long ago, even before he had taken Svannehals as his mistress, Harold had learned the wisdom of listening to her thoughts. As savvy in her own way as Leofwine or Aethelwine, Svannehals brought a unique woman's perspective to whatever issue she deigned to examine. Although Harold knew that his enemies would ridicule him for taking the *rede* of a woman seriously, they would be surprised to learn how frequently that council had been their un-doing.

"With Morkere and his allies on the loose, the battle at Hrypadun is only the start of something bigger. You're going to have to be on your guard against Morkere while planning to meet the host which Alexander is marshaling against you on the continent."

"My intention is to finish with Morkere long before Alexander's armies can get anywhere near the coastline. Morkere's men are disunited right now. His allies are scattered across the middle of England, trying to make their way back to the safe havens of the North. Few, if any, have had the time to get back to their lands. If I strike now, I can crush them before they can make another attack."

"OW! That hurts," Svannehals yelped as Harold's hand squeezed her breast too tightly. She wriggled out of his reach on the bed and sat up with her back pressed against the wall. "What are your plans then?"

"Although a few of Morkere's allies were from the South, the vast majority were from the North. I plan to wreak my vengeance on them as a demonstration to all those in the South who would question my rule. Northumbria shall be harrowed so that nothing grows there for years to come, even until the reign of our son, Godwin. None shall be able to rise against me, for the menfolk shall be put to the sword. My name will be feared in the North and I will be seen as another Pharaoh who brought about the death of the firstborn children, or Herod who ordered the death of all those who would assail his crown. When I have finished with Northumberland, none there will ever rise up against the House of Wessex again." A fierce light seemed to glow in Harold's eyes.

Svannehals shifted again on the bed. Although physically comfortable, Harold's urgency made her discomfited.

"I think you'll find, if you ask Archbishop Colum-cille, that Pharaoh was not responsible for the deaths of the first born. Moses brought down the wrath of God against his enemies, the Egyptians." Svannehals was, perhaps, the only person who could correct Harold when he was fired up without worrying about his reaction. As such, she made the most of this ability, never letting an opportunity to exercise it pass her by.

"Furthermore, if you stop to think about your plan for vengeance on the North, I think you'll find there is a better way. Whether you like it or not, you're going to need those Northerners. Alexander is very likely going to contact Malcolm of Scotland to try to attack you from the North. The Northumbrians could serve as a shield-wall against their incursions. Even if Malcolm doesn't try to aid the pope, you'll need the might of the Northumbrian fyrds against the Franks, Normans, Germans, Spanish, Romans, and anyone else Alexander manages to recruit into his campaign against you."

"Are you suggesting I let Morkere and his renegades get off free as Scots from a raid? I'll never have peace then, nor will your son."

"I did not say that Morkere should escape retribution. You know well I have no love lost for any in that family. Do with Morkere, Gottcund, and the others what you will. But stop with the leaders. The thegns and ceorls were merely following the orders of their true lords. Would you have your men do any differently had you been in Morkere's situation?"

Harold hadn't thought about that, although he had frequently been in situations similar to Morkere's. Slightly more than a decade earlier, the entire Godwin family, with the exception of his sister, Eadgyth, was forced to flee England when Edward brought in his band of rampaging Normans and succeeded in humiliating Godwin. Unlike Morkere, Godwin had successfully negotiated his family's return to the king's Grace instead of resorting to force of arms.

AFTER HASTINGS

While Harold lay on the bed thinking over Svannehals's comments, she rose from the bed and wrapped herself in a fine linen gown. In the darkness of the room, the normally translucent material was opaque enough not to cause Harold any distraction. With a fluid movement, Svannehals glided over to a chair and flowed into it. She picked up a horsehair brush and began to stroke her long hair while looking at her reflection in a speculum of polished silver, enough metal, she reflected, to pay a medium-sized village's tithe to the church for well over a year. At one time, Svannehals had been in a position where she and her family had needed to worry about such matters as where their next meal would come from, but her father had managed the difficult task of moving from the ranks of the ceorls to the thegns by demonstrating his capability in Godwin's armies thirty years earlier when Svannehals was just a babe. Behind her, she could see the distorted reflection of Harold as he rose from the bed. Despite the murkiness of the image, she could still see the muscular legs which the king had battled and rode to attain. With the active, military life that Harold had been forced to lead his entire adult life, very little in the way of fat had ever been able to attach itself to him.

"You are, as always, right, my *claene svanne*." Harold's words could mean either "chaste swan" or "intelligent swan." Svannehals chose to believe the king meant the latter. "I will not harrow the Northlands. They are too valuable and necessary an asset at this time. But the leaders of the rebellion will perish and I will not forget that few in the North stood for my rule. I will return my attention to the North once I have settled with Rome!"

Svannehals smiled at her reflection. Although she cared little for warfare in the abstract sense, she was well aware that her continued well-being was closely tied to Harold's enduring rule. If Morkere, or some other *aetheling*, should replace Harold, he would most likely have little sympathy for the former king's concubine.

CHAPTER IV

Edith sat in the gardens at her manor in Gaddesby. Although late in the spring, there was still a bite of chill winter air and many of the trees were putting on their first leaves. Next to the queen, a small brook bubbled through the garden, ignorant of the honor being paid to it by the royal presence as well as of the thoughts lurking on the queen's mind.

Edith found the spring weather conducive to thoughts of subversion. Soon, she knew, her brother would be marching against her husband. Although Morkere was careful to prevent Edith from discovering his plans, both in order to shield her from Harold and to protect his plans from the king, some inkling of the earl's plots had worked their way into Edith's cognizance. She knew that Morkere and a coalition of Northern aethelings and thegns were planning an attack on Harold sometime in late June or early July, but not when it would happen. When Morkere's advance began, Edith would have to be in a position to enact her own means of supporting her brother and the Roman church against Harold.

Her thoughts were interrupted by an outbreak of barking and growling coming from the kennels were her servants were training the hounds. The incessant yelping of the hounds quickly began to get on Edith's nerves, and she resolved to leave the garden which should have held a contemplative stillness and return to the manor house where the thick stone walls would serve as a buffer to the continuing canine noises.

Gaddesby Manor was a relatively new building, having been built during the first reign of Aethelred at the beginning of the century. When Cnut had taken the kingdom from Aethelred and his son, he had bestowed Gaddesby on one of his new men, Godwin. Godwin had expanded the main building of the manor slightly, mostly focusing his attention on the addition of out-buildings, such as the kennel where the dogs were still raising such a ruckus. When Godwin was forced into exile by King Edward, the king granted Gaddesby to one of his other earls, Alfgar, who gave the manor to his daughter, as a gift. With Edith's marriage to Harold, Gaddebsy was once more united with the lands held by the Godwin clan.

Walking quickly from room to room, Edith discovered that the dogs' cacophony was most mute in the upper front room which she used for storage. Having resigned herself to a lack of quiet for thinking about how to go about twitting her husband, Edith set to work looking through the antiquities which had managed to make their way to the small storage chamber. Although Edith could easily have set her servants or slaves to work on the room, she had the desire to get her hands dirty doing work which she would normally envision as being beneath her dignity.

During one of her trips downstairs carrying the remains of an old, moth-eaten tapestry, Ordgar, her steward, approached her.

"My lady, A band of your husband's men have arrived at the manor. They have requested an audience with you and are waiting in your audience chamber."

"What is their desire?"

"They would not state their business, my lady, but they look as if they have been many days on the road, and perhaps in battle."

"Do they require a surgeon or are they simply seeking the hospitality of their king's wife?"

Ordgar shook his head, "They do not look damaged, nor have they requested lodging."

"If it is not urgent, I should like to clean up and make myself more presentable." Edith was suddenly aware of her disheveled hair and the smudges of grime on her face. "I'll be in my chambers. Please send Vala to attend to me with hot water."

As Ordgar muttered acknowledgment of her command, Edith walked quickly through the halls to her chambers. She was halfway undressed when Vala entered.

"Take care of this," Edith commanded, as she moved toward the bowl of water Vala had set down on a small table with a small cake of soap. Vala took the offered clothing as the queen sat in front of the silvered mirror and began to wash the grime from her arms and face. As the queen finished, Vala returned and began to let out the long braids in Edith's hair in order to comb the queen's long golden tresses.

"What are the servants and slaves saying?"

"About what, my lady?"

"About my husband, my brother, perhaps these visitors at the gate. Our land is going through a time of upheaval. Surely you must talk about something."

Vala sat in silence, biting her lip as she combed out Edith's hair. Although the queen was usually fair, it did not do to offer advice and gossip, even when solicited. Vala quickly decided the men waiting in the rooms below were the safest topic of conversation.

"I saw the group of men ride up while I was cleaning in the entry hall. They were rough looking men covered in grime and dirt and mud as if they had been on the road for a long time. There was blood on some of them, too, as if they had been in a battle or attacked by animals or something. In truth, they scared me." As Vala spoke, the queen noticed her slave's voice was getting a little agitated. If the queen permitted her to continue, it wouldn't be long before she had reverted to her own barbaric Welsh tongue.

"Thank you. Please tie up my hair and help me find a gown to wear."

By the time Vala had finished making the queen presentable, the king's men had been waiting in the audience chamber for nearly two hours, putting their leader into a dark mood in which he roundly cursed any of his men who spoke or moved in a manner not to his liking. Nevertheless, when Edith entered, he rose and acted like one of the French courtiers from old King Edward's court.

"My lady," he said, dropping quickly to his knee, "My band has come from battle between King Harold and the traitorous Northern Earl Morkere. We are here to see that you are safe from any fleeing traitors who escaped their just reward on the battlefield."

AFTER HASTINGS

Edith looked over the man and decided that although the leader of this band of warriors he was not of particularly high rank.

"And the battle? What became of my . . . husband? My brother?" The queen's voice had a wintery chill to it.

Realizing his mistake, the warrior swallowed before replying. "Although the king was victorious and many of the traitorous Northerners were slain, my lady's brother is believed to have fled the battlefield with his life." Even as the words were leaving his mouth, the man realized he had practically called the queen's brother a coward.

"I have neither seen nor heard of any renegade men in the area. In fact, your words are the first I have heard of this battle. I must go now, and pray for my brother's, and husband's, souls."

Edith walked out of the room as Ordgar appeared to show the men to the door. Their leader couldn't help thinking that he had waited two hours to be summarily dismissed by the queen after such a short interview.

After showing the band of men to the gate and making sure they were walking away, Ordgar returned to the queen.

"Did you know anything of this battle or my brother's fate?"

"Yes, my lady."

"And you decided not to tell me?"

"Yes, my lady."

"Might I ask why?"

"A short time ago, a group of five men, looking even worse than those with whom you just met, showed up in the back fields. They did not know whose lands they were on, but begged for mercy and asked to be hidden. They told me about the battle and that they had fought for Earl Morkere, who managed to escape the battlefield. I believed that it would be your lady's wish that they be hidden, but before I had a chance to tell you, your husband's men arrived at the front door. I thought it would be safer for you to know nothing of the battle or these men before your interview."

Edith thought about her steward's words and gave a small, brief smile. "You did the right thing, of course. Now, show me to my brother's men."

Ordgar led the queen across the fields behind the manor to a small storage building near the dog kennels. When Ordgar opened the door, the interior of the building looked empty of men until he called out. As his voice sounded in the room, three men suddenly appeared from behind the walls of the dogs' stalls.

One of the men had the air of a leader, and it was he who addressed the queen.

"My lady, I would thank you, on behalf of my men, for the hospitality you have shown to men wounded in your brother's cause, even though we fight against your husband."

Edith looked around the dim room and glanced at her servant. Ignoring the man who had just spoken to her, the queen asked Ordgar, "You said there were five men. I only see three."

Before Ordgar could respond, the band's leader spoke again, "Iethe was wounded in the battle and is being treated by Guthbeorn in one of the stalls. Guthbeorn, declare yourself!"

From a stall at the back of the kennels, Edith could hear a deep, growling voice announce, "I've stanched Iethe's bleeding, but he has yet to wake from his wound. I'm rather worried he may not pull through. I'll hate to have to bring the word to his wife."

Edith looked back at the warrior standing in front of her. "Why did you come here? Although I'm Morkere's sister, I am also wife to the man you fought against. What would make you believe that you would receive succor from this house?"

The large man shifted uncomfortably under the queen's gaze. "When we arrived, we had no idea who lived in this manor. In fact, it wasn't until you entered the kennels that we knew whose manor this was. I recognize you from your father's house where I saw you long ago."

Edith glanced at Ordgar, "See that these men get whatever they need and move them somewhere more suitable, if not quite as hidden. I hope your man survives. If its necessary, I have a priest who can give him the last rites, but my priest is loyal to my husband's new church and I would prefer not to inform him of your presence."

"I'll arrange a place for them to be put, my lady," Ordgar responded.

The large warrior said, "Thank you," in a quiet voice as the queen and her servant left the kennels.

Walking across the yard, Edith turned to Ordgar and broached the important matter which the appearance of these men had made necessary.

"By accepting this band into my house and offering them succor, I have as much declared myself for my brother against my husband." Edith's voice held a mixture of sadness and jubilation at the thought of the king.

"It's only a declaration of defiance if their presence here becomes known."

"Of course their presence here will become known. Eventually, they'll leave and tell others where they received aid. Even if we arrange for them to stay at Gaddesby, their presence would become known. Do you think we could hide four or five men from Father Spiwtha? As soon as he discovered we were helping Harold's enemies, he would bear tales to my husband and I would find myself in a monastery like the king's sister. And, whereas that life might suit my sister-in-law, I personally find it a rather cloistered existence."

For a while, neither spoke as they walked across the fields, just now becoming warm in the noonday sun. Both were entirely within their own thoughts, ignoring the sounds of spring birdsong and the creek as they sorted through the dilemma which their good intentions and beliefs had landed them in. Eventually, as they approached the manorhouse, Ordgar spoke the words that Edith knew would have to come.

"My lady. You and I both know where you stand in regards to your husband's current course of action. You have told me of the recriminations exchanged between you and your sister-in-law when she visited before leaving for the continent and its nunnery. It seems to me, if it is not out of my place, that now is the time that God has chosen for you to make your own stand against your husband's apostasy. These men can provide you with an escort to the Northlands and your brother's strongholds. Perhaps you will even be able to join with your brother against the king."

Edith slowly nodded. "Tell those men that I will be prepared to leave with them in a week's time. That, I hope, will give their man enough time to heal."

The queen turned and entered the house, leaving her trusted servant to make all the required arrangements for the band of renegades.

CHAPTER V

Lanfranc tapped lightly at the door to the sick man's bedchamber. Although he had not yet seen the occupant, all rumors he had heard told that the bed within the chamber would soon turn from sickbed to deathbed. Given the previous stature of the room's occupant, Lanfranc felt a visit was necessary in order to offer the dying man whatever consolation he could.

The bishop repeated his knock, a little harder this time. Although the monk at the front door had offered to show the bishop up to the room, Lanfranc had simply taken directions and navigated the halls by himself. The second rapping resulted in the door being opened by a monk who attended the ill man inside the room.

Although it was obvious to Lanfranc that the monk tried to keep the room clean, the task was beyond him. A strong smell permeated the room, giving mute, but aromatic testimony to the multiplicity of times the bed's occupant had fouled himself and his bedclothes.

"He is awake, but not particularly strong. Although I will admit you to his presence, I must have your agreement that you will leave as soon as he or I ask you to." The monk refused to move from his place barring Lanfranc from the room until the bishop nodded his head in agreement to the monk's demands.

AFTER HASTINGS

Lanfranc found himself led, like a novice, to the low bed. He looked down on his predecessor, Stigand, the last archbishop of Canterbury. Although legend told of the man's ruddy complexion, large build, and neatly trimmed tonsure, his final, wasting illness had destroyed his coloration and taken all the fat and muscle from his body. The monks had allowed his hair to begin to grow back, giving him a strange look of short cropped hair on the crown of his head, surrounded by long strings of hair on the sides.

As they approached the bed, the monk left Lanfranc's side to help Stigand maneuver into a sitting position.

When Stigand was sitting with his back against the wall, a pasty-white tongue flicked out of his mouth to moisten his thin lips. When he spoke, his voice was faint and harsh, reminding Lanfranc of the sound of aged crumbling vellum. "The 'bishop' of Canterbury. Come to gloat over your predecessor?"

While a wheezing chuckle escaped from Stigand's emaciated face, Lanfranc examined the cleric's rheumy, red eyes and saw only sadness and despair. Stigand knew he was dying and knew there was no hope that any of the surgeons who attended him could avert the fate God had chosen for him.

"I've not come to gloat, but rather to offer you succor and sustenance in your final days. It is not too late for you to return to the warm embrace of Ecclesiastica and spend eternity in the contemplation of His Divine Glory instead of being tormented in the fiery furnaces of hell." Lanfranc spoke without the hint of malice or sarcasm, both of which he expected Stigand would imagine existed. He was surprised, therefore, at Stigand's response.

"I can see you speak as one who believes in what you say. I truly wish we had met under different circumstances. No matter what you, or Pope Alexander, may believe, I have always done what I felt was right for the Church."

Stigand was interrupted by a coughing spasm which persisted for some time. Lanfranc stood quietly while the monk who had been assigned to serve Stigand rushed to the former archbishop's aid. By the time Stigand finished, Lanfranc was acutely aware of how awkward and ill at ease he felt.

Once Stigand's breathing was back to normal and his body had passed through a stage of involuntary shuddering, the archbishop continued as if he had never been interrupted. "Unlike the monastery over which you presided at Bec, or the chapels in the shadow of the Lateran Palace, England is very far away from Rome, in more than just the physical sense. The channel of water which separates us from the continent has great ramifications of which His Holiness may be unaware.

"My people, the English, have lived in this land for hundreds of years. Before we came, the Celts had lived here for uncounted centuries. Although our two races fought at first, eventually we merged. We slowly accepted faith in Jesus Christ, but that faith was tempered by our older beliefs. His Holiness's predecessor, the blessed Gregory, saw the importance of allowing the English to retain their own practices as long as they espoused the vastness of Christ's glory.

"To this day, the English view their agreement with Gregory as an integral part of their religion. Oh, the common peasant working in the fields, or even a nobleman in his great hall, wouldn't put it like that. It is so central to their belief that it need never be stated. Nevertheless, this part of religion exists in this island. Occasionally, that means the English will seem to worship in a way which offends Rome but I promise you, it is dear to His heart."

As he finished speaking, Stigand's face rapidly changed to the brilliant red which was legend throughout England and the archbishop motioned toward his throat. Before the monk-servant could move back to the bed, Lanfranc had moved forward to help Stigand clear the obstruction from his throat. As the archbishop reclined on his bed, his coloration returned to the sickly pale Lanfranc had seen upon first entering the chamber, all three men in the room remained silent.

A gentle knock on the door sounded loudly into the silence. A monk stuck his tonsured head, Roman style, Lanfranc was pleased to note, through the doorway and announced, "The archbishop of York has arrived to pay his respects to the archbishop of Canterbury."

Stigand raised himself on the bed and said softly, "Show Ealdred in."

Lanfranc was stunned to discover that Stigand knew nothing of Ealdred's death and replacement by the Celtic Colum-cille. Stigand would discover the truth soon enough and Lanfranc turned to reply to Stigand's comment.

"Although at one time He may have looked upon the idiosyncracies of England's worship with a kind eye, the situation has changed. The Church is at a crossroads and must remain strong and united against the mistaken practices of earlier days and other places." Even as he spoke, Lanfranc realized that his argument was unlikely to sway Stigand. Although Stigand's opinion no longer held any political value, Lanfranc was attempting to save the dying man's soul.

A slight tap on the door immediately preceded the appearance of Colum-cille, his head shaved in the outlandish tonsure used by the Celts. The archbishop moved toward Stigand's bed and knelt beside the confused Saxon.

"Your grace," Colum-cille said quietly. "I heard you were dying and came tae offer any comfort Christ would allow of such a humble servant as I."

Stigand looked from Colum-cille to Lanfranc to the novice and back to Colum-cille. "Who are you?" Stigand asked, giving Lanfranc the barest hint of what his voice must have sounded like when he was a healthy, younger man.

Colum-cille looked up from his place on the floor. "I am the archbishop of York, Colum-cille of Scotland. I thought you knew I had succeeded Archbishop Ealdred upon his death last Easter."

Stigand looked amazed and stared off into space as he repeated the words "last Easter" in a low voice.

Colum-cille looked almost as startled as Stigand. "I thought you had been informed of Archbishop Ealdred's death. I'm sorry."

The three men stood in an awkward silence, each trying to avoid looking at each other, but not able to find anything else in the room to turn their gaze on. Eventually, Stigand broke the silence with a rasping cough.

"Some ale, please," he wheezed to the novice who sat in the corner. As the young monk moved to exit the room, Stigand added, "Three cups."

Once the boy left, Stigand turned his attention to his two visitors. "As you have surmised, although Harold permits me to live in the relative comfort of this manor, he severely limits the news which manages to find its way in. I probably know less of what is happening in England than the rulers of St. Brendan's Land, wherever that may be. Allow me to tell you what I believe has happened and then you can fill me in on the details.

"Harold sacrificed me to Pope Alexander in return for which you," Stigand motioned with a weak hand to Lanfranc, "replaced me as archbishop of Canterbury. Shortly after, Ealdred died and the pope appointed this Scot to replace him, although I've never heard of you and can't imagine why Alexander would appoint an islander when he seems so intent on homogenizing the Church in his own image.

"As I've told you, Harold permits me very few visits. I'm rather surprised that he agreed to allow not just one, but both of you to visit me, even dying as I am."

Lanfranc replied, "Actually, I think we were both able to visit you because Harold is too busy with other concerns to worry about who a dying prelate is getting information from."

Lanfranc preceded to bring Stigand up to date on the events in England and on the continent, with frequent, and sometimes loud, additions, amendments, and opinions from Colum-cille. While the two clergymen spoke, Stigand sat up in his bed, his face registering, at various times, anger, amusement, surprise, and indignation. When Lanfranc finished relating the state of Morkere's revolt, Stigand lay back on his bed.

"I almost think I should be grateful that He has chosen this time to call me from this wretched land. Although I know that He will not permit Harold to win, sad is the country which has fallen under the devil's sway. I will be long in my grave before England has recovered from this insanity which grips Harold. Morkere may fail, but Alexander, or his successor, will return England to the fold of the Mother Church."

Stigand slowly, painfully, raised himself onto one arm. "It is amazing the amount of insight and wisdom the oncoming of death grants."

Lanfranc and Colum-cille both began to speak at the same time, Lanfranc once again offering clemency for Stigand from the Church for all his sins, Colum-cille trying to explain why Harold's new way of thinking was proper. Their words fell on deaf ears, however, for Stigand had fallen back onto his bed and into a deep sleep, exhausted from the strain of the bishops' visit.

As the two clergymen were ushered from the room and the palace, they walked in silence as complete as any monk's. Both men were trying to avoid the discomfort they felt in the other's presence, as if by ignoring him, he would go away. As they exited the palace into sunlight and began to walk apart to their horses and retinues, Colum-cille turned to Lanfranc and spoke the only words he had directly addressed to the bishop of Canterbury all afternoon.

"Your mother Church thrives on hatred for all who are different: Jews, Moors, 'heretics,' it doesn't matter, the hatred is there."

"Not hatred," Lanfranc interrupted, "Pity."

Colum-cille waved him off, "My Celtic Church welcomes all and permits diversity to exist where your Church sees only enemies. That is why we are stronger and why He will permit us to retain the British islands."

By the time Colum-cille's words had fully registered in Lanfranc's brain, the two men were already riding off in their own directions.

CHAPTER VI

The cool days of spring had given way to the warmth of early summer. Nevertheless, the ground over which Morkere's army walked on their trek back North was broken and muddied by the passage of so many feet, both human and horse. In the first few days after the disastrous defeat at Hrypadun, Morkere had been able to move in quiet anonymity around the English countryside. As the days and weeks moved on, more and more men had managed to find their way to Morkere's banner until none couldn't recognize an army on the move. Without a doubt, Harold knew exactly where the rebellious earl was.

Morkere hoped he would have time to regain the Northlands before Harold's armies set upon him, but he knew such a wish was just a wish. Harold would give battle sometime soon, before Morkere's men had a chance to scatter to their far flung fields and villages. Before they had a chance to get some good food and rest into them. Before they could get a good night's sleep to relieve the weariness which beset all soldiers after tedious days of walking or riding across the countryside. Morkere knew the final battle was coming and also knew that there was little he could do to rebuild his men's morale. He needed merely to look into their eyes and see that thoughts of home, not victory, were what enabled these men to put one foot in front of the other for the many steps that would take them back to their wives and mothers.

Despair was never far from Morkere's mind, but he continuously tried to squelch it. If he simply looked at the forces surrounding him, without giving thought to the battle which would have to be fought all too soon, Morkere could see reasons to rejoice. His army was stronger now than at any time since Hrypadun. Deaths due to battle injuries and disease had fallen off while more men still managed to link up with the army. Morkere was also lucky that so few men had deserted, although he knew this was mostly due to the fact that the army was moving in the same direction any deserters would want to go.

AFTER HASTINGS

Unlike the journey south, which had been convivial and filled with last minute planning on the part of the barons, the long hike north was under a cloud of gloom and despair, men mostly walking in silence in the hopes that the southern English would ignore them or flee from their dour presence. The Northerners moved slowly north, one tedious day following another tedious day.

Morkere knew that eventually the monotony would break. That day was not one he relished, for it would mean that Harold's men had finally decided it was time to attack the defeated army. Despite the counsel of his father's ghost, Morkere knew that Gottcund was right. The fight against Harold within England was over. If there was to be any successful attack against the English king, heretic or usurper, it would have to come from the continent.

Several times over the past few days, when Morkere was at his most depressed, he thought about deserting his own army and making his way to the coast where he could hire, or steal, a fishing boat and make his way to the continent. Nevertheless, a sense of duty to the thegns he had brought down from Northumberland kept him from trying to escape the way Gottcund had. Besides that duty, Northumberland was his home, as it had been the home of his families for generations. He could never leave that land behind.

As Morkere topped a hill, he thought he could make out a river snaking its way across the land at the horizon, almost out of sight. He called to the warrior who was keeping pace with him.

"My lord?"

"Can you make out a river to the north?"

The foot soldier squinted and looked toward the horizon where Morkere indicated.

"I see it."

"Is that the Humber? We're almost home. Just another day or two until we're on our side of the river."

The man looked at Morkere skeptically. "It might be the Humber, but I wouldn't swear to it. I've lived on the North bank of the Humber my entire life and have many times made trips along nearly its entire length since my home is near its mouth at Barton, and I've frequently taken grains to York. I think we're too far west for that to be the Humber. Perhaps it's the Aire or Nidd River." The man suggested.

Although Morkere's first response was to scoff at the man's lack of faith, he paused to hear what the man had said. Although Morkere had made many trips across the Humber, this man had spent his life on the river. If he doubted its identity, perhaps Morkere should listen to him. The earl summoned another man and gave him orders. Within moments, the man was riding on horseback ahead of the slowly moving army to discover what river they were about to cross.

By the time the man returned, nearly three hours later, Morkere's army had only covered a couple of miles, and were in a valley which obliterated their view of the disputed river. Twilight was setting in and Morkere had decided to make use of the last rays of the sun to have his men make camp in the unknown valley somewhere in West Riding or Derbyshire.

The horseman picked his way through the growing camp, frequently stopping to ask the location of Earl Morkere. Eventually he found the Northerner sitting outside his tent with the Barton man. Morkere was listening as the man told about his pastoral life near the mouth of the Humber to the great earl. Nothing seemed incongruous about the scene to the rider as he walked up to deliver his message.

"My lord. I rode ahead and found a village. I'm afraid the villagers think me something of an idiot. When I asked what river we were approaching, they looked as if I were daft to be able to misplace an entire river. It is not the Humber, nor is it the Aire or the Nidd as was suggested earlier." He nodded in the direction of the farmer who sat with Morkere. "I'm told that we are in Chester's shire, near the village of Altringham and will soon be at the south bank of the Mersey River, north of which is Lancashire."

AFTER HASTINGS

Morkere allowed a shocked expression to play across his face. If this man's intelligence were correct, Morkere had led his army scores of miles west of where they wanted to be. Instead of moving to the relatively safe lands of Northumbria, Morkere was headed straight for the lands held by the treacherous Sigeweard Bearn and his equally traitorous partner Arnketil.

He turned to the Barton farmer, "Thomas, go through the camp. Try to find out if any of the men who are still with us are Cheshiremen or Lancashiremen. If so, send them back to my tent. Be quiet about it. If our men don't know how far we are from home, I see no reason to give them that knowledge. It could only cause a panic and more desertions."

As Thomas left to search through the camp, Morkere sat down and tried to remember the geography of England. With a stick, he tried to sketch the landscape in the mud in front of him. A large triangle with the top cut off. On the right side a cross to mark the general area of his strongest holdings. Somewhere on the left, and a little toward the bottom was a circle to denote the general area in which he found himself. He took the stick and drew a ragged line through the thick mud. Everything south of that line belonged firmly to Harold. With a slow deliberate motion, he drew another line perpendicular to the first heading north. Everything west of the second line and north of the first belonged to the traitors. The small triangle left was his safe land.

Morkere looked at the small area he could call home. Although he had holdings in the other parts of England, Northumbria was the only place where he could be assured of something approaching safety. In fact, there was a good chance that Harold had already confiscated all his other lands and probably given them to Arnketil and Sigeweard Bearn.

Morkere sank back into the mud. The soft, squishy feeling of the ooze perfectly reflected his current state of mind. He had led his rebellion against Harold, and through poor luck and poor timing he had been defeated. Perhaps now was the time to head for the continent after all. The only other future Morkere saw, despite his long dead father's protestations, was defeat and death at the hands of his brother-in-law.

Thinking of his father, Morkere raised his head to the grey, clouded heavens and beseeched, "Father, what am I to do now? I have led my army into the hands of my enemies and am in need of counsel."

The only response Morkere received from the heavens was a light, misty rain which began to fall as the first of his men gathered by Thomas began to approach his tent.

The earl stood to greet his men, trying as best he could to disguise the anguish he felt in his heart at his failure to lead his men to victory, or, failing that, safety. Within a few minutes, a group of nearly a dozen men were gathered around the earl. Morkere waited a few moments to allow Thomas to join them before he began talking to the men.

"As I'm sure many of you have realized, we are not near the Humber as I had intended. Instead, we are just south of the Mersey. I've asked Thomas to gather all you men who make your home near the Mersey in hopes that you can help me form a plan to get the army to an area where we are safe. Once this plan is formulated, we'll begin our movement across toward Northumbria. You will be free of you obligations as we pass near your homes."

The already overcast sky began to darken as night added its darkness to the gloom of the day. Morkere and his Merseymen sat in front of his tent, lanterns and torches lit around them, arguing the best route from Altringham to the lands of Eastern England. Despite the earl's desires, rumors were rampant throughout the camp concerning the location of the men. Shortly after the sun had set, Morkere detailed Thomas to go through the camp and reassure the men, while getting them to bed down for the night. The army of Morkere would be on the move early the next day.

CHAPTER VII

Leofwine rode his horse at the head of his army through the hills of central England. While Harold was back in London trying to keep the population of the city content with his rule, Leofwine was left to mop up the remains of Morkere's army.

Searching throughout the Midlands and into the North was a tedious job, but Leofwine had split the task into three parts. Arnketil led his troops along the Welsh Marches and up into his native Deira. Sigeweard Bearn took the middle road and searched the Pennine Hills for remnants of the rebel army. Leofwine's own band had moved up along the Eastern coast of England, trying to find Morkere along the most direct route back to his Northumbrian stronghold or for flight to the continent. So far, none of the three had managed to ascertain the location of the rebel earl.

Upon reaching Morkere's disseized castle of Morpeth, Leofwine had swung his army inland. He sent riders ahead to arrange a meeting with Sigeweard and Arnketil at Bellingham, near the disputed Scottish March. If Morkere hadn't been sighted by the time of their meeting, Leofwine planned to take the army across into Scotland as a show of strength to keep King Malcolm where he belonged. . . out of English business.

Leofwine had only been traveling westward for a couple of days when a lone figure on horseback appeared on the horizon. As the rider came closer, Leofwine recognized him as Thurlkill, Aethelwine's son. Leofwine had not seen the boy since Harold had sent him off as a hostage to Arnketil, but the king's brother viewed his appearance as a well-founded omen.

Thurlkill rode into the army shouting Leofwine's name. Since Earl Leofwine was aware of the boy's arrival, it didn't take very long for the two to be re-acquainted.

"Welcome to my forces. Bring you news of our comrade Arnketil?"

As he dismounted from his horse, Thurlkill answered the earl, "Not Arnketil, as such, although he is well, but of our enemy, who has been spotted. Might I have something to drink?"

Leofwine motioned for a slave to bring Thurlkill a wineskin and then gestured for the boy to have a seat. When his thirst had been quenched, Thurlkill continued his report.

"Earl Morkere moved up the Welsh Marches until he reached the Mersey. At that point, he seems to have held a meeting before turning to the east. Arnketil caught up with him at Stayley Bridge when Morkcre's men moved across the Mersey. Rather than give battle, Arnketil has been shepherding Morkere and his men, bringing them north. While Arnketil's troops are playing sheep dog, Sigeweard has joined with Arnketil and is playing wolf, harassing and harrying the Northumbrian on their journey north and ensuring that Morkere can not get too close to any of his centers of power. Sigeweard and Arnketil plan to make their final attack on the traitor when they reach Skipton in the West Riding. They hope that you might be able to join forces with them before that time in order to totally crush the rebel's might."

Leofwine looked at Thurlkill. When the boy had left Harold's court last year, he had been a practically worthless child who had barely learned which end of the sword to hold. Leofwine had thought Harold daft to send such an inexperienced youngster as a diplomat and hostage to Arnketil. The time Aethelwine's son spent with Arnketil in the North had obviously caused the boy to become, if not a man, at least on the verge of manhood.

"Have you fought in battle?" Leofwine asked the youth.

"No. Arnketil had left me at his manor whilst he and Sigeweard Bearn went off to battle. I think he was afraid of my reaction to seeing him line up with Morkere's men against the king's forces, nor did he trust me enough to confide his loyalty to Harold and his treachery against the traitorous Morkere. This coming battle at Skipton will be the first time I'll have the chance to shed blood."

AFTER HASTINGS

"It looks like you're about to get your chance." Turning around in his saddle, Leofwine called for his men to start forward again. As they did, Thurlkill pulled his horse around into stride next to the earl.

The army moved at a slow, but steady pace. They had a long ride ahead of them and Leofwine did not want the men to arrive at Skipton tired as they did at Senlac a couple years earlier. Leofwine knew that by reaching the battle as quickly as he could, Harold had nearly lost his throne and crown to William the Bastard. Leofwine would not make the same mistake.

"Thurlkill," he said to the instantly alert boy, "I have another mission for you. You'll still be able to take part in the battle, don't worry. I may not be able to make the meeting at Skipton when Arnketil and Sigeweard Bearn are ready. I want you to ride ahead and make sure they delay until I am in the area and can join in the attack. Ride as fast as you can."

Without another word, Thurlkill kicked his steed into a gallop. It wasn't long before he put Leofwine's army behind him. The Northern country through which he rode was new to him. While the Southern and border lands in which he was raised had hills and the occasional mountains, the North seemed to be a constant string of mountains, one after another. His horse's speed was restrained by this as it wouldn't have been in the South, but he still was able to ride faster as a single man than an army could. He would arrive at Skipton several days before Leofwine's forces possibly could, and probably even before Arnketil had managed to herd Morkere to the village.

Thurlkill pushed himself to arrive at Skipton as soon as possible. He slept for only a few hours each night, allowing the moon's light to guide him. Although he only had a single horse, he continuously changed the animal's gaits in order to increase its endurance. Despite this precaution, it was obvious to Thurlkill that he would have to find a replacement horse relatively soon.

On the second day after leaving Leofwine, Thurlkill was riding through a mountain pass. Although his horse was galloping, it had lost much of its initial speed. Thurlkill knew the horse was tiring. Suddenly, Thurlkill was knocked from his seat as the horse galloped under a cord stretched tight across the pass.

Although winded by the fall, Thurlkill quickly rose to his feet. By the time he stood erect, sword slipped from its scabbard, Thurlkill found himself facing two men.

The men were unshaven and unwashed. Their clothing was torn and both showed signs of having been in a battle. Most likely refugees from the Battle of Hrypadun. Neither man bore a sword, although each was armed with a heavy looking cudgel. Thurlkill's head was ringing from the fall he had taken and he missed the first words spoken to him by his ambushers.

"Drop yer sword now and we might let ye live. Ye have no escape since yer horse bolted."

Looking around slowly, Thurlkill realized there was no sign of his horse. He turned his full attention back to the bandits.

"All we're askin' fer is yer sword and coins and food. Whatever ye have on ye. We'll get yer horse later."

While the bandit was speaking, Thurlkill's head was beginning to clear. He didn't let it show but continued to act addled by the fall. His head must have fallen in a patch of soft mud, although, by the ache he felt in the rest of his body, most of him had found hard, rocky terrain to land on.

The second bandit had begun to move around to Thurlkill's left, away from Thurlkill's sword, while the first bandit spoke. As Thurlkill glanced in his direction, he heard the first bandit grunt with the effort of swinging the cudgel around for a blow. Thurlkill raised his sword as he bent out of the way, catching the blow on the blade enough that when it connected it knocked him off balance rather than cause any real damage.

Thurlkill managed to stumble away from both of his adversaries, maneuvering both of them in front of him. No longer outflanked, he swung his sword in a wide arc, trying to let it bite into either of the two men he faced. The swing left his left side open for a moment which allowed one of the bandits to reach in with his club and knock Thurlkill in the ribs.

The boy grunted from the pain and reversed the swing of his sword. He was rewarded by a yelp of pain from the second highwayman, but he knew the wound couldn't be too great considering how slowly the sword was moving when it connected.

As Thurlkill worked to parry the blows which rained toward him from the two cudgels, he had a brief thought that this nameless ambush in the mountains of Northern England was his first battle. He tried to remember the strategies which his father and the king had tried to drill into his head, but failed. In any event, he discovered, a real battle, in which one's life was in jeopardy, was very different from a practice session in the safe courtyard of Winchester or Sarum.

That thought was driven from his head by a strong cudgel blow which connected with his lower right back. The strength of the blow was enough to make Thurlkill drop his sword in pain. Before he could even bend to retrieve it, a second blow of the cudgel against his head drove all conscious thought from his head.

CHAPTER VIII

Morkere knew he was being herded. He knew that there were two armies trying to avoid attacking him. He also knew that his men knew the truth of their situation. After he had crossed the Mersey, his force had begun to dwindle. Men were returning to their abandoned farms when the army passed nearby. Most of the desertions occurred at night, although a few had happened during the day. With his diminished army, there was no way to successfully defend against the attack he knew was coming when the two harrying forces joined in a final assault. Morkere simply had no idea when that would be or why they were delaying.

The two enemy forces had served, however, to stem the tide of desertions. After a few mornings of discovering corpses of the deserters, killed, usually cleanly, but sometimes viciously, by the enemy armies, Morkere's troops decided there was safety in numbers, at least for the time being. All the bodies were found holding a placard with the Latin word *"Proditor,"* traitor, printed on it.

Morkere did not like the situation, but was past the point of being able to do anything about it. He had led his army into a disaster. He had held the army together through battle, defeat, rain, mud, and hunger, only to have them suffer this long drawn out fate. Death in battle after a long, demoralizing march through enemy territory.

Spies sent out by Morkere had determined that the two armies were probably being led by Arnketil and Sigeweard Bearn, although their reports differed as to which of Morkere's enemies were controlling which of the two forces. After the first few scouts had reported back, any other men Morkere sent out had failed to come back. A few of them had been found killed, holding the placard which had become customary for those of Morkere's troops killed outside of the camp.

Morkere had appointed Thomas of Barton as leader of the houseceorls, a group of ten hand picked men whose sole duty it was to protect Morkere against attack. Unlike previous times when the houseceorls guarded against attacks from without, Thomas had been given instructions to protect Morkere from the men in his own army. Morkere now feared that his troops would rise against him in order to deliver him to Arnketil almost as much as he feared Harold's rage against him.

When he thought about his situation objectively, an occurrence which was becoming more and more rare, Morkere realized that he was being shepherded in the general direction of his own estates. That tactic on the part of his enemies made no sense, but then, neither did their delaying tactics and refusal to face Morkere in a straight battle. The only reason Morkere could see for not having already attacked him was if they were planning to meet up with another force. But either Arnketil or Sigeweard Bearn alone should have been able to defeat Morkere at this point.

CHAPTER IX

Although the Northlands were his home and his base of support, Arnketil hated being on campaign here. The climate was much colder and wetter than in the South of England. The rain was only relieved by a low-lying cold mist which crept in through the links of his chain byrnie. The ground was cold and muddy when one lay down and the hills over which they rode, Arnketil refused to call them mountains, caused delays and made travel more strenuous.

Matters weren't helped by his earlier decision to shepherd Morkere to Skipton. That decision had been made before he or Sigeweard Bearn had realized how small and demoralized a force Morkere had been leading in his quest for home. Arnketil had pressed Sigeweard Bearn to attack now and have the whole thing over with, but the lord had insisted on waiting either to hear from Leofwine or to arrive at Skipton. As yet, there was no word from Leofwine and Aethelwine's brat Thurlkill had yet to make a reappearance.

The only thing which made the war against Morkere bearable for Arnketil was the knowledge that when the earl was finally defeated Arnketil's daughter would marry the king's son. Although the marriage would only be to Edmund rather than Harold's heir, Arnketil would still receive many of Earl Morkere's lands as the bride-price for his daughter. Although Sigeweard Bearn might now be able to command Arnketil and his army, soon Arnketil would be powerful enough to let Sigeweard Bearn know exactly what Arnketil thought of him.

Arnketil could see a man approaching his mob which moved anything but silently through the Northern English countryside. When the man closed the distance somewhat, Arnketil could recognize him as some messenger or other sent to him by Sigeweard Bearn. One of the thegn's annoying habits was to attempt to maintain constant contact with Arnketil although their armies were separated by several miles. Few of the emissaries brought anything noteworthy, yet Sigeweard Bearn's exalted rank required Arnketil to meet with them personally and act graciously in their presence. This one probably brought word of how many times his master made water this morning, Arnketil thought dismally.

By the time the messenger arrived within hailing distance, the light rain had picked up and the soaked men were trying to slog through a viscous ooze. Arnketil thought about calling a halt while he met with the boy, but changed his mind. Whatever "news" Sigeweard Bearn was sending him could be received on the march and if they kept moving there was the possibility of finding a dry, or at least drier, area in which to spend the night.

The messenger turned out to have a couple of pieces of worthwhile news. Arnketil almost found himself disappointed not to be informed about the condition of Sigeweard Bearn's bladder.

Although Sigeweard Bearn had still not been able to ascertain Leofwine's location, he seemed to be more amenable to the idea of fighting Morkere without the earl's assistance. Although he still desired to wait until they reached Skipton, he seemed to be wavering in that resolve. Finally, knowing that battle soon approached, Sigeweard Bearn decided that he would allow Morkere's men to begin desertion once again, in the hopes that the Northumbrian earl's army would vanish and Sigeweard Bearn would have fewer fatalities among his men.

CHAPTER X

Harold sat at table in his castle at York. Across from him, Archbishop Colum-cille was seated. Although the table was built to seat ten times their number, the two potentates were the only ones occupying the room, with the exception of several servants who continuously entered and exited, bearing in trenchers filled with food and vanishing with the empty plates.

"How do you like your city?" Harold asked the archbishop around a mouthful of baked pimpernol.

Colum-cille reflected on the question as he drank from his goblet. He had arrived in York only a few days earlier and was still trying to get used to the city. "It isn't as large as London, but is still a far cry from my simple hermitage in Aberdeen."

"This is your first visit to your see?" Harold tore off a piece of light bread to soak up the juices which spilled from the eel. He popped the oily bread into his mouth and chewed slowly.

"Nae. I passed through here with your renegade earl on my journey southward from Scotland. Of course, we were in a hurry, so I did nae have a chance tae explore the city. It seems it will prove as pleasing tae me as possible. Although I must admit tae missing Aberdeen."

Colum-cille looked down at his trencher. The food sitting on the plate was far richer than anything he had eaten prior to coming down into England. Although he enjoyed the food, he felt guilty about eating so richly. Christ had never eaten so well, nor had his apostles. He could feel the censure of the most holy of all saints: Columba, Patrick, Cuthbert, and Columbanus. They had frequently survived on bread and water. Food was given to them by the people to whom they preached, or food they could grow or catch themselves. When Colum-cille looked at Harold, he could see the towers of Yorkminster through the window, rising high above the city. The tall spires only served to make Colum-cille feel worse about his decision.

The Celtic Church, which Harold claimed to want to restore to all of England, did not condone the massive edifices which the Roman Church had erected throughout all of Christendom. Even in Scotland and Ireland these piles of rock stood towering over the natural landscapes and the people, monuments to God's glory, but also monuments to the avarice and corruption which existed in the Roman Church. Colum-cille had come south to cure England of these ills. To teach the English that the true way to worship God and study His teachings was to live a simple and contemplative life. Instead, despite all the king's promises to the contrary, Colum-cille found himself sitting in a lavishly appointed chamber eating rich foods which focused the attention on one's stomach rather than one's soul.

"If you'll excuse me, I do not feel well." Colum-cille murmured toward Harold. Even as the king was gesturing toward the door, the archbishop was hurrying out of the room. There was a chamber pot sitting in the hall and Colum-cille vomited the contents of his stomach into the brass receptacle.

Colum-cille used the finely embroidered sleeve of his tunic to wipe his mouth and then moved slowly down the hall, away from the king and his sumptuous feast. Just now, Colum-cille needed to reflect on himself and his soul rather than share an extravagant repast with Harold. The archbishop moved through the castle without paying attention to his surroundings, attempting to avoid thinking about his predicaments.

Leaving the castle grounds, Colum-cille moved through the crowded streets of York in the general direction of Yorkminster. Years earlier, this was the site of a great *schola* led by Alcuin Albinus before he had trotted off to a foreign land to do another king's bidding. With this thought of Charlemagne's summoning of Alcuin, Colum-cille suddenly felt a strange kinship with the Saxon who had left York nearly three centuries before Colum-cille had arrived.

Although Colum-cille had planned to retire to his apartments in the Minster, he turned and headed for the wall which was built around the city either by the race of giants who lived in England before the Celts or by the Romans, depending on which story one chose to believe.

Passing through the city gate, Colum-cille found himself walking through the small city which had sprung up outside the walls. Although this city covered more area than the walls encircled, the population was much less dense, mostly clustered near the gates where they could rush into the city in the case of a Viking attack. Colum-cille, who had decided that he needed to get away from people, moved parallel to the city wall in order to get away from the crowds and into the open country. Once he left the people behind, he turned his back on York and walked through fields until he came to a small coppice-wood.

Moving through the thickets, Colum-cille tried to formulate the questions which he needed to contemplate. His attention was broken by the unending brambles and thistles which clung to his arms and legs, and he broke through the dense forestation. Eventually, he emerged into a small clearing, almost, he reflected, as if he had been led to it.

The glade was small, hardly large enough for a man to lie down in. On one side of it, a large rock jutted out of the ground at an angle. In the distance, Colum-cille could hear the gentle bubbling of a water rilling. Colum-cille walked to the stone and leaned up against it. Although hard, Colum-cille welcomed the rock's harshness for it reminded him of the life he led when he lived in Aberdeen. His life in Aberdeen, only eighteen months earlier, seemed so much more spiritual.

Colum-cille realized that he missed Aberdeen and the solitude he had known there. England was a very different land. Colum-cille hardly understood the monks of this Southern realm. They lived a soft life, studying and praying and sleeping and waking. The thought of lifting a hand to do any honest work was anathema to them. Although they paid lip-service to the *regula Benedicti*, which called on all monks to "work at manual labor from Prime until the fourth hour," these cenobitic monks called prayer and reading work, letting peasants do all their labors for a less than fair wage. In the Celtic Church, monks lived as cenobites as well.

Celtic monks, however, would never presume to tell an anchorite such as Colum-cille that his hermitage was a lesser form of monastic devotion. Nor would Celtic monks shirk the physical labor which brought them closer to God and provided their sustenance.

As he sat thinking about the differences between the Celtic Church in which Colum-cille was raised and the Roman Church which had infested England since the infamous Synod at Whitby, Colum-cille realized that Harold did not really desire to give up the Church as the English knew it. The Church was too valuable to the king, both politically and economically. What Harold wanted was the Roman Church to be under his control. However, Colum-cille could refuse to be Harold's *Papa Anglorum*. If Harold wanted to call his Church Celtic, Colum-cille would insist that it become a truly Celtic Church.

Colum-cille held the position of archbishop of the English Church. Although he disliked the idea of an archbishop, he could reconcile himself to the title of bishop. After all, had not Patrick, who first brought Christianity to Ireland been named bishop by the pope? Of course, the Roman form of Christianity had changed much since that time six centuries earlier. The Christianity which Patrick brought to Ireland had been preserved better than the Romans could preserve it. Since Patrick's religion was so much closer to Christ's life than the present form of Christianity, it must have been closer to God's own form of the religion. Colum-cille would retain the title of archbishop, not because it pleased him, but rather because the reformation he had in mind would require a strong, guiding hand to return the Church to the way it had been.

The first thing to change would be the monasteries. Already, Colum-cille had gathered a band of monks from Ireland and Scotland who he could trust to go throughout England and purge the monasteries of their laziness and laxness. Upon returning to York, Colum-cille would issue an *ex cathedra* decree stipulating that all who would worship as monks in England follow the ways of the anchorites who lived alone or the *regula Columbani* as laid forth by St. Columbanus in the sixth century after Christ.

Once the monasteries were reorganized, Colum-cille could turn his attention to the secular clergy and then the political relations of the Church.

With his new plan of action resolved, and his stomach feeling better for its purging of food and bile, Colum-cille leaned his head back on the rock and fell asleep to dream of his small cell in Aberdeen.

CHAPTER XI

Tomorrow morning would be the day. In his besieged camp Morkere knew his fate would be resolved. Only a few miles to the south, Arnketil was planning for battle, just as Sigeweard Bearn was preparing a little to the east. Of Leofwine, there had been no news, but Arnketil had finally managed to convince Sigeweard Bearn that the time to strike was now. Over the past several days, Morkere's army had been melting away. If they waited for word from Leofwine, the army might totally vanish. What Harold needed was a decisive victory, not a spectral army which was never punished.

The skies above Skipton were dark and clear. Stars sparkled brightly in the cool nocturnal air. In three warcamps, three leaders of men sat outside, preparing, both mentally and physically, for the battle which was to come in the morning. Between two of the men, messengers ran throughout the early evening hours, laying out battle plans in their attempt to utterly destroy the third.

In the center of his camp, Sigeweard Bearn looked up to the heavens and was the first of the three to notice a wondrous sight. Curtains of color, red, yellow, and green, were billowing high in the night sky. Dense tapestries which almost seemed to eclipse the stars above. Although the magnificent lights were not bright enough for real illumination, Sigeweard Bearn could make out the silhouettes of his men where the lights touched the northern horizon. Calling out to his men and pointing at the sky, Sigeweard Bearn declared the lights to be an omen of victory against Morkere.

Arnketil noticed the strange glow as well, for as the illumination grew, none could miss seeing the brilliant colors. Although Arnketil knew that victory would be achieved the next day, he was unsure of the exact meaning of the omen and called for a priest to explain what God's will was.

Morkere also saw the lights, but so deep in thought was he that Thomas had to touch him on the arm before he noted the ghostly colors which seemed to rise from the north. He and Thomas stood watching the curtains billow in the sky and then Morkere slowly began to walk away from his companion. Thomas called after the earl, but his voice went unheeded and Morkere, entranced by the strange sight, tried to walk toward it.

"Father," the earl called softly, *"lema sabachthani?"* A priest, more learned than most, heard Morkere cry out and believed he was addressing a prayer to God, saying the words that Christ said on the cross. Unlike Christ, Morkere received a reply.

"I have not forsaken you in your moment of need." Alfgar's bass reverberated at the very threshold of hearing. Above, the curtains of light seemed to ripple to the sound of Algar's voice. "I have led you to this spot where you can make a stand against the tyranny of Harold's men. I have given you illumination this night in which to prepare. Look, can you not see the radiance of the North? Even as these lights come from the North, so, too, will the light of England flow from the North to defeat the darkness of the South. I have told you that you will rule in Harold's stead, yet you have doubted the wisdom and words of your father. Tomorrow shall be your day. You shall come among your foes and I shall be with you, making your shield lighter and your axe fall rhythmically among your foes."

Morkere's spirits were buoyed by these words from his father and he returned to camp. Ready to interpret the lights of the north as a sign that his army would shine amid the southern darkness, he wandered, quietly, among his men.

CHAPTER XII

The village of Skipton resembled the wishbone of a duck. Two roads converged from the southeast and the southwest. When the paths met, they merged into a single road heading north. Around this fork, the hovels and homes of Skipton had been erected. Just north of the juncture, a stream ran perpendicular to the northern road.

Dawn broke to find three armies facing each other in the open fields just south of the village. Earl Morkere of Northumbria stood with his men arrayed, their backs to the southwestern road. Immediately to the east, Sigeweard Bearn's army stood ready, a Celtic priest loudly chanting the morning office as he walked among Sigeweard Bearn's men. Directly south of Morkere, Arnketil had set his forces, who stood grimly waiting for the day and the battle to begin. Behind each of the three armies baggage trains of various sizes remained outside the battlefield, horses tethered to them to become spoils for the victors.

As the sun rose above the horizon, men were still moving into position. Despite the rapid activity a hush seemed to have fallen over the armies. To the north, standing and sitting in the "V" shape where the roads met, villagers had gathered to watch the carnage which was about to occur just south of their hamlet.

Sigeweard Bearn's priest stopped chanting prime, plunging the entire area into silence. Within moments, a standard was raised above the center of Sigeweard Bearn's lines and with a great roar, Sigeweard Bearn's forces and Arnketil's forces began to move forward. As they moved, Morkere began to hustle his men toward their enemy. Lines broke against each other as battle began.

CHAPTER XIII

The press of people around him was greater than Thomas had expected. Although he had fought at Hrypadun, it had not prepared him for this smaller battle. Despite the fewer number of men on the field, this battle seemed more personal, perhaps because he now knew Earl Morkere as a comrade instead of merely his leader.

A sword came down at him and Thomas moved quickly to block the swing with the tines on the pitchfork he carried. As the swing went wide he swung the pitchfork around and felt the shaft meet the resistance of a body. Without pausing to see who he had hit or the damage he had caused, Thomas pressed on, deeper into the fray.

CHAPTER XIV

As Sigeweard Bearn had expected, the attack on Morkere, coming from two angles, had bent the earl's line into a "V"shape. If everything worked as he and Arnketil had planned, Morkere would soon be caught entirely between the two armies. Sigeweard Bearn was in the thick of the fighting. He hardly recognized any of the men whose sword rose and fell and whose battle-axes swung around him. Where he was standing, the mass of men was almost too dense for him to move his own weapon, a Norman sword he had found at Hastings. Nevertheless, he attacked almost indiscriminately, using the extra length the sword had over Saxon swords to thrust with the sharp point whenever he thought he saw one of Morkere's Northumbrians.

Sigeweard Bearn's efforts to distinguish foe from friend were aided by the various battle cries shouted by both sides. Shouts of "Morkere," "Harold," "Arnketil," and "Bearn" filled the air, rising above the clamor of sword and axe against shield and armor.

Within moments of the start of the battle, other cries filled the air, almost drowning out the battle calls of men and the metallic noises of their tools. Because men were swept from place to place by the inconsistent tides of the battle, many of the wounds were superficial or not fatal. The cries of wounded men began to join those of battling men.

CHAPTER XV

Blood was streaming from a wound in Edwig's forehead. Although he was occasionally blinded by the blood flowing into his eyes, he knew that the wound was not particularly dangerous. The scythe which had injured him had also thrown him off balance, making the wound a broad, but shallow cut. Ignoring the slight pain and the copious blood, Edwig continued to press into the writhing mass of flesh, knowing that this battle would secure King Harold's throne against his treacherous brother-in-law.

Edwig did not care about the political issues or religious issues which Arnketil claimed were behind the battle. The important thing was that Edwig establish himself as a great warrior and, even more importantly, be alive at the end of the battle to reap the rewards. If Arnketil or Sigeweard Bearn noticed his valor, life could only get easier.

As Edwig pressed deeper into the battle, thrusting occasionally with his sword, other, more grievously wounded men were pushing their way trying to retreat from the battle. In his haste to get away from Morkere's forces, one man tripped over a corpse. He fell, trying to steady himself with a no longer attached arm, onto the tip of Edwig's sword. As the sword pulled down with the weight of the body, the man's face twisted toward Edwig, who could see the glazed, painful look of death on the man's face.

Edwig tried to wrench his sword from the man's chest, but the blade caught between two ribs. Dropping his own blade, Edwig fell to his knees in order to search for a free weapon. The blood from his head wound streamed into his eyes, blinding him with a stinging pain. He groped blindly, first putting his hand into the gaping wound of a corpse. The man's organs moved softly, sluggishly aside, covering Edwig's hand in a warm, thick liquid. The stench at so close a distance made Edwig gag.

As he crawled around the battlefield, Edwig was continuously kicked by men who were either attacking or retreating. One time, a severed finger landed on top of Edwig's hand, causing him to sit up. He promptly was hit in the back of the head by the blunt end of a sword and knocked back to the ground.

Around him, the screams of wounded filled his ears while the stench of blood mingled with the odor of men whose bladders and intestines had failed them. The blood filling his eyes meant that Edwig was groping around blindly in the carnage and butchery of his own personal hell.

The dagger Edwig finally found was much shorter than the sword he had left embedded in the stranger's chest, but it was a much higher quality of craftsmanship. Wiping the blood from his eyes, Edwig saw that a stone of some sort was set in its hilt. He stood quickly, trying to get his bearing, but quickly found himself engaged with a dirty fighter who, Edwig hoped, was fighting for Morkere rather than in the king's name.

CHAPTER XVI

Arnketil was caught in the thick of the battle. He could not recognize any of the men around him, partly because he had never seen many of them, partly because those he did know were caked in mud and blood, but mostly because he didn't have the time to look around to see who he was surrounded by.

When the battle had first begun, Arnketil tried to pick out enemies who were of the same social rank or higher as he was. This quickly became impracticable as the battle took on the form of a general *mêlée*, to use a term of which the hated French were fond. Once the tone of battle had changed, Arnketil simply made it a habit to try to slice or skewer anybody who got in his way, regardless of their allegiance.

Suddenly, through the haze of the battle, Arnketil saw a fiery blond head of hair. The face beneath it seemed familiar and the Northern lord moved in its direction. Although he was continuously jostled by the men fighting around him, Arnketil somehow managed to keep the blond man in his view. As he fought his way closer, his identification became more and more certain until he absolutely was able to recognize the features of Earl Morkere.

When Arnketil approached Morkere, the earl had his back toward the lord. Something caused Morkere to turn around and he faced his enemy for a moment before reacting to Arnketil's presence.

Both men raised their swords for great blows against the other at the same time. As the blades swept downward, Morkere twisted his body to the right to avoid Arnketil's swing. Although Arnketil moved his body as well, Morkere's movement altered the course of his blade and Arnketil felt the bite of the blade, no longer particularly sharp, into the muscle on his upper arm. Arnketil's flesh was further torn as Morkere pulled his blade free and several small nicks on the blade ripped at the ragged edges of Arnketil's wound. Before either man had a chance to swing another blow, the forces of the battle moved them apart and Arnketil lost sight of his quarry.

CHAPTER XVII

Morkere's encounter with Arnketil left him slightly disturbed. For moments after he was forced away from his opponent, he was unable to field an attack against any of the men pushing and shoving at him. He was immensely lucky during this time, for none of the myriad blows aimed at him managed to find their mark. One would glance off his helm while another would miss because he was jostled out of the way by the incognizant mass.

Eventually, Morkere regained his head. He found himself in a quiet glade amidst the forest of battle. Looking out over the heads of men, he was able to pick out certain individuals: Thomas, his white jerkin dyed crimson with blood, battling against anonymous fighters, Sigeweard Bearn, striking all who opposed him, but of Arnketil, Morkere could find no sign.

Morkere elected to move toward Sigeweard Bearn. Although the earl held greater personal loathing for Arnketil, he recognized that Sigeweard Bearn held more real power and was closer to Harold than Arnketil would ever be, even if one of Harold's sons were to marry Arnegifu.

The crowd was tight around Morkere, but he was able to force his way through the mass much as a man would plough his way through a muddy river. Sometimes the flow of the crowd would work to Morkere's benefit, carrying him toward his quarry, more often it tried to prevent him from reaching Sigeweard Bearn.

Morkere's foot hit a corpse submerged beneath the fighting crowd. A cloud of foul gas was released from the body's gaping wound choking the earl. Morkere had to restrain the impulse to gag. Looking around, he saw his standard raised high above the battle near one edge of the fighting. Arnketil's banner could also be seen fluttering in a different part of the battlefield. There was no sign of Sigeweard Bearn's banner. As Morkere looked for the third banner, he noticed that the townspeople watching the battle had begun to scatter. They were no longer sitting and cheering for Morkere or Arnketil or Sigeweard Bearn or Harold.

CHAPTER XVIII

Sigeweard Bearn's wounds were streaming blood over his body. Miraculously, he had not suffered any blows to the head and his vision was still clear. Nevertheless, he was beginning to feel the strain of the hour of battle. Morkere's forces were fighting much better than Sigeweard Bearn would have given them credit for had he not been in the thick of the battle with them.

Suddenly, Sigeweard Bearn found himself in the open. No foe threatened him. In front of him was a teeming mass of men, swords, picks, and pitchforks rising and falling indiscriminately, but none of them reaching for him. The tide of the battle had pitched him onto the deserted shore, giving him a chance to breathe before once again entering into the fray. Although Sigeweard Bearn would never admit to it, he was feeling weak and old. His time for battles was in the past. *Sometimes battle was required to prove manhood and loyalty*, Sigeweard Bearn thought as he stood free of the battle.

Cautiously, Sigeweard Bearn turned his back to the battle. He looked to the north where the villagers of Skipton had been arrayed watching the battle. The crotch of the roads had emptied leaving only a muddy field where there had once been assembled an entire village worth of spectators. Sigeweard Bearn moved away from the battle's edge and looked more carefully to the north. It took him a few moments to spot it, but eventually he saw a faint cloud of dust on the northern horizon. He waited a few moments before deciding that there was only one thing the cloud could portend.

Sigeweard Bearn turned and forced his way back into the battle. As he did so, a new battle cry arose from his throat. Joining the calls of "Harold," "Bearn," "Arnketil," and "Morkere," Sigeweard Bearn raised his voice in a deafening cry of "Leofwine!"

CHAPTER XIX

The worst blow Morkere received all day was not physical. It came when he first heard the cries of "Leofwine" coming from the throats of his adversaries as the king's brother rode down from the north. Morkere had known that he could not hope to carry the field of battle just south of Skipton, but he had a chance of escaping. With Leofwine's arrival, that chance had virtually vanished.

God, Morkere thought, *If I manage to escape from these men on this day, I pledge to leave England for the continent where I shall aid your representative, Pope Alexander, in his holy war against King Harold.*

Even as Morkere thought the prayer, he felt the deep bite of a blade in his side. He turned to see Arnketil standing next to him, a huge grin on his face. Without even thinking about the pain which seared his body, Morkere thrust his sword at his adversary.

Arnketil parried the earl's blow and reposted, only to find Morkere's blade blocking his advance. The two faced each other in a calm amid the swirling sea of battle, able to trade multiple blows against each other. Blood streamed into Morkere's eyes, but he forbore wiping it away lest the pause in combat give Arnketil more of an advantage than his half-blindness.

Though the red haze blurred his vision and stung his eyes, Morkere was able to make out the shadowy figure. The earl had no idea of how badly Arnketil was injured, but knew that his own strength was fading fast. He summoned his remaining strength from wherever it hid deep in his gut and launched a great blow where he believed his adversary's head was. As he felt his blade meet with a little resistance, Morkere also felt his knees buckle beneath him.

CHAPTER XX

When Leofwine's forces descended on the battlefield from the North, the remnants of Morkere's army attempted to flee to the South. There was no order to the rout, mere flight fueled by panic. At the same time, Arnketil and Sigeweard Bearn's men were refreshed by the appearance of allies. Newly invigorated, they chased after the fleeing rebels.

From the time Sigeweard Bearn shouted the name "Leofwine" until Morkere's rebels were broken, the sun had barely passed through a half handspan on its journey across the sky.

While their armies were destroying the rebels and looting the battlefield, Sigeweard Bearn and Leofwine managed to link up on the side of the battle field.

"I'm sorry we didn't arrive sooner, but I thought you were going to wait for us. Wasn't that the agreed upon plan?" Leofwine carefully stepped around a bloody body lying in his way. There was no way to tell on whose side the man had fought

"That is what we had planned, but when our messenger never returned we did not know if you had received our word."

"Thurlkill didn't return? That's odd. He should have made contact with you several days ago."

"He didn't. We waited as long as we could, but Morkere was losing men right and left to desertion. If we didn't attack now, there wouldn't have been a rebel army, but neither would we have won a victory for your brother." Sigeweard Bearn, exhausted, weakly waved his sword at one of the ravens which circled and landed on the battlefield. The bird pecked at the blade and let out a loud squawk before returning to the corpse it was feasting on.

Leofwine paused and looked at the carnage of Skipton field. As he surveyed the dead and broken bodies of young Anglo-Saxons, a living one picked his way across the mounds of once living flesh.

"Lords Leofwine and Sigeweard Bearn, we've found something you should see."

The two lords looked at each other and then followed the man back into the heart of the battlefield. Around them the screams of the wounded mingled with the cawing of the crows. Hunched figures of men moved among their former opponents and comrades, looting where the dead lay and slaying the wounded. Neither man paid any attention to the looters. It was part of battle, or rather the aftermath. Any man who Leofwine or Sigeweard Bearn caught looting during a battle would find himself among the fatalities shortly after the battle was won.

A group of men stood clustered around something where Leofwine and Sigeweard Bearn were being led. The warrior, who had given his name as Edwig, was very quiet as he led the way to the men. His face was covered in blood, although it didn't seem to bother him. As he approached, the men moved aside, allowing Leofwine and Sigeweard Bearn to look at their discovery.

Lying on the ground were Arnketil and Morkere. Morkere still gripped the sword which was embedded in Arnketil's neck. The blade had been on its way to decapitating the Northern lord until the sword's edge wedged itself into Arnketil's spine. Blood and cuts covered Morkere. As Leofwine knelt beside the earl, Edwig spoke for the first time since he had summoned Leofwine.

"He isn't dead. He seems to almost be asleep. I imagine he was exhausted, although I can't imagine falling asleep during a battle."

"Loss of blood probably also played a part," Sigeweard Bearn commented, "At any rate, we can't leave him like this. Tie his hands. Since he did not have the grace to die in battle, we'll have to give him a trial. Of course, there is no question of his guilt."

Leofwine looked up at Sigeweard Bearn. "There's no need. Edwig, give the traitor his due."

The young Anglo-Saxon looked at his lord lying dead next to the unconscious Morkere. He looked up at the disapproving face of Sigeweard

Bearn and the stern, commanding face of Earl Leofwine. Finally, he looked down at the soft, relaxed face of Morkere. He reached to one of his comrades who handed him a sword. Before he could really think about what he was doing, Edwig lifted the sword and let it fall.

It took three blows of the sword to completely sever Morkere's head. The earl never regained consciousness during his final ordeal. When it was over, Leofwine reached down and picked the head up by the hair. Leofwine held the head as high as he could and proclaimed, "So will all the enemies of King Harold meet their end. We ride now for Durham. Morkere shall look over the city."

CHAPTER XXI

Edith knew what to expect long before she reached Durham. Soldiers, both victorious and fugitive, were moving south and sharing the news. Edith and her band were able to piece most of the story together. Nevertheless, she was unprepared for the reality of seeing her last surviving brother's head on a pike next to the gate of Durham.

Edith looked up at the sightless eyesockets of her brother. Tears filled her eye for the first time since Harold had rescued her from Gruffydd and she spoke in a voice so low that even those men who stood closest to her couldn't be sure they heard her say, "You will be avenged."

Steven H Silver

AFTER HASTINGS

BOOK V: INTERLUDE

> *When King Harold thought his realm was secure against the internal threat, Archbishop William of London, whose see the king had elevated from a mere bishopric, made a sermon against the king on the steps of Saint Paul's in London. At the height of his treacherous sermon, a shaft of light sprang through the clouds from the heavens, like the accusing finger of God and lit the archbishop in its radiant glow. As the crowd watched, Archbishop William fell to the base of the steps, never to arise.*
> —HISTORIA NOVARUM GESTARUM ANGLORUM,
> ERKENWALD OF BATH

CHAPTER I

Lanfranc stood inside the monastery doorway dripping wet. A sudden downpour had caught him in the middle of the courtyard and he had run for cover in the nearest alcove.

Three geese waddled in the courtyard, oblivious to the rain. Beyond them stood the hulking mass of the half-destroyed cathedral—partly burned and partly torn down. Laborers continued tearing apart the unsafe parts of the building despite the storm. The peal of a distant crash of thunder caused Lanfranc to cringe. Since the fire in the cathedral, he could no longer hear thunder or see lightning without a sense of dread.

The door opened behind him and he could hear Brother Beornred's deep voice.

"Come in, Your Grace. Not only is the rain wet, but it is cold as well."

When Lanfranc entered the monastery, Brother Beornred offered him a towel. While the bishop dried off, Beornred poured him wine and carefully diluted the thick syrup with water. Before giving it to the bishop, Beornred held the goblet over the flames in the small fireplace. He handed the mulled wine to Lanfranc who accepted the drink gratefully and drank it in one quick swallow.

Lanfranc looked at the brawny monk. Since coming to Canterbury, he had come to trust and confide in the monk. Beornred usually didn't offer good advice, he wasn't intelligent or imaginative enough for that, but after talking to him, and hearing his own voice, Lanfranc was often able to come to a decision.

"Word has come down from London that the king's wife has been sent to a nunnery in Flanders and King Harold is now flaunting the harlot Svannehals." With Beornred, Lanfranc did not have to pretend. He permitted the full measure of his scorn to enter his voice.

Beornred looked scandalizaed. "The king has torn asunder the holy bonds of matrimony which He has blessed! How is it possible for him to do such a thing?"

Before Lanfranc had met Beornred, he would not have believed such naivete could exist. The monk had witnessed the king's dismantling of ties to Rome, yet still could not fathom his dissolution of a marriage.

"The king shows no sign of remorse or contrition. He sees no reconciliation with the Church. When I agreed to remain in their heretical land, I had hoped to effect a change. Instead, he keeps pushing me further aside. I feel like marginalia. I can sit by and comment on the evils I see, but I can't do anything to change what I see. Every sermon, I loudly denounce the king, yet I am ignored. Rather than fear for their souls in eternity, they fear for their lives on earth."

"But all those noblemen followed Morkere when he tried to overthrow the king," Beornred protested. Lanfranc could tell the situation confused the monk. The king was duly elected by the witanangemot, and therefore should not be overthrown, yet he was a heretic and therefore could not retain the throne. Facing a paradox, Beornred ignored the difficulty and permitted the differences to stand side by side, resulting in contradictory statements in which the monk failed to see any failure of logic.

"Since Morkere's head appeared on a pike, all opposition to Harold has either vanished or fled to join the pope's *Magnus Foedus*. It seems I alone stand against Harold in his realm."

The two men sat in silence as Brother Beornred prepared another goblet of wine for Lanfranc. When the monk placed a goblet in front of the bishop, Lanfranc lifted it and drank slowly. He let the wine sit on his tongue for a few moments and realized how much he missed Italia, the birthplace of civilization. Although the French could make a wine which was palatable, the English had never learned the process. Only in Italia, only in Tuscania, could real wine be made. However, when all He gave you was the fruit of a pitiful English vine, you must learn to make do.

"I did not think it would have been possible for him to be even more deplorable than he was when he announced his bizarre intention to create a Celtic Church, yet he goes and lives in sin with this hussy, openly, when his wife is devoting herself to His work."

Beornred sat silently, watching the bishop's anguish, allowing Lanfranc to vent his rage at Harold and his mockery of a church.

CHAPTER II

Aethelwine stood at the prow of the ship as it sliced its way through the warm waters off the Oviedan shore. He stood with his eyes firmly rooted to the imaginary point in the ocean where his chilly island home stood, resolutely not turning his gaze on the warm-baked lands of the Moors which he left behind. When Harold's summons came, along with the king's explanation of Morkere's revolt, Aethelwine cried at the thought of leaving the strange land which had managed to grasp his heart in a way he hadn't believed possible when he first arrived.

His heart was broken further when he opened the letter which came from Leofwine. While Harold's epistle was brief, and to the point, Leofwine had been at Skipton and was able to describe the carnage of that battlefield. Worst of all, Leofwine informed him that Thurlkill had vanished before the battle of Skipton, either turned coward and fled, or set upon by bandits, none knew which.

The loss of his son made him yearn to stay away from England more than he would have thought possible. At the same time, he needed to go back to her white shores `and look for signs that Thurlkill was alive and not a coward.

The thoughts of Thurlkill's loss turned Aethelwine's mind back to the days after his wife had died, shortly after Thurlkill was born. She was still young, hardly older than Thurlkill was now, assuming he was still alive. Although Harold had chided Aethelwine constantly about having married a Welsh woman, Aethelwine actually had more in common with her, or at least her male kin, than he did with Harold.

Although there was nothing in the warm seas of Spain reminiscent of their time spent on the Welsh Marches, every breeze of wind and spray of brine made Aethelwine think of their few years together before she had been taken from his side by illness. Just as he did not have a chance to say goodbye to Thurlkill, Aethelwine was on campaign in the North Country when Gwynyfyr died. Despondency settled over Aethelwine as he thought of Gwynyfyr, Thurlkill, and Moorish Spain, all lost to him. He gave up trying to remember the good times he and Gwynyfyr had shared, the carefree days of teaching and playing with Thurlkill and the strange, early days of his brief sojourn to the court of Ishbiliya. The waves suddenly took on a grayish, almost sluggish mien as clouds moved to block the sunlight from their formerly glistening crests.

Aethelwine turned to go to his cabin below decks, grabbing a meadhorn as he left the open air.

CHAPTER III

Rodrigo Diaz de Vivar sat on an outcropping of rock near the mountain village of Roncevalles. Behind him, shielded from his view by a low, rocky peak, lay the army of King Sancho II of Castile. Rodrigo scanned the dark, starlit night, trying to pick motion out of the shadows with the corners of his eyes. His ears pricked at any sound which reached them, from the far-off, muted cries of his compatriots to the scrabble of a mountain cat as gravel gave way beneath its feet. Although Rodrigo had been charged with keeping watch for the armies of the Moors, he was more concerned with the possibility of an attack by the ancient Basques who lived in these mountains.

The Basques had lived in the Pyrenees since time immemorial. Although nominally Christian, they wanted nothing to do with the Christian kingdoms of Spain or France, or with the pope. For that matter, they had no desire to have any sort of relations with the Moors. For all their claim to want to be left alone, however, the Basques seemed to attack both Christian and Moor with surprising regularity.

Suddenly, the calm air was split by an eerie undulating sound Rodrigo knew to be the strange warbling battle cry of the Moorish forces. Rodrigo quickly raised his horn to his lips to blow a warning. He sucked in a deep breath to rouse Sancho's men, who must have heard the same cries as Rodrigo. Before he could exhale into the horn, a Moorish arrow caught the Spanish warrior through the throat and he fell lifeless, dropping the horn over the precipice on which he had sat.

CHAPTER IV

The hamlet of Senlac was normally a nondescript Saxon town, like every other Saxon village from Kent to Northumbria. A narrow dirt road ran from cottage to cottage, scuffed by the feet of villagers, chickens, and pigs. A large barn at one end of the village housed the communal oxen, used by each farmer in turn to pull the ploughs across their fields. Outside the small, close cluster of houses spread the villagers' fields, separated by the tall hedgerows which dissected the English countryside.

What made Senlac different, a feature which would draw the eye of any visitor who happened to pass near the village, was the abbey being built on a hill outside the village. Around the base of the hill stood four perfectly symmetrical mounds. Surrounding those mounds was the camp where the workman lived who were building the abbey.

On this day, however, the workman had abandoned their work on the holy edifice at the top of the hill. Large tents had been erected on the flat ground between the mounds and the smell of roasting meat filled the air almost as thickly as the sound of minstrels singing to be heard over the constant noise of the crowd.

Although all England was supposed to be celebrating King Harold's victory over his brother-in-law, the outlawed Morkere, the celebration at Senlac was particularly riotous, for Harold had announced his intention of visiting the village where he had defeated William the Bastard during the first year of his reign.

AFTER HASTINGS

Senlac had not had so many living nobleman in it since that fateful October day. The first to arrive had been Bishop Lanfranc of Canterbury. Many were surprised to see the bishop arrive so early, given his disagreement with the king. Others pointed out that the proximity of Canterbury to Senlac meant Lanfranc had the shortest trip to make. All noticed that Lanfranc mentioned Pope Alexander several times during the Mass he performed and sermon he taught before the king's party had arrived. Once Harold arrived, Lanfranc managed to keep a very low profile and many wondered if the bishop had returned to Canterbury.

Harold walked through the winding streets of the city of tents which surrounded the burial mounds of Senlac. At his side, Svannehals walked silently, her bright eyes taking in the sights of the strange, impromptu town. Queen Edith's departure for the continent following Morkere's death irked Harold, but the king saw no reason not to use her flight as an excuse for making his relationship with Svannehals even more public.

Svannehals paused to look at a booth selling lead badges depicting the symbols of a wide variety of saints' symbols. Harold spent the time looking around the crowd which milled between the vendors' stalls. He saw Leofwine come around a corner, followed by one of Harold and Svannehals's sons, Edmund.

"Leofwine!" Harold cried out, forgetting any decorum which might be associated with his royal status.

Leofwine hurried over to his brother, Edmund running behind, tried to keep up with his uncle.

"It's good to see you. I can't believe we haven't been in each other's company since before Skipton. I must tell you all about the day." Leofwine was more excited than Harold could remember seeing him in a long time.

"Now is not the time for your tale. We're at a fair in my honor, and yours. Let us enjoy the sunshine and warm air. There will be time enough to talk about death later." Harold found Leofwine's enthusiasm to be infectious. He had not really been looking forward to strolling through the fairgrounds, but duty had called him to the celebration. Now, however, he realized that England was enjoying a rare day when the weather was warm and sunny. Harold wondered if this was like the weather Aethelwine had reported having in Iberia.

Harold gestured for Svannehals to join them and she reluctantly turned her back on the badge vendor. When she caught sight of Edmund, she hurried over to where the three men stood. It wasn't often that she got to see any of her children and Edmund's near engagement to Arnketil's daughter had caused him to be even more absent from her sight than normal.

As the foursome walked through the fairgrounds, they enjoyed the warmth of the sun beating down on them. A cool, gentle breeze brought the distant tang of the sea to their nostrils. As far as Harold could remember, this was the most perfect day he had lived through since being placed on the throne by the witanangemot. As they moved from stall to stall, jostling with the crowd like any commoner, Edmund pleaded with Leofwine to continue telling him about his adventures on campaign in the North against the evil Morkere. Harold refused to allow Leofwine to talk about the campaign, but noted that Svannehals took great glee in her son's attitude toward Harold's traitorous brother-in-law.

Eventually, as they sat on a small bridge eating meatpies, Harold relented and Leofwine began to tell Edmund about the Battle of Skipton. Although Harold was paying more attention to Svannehals than his brother or their son, Harold noticed that Leofwine had gained in his ability to tell stories. In spite of himself, he found his attention wandering from Svannehals to his brother's voice.

"I stood at the crest of a hill and looked down on the battle. You could hardly tell the one side from the other, even though all the warriors were laid out below me like pieces on a gameboard. I saw that the men were rallying wherever your father's banner flew. I almost did not enter the fray, but then I saw Morkere, standing head and shoulders above all other men on the field, move toward your father's trusted aide, Arnketil. I saw that

Morkere would slay the lord from behind if left to his own, so I motioned my men forward."

Harold knew enough of the story to know that Leofwine was elaborating enormously, but decided to allow Edmund to enjoy the picture Leofwine was painting. Suddenly, Harold's attention was attracted to a man shouting as he approached the quartet.

"I'm looking for the rightful king of the English. Some peasant who calls himself Harold Godwinsson."

Harold stood, motioning for Leofwine to stand behind him. He felt Leofwine slip a knife into his hands and assumed his brother had retained one for himself. Svannehals moved behind the brothers. Although she tried to walk with Edmund, her son joined his father and uncle in standing against the threatening stranger.

The crowd thinned as the man moved toward the king. His head was wrapped in cloth, leaving only his eyes visible through a narrow opening. Despite Harold and Leofwine's stance, the stranger continued to stride purposefully. When he was only about ten feet away, he slowly reached up and touched his temple.

The cloth fell away from his face to reveal a dark brown face with the light beginnings of a blonde beard. Despite the changes, Harold couldn't help but recognize his lifelong friend.

"Aethelwine!" the king shouted as he ran to hug him. He dropped the knife to the mud as the two men embraced. "When did you arrive back in England? What happened to you? You look like a Saracen!"

"If you'll be quiet and stop asking questions, I might be able to answer some of them." Aethelwine turned to Leofwine, who had retrieved his knife from the mud where Harold had dropped it. "Leofwine, is it true my son is dead?"

"I don't know. I wish I could tell you more. Arnketil sent him to me with battle plans before Skipton. I gave him the chance to get back in time for the battle. I thought it was a good idea. It wasn't until after the battle that I discovered he never arrived back at Arnketil's army. Whether or not he's dead, I can't tell you. He may have gotten lost. He may have been killed. He may have . . ."

"He wouldn't have done that." Aethelwine spoke authoritatively to cut off Leofwine's suggestion of the unthinkable.

"You would have loved Ishbiliya and Spain," Aethelwine said to Leofwine. "The weather is always warm. Today would be chilly down there.

"In brief, muluk al-Mu'tadid bi 'Illah, Abu 'Amr 'Abbad ibn Muhammad ibn 'Abbad has agreed to send his men against the Roman Spanish and the French if he is able to reach them through the mountains. If all has gone as should, he has already attacked the forces King Sancho was moving to join with the pope. I imagine we'll soon hear of a confrontation.

"Now, what are the happenings here in England? All I have heard since landing are reports of Leofwine's victory over Morkere at Skipton."

"Don't listen to what Leofwine has to say on the subject or you'll never hear the truth," Harold laughed. "He did manage to defeat Morkere, and the traitor's head adorns the wall at Durham, but he had help from Arnketil and Sigeweard Bearn. In the aftermath of the battle, Edith has gone missing, although there are reports she's fled to join Edward's wife in a nunnery. With Edith gone from the island, I've tried to convince Archbishop Colum-cille to annul my marriage to the ungrateful wretch and instead marry Svannehals and me, but he refuses."

"So your tame monk isn't as tame as you hoped he would be?"

Harold shot a stern glance at his friend. "I never meant for Colum-cille to be my 'tame monk,' as you call him. I was trying to protect England from the foreign invaders who started coming over during good King Edward's reign." The king put as much contempt into his predecessor's name as possible. "If I had rolled over to Hildebrand and Pope Alexander, I would be joining Hardraada and my good brother, Tostig in the rich English soil."

"Forgive me, Harold. I didn't mean my words to sound as they did."

Harold was silent for a moment. "It's too nice a day to let Edward's spectre haunt me. No more talk of dead kings or brothers . . . or brothers-in-law," he glanced at Leofwine meaningfully. "I would hear of the exotic Moorish lands. Some other time. For now, let us enjoy a carefree day at the fair."

Harold offered his arm to Svannehals and began walking away from the bridge they had been standing on. After a moment, Aethelwine, Leofwine, and Edmund began walking after them.

With Aethelwine back in England, the fair became an even more colorful and joyous celebration than before the two friends had been reunited. As they walked back and forth between the booths, Harold laughed, nearly forgetting for moments that he was the King of England and not just the Earl of Wessex. He reveled in the freedom he felt, buying a comb for Svannehals at one booth, looking at a broach that Edmund called his attention to, bestowing largesse on any minstrel, mime, or juggler who happened to cross his path.

The small group stood watching a band of mummers re-enacting Harold's victory over William when a loud voice boomed from the crowd on the far side of the display.

"All here imperil their immortal soul! You keep the company of a heretic! Worse, you allow a heretic to thrive in your midst! Denounce him as the devil's pawn and turn to a king who supports the True Church."

The robed man moved slowly toward Harold, his right hand extended in accusation, "Turn out this evil creature who lives in sin with his harlot while his *huswyf* seeks her spiritual redemption! Does not Matthew tell us that Christ said, 'Whosoever shall put away his wife, except it be for fornication, and shall marry another, committeth adultery: and whoso marrieth her which is put away doth commit adultery.'."

Leofwine and Aethelwine moved forward to grab Harold's mocker. They laid hold of his arms at the same time and discovered that the robes concealed muscular arms. Wriggling his right arm free of Aethelwine, the monk smashed his fist into Leofwine's stomach. As the earl bent double, the monk tried to run from his captors. Intent on Aethelwine, the monk did not see Edmund standing in his way. Monk and *aetheling* fell to the ground in a tangle of arms and legs.

Edmund grappled with the monk, but the man broke free from his grip. As the monk rose, Leofwine aimed a kick at the small of his back, sending the holy man sprawling. When the monk tried to rise, he found himself looking at the sharp end of Aethelwine's sword.

"Your name?"

"*Servis diabolo!*" The monk shouted at Aethelwine.

Aethelwine glanced at Harold. "Why is it that every time one of these priests goes mad he starts cursing you in Latin? You would think one could come up with something original to say instead of 'You serve the devil' or 'Your master will burn in the fires of hell.' What are we going to do with this one?"

Harold looked at Aethelwine's captive. The man looked familiar. He was burly, looking more like a warrior than a monk. His head was tonsured in the Celtic style, the front half shaved and the back covered in hair. From the shortness of the hair at the top of his head, Harold guessed that he had only changed his tonsure recently. Trying to imagine the man with a Roman tonsure, Harold still couldn't figure out why he looked familiar.

"Brother Beornred of Canterbury," Leofwine pronounced the mad monk's name slowly, as if not entirely sure of what he was going to say until after the words were out of his mouth. The monk did not voice a response, but shifted uneasily at the end of Aethelwine's sword, as near an admission of his identity as he was likely to give. Seeing this movement, Leofwine turned to Harold and continued, "Brother Beornred has been a monk at Canterbury for several years. He once served Archbishop Stigand, and I think was even there when Edward tried to foist the Frenchman on us. When you deposed Stigand and the Hildebrand put Lanfranc in his place, Beornred was among the first monks at Canterbury to welcome the foreigner. If he is still at Senlac, I imagine his master, Bishop Lanfranc, must be somewhere nearby."

"Bind this miscreant's arms and legs and hold him in the pens with the pigs and chickens. I wish to hold an audience with the bishop of Canterbury."

As Harold announced his desires, four men emerged from the crowd to help Aethelwine deal with Brother Beornred. Boys vanished from the crowd to try to find Lanfranc, although few would be able to recognize the bishop if they saw him.

Harold sat on a tree stump and watched Aethelwine haul Beornred away. He glanced around at the crowd and saw that Svannehals had melted into their midst, trying to absent herself from Harold now that he had to act as the king. Their son, Edmund, however, had drifted to his father's side, standing next to the stump, listening to every regal decision Harold had to make, as if remembering them for his own holdings.

The sun had hardly moved when Lanfranc was brought before the king. The prelate's clothing was disheveled and torn, as if he had struggled against his captors before they were able to bring him to the royal audience. Knowing Lanfranc, Harold had a feeling the townspeople who found him had taken joy in the ability to rough up a prince of the Church.

"My lord bishop," Harold looked up at Lanfranc, "Are you in acquaintance with a monk of Canterbury who is known as Brother Beornred?"

"Brother Beornred is a great aid and comfort to me. He guided me on my first visit to my see. What has brought such a humble monk to the attention of a monarch?"

"When did you last see the monk we are discussing?"

"I was watching an archery contest on the other side of that hill. When I turned to ask Brother Beornred a question, I discovered he had gone off."

Lanfranc had thought for a few moments before answering, which caused Harold to believe the bishop. If Lanfranc had known what Beornred was about, he would have known exactly when he was supposed to have lost sight of his aide.

"I regret to inform you that your wayward monk seems to have been infested by a demonic influence. It seems many clerics throughout England have been behaving in treasonous fashion lately and Brother Beornred has succumbed to the evil spirit."

Harold waited for Lanfranc to defend the monk or agree with Beornred's rantings. If the bishop were to espouse Beornred's harangue, Harold would be able to conveniently rid himself of the Roman bishop. Lanfranc, however, was too wily to give Harold the opportunity.

"I see," he replied, slowly, "Treason. This is certainly regrettable. The Church has always tried to instill a respect for authority in all her sons. When will you be able to return Brother Beornred to my care?"

Harold stared at the bishop's affrontery. "Why should I return Beornred to you? He will be tried and sentenced for treason."

"Brother Beornred is a cleric. As such, he is immune to the secular laws."

"Such may have been the case when the archbishop of Rome tried to undermine the laws of this kingdom. The Church in England no longer heeds that foreigner's will. Clerics can retain their immunity as long as the crime does not impinge on the royal estate," Harold thought for a moment, "or murder."

"I must protest this decision. I would present my case, and Brother Beornred's, before Archbishop Colum-cille."

Against his better judgment, Harold assented to Lanfranc's demand.

CHAPTER V

Swaefred rarely went into Grantham. Although the journey from Heorlafestoun to the city only took a half hour by cart, the cleric found something about the distance to be daunting. However, when Father

Egmund summoned him, there was no way he could refuse to make the trip into town.

Swaefred hadn't seen Father Egmund since the day Earl Leofwine had executed Heardcwide outside the Heorlafestoun Church. This visit would, in fact, only be the third time the village priest had spoken to his new spiritual leader. Father Egmund had made a progress of the parishes surrounding Grantham when he first replaced Father Maegleas and then vanished until the day he was summoned to mediate the dispute between Swaefred and the earl. Thinking back on that day, Swaefred could hardly believe he had stood up to the earl and his soldiers as he did. Especially when Father Egmund came and explained why Swaefred was wrong to stand defiant against the king's brother.

Swaefred had, in fact, no desire to speak to Father Egmund. Their first visit could be discounted. He thought Father Egmund was only in Heorlafestoun for a quarter hour between the time he rode in from the east side of the village and rode out again to the north, scarcely enough time to even see the church, let alone speak to Swaefred. The second time, of course, Swaefred would rather not have had the priest's support. After the close relationship Swaefred had with Father Maegleas, it felt strange to think of his superior as someone who, if not an enemy, did not think the way he did.

When Swaefred arrived at Saint Wulfram's, he was admitted by the sexton, Adric. The sexton motioned for him to have a seat near the door and disappeared further into the dark interior of the church. Although the church was not huge, the darkness effectively swallowed up Adric before he had gone too far. Only a few candles relieved the pitch blackness of the church's interior.

When Adric returned with Father Egmund, they found Swaefred working to pull a small insect of some sort, a louse or flea, from his bushy red beard. The village priest quickly ceased his activity when he realized he was no longer alone. Without saying a word, Adric presented Egmund to Swaefred, and then vanished once again into the darkness.

"I've been told it is a nice day out. Let's walk outside." Egmund opened the door and motioned for Swaefred to precede him through it. Even after a short while inside, Swaefred found the day to be blinding. He could not imagine how Egmund made the transition from darkness to light as easily as he seemed to.

The men began to walk around the Church. The walked slowly, moving aside for the gravestones which dotted the churchyard. Swaefreed waited for Egmund to begin speaking. It almost took more patience than the village priest had, but finally his superior began to talk.

"Whenever I see clouds in the sky or a blade of grass, I am reminded of His majesty. No earthly master can compare with the splendors which He can perform. They say that the late king, Edward, could heal a man with the touch of his hands, truly a miraculous event. However, what could Edward do if He wasn't there to guide his hand to the poor wretch?

"Kings change. One year England was ruled by the Saxons, then the Danes came, the Saxons regained the throne, the Normans almost took it from the Saxons. The only thing which remained constant throughout was that God sat in heaven looking over the events of England.

"I hope you can understand what I'm about to tell you. It doesn't matter who rules on Earth, and that applies to the Church as well as the kingdom. The important thing is to do what He wants. If that means bending to the will of this so-called Celtic Church which Harold has created rather than the true ways of the Roman Church, we can do more good for the people by following Harold's Church."

"How can God be separate from the Church? The two are linked. He told us how to worship, He ordained the pope as head of the Church. Did He not give Peter the keys to heaven?"

Father Egmund sighed. It was obvious that Swaefred would not be able to handle the truth he was being told. "We live in a dangerous world when kings set up their own church. Just continue in your parish as before. I'll advise you on the proper date of Easter. Try to stay away from politics. You may have made a dangerous enemy when you opposed Earl Leofwine, but I think he'll forget about you. A minor village priest is not his major concern."

"Thank you for your advice. It is similar to what I was told by Father Maegleas before he left Grantham."

The two men walked in silence until they returned to the entrance of Saint Wulfram's. As Father Egmund opened the church door, he turned back to Swaefred, "You have also been summoned to appear before Archbishop Colum-cille at his convocation in York next month."

Before Swaefred could respond, Father Egmund entered the church and closed the door.

CHAPTER VI

Hildebrand stormed around his chambers in the royal palace on the Ile d'Paris. Piled high around him were letters and dispatches concerning the great alliance he had painstakingly built up to regain England for the Holy Church. Unfortunately, many of those letters detailed setbacks which he had tried at all costs to avoid. In Spain, the Moors had launched an unexpected campaign to rid the peninsula of its Northern Christian kingdoms. The Christian forces of King Sancho of Castile had been forced into retreat and been soundly defeated outside the village of Roncevalles. The Moors had continued their push north and none of the Spanish kingdoms would be able to give aid to the attack on England. In fact, if the Moors were not halted quickly, Hildebrand would not be able to count on Provence being able to help in the war either.

In the East, the Byzantine potentate, who called himself a Roman Imperator, had sent a lengthy letter in his infernal Greek language which, once Hildebrand had managed to translate it into Latin and then remove all the courtly gibberish, seemed to state that Byzantium was friendly with the English who desired to learn the true ways of Christ as practiced in the

Roman Empire and would regard any attack on the English as an attack on Constantinople itself.

Although Hildebrand wanted to laugh at the thought of the English following the lead of the Byzantine patriarch, he knew that Harold's emissary must have covered the eyes of Romanus Diogenes to make him believe that England would become Byzantine. The archdeacon also had a brief missive from the papal emissaries which told how two legions had been pulled from the Seljuq marches and were moving into a position to attack either Calabria or Sicilia.

Hildebrand hadn't really expected much support from the Spanish monarchs, who seemed to view themselves as part of the Catholic Church, but not really part of Christendom, so their battles against the Moors did not really diminish the strength of the army which Hildebrand planned to send against Harold. The threatened attack on Calabria and Sicilia, unfortunately, would require a small army of men stationed in Italy's south in case the attack materialized. To make matters worse, the most likely candidates for that action were the Normans who already lived in Sicilia and who were among the greatest warriors in Christendom, second, perhaps, only to their cousins who had remained in Normandy where Duke William had forbidden his vassals to fight in what he termed a misguided effort to gain a crown which William no longer desired.

William's illness showed no sign of either killing him or abating. Nevertheless, his sons, particularly Robert and Richard, were forced to defend their weakened father's realm from barons who were tasting freedom after being subjected to William's steady hand over the past decade and more. Even if William hadn't made his announcement about the battle against the English, the Normans were not in a condition to fight against any but themselves.

Hildebrand threw the offending papers and letters onto the oaken table which rested in the center of the room. He walked over to the small window which hardly permitted enough light to see by into the room and looked out over the city of Paris. The city was crammed together, just as

AFTER HASTINGS

Rome or London or Aachen, or any of the other great cities of Christendom were. Church spires poked above the heights of houses and shops, pointing, like fingers, to the heaven which they promised to those who worshiped within.

Paris was the only land which had remained in the hands of the French kings since the days when Merovech had ruled the Frankish people. When the Pope displaced the last of the Merovingian kings with Pepin's line, and later Hugh Capet's family, Paris remained as the base of the royal support.

While the Holy Roman emperor, who claimed descent from Charlemagne, tried to be a pope-maker, the pope succeeded in being a king-maker among the French. That, Hildebrand reflected, was the only way he had been able to gain King Philippe's support for the Great Alliance. Even then, Philippe's desire to break away from under the pope's benevolent yoke almost cost the Foedus Magnus its French support.

Hildebrand dropped heavily into a hard, wooden chair placed in front of the fireplace. The resistance Philippe and Heinrich had put up to the proposed alliance was enough to make Hildebrand wonder if they realized what a threat to the Church Harold's rebelliousness was. Even if they did, it was obvious that they did not realize that a threat to the Church was also a threat to their right to sit on their thrones. Harold had already had to face one uprising from his subjects. Without the backing of the Church, he would face an infinite number of similar revolts until he was finally overthrown and a pious man was made King of the Saxons. These thoughts set Hildebrand to chuckling. His first moment of levity in weeks, brought on by the thought that he wanted his allies to learn a lesson from his enemy.

Rising from his chair, Hildebrand opened the door and called for Giovanni. The short man had a room just down the corridor from the legate and appeared within moments of hearing his master's voice.

"Giovanni, I find that I have need to discuss the plans of the war. Could you arrange for an audience with the king's ancient advisor,

Guillaume. I would prefer that he come to me rather than me going to him, but I must see him soon."

"Of course, Your Excellency." Giovanni bowed and turned to leave the room.

Once alone, Hildebrand began to straighten the randomly strewn papers into neat stacks. Although he could easily have called a servant to return his chambers to order, he preferred to do so himself. He had found, over that years, that servants never could figure out the proper order for papers. Hildebrand reflected that their inability to read or write even the simplest sentence had a lot to do with that deficiency. Laughing again at that thought, he began to sift through the pile until he found the missive he wanted to look over in preparation for his meeting with Guillaume.

Hildebrand was pouring himself a goblet of wine when Giovanni rapped lightly on the door. Hildebrand recognized his servant's distinctive knock and translated it in his mind to mean that Guillaume would be right behind Giovanni. Rather than answering the door immediately, Hildebrand took a long sip of wine and settled into a comfortable, but austere-appearing, chair which stood next to the table. He lit the candle sitting in the middle of the table and pulled the letter he had been reading in front of himself.

"Enter," he called, when he deemed that Guillaume had stood outside the door long enough.

Giovanni opened the door and stepped in. "Guillaume, advisor to King Philippe of the Franks, stands outside and begs an audience with Your Excellency."

"Of course I will see the servant of our illustrious host, the King of the Franks." Hildebrand hoped Guillaume's hearing was good enough for his words to be heard in the hallway.

The man moved slowly into the room, his gait a shuffle where once it would have been a proud step. The Frank's snowy white beard hung in limp strands against his chest. His face, peeking from above his long moustache, was a bland gray, hardly a contrast to his beard. Although the

Frank sported long beard and moustaches, his hair was short. While long hair had once been a badge of royalty among the Franks, now all still wore it short in revolt against the downfall of the Merovingians three hundred years before.

When Guillaume stopped his slow, but steady, movement into the room, Hildebrand motioned that he could begin.

"Your Excellency," Hildebrand was surprised at the strength behind Guillaume's voice, "I have served my master, King Philippe, for many years, since he was but a child. Before he was born, I was permitted to give advice to his father Robert. I even was known to make suggestions to King Hugh in the years after he was made king by your own master's ancestor nearly eighty years ago. Permit me to suggest that one who has outlived his biblically allotted years by nearly a score may have acquired, in that time, wisdom beyond even that which He has granted His vicar on Earth. For although I may look like a man who should have long ago been placed on a bier, I assure you that I am as capable as any other man. Perhaps not in fighting or in love, but certainly in thought."

Hildebrand found himself getting distracted by the man's words, almost as if he wove a spell around the legate simply by rambling about himself and the past to which he could look. Hildebrand deigned to ignore Guillaume's slight against the pope in the interest of hearing the old man's thoughts. Rather than the confused elder most people perceived, Hildebrand saw Guillaume as a shrewd man, hiding behind a mask of incomprehensibility. Instead of interrupting Guillaume's ramble, Hildebrand nodded for him to continue.

"I would share my thoughts on your war, if I may, for I have seen many wars and battles throughout my long life, and although you may laugh to look on me now, I was, at one time, a participant in such august and glorious affairs. I remember fighting beside my first lord, King Hugh, as he defended the crown set upon his head by God's vicar. I did such wonderful deeds when I was near King Hugh, who served as inspiration to all who saw him on his horse wielding a sword and putting his enemies to rout. None of these kinglets who parade around Christendom, from Usurper Harold to Emperor Henri were any part of the man my lord Hugh was. He could have bested all of them before breaking his fast. However, instead of warring against his fellow monarchs for his own glory on Earth, my lord Hugh waged battle only for His greater glory in heaven at the command of the Pope.

"Although I tell my current lord, Philippe, legends of his grandsire, I fear that he is merely of the lot who rule in foreign places and not, it seems, truly descended from the loins and limbs of Hugh the Great. Instead of listening to my hoary words of his illustrious ancestor, Philippe prefers to hear the gilded voices of his Provencal minstrels as they strum their lyres and lutes and sing of ancient Charlemagne and the fallen Merovechs. Philippe does not seem to understand that the only deeds which reflect well upon his soul are the deeds which are worth doing, or singing about."

Guillaume was seized by a coughing fit and Hildebrand motioned for Giovanni to offer the man a goblet of wine to clear his throat. When Guillaume had sipped from the goblet, he continued, his voice rheumy with humours.

"I call upon you, my lord, to beg guidance in finding some way to convince my lord Philippe that he must follow the path laid for him by our father in Rome."

Having completed his speech, Guillaume turned and sat on a chair without Hildebrand's invitation. Given the man's extreme age, Hildebrand refrained from a reprimand for Guillaume's insolence.

"What you say is very sensible," Hildebrand said gently, "I wonder that your young charge does not heed your advice."

"Philippe has eyes only for posterity. He believes, rightfully or wrongfully, that should he do the bidding of Pope Alexander, all of history will see him as merely a lapdog of the papacy, fit only for His Holiness to wipe his greasy fingers on. I've tried to convince my lord that he would in reality be the hounds sent off to the chase, trusted to bring down the mighty stag."

"And he doesn't see himself as a warrior? That's very unusual."

"No, he sees himself as a warrior. He merely sees himself as an *imperator* rather than as a *pedes*. If he follows the orders of Alexander, he fears he will forever be seen as a foot-soldier instead of a general. Remember, he is but a mere lad of sixteen years, only recently out from under his mother's regency."

"But in the eyes of the Lord, he will be seen as a defender of the faith."

"Forgive me, but when one becomes my age, one's immortal soul becomes very important as one reflects on all the evil one has done over the course of many years. When one is just entering adulthood, as Philippe is, he believes he can not be killed. His concern, therefore, is for *gloria mundi*, not *gloria coeli*."

Hildebrand was surprised that Guillaume was able to sprinkle Latin phrases throughout his speech. Despite his white hair and wrinkles, the old servant still had the use of his faculties. Hildebrand began to mentally re-categorize the man who sat opposite him.

The voice of a minstrel, singing in the courtyard, interrupted the silence between the two men.

> "When Charles, who was king, our great emperor,
> Had been in Spain for nigh on seven years
> He conquered it from the high lands to the sea
> No castle, wall, or city remain standing
> Where he has visited the countryside
> Save Zaragosa, high up on a mountain
> Held by Marsilius, who does not believe in God
> But who worships Mohammed and Apollo
> So, like all pagans an evil end awaits him."

The lyrics the minstrel sang sounded vaguely familiar to Hildebrand. He listened closely, missing something Guillaume said to him. Once he recognized the troubadour's song, he rose and went to the door. Giovanni sat in a chair just outside the door. A small hymnal was clasped limply in his hand. Hildebrand gently nudged his shoulder until the man woke.

"There is a minstrel in the courtyard. Please bring him to me."

By the time Hildebrand had finished issuing his instructions, Giovanni was fully awake and had begun to move down the hall toward the staircase. Hildebrand turned and re-entered his chambers. Guillaume was in the middle of refilling his wine goblet when Hildebrand took his seat again.

"Do you think the king will put his stubbornness behind him?"

Guillaume looked at Hildebrand for a moment with a strange look on his face. "As I said, King Philippe is young. He will eventually come around. Assuming, of course, that his advisors, most importantly Théobald, indicate that to be the prudent course of action. Théobald will naturally be willing to support the papal party for the right price, as I'm sure you can tell."

"And what would that right price be?" Hildebrand hated bribing others to follow the papacy. It was something which should be done naturally. He had heard Emperor Heinrich use a word to describe what he was doing. A coarse, Germanic word to describe a coarse barbarian practice. *Realpolitik*.

"I'm not really sure. I wish I could offer a guarantee, but at my age, the only guarantee is that I won't be on this earth for very much longer. On the other hand, when you get to be my age, if you get to be my age, you'll wonder if He will ever call you to His feet."

"I'm glad you were able to come and have this talk." Hildebrand noticed that Guillaume was a well enough trained courtier to know a dismissal when it came. He would have to be to survive nearly a century in the Frankish court. Even before Hildebrand could formally dismiss him, the aging advisor was shuffling backwards toward the door. Hildebrand had timed things perfectly. As Guillaume reached the door, Giovanni's knock, indicating the presence of the minstrel, sounded on the boards.

Guillaume opened the door to exit and allow the minstrel into the legate's presence. Hildebrand motioned for the minstrel to close the door behind him. A look of apprehension appeared on the man's face as he complied with the order. He stood near to the door, nervously shifting his weight from one foot to the other while Hildebrand enjoyed his discomforture. Eventually the Italian began to speak.

"What was that song I just heard you singing in the courtyard?"

"Forgive me, lord, if I disturbed your thoughts. I was merely practicing a tune of my own devising. I shall do so more quietly."

"And what were the lyrics?"

"The song tells the heroic story of Roland, one of the great nobles of Charles the Great. I thought you liked the tune, Your Grace. The last time you were near when I sang part of it you presented me with a small token."

Hildebrand sat down trying to recall the incident. He had no doubt the singer was recounting the truth. The man was obviously too frightened to even consider a lie. Hildebrand absent-mindedly poured himself another goblet of wine.

"Roland," he mused, "died while fighting the Moors, did he not?"

"Yes, lord."

"In Spain?"

"Yes, lord."

"Where, might I ask, did he fall?"

"He was ambushed outside the village of Roncevalles, lord."

As the minstrel was answering questions related to his song, he seemed to gain some of his confidence back. Hildebrand crushed that confidence with his next words.

"His Holiness, the pope, would appreciate you never sing that song again as long as you shall live in this world."

"But I have to make a living. My song of Roland has been very popular. Why would the pope care whether I sing it or not?"

"There are other songs you can sing to earn your living. This is not one of them."

Usually when Hildebrand feigned losing his temper, it was enough to cause most men to back down. Surprisingly, this minstrel was made of sterner stuff.

"I would like to know why Pope Alexander disapproves of my lay," the minstrel demanded.

Hildebrand thought for a few moments and then looked at the minstrel warily. "What is your name?"

Hildebrand's apparent calmness took the minstrel by surprise and he slowly said, "Gilles d'Argyre, my lord."

"Gilles, you may have heard about the destruction of King Sancho's army. I'm afraid your song of Roland is a little too close to the treachery the Moors perpetrated. We are on the edge of a major war with the unbelievers. Your song may make people think the Moors can defeat us. That is why His Holiness desires that you no longer play it. I'm sure there is no need to strengthen our position to you."

Gilles listened to the threat behind Hildebrand's words and quickly nodded his acquiescence.

CHAPTER VII

Harold sat surrounded by his sons. He could not remember the last time they were all in the same place. He was sure all had attended his coronation only two years earlier, but he had hardly noticed Edith standing by his side, let alone Svannehals and their bastard sons standing in the shadows.

He had gathered his sons together with great difficulty. With the exception of Edmund, who he had kept near him since the fair at Senlac, Harold's sons were scattered throughout the kingdom. He looked around at the boys and prepared himself.

"Today, I want to tell you two stories. That may seem a strange reason to have summoned you from across the kingdom, but its important that you hear these stories and important that you learn from their morals.

AFTER HASTINGS

"The first story is of an ancient king of Briton. He lived long years ago before the Angles and Saxons came to these shores, when the barbarous Welsh ruled the entire land. This king, whose name was Llyr, had three sons, Cunegund, Reagan, and Guthrum. When Llyr began to get old, he decided to train all of his sons in the proper way to rule the kingdom. He thought this would ensure that his reign, which was prosperous and peaceful, would continue after he died.

"Llyr divided the country into three. The part we now call Wales and Cornwall were given to Guthrum. The land known as Scotland he gave to Reagan. Finally, the land we know as England was given to Cunegund. Llyr retreated to his castle at Winchester to allow his sons freedom in their reigns.

"Although they were brothers, Llyr's sons quickly began to plot and scheme against each other. Each wanted all the land Llyr ruled. Llyr saw what was happening and went first to one son, then to another, trying to make peace between his children, all to no avail. Each tried to take what was rightfully his brother's, first Guthrum and Cunegund uniting against Reagan, then Reagan and Guthrum against Cunegund.

"When Llyr died, his sons still squabbled. To this day, Llyr's land remains divided."

Harold looked around at his sons. They sat quietly, listening to his words. Godwin looked thoughtful, and Harold could see him savoring the kingdom which would one day be his. Edmund looked hungrily at his older brother, desiring what would probably belong to Godwin.

"I will not make the mistake Llyr made. While I live, I will rule England. You will all learn to govern well, since each of you will have your manors. When I die, the witanangemot will perform its proper function and select my successor, just as it elected me to succeed Edward and elected him on Hardecnut's death.

"I have another story for you. I think you'll like this one more." Harold called to a slave. The man entered and handed a bundle to the king. Harold unwrapped one end and pulled out an arrow. He handed the slender shaft to Magnus, his youngest son..

"Can you break this?" Harold asked.

Magnus snapped the stick in two with ease and handed the broken sticks back to his father.

"I didn't expect anything less. That arrow was you, Magnus, or you, Godwin, or you, Edmund." As the king said each name, he pointed to each son.

"Alone, each of you may be deadly, but you are also vulnerable. This arrow is my brother Tostig." Harold snapped another arrow in two.

"He stood against me at Stamford Bridge. These two arrows are me and my brother Leofwine." With more effort, Harold was able to break the two arrows.

"We are stronger together than I would be alone, yet we may still be broken. Not as easily as one brother, but it can be done. I have four sons. Here is an arrow for each of you. If I wanted to break a single arrow, I've already demonstrated how easy it is. But look what happens when I try to break four arrows together."

No matter how hard the king strained, the arrows, grasped firmly together, would not break. He handed the bundle to Godwin and bade his son try to break them. The arrows went around the circle until each son had a chance to try and break the arrows.

"Remember that you must stay together. It is the most important thing. To remind you of this story, I have a gift for each of you."

Once again, Harold called to the slave. This time, the man carried in four bundles. When Harold unwrapped the first one, he presented Godwin with an Anglo-Saxon battle axe, the haft of which was made of four arrow shafts banded together with iron. He repeated the presentation to each of his sons before dismissing the boys to think about his two stories.

CHAPTER VIII

The room in which Pope Alexander sat was the finest available in Dunkerque. Nevertheless, it felt small and cramped. More suited for a monk than a pope. Alexander quelled that thought as soon as it crossed his mind. He belonged to God and was no greater than a monk. The day on which he forgot that basic tenet of humilty was the day when he served riches and worldly power rather than Christ. He tried to settle comfortably onto the hard wooden chair, but was unable to find a position in which the wood didn't pinch or bruise his posterior. He felt a momentary sorrow for the monks and peasants who knew no better than this. However, he reflected, if they've never sat on cushions, they don't know how uncomfortable a wooden chair really is. Back in the ancient days when Alexander was Anselm, he had sat on wooden stools in ingorant bliss, happy merely to raise himself off the ground. Alexander yearned for the days when he was Anselm, not for the discomfort that Anselm must have constantly been in, but for the ignorance of that very discomfort.

Lotario cleared his throat, interrupting Alexander's dialogue with the long hidden Anselm. The pope's aide approached the spurious throne and bent to the pope's ear.

"The Englishman Gottcund has arrived." Alexander was certain that Lotario, willing only to speak in Latin or Italian, had completely mangled the Englishman's name.

As if by magic, as Lotario announced Gottcund, the door to the room opened and a man walked in, surrounded by four of the pope's guards. Gottcund's moustache was neatly trimmed, falling loose around the corners of his mouth. His bare chin jutted out, nearly as far as his nose, giving his face a strange pinched look. His large eyes were set close together, partly obscured by his blond hair. Overall, Alexander reflected, Gottcund was not an attractive man. Anselm quickly and quietly pointed out that a man's true measure was in his relationship to God. By all accounts, this Gottcund, whose name, Alexander understood, was Anglo-Saxon for "pious," lived up to the full measure of his name.

He knelt on the floor in front of Alexander and reached for the pope's hand to kiss his ring. It was obvious from the man's bearing that he wasn't going to say anything until Alexander granted him permission.

"Rise, my son." Alexander had come across Gottcund's type several times over the years since he had been named pope. Gottcund's religion was one which could not separate the trappings of the Church, in this case the papacy, from God, Himself.

You were once like that as well. Anselm nagged at the back of Alexander's mind.

"You were one of the men who fought against Harold in England, were you not?"

"Yes, Your Grace." Gottcund's voice was full of awe that he could be standing so near the pope.

"You pledged your allegience and loyalty to Harold upon the death of King Edward?"

"Yes." The awe was fading into a mix of uncertainty and fear.

"Did you pledge that you would support Edward's choice of William of Normandy?"

"No."

"I see." Alexander paused. "I am given to understand that you are a pious man. Why, then, did you break your oath, freely given?"

Sweat began to bead Gottcund's forehead, despite the cool French weather. His words came out in a stammer. "I thought, and my confessor agreed, that when Harold defied your emissary, the legate Hildebrand, he removed himself from the Grace of the Church and thereby released all Christian men of any vows they made to him."

"Did you make your vow to Harold or to our Heavenly Father?"

Gottcund fell silent. Alexander took the moment to look at his visitor and found himself reprimanded by Anselm. *You took pleasure in humbling a man who honestly believes in his convictions. He knows what he did was right but is looking for you to affirm that knowledge. You serve no purpose of His by humiliating His faithful.*

"Although He does not usually release a man from his oaths, unless the man is unable to accomplish the task no matter how hard he tries, in this case, He has discharged your vow, for a Christian shall not be in thrall to a heretic. In fact, there is another who He has discharged from a vow made to Harold."

As Alexander spoke, Lotario moved to the door and opened it, allowing a woman to enter the room. It took Gottcund a moment to realize who she was, but when he did, he faced her direction and dropped to one knee.

"My lady."

Queen Edith walked over and gently laid a hand on Gottcund's shoulder. The baron took this gesture as a signal for him to rise.

"It is good to see an English face in this foreign land." Unlike Alexander and Gottcund, who had been speaking in Latin, Edith spoke in the language of her host country. Seeing Gottcund's question in his face, she continued, "Of course I learned French from all the Normans my brother brought to England. As long as I must remain in Normandy and France, I will not use my native language. That pleasure, I reserve for the day I can return to an England where God is once again supreme."

"The question before us is your role in the invasion of England and its subsequent return to the flock." Alexander lifted his bishop's crook, "It's too bad your brother moved so quickly. If he had waited, the alliance might have been able to offer him aid. As it was, he chose to attack Harold alone, without even consulting us. I regret his decision to act in haste. Everything I have heard of Morkere shows that he was a good man.

"Before I go any further, is there anything you wish to confess to me?"

Gottcund sank to his knees. "I have taken up arms against my rightful overlord, a man who I helped elect to the kingship of England, a man to whom I had pledged a vow of obedience. I took up these arms in the belief that this man had violated a greater vow, a vow sworn to God, and had turned his back on the one true faith given to us by our Lord, Jesus Christ, who suffered on the cross to redeem our sins. I repent that I am an oathbreaker no matter whether I feel the circumstances warranted my actions."

"*Absolvo te.*" The ritualistic phrase was not enough, it never was. Alexander tried to think of the penance which would strengthen his words. Anselm made the suggestion, "Although I can offer you forgiveness, only He can fully grant you absolution. For your penance of oathbreaking to your lord, you must look into your heart and swear an oath, a truthful oath, to a greater Lord, an oath which cannot be broken."

Gottcund looked up at Alexander, and Anselm thought he saw hope on the Englishman's face. "I will do as you ask. I beg Your Grace's permission to retreat to a monastery to consider whether my place should be as a regular or lay clergyman or to serve Him in another way altogether."

"I grant you permission to journey to the monastery at Fleury to contemplate the monastic life, removed from the rigors and trials of this world."

Lotario ushered Gottcund from Alexander's presence. Already Alexander could see a change in his walk. Absolved by the pope, Gottcund no longer walked like a man on his way to the gallows. Contemplating monastic life, he no longer walked like a proud aristocrat.

I have acted with wisdom, Alexander thought, only to be rejoined by Anselm, *God has bestowed wisdom upon you.*

The English queen cleared her throat and Alexander looked at her. He had nearly forgotten she remained in his presence.

"And do you, too, wish to contemplate life in a nunnery?"

The queen, Edith was her name, thought about his question before answering. "When I first thought to leave England, at the urging of my husband's sister, I thought to enter a nunnery. My decision to leave, however, was sparked by seeing my brother's head on a stake outside the city of Durham. I know it is not a virtue recognized by the Church, but my first husband's people strongly believed in vengeance. I would see vengeance meted out to my current husband. I would help in any way you would deem proper."

Alexander was taken aback by this woman's passion. Nothing in her demeanor would have suggested that she was capable of the brutality her words demonstrated. Her body was relaxed and her voice calm as she spoke of her desire for revenge. The lack of warmth sent a shiver down the pope's spine and he thought of the demonic French queens Gregory of Tours had described in his books on Christianity's introduction to the Franks.

"I will take your desires into advisement while I consider your place in these events," he eventually was able to murmer.

CHAPTER IX

Gunnlaug had never failed in his duty to Harold ever since the king, then merely an earl, had first commanded him in battle. Over the years, Gunnlaug had risen in Harold's service until the king only used him for the most important assignments. Although Harold would never raise him to the nobility, the king provided for Gunnlaug with three manors scattered across England. Most of the time, Gunnlaug was able to relax on one of the estates. About once a year, Harold would send a messenger with a task for him to accomplish. Gunnlaug hadn't seen the king since before Edward's death. He merely carried out the assignments he was given and enjoyed living like a thegn.

Gunnlaug was nervous about his latest assignment. It was the first time he had left England since Harold and old Godwin had been exiled nearly eighteen years earlier. He didn't like being in a land where hardly anybody spoke Saxon. However, when Harold sent a message, Gunnlaug responded.

He was part of a large crowd around a hastily erected dais near the Nordsee. King Philippe's army was camped outside Wissant, waiting for Heinrich to bring his Germans to fight against King Harold. Philippe was talking to the crowd, but Gunnlaug could only hear bits and pieces of the king's exhortations. Those who were near the platform were passing the king's words back to those who couldn't hear. Gunnlaug joined everyone else in trying to press as closely to the dais as they could, although he could not care less about what Philippe's advisors had told the king to say.

Gunnlaug's attention was on the young man who stood next to Philippe. He hadn't said anything to the crowd yet, but he was one of the reasons Philippe had come to talk to his army. Wulfnoth seemed not to care about what Philippe was saying either. He was watching the army, trying to gauge their feelings. Gunnlaug recognized his expression. It was the same one Harold, Leofwine, Svegn, Tostig, and Gyrth had when they were trying to decide on a course of action. Old Godwin had gotten the same expression when he was examining King Edward. Although Gunnlaug had come to recognize the expression, he had never been able to read the thoughts which ran behind it.

Gunnlaug was nearly to the dais when Philippe finished his speech. A tremendous roaring sound rose from the army and the Wissanters who had come to hear the king speak. Philippe sat on his throne and nodded as if the crowd's response were his due, as much as the copper coins they paid into his treasury. When the cheers died down, Wulfnoth moved to the front of the platform to address the crowd.

Toying with the knife at his belt, Gunnlaug thought about his goal. If all went according to plan, these would be the last words Wulfnoth spoke. As Wulfnoth came down from the dais, Gunnlaug would plunge the dagger into the prince's heart, committing, on Harold's behalf, fratricide. If he thought about the murder in those terms, Gunnlaug found it distasteful. It was just another death, one of many he had committed for Harold over the years. Although the pope might condemn his soul to Hell for all the murders, Gunnlaug knew that Harold's new archbishop would offer him salvation. Wulfnoth's death, martyrdom, would increase the glory of the Celtic Christian Church which Harold and Colum-cille were re-establishing in England.

As Gunnlaug finally stood near the steps down from the dais, he took the liberty of listening to what Wulfnoth said. He had expected to be able to understand Harold's brother. After all, Wulfnoth was a Saxon of Godwin's clan. Yet his words made no sense to Gunnlaug, who quickly realized that Wulfnoth was speaking in the barbarous language of the Franks. It made no more sense than the mass chanted by the Roman priests Harold had thrown out of England.

Wulfnoth's inability to address the army firmed up Gunnlaug's resolve to kill him. He might be the Harold's brother, but he was an imposter Saxon. *A Saxon should speak Saxon*, Gunnlaug thought.

Suddenly, Wulfnoth's features took on a strange, greyish color. The prince grabbed his left arm and collapsed onto the platform like a child's doll. Philippe's advisor's rushed around the fallen prince as a murmer reverberated among the crowd. One of the men rose from his examination of Wulfnoth and walked to Philippe, whispering something in the king's ear. Philippe, a shocked expression on his face, nodded back to the man, slumping on his throne in a manner which emphasized his belly.

Gunnlaug pressed against the platform, trying to hear what was being said. When he got close enough, he realized the discussion was being carried on entirely in the language the Franks used among themselves. Unable to understand their conversations, Gunnlaug was now able to get a closer look at the supine form of Wulfnoth. Harold's brother had definitely gone to his final reward. His body lay crumpled on the dais. Philippe's servants were moving around it, trying to lay him out in a restful looking position, not that it mattered to Wulfnoth.

Gunnlaug moved away from the dais. Although he had no qualms about killing Wulfnoth for Harold, he was somewhat relieved that he no longer actually had to stick his knife into the *aetheling*.

Fighting his way against the crowd was like swimming into the surf off the Kentish shore. The waves of Frankish soldiers seemed to continually roll Gunnlaug back toward the dais as surely as the sea defied Cnut's commands.

Eventually, Gunnlaug was able to break free. The relatively sparse crowd which surrounded those closest to the dais allowed him enough air so he no longer felt confined. He paused to gain his bearings before setting off toward Wissant. He was sure a priest in the Flemish city would be willing to offer him absolution for a sin committed only in thought and not in deed.

CHAPTER X

The cathedral at York was sandwiched between the ancient Roman city wall and the winding streets of the Shambles. Although the Roman wall had once delineated the city, as York grew in importance more and more citizens were building outside the wall. Some only enterred the city proper when news of Viking raiders swept through the community. Like the Shambles in the city, the haphazard construction outside the wall consisted of narrow alleys between houses and shops. The cathedral grounds were the only vacant land in the area not given over to farming.

Lanfranc sat in the cathedral library, a small room in a building next to the cathedral proper. One of the local monks had brought him several books and he was working on his long forgotten treatise *De Toleratio*. He rubbed his eyes with an ink speckled hand, becoming aware of the change in light when he opened his eyes. It was later in the day than he had realized. He looked at what he had just written, a brilliant passage concerning why tolerance to the Jews was admirable, but not necessary, and decided to put down his quill.

Lanfranc gently blew a fine sand over the parchment to help dry the ink and began to pack up his supplies. While he was working at this task, the door opened and Archbishop Colum-cille entered the room.

"Preparing for your case against the king?" Colum-cille asked in a guarded voice.

"As a matter of fact, no. I was working on a treatise I had begun quite a while ago. Yorkminster library had some rare books dating back to the time of Alcuin which had some bearing on the topic. I could hardly pass up the chance to make use of them for my work. Have you come looking for a volume?"

Colum-cille was walking along the library's outer wall, looking at the tomes chained to the shelves while Lanfranc spoke. "No, I had heard you were here and thought to stop by. It is somewhat traditional for visiting clergy to make their presence known to their superiors."

"Forgive me. I assumed you were busy with more important matters. King Harold is arriving tomorrow, as I understand. Surely you have much to attend to."

"My servants have much to attend to. Monks and priests and laity have much to attend to. I have very little requiring my attention at this particular moment. I see you have finally adopted the proper tonsure. I had begun to wonder if you ever would."

Lanfranc moved his hand to touch, not the bald front of his head, but the hair growing on the crown. It was not yet long enough for him to run his fingers through, resembling instead the fine down which graced the backs on new-born chickens.

"If I'm presenting myself to you for judgement, it seemed only fitting that I adopt the ways you espouse. I'm sure He will forgive me for altering my hair style if it serves His greater purpose."

The two men looked at each other in silence for just a moment before the archbishop turned from the Italian. A small lamp burned on the table, giving the room its only, dim, illumination now that the sun had set. Colum-cille picked the lamp up and walked to the window.

"If this light is in the midst of this small room of the Yorkminster library, it gives off enough light and heat that we stay warm and can see each other. If I apply it outside, its heat gets lost and its light swallowed up by the darkness. If it is daylight outside, its heat is still lost and its light is swallowed up the by brighter light of the sun. Does that mean that within this room its light is not useful and true?

"This light is the light of Celtic Christianity. This room is the island of Britain. Within these islands, England, Alba, Cymru, and Erin, this light provides true illumination. Outside these islands, it may be swallowed up by your Roman Church, but that does not make its light any less legitimate. Within this room, these islands, if the light is snuffed out, where are we if not cold and in the dark."

Having moved next to the door, Colum-cille blew the flame out, set the lamp down on the table and quickly exited, leaving Lanfranc alone in the dark to consider the archbishop's arguments.

CHAPTER XI

Needlework and weaving no longer held any consolation for Gytha. Those were tasks for younger women. She had once ruled by the side of Godwin, the greatest earl England had ever known. Although Godwin would have claimed he made all decisions himself, he would never have dared make any of those decisions, large or small, without first consulting Gytha. Time and again she had demonstrated her understanding of people and events. Her strength of character made her a formidable opponent. Godwin had only crossed her once in all their years of marriage. That mistake had resulted in a two year exile for his entire family.

Harold had many of Godwin's traits. His major failing, in Gytha's mind, was that he never listened to the advice of his mother. She realized, now, that she was mistaken for berating him for his decision to break with the Roman Church. Her input most likely solidified his desire to be free of Roman influence. Gytha should have recommended that he follow the asinine course he had started on. She realized that would have been the surest way to promote a reconciliation with Pope Alexander.

Gytha did not desire reconciliation with Rome for any deep religious reasons. She felt Rome was arrogant and overbearing. However, the pope's power was a reality she, and Harold, could not ignore. Even if none of Alexander's "great alliance" ever set foot in England, the pope could stir up malcontents, as he had with Harold's brother-in-law. Although Alexander wanted to remove Harold from the throne, Gytha realized the surest way for her son to retain his crown would be for him to maintain his links to Rome, no matter how painful that action might be.

"Damn it, Arne, get your holy ass in here. I need to send a letter."

Arne meekly entered the chamber and bowed low to Lady Gytha. He had served her since before Earl Godwin's death and had long ago grown accustomed to her coarse language. He had also learned how to interpret her swearing to determine her mood. Today's session would hardly prove to be one of her more peaceful outbursts.

"Would milady seek to offer confession for any transgressions?" He knew the answer, but hoped it might be a way of creating a sense of humility in Gytha.

"Hell, no. I know what my transgressions are. I'll tell them to you when I damn well feel like it. You'll tell me to say fifty *pater nosters* and fifty *Ave Marias* and flog my back bloody with a birch twig and I'll ignore your asinine suggestions so you'll just add more the next time. Forget that kind of bullshit. I want to discuss my son and his head full of shit."

Arne nodded. When Gytha indicated a hard wooden chair, he sat down gratefully. He had a feeling it would be a long session.

"Have you heard any news from the continent?"

"I understand the Foedus Magnus is gathered in Flanders, waiting for a portentious wind before sailing," Arne replied, his voice soft.

"Who has joined this unholy alliance?"

"I am told it contains men from the Germans and the Franks. Pope Alexander tried to get the Spanish to join, but they are too busy fighting the Moors. Apparently the heathens have launched a campaign to push the Christians out of Iberia entirely. I am told Alexander even tried to make common cause with the Byzantines, but they refused even to meet with his emissary. The Great Alliance has proven to be much less than Pope Alexander or Hildebrand ever thought it would be."

A deathly quiet fell over the room as Gytha thought about Arne's words. The priest doubted he had said anything new to the king's mother, but he hardly wanted to draw any more attention to himself than necessary. He would wait until Gytha was ready to speak again.

Gytha poured wine from a decanter into a chalice. The dark liquid looked black when viewed through the blue glass of the bowl. She rose and took the glass to the window, staring into the wine as if it held all the answers to her future and her past. Abruptly, she turned to Arne.

"I've never asked you for your opinion of my son's behavior."

"I would be lying if I said I supported everything the king has done." Arne knew that while his problems with Harold were mostly based on the king's actions against the Church, Gytha's difficulties arose out of her perception that Harold was not acting in the most politically advantageous way. He had also heard that Gytha asked all priests their opinions of Harold's policies. The intelligent priests had learned to dissemble. He would have to finish his answer with care. "Much of the problem seems to stem from your son's rash behavior. If he had paused to think about his problems, it seems to me he would have been able to chart a wiser course of action."

"You're damn right he would have. I never thought I would raise a son who could be so God damned headstrong that he couldn't even see where his own interests lay."

Arne was pleased with his answer. He had not compromised his integrity while diverting Gytha's attention away from her question. She had taken his answer as he had hoped she would and had not probed further into his opinions.

CHAPTER XII

The Mass celebrated by Archbishop Colum-cille in Yorkminster would, on first glance, seem no different from the Mass celebrated in cathedrals and churches across Christendom. All the hymns and prayers were sung in Latin. The priests stood with his back toward the audience. Even though the primate of England was leading the service, people wandered among the pews, speaking in quiet, and not so quiet, voices to each other. Late arriving worshippers greeted their friends loudly.

There were subtle differences. The tonsures worn by the priests differed from those worn by their continental brethren. The albs worn by the priests were, perhaps, a touch less ostentatious that would normally be found in an archbishop's cathedral. On occassion, a word, or even a whole phrase of the secular language would find its way into the service.

King Harold sat in a royal pew set aside from the pews used by the nobles and citizens of York. He wasn't paying any particular attention to Colum-cille. The Mass was the same abracadabra priests chanted at church and chapel every Sunday. The only difference, Harold reflected, was that Colum-cille probably understood the language he was speaking.

Leofwine sat on the king's left. To the king's right sat Edwy, Harold's advocate. Throughout the service, Harold and Edwy whispered back and forth, discussing the case Lanfranc was bringing against Harold in front of Archbishop Colum-cille.

"The behavior of the monk, Beornred, was criminous in a way priests usually avoid. He spoke treason against the king. There is no doubt he is guilty of this crime. The question is whether Colum-cille will support Lanfranc's contention that because he is a clergyman he is subject only to the laws of the church and not those of the king. Lanfranc's position is that if Beornred is tried in a royal court after he is dismissed from the Church, he is being tried twice for the same crime," said Edwy.

"Do you believe Lanfranc will prevail?" Harold asked.

Edwy thought for a few moments before answering. "It is hard to say. I am familiar, of course, with the laws espoused by Rome, which we have followed for the past four hundred years. What Colum-cille will claim the laws of the Celtic Church are is unknown. If the Celtic Church has precedents, Colum-cille will surely abide by them. If they don't, he may break from the Roman tradition to be different. He may also remain within the Roman sphere of influence to keep the Church's power."

Leofwine leaned over his brother and whispered, "I've informed that priest in Grantham and his subordinate that I want them to appear in front of Colum-cille."

Harold threw a confused look toward his brother. "That sounds vaguely familiar. Why do I know that town?"

Before Leofwine could answer, Edwy reminded Harold of Maegleas, the mad priest who tried to kill Archbishop Colum-cille.

"I had more dealings with Grantham after that priest was put to death. After Hrypadun, one of Morkere's rebels tried to claim sanctuary in a villege near Grantham. The traitor's successor supported my contention that sanctuary was a Roman concept and no longer applicable. I thought he might be a good person to have speak before Colum-cille."

Harold nodded, but Edwy whispered, "I'll need to speak to you about this in a more private setting. I would also like to speak to these priests you called. Can we trust them?"

"The priest from Grantham can definitely be trusted. He was behind me entirely. The village priest might be contentious. He liked the assassin-priest and tried to protect the traitor, Heardcwide, after he took part in Morkere's revolt. I imagine he will be too awed by royalty to make any problems."

AFTER HASTINGS

From his pulpit, Archbishop Colum-cille turned to face his audience. It was time for the sermon.

"Matthew tells us that Christ said, 'Render therefore to Caesar the things that are Caesar's, and to God the things that are God's'," Colum-cille's Scottish accent reverberated against the vaulted arches of Yorkminster.

From the first line, Harold knew he wouldn't like anything the archbishop was going to say. The text he had chosen to discuss was one which clearly delineated the powers of the king. It was part of Rome's reason for not allowing the royal courts to place priests on trial.

Unlike the king, Edwy was paying close attention to the archbishop's words. Despite his text, Colum-cille was trying to keep his sermon abstract, avoiding any direct reference to Harold, Lanfranc, or Beornred. Those who heard the sermon would come away with the impression that the archbishop was opposing the monarch, but Colum-cille was being extremely careful not to say anything which the king could point to as offensive. While the sermon caused Harold to despair, it gave Edwy reason to hope that Colum-cille would rule against Lanfranc's case.

Leofwine was paying even less attention to the sermon than Harold. His attention was focussed, instead, on his brother. For the first half of the sermon, Harold was restless, which Leofwine took to be a good sign. As long as the king was playing with his rings and shifting in his seat, he wasn't too concerned. About halfway through the sermon, Harold became more still. His hands dropped to his sides and his face became a scowling mask. Without listening to the archbishop's words, Leofwine knew that Harold was upset with the archbishop.

Tapping Harold on the hand, Leofwine rose and made his way through the jostling crowd, still talking as loudly as when the archbishop was speaking in Latin. Leofwine reflected on how much a Sunday Mass reflected a marketplace or the fair at Senlac.

He left the minster through a door set in the side of the nave. A light rain had begun to fall and he ran toward the ancient Roman wall which surrounded the city. Once on the wall, he walked quickly around the city until he came to the defensive castle on the other side of York.

The guards let him in without questioning him. Leofwine had made sure he was known as soon as he arrived. He made his way through the narrow passageways of the castle, built for defense, not for luxurious living, until he found Aethelwine.

Aethelwine was sitting over a board with an arrangement of black and white pebbles laid out on a grid. He was examining the placement of each piece while rolling a small white pebble in his hand, trying to determine his next move. There was nobody else in the room. Leofwine watched as Aethelwine carefully placed the piece at one of the grid's intersections. When the baron turned the board around, Leofwine announced his presence.

"Archbishop Colum-cille has given indication that he is opposed to the king in the Lanfranc matter."

Without taking his concentration from the board, Aethelwine asked, "He said that during his sermon?"

"Of course not. Colum-cille is too wily to come right out and say he was opposing Harold. If he did that, my brother would send him right back up to Malcolm in Scotland. I don't think Colum-cille would care for that. He preached on the passage 'Render unto Caesar.'"

"He's going to support Lanfranc against Harold."

"That's the way it looked. Harold got very serious as he spoke."

"Edwy is at the Mass. Did he have any sort of reaction?"

"He had been plotting strategy with Harold. I let him know about those priests from Kesteven. No, he didn't really seem to be paying attention to anything Colum-cille was saying in either English or Latin."

"We'll have to talk to Harold when he comes back. He's likely to take rather ill-advised action against Colum-cille if we don't."

"We simply have to decide what actions we should advise him to take."

"It's simple. He must not do anything against Colum-cille, especially if the archbishop rules against Harold. There are enough people who disagree with Harold's reaction to the pope's envoy. If he demonstrates just how much of a secular move his break with Rome was, he'll be facing even more revolts than he has since he sent Hildebrand away," Aethelwine pointed out. "You and I know that Harold hasn't suddenly found a new religion. It is all just a political game to him. If Colum-cille proves unreliable, he'll set off in another direction again and that will be dangerous for him."

"It may be simple enough to say that, but how are we going to convince Harold not to take any action? My brother, as our mother would be the first to tell you, has never been very good at looking to the future. He is king, he wants to remain king, he must rid himself of all opposition."

"Your mother would be the first, middle, and last to tell you anything. She is like Christ, the alpha and the omega."

"You blaspheme," Leofwine's grin showed he did not take Aethelwine's words too seriously. "We must return our attention to Harold."

As he spoke, Leofwine looked down at the board and tapped one of the black pebbles. The piece skidded sideways along one of the lines etched into the wooden board and came to rest as it hit a white pebble. The white pebble skidded off the board and dropped to the floor.

Aethelwine started to bend over to retrieve the piece. He stopped halfway to the floor and looked up at Leofwine. "What if Harold does nothing? Let Colum-cille lie where he falls." The earl indicated the white pebble. "Surely if Harold indicates Colum-cille's speech does not worry him any problems can be avoided."

"It might appear good to the people and the barons who are on the hedge, but if Colum-cille decides for Lanfranc, what happens then?"

"Colum-cille won't decide in favor of Lanfranc. You and I will ensure that he sees your brother's point of view."

CHAPTER XIII

King Philippe of France sat on a cushioned chair. Théobald stood in front of him, holding a piece of parchment.

"According to this letter from one of your agents in England, King Harold is claiming the right to place clerics on trial. This action, of course, is a further affront to the dignity of the Church and God."

"I thought Harold no longer claimed to belong to the Church. If this is so, how can his actions reflect on Rome?" Philippe's beard had just begun to come in over the previous couple of months and he was playing with the fine down which nearly covered his cheeks.

"What effects the clergy in one kingdom effects the clergy in every kingdom, whether in the heretical West or the heretical East."

Philippe's face took on what he thought of as his royal expression. The royal expression was a mask Philippe wore when he had to listen to Théobald or some other advisor try to explain to him why he shouldn't use his power to achieve his own ends, but rather allow himself to be ruled as if he were still a minor with a regency.

Instead of listening to Théobald's arguments, Philippe tried to think about what Harold's claim regarding the right to judge clergy could mean to France. Naturally, Théobald would champion Pope Alexander's cause. The man seemed to firmly believe that Alexander was God come once again to Earth. Although it would be nice to be rid of Théobald, Philippe could not think about any way to put his advisor aside. Perhaps Guillaume would have suggestions. The old man seemed to honestly care about Philippe. In any event, Guillaume and Théobald hated each other.

As far as Philippe could tell, if Harold had the right to judge clerics who committed crimes, it meant that the clergy's power would be limited. Churchmen would be accountable for their actions. They would even be accountable for their speech. The thought of putting a bishop on trial for *lese majeste* was fantastic.

"What is the crime the cleric is being tried for?"

"I'm sorry?" Théobald had a confused look on his face and Philippe realized his advisor had gone on to other topics.

"In England. What crime did the cleric commit?"

"Apparently the monk tried to kill their heretical usurper. Now, returning to the Count of Blois. He insists that he only owes thirty knights for service instead of thirty-two. Despite this, I have a parchment here which clearly shows the number thirty-two. I know two knights may not seem like a lot, but we cannot allow your barons the luxury of being allowed to alter their terms without your permission and assessment."

Philippe once again blocked the officious drone of Théobald's voice. Although the king knew the issue of the Count of Blois was important, the English events were so much more vibrant. They offered a chance to be remembered by posterity as a great monarch, a ruler who helped break the iron grip of the papacy.

After an interminable period, Théobald ran out of topics of discussion and begged Philippe for permission to leave. When his advisor was gone, Philippe pulled a wax tablet from his desk and began to compose, the stylus digging neat grooves into the soft wax. When he finished his letter, he copied the text onto a piece of parchment and called for a messenger. The man appeared at his door within moments.

"Louis, here is a letter. It is extremely important that it be presented to Earl Leofwine of England as speedily as possible."

Without saying a word, Louis accepted the sealed parchment and walked from the monarch's presence, making sure not to turn his back on the young king.

CHAPTER XIV

The village of Al-Yāj was located on the eastern coast of Sicilia. Its inhabitants went about their business, hardly caring about the outside world, except when that world impinged on their corner of it. In recent years, they could hardly help taking a notice of the world as a whole. In addition to the Saracen pirates who had ruled and raided their lands for centuries, the Italians were showing signs of interest, and the recent Norman invasion of the island had turned their entire land upside down as the new conquerors imposed laws as different from the Saracens' as the Muslim laws were from the Italian. Mostly, the Al-Yāji wished the Muslims, Normans, and Italians would all return to their distant homelands and leave Sicilia for the Sicilians.

When the ship first appeared in the harbor, nobody took much notice aside from the stevedores on the docks who saw a chance to pick up a little extra money. Although no ship had been expected, the laborers and merchants of Al-Yāj would hardly begrudge the traders a chance to unload their wares. Chances were the ship had gotten lost on its way to a larger port, perhaps Siracusa. When the merchant came ashore, they would either decide to sell their cargo in Al-Yāj, or they would find their cargo had a tendency to disappear before they could leave port.

Vittorio Caltanissetta normally did not spend much time on the docks. In fact, he normally stayed outside of Al-Yāj entirely. As a winemaker, he preferred to remain at his villa on a hill overlooking the city. On occasion, he found himself having to come into the city to correct a misunderstanding between his representative and the innkeepers and merchants who bought his vintage. Such a dispute had brought Vittorio into Al-Yāj on the day the ship arrived.

Santino Giarristi exported Vittorio's wine to Italia. His business was filled with dangers, some of which could be guarded against, like pirates, others would happen despite all precautions. One of Santino's recent shipment's of Vittorio's wine to Italia had the misfortune of being lost in a storm as it crossed the channel between Sicilia and Italia. Normally, this type of loss would not effect Vittorio, but in this particular case, Santino was carrying the shipment on consignment. When the wine was lost,

Santino refused all Vittorio's requests for payment. Vittorio now was coming into Al-Yāj to arrange a satisfactory agreement.

When he saw the strange ship arrive, Vittorio decided to delay his visit to Santino. Before confronting the greasy little exporter, he would watch the ship tie up to the dock. Although he did not recognise the vessel, he realized he was no expert in shipping.

Vittorio Caltanissetta, therefore, was one of the first people in Al-Yāj to learn they were under attack.

Even as the invaders swarmed from their ship onto the pier, Vittorio was racing to sound the alarm to alert the town. The stevedores pulled knives and swords and rushed forward to face their opponents before too many of the foreigners could make their way off the ship.

The stevedores proved to be a reasonably good match for the raiders, who were not prepared for such a quick response. Although there was no way the laborers could possibly defeat the invaders, they were able to hold them off long enough for the townspeople to rally to their aid.

Although the raiders were highly trained warriors, the Al-Yāji's fighting skills were honed from years of fighting against Saracens, Italians, and Normans. Once reinforcements arrived, the invaders fled to their ship and pushed away from the pier. Vittorio found himself guarding a wounded prisoner.

Nothing Vittorio said to the man elicited an intelligable response. Vittorio tried to ask him questions in both Italian and broken Latin, but the man showed no understanding of either language. He tried the few words of Arabic he knew, but the man remained silent. Eventually, when Vittorio tied a strip of cloth around his wounded arm a little too tightly, the man let forth a stream of babble which, although the language was foreign, had the feeling of cursing.

One of the stevedores nearby walked over to Vittorio upon hearing the cursing and began to speak to the man in a language which sounded to Vittorio like it might be the same tongue.

"What are you saying? Where is this bastard from?" Vittorio demanded of the laborer.

"He says his name is Theophanes of Gelibolu. These invaders were sent by the *imperator* Romanes Diogenes. He also claims that we Sicilians are not true Christians."

While the stevedore spoke, a crowd had gathered to listen. Apparently Theophanes was the only surviving Byzantine, the others either were killed or escaped. Upon hearing the declaration that Sicilians were not true Christians, the armed crowd began to push in. Vittorio and the stevedore tried to protect the wounded man but he pushed them aside, speaking rapidly.

The two Sicilians were unable to protect the Byzantine warrior who seemed intent on allowing himself to be torn to pieces by the enraged crowd. When the crowd had destroyed his body, the stevedore invited Vittorio to join him in a nearby tavern.

Although it was still relatively early in the day, the tavern was packed with people. Vittorio thought he recognized some of Al-Yāj's defenders in the crowd, he would have been surprised if they hadn't gone to taverns when they left the bloody wharf. Despite the crowd, the stevedore was able to find a table relatively quickly. The two men sat and a servant brought them a bottle of red wine. Vittorio noted with glee that it was a bottle which had come from his own vineyards.

"My name is Reggio di Calabria. As you can tell, I work on the docks here and in Italia loading cargo onto ships. Occasionally, I find the need to load myself onto a ship and then I work on the other side of the Straits of Messina."

Vittorio introduced himself and permitted himself a sip of wine. It was from a vintage he had pressed about three years earlier.

"Why did that Greek let himself be killed? What did he say when the crowd came for him?"

"It was a little disjointed, as you might imagine. I don't think anybody can really be coherent when a crowd is coming to tear them to pieces, no matter how brave they are.

"This fellow was shouting about how he was doing God's duty by trying to bring true Christianity back to Italia and the West."

"I had heard that the Greeks perverted the ways of Christ. That they think our ways are false shows how far they have taken their strain of heresy."

"The Greeks aren't the only heretics. A sailor who put into Palmi when I was working there told me that the English had also embraced a heresy. Something he called Pelagianism."

Vittorio took a much larger drink than he normally would allow himself. "The Greeks in the East, the English in the West, the Muslims to the South. Truly we are facing the coming of the Antichrist. The millennium was over, yet He chose to delay His judgment until today."

Reggio signalled the waiter and ordered a wheel of cheese and several loaves of pita.

"It does seem Christianity is under attack from all sides. But if He has chosen this time for the Apocalypse, there is nothing we can do except try to live as good as we can as good Christians."

As Reggio was speaking, Vittorio found himself thinking, not of the battle he had just participated in or even being a good Christian. He was thinking of the bottles of wine which Santino Giarristi claimed were lying in one of his ships at the bottom of the Straits of Messina. The wine was worth a lot of money, but as the priests said, "A camel will go through the eye of a needle before a rich man gets into heaven." By the time the cheese arrived, Vittorio decided to forgive Santino Giarristi for the lost tuns of wine, although he would still instruct his agents not to ship any more wine with him.

CHAPTER XV

The North Sea rushed against the East Anglian coast with the rage of an advancing army. Thurstan of Gippeswic stood watching the raw natural force of the sea constantly barrage the rocky shore. The difference in color between the white-capped waves crashing against the shore and the icy gray waters further out in the sea was minor compared to the contrast between the forcefulness of the waves and the calm appearance the water gave.

The weather had turned autumnal and a cold wind had sprung up, blowing the salty brine over the land in great misty clouds. Thurstan turned his back to the water and walked toward a small stone house overlooking to beach. Two peasants sat close to the fire in the house, trying to stay warm against the weather. One of the peasants, the woman, was stirring a cauldron. When she saw Thurstan, she quickly stood up, her mate following quickly.

"Your lordship! Please, have some porrage to warm yourself. It must be freezing outside."

Thurstan made his way around the four sheep which shared the peasants' house and accepted the bowl the woman offered him. He looked at the watery liquid inside but refrained from commenting on it. The important thing was that the thin mess of barley was warm. He ate quickly, hoping to ward off the chill he felt in his bones.

While Thurstan ate, the woman's husband walked over to the door and looked out to the sea.

"The waves are coming in stronger than they were. The wind from Oostend must be very strong."

Thurstan nodded as he ate his porrage. He had noticed that peasants tended to point out obvious facts. The waves are bigger. The wind from Oostend is stronger. Thurstan had just come in from the bitter cold. He knew there was a strong wind from Flanders.

AFTER HASTINGS

Suddenly, Thurstan dropped his bowl. He ran to the door, wrapping his cloak tightly around his body. A blast of freezing air hit him as he emerged from the hut, pushing the peasant before him. The wind was coming from the East.

Jumping on a horse, Thurstan began to ride for his manor at Gippeswic. If a strong wind was coming from Flanders, it meant that Alexander might be able to launch his fleet of Germans and Franks against the English. Thurstan would have to send a warning to Harold in York.

Normally, Thurstan would have sent a messenger to York, but this news was too important. Thurstan would be able to get in to see the king without delay. A messenger might have to wait. Thurstan's name alone would not have been enough to get him in to see the king.

Before riding north, Thurstan picked up four servants from Gippeswic. The five men rode off on horses. There was nothing to set any single man off from any of the others. Since Thurstan had put down the revolt at Colchester, the malcontents who opposed Harold's religious reforms had marked him as one of the king's staunchest supporters. Thurstan did not care one way or the other about religion. Priests had always been an annoyance, claiming lands and rights which a normal man could never claim and then refusing to give the lord his due. If Harold could change that, Thurstan would stand behind him until Armageddon.

Their ride was slow. The horses had to pick their way carefully through the fens which saturated Anglia, muddy rivulets meandering through muddy islands. In many cases there was little difference between land and water. Every time a horse took a step, its hoof would sink into the mire. Thurstan had made sure that all of his servants knew the message. At least one would be able to make his way to York to deliver the message to Harold or his representative.

CHAPTER XVI

Colum-cille sat listening to Lanfranc and Edwy argue about Church prerogatives, rights of clergy and whether the Celtic Church was bound by anything decreed by the Roman Church. Colum-cille could tell Lanfranc did not agree with his own arguments, but he still tried to convince the archbishop that the Celtic and Roman Churches could be different and still share the some of the same practices. Edwy's arguments generally boiled down to the observation that deciding in favor of Lanfranc was the same as signing the death order for the Celtic Church, giving it a subordinate status to the bishop of Rome.

Although Harold did not need to sit in on the hearing, and Colum-cille would have preferred his provider to absent himself, the king sat next to the fireplace in the aAchbishop's chamber, not speaking, but making his presence felt. Occasionally, Colum-cille would glance over at the king. While Lanfranc was discussing the history of the Church since the Dunstanian Reformation, Harold was copying a letter from a wax tablet to a scroll. Colum-cille tried to read the letter while half-listening to the bishop's lesson.

Harold, by the Grace of God and the choice of the witanangemot, King of the Angles, the Saxons, and the Jutes, ruler of Wessex, Northumbria, Kent, and Anglia to his fellow king, Malcolm of Scotland and Skye, greetings.

Harold's attempt to influence the archbishop did not surprise Colum-cille. Even before Colum-cille had travelled south with Morkere, he knew the day would come when Harold would use Colum-cille's link to MacBeth's lost cause to make him do something Harold desired. Colum-cille had long ago decided not to let Harold intimidate him. If he agreed with Harold's cause after Edwy's rebuttal to Lanfranc, he would order Beornred given to Harold for judgment and punishment.

"The issue really is not even an issue of the Church. The issue is double judgment. Harold is asking to judge and punish a man who will already be judged and punished by the Church. He would never ask to do this to a secular criminal. He's trying to further exert his influence over the Church."

"The king is not asking to have the right of double judgment. The king claims that he has a right to try this criminal, not the Church," Edwy spoke forcefully, like Lanfranc, ignoring the king's presence in the chamber.

"The Church has the right to try clergymen who are accused of crime. It has always been that way. If you allow King Harold to take away that right, no cleric will ever be safe."

"The Church will retain its right to try clerics. King Harold admits that his right to try clergymen should only extend to cases which are treasonous or murderous."

"If you grant the right to secular trial in these instances, how long before the king or his successor demands the right to try clerics for burglary or rape or blasphemy."

Edwy got a disgusted look on his face. He turned to face Colum-cille directly, turning his back on Bishop Lanfranc. "Surely you see what he is trying to do, Your Grace. Despite Christ's admonishment to render unto Caesar, there is no reason a Christian monarch can not work in conjunction with the Church. The bishop would have you believe that the Church exists in opposition to the king. Both are responsible for the well-being of their followers."

Colum-cille glanced out the window. Neither Lanfranc nor Edwy were saying anything he did not already know. His decision would come down to precedents of England and the Celtic Church. Rome had no place in his choice, except that English precedent was based on the Roman Church since St. Augustine first arrived in Kent. No matter how much Harold wanted to ignore that fact, Colum-cille knew he had to take it into account.

"With your permission, Archbishop, I would like to bring in two priests." Edwy's voice broke Colum-cille's reverie.

"That will be fine."

Edwy walked to the door and called to one of the ceorls who stood outside. Before he could close the door, Harold rose, dipped his head to Colum-cille, and exited, taking his housecarls with him. Although several men remained in the room, Colum-cille suddenly felt as if the room had completely emptied.

Lanfranc stood calmly next to the window. Colum-cille could not tell if the bishop of Canterbury had any idea what Edwy was trying to do. Colum-cille wondered what two regular priests might be able to add to a debate which already included the bishop of Canterbury, the archbishop of York and the king's advocate.

When the door opened, two men were ushered in. More striking in appearance was a short, burly man with a flaming red beard. His eyes were dark and set closely above an almost comically long nose. His crimson hair was tonsured in the manner appropriate to a priest of the Celtic Church, although it betrayed a shortness near the crown which demonstrated the man's Roman origins.

The second man was of a more normal height. Clean-shaven, he kept his hair short so you could not tell how recently he had changed from a Roman to a Celtic tonsure, although Colum-cille had no doubt of the man's Roman Church origins. His hair was the color of sand. His eyes were a brilliant blue, detracting from the high forehead occasioned by the Celtic tonsure. Although he was more normal in appearance than his short companion, his eyes tended to draw attention and mesmerize.

"Are these members of the jury?"

"No," replied Edwy, "they are not here to speak to Brother Beornred's character. These are Father Egmund and Father Swaefred." Colum-cille found it difficult to pull his attention away from Father Egmund's eyes to look at Edwy. "Father Egmund is the priest of Saint Wulfram's in Grantham. Father Swaefred holds a parish at Saint Andrew's in the village of Heorlafestoun, just outside of Grantham. Both have had some dealings which I believe Your Grace will see as a precedent for the rights the king claims."

AFTER HASTINGS

When Edwy referred to the archbishop, Father Egmund bowed his head and moved to kiss the archbishop's ring. Father Swaefred fell to his knees, practically groveling before the higher clergymen and lawyer. No words Edwy spoke could calm the village priest, and Father Egmund eventually had to pull him aside and speak to him in quiet tones. When Father Swaefred was finally calm, Edwy began to explain their presence to Colum-cille in more detail. Edwy finished and Colum-cille turned to the two clerics.

"Father Egmund. You supported Earl Leofwine in his contention that Sanctuary was a Roman concept and not a part of the Celtic Church. May I ask what information you based that decision on?"

"When I received my appointment to Saint Wulfram's, my superior, the bishop of Lincoln, made it clear to me that the purpose of the Church was to support the king. The man who was trying to hide from the king's brother in the church was doing so both in opposition to the king and in support of the foreign Church. Given my instructions from the bishop, there was nothing else I could have done."

Despite his calm demeanor, Father Egmund was nervous. Colum-cille watched the man closely while he spoke, saw the way he scratched his chin with the back of his hand. Despite the cool air and his distance from the fire, the priest had beads of sweat on his brow. Obviously, Father Egmund had been given poor advice by the bishop of Lincoln. However, the subordinate could not be held accountable for the superior's mistakes. After this business with Lanfranc and the king, Colum-cille would have to send out an encyclical letter to all his bishops. With luck, he would be able to get rid of the bishop nonsense within a few years. It was clear that the English priests who were so staunchly opposed to Rome had no idea what Celtic Christianity actually meant.

"I see. Did you know your predecessor at Saint Wulfram's?"

"No, I did not. I was brought to Grantham after Father Maegleas fled his position. Until then, I was a priest at Saint Dogmael's in Tintagel."

"I'm afraid I'm still not very familiar with all the little towns in England. Where is this Tintagel?"

"It's near where Cornwall meets the rest of England. On the Cornish side."

"That's quite a distance. Do you like your parish in Grantham?"

Colum-cille's question clearly caught the priest off guard. It took a few moments before he was able to answer, "The people do speak a little queer, but I've gotten used to it. The city is nice, but it's different than Tintagel. I suppose part of me will always wish I were back home."

Colum-cille ignored Father Egmund's reply, or lack thereof, and turned his attention to the shorter priest.

"Where did you preach before being given Heorlafestoun?"

"I've lived my whole life in Heorlafestoun, Your Grace, with a few trips each year to Grantham once I became a priest, Your Grace. That was the furthest I ever traveled, Your Grace, until I was summoned to York, Your Grace."

"You knew Father Egmund's predecessor at Saint Wulfram's, then?"

"Yes, Your Grace. Father Maegleas taught me everything I know about being a priest, Your Grace. At least, until Your Grace came down to England, Your Grace. Since then Father Egmund has been helping me, Your Grace."

"Can you tell me about Father Maegleas?" A strange desire to hear about his would-be assassin filled Archbishop Colum-cille.

"Father Maegleas was like a father to me, Your Grace. Not a priest, mind you, but a father, Your Grace. My own father died when I was little, Your Grace. He worked a plot of land in Heorlafestoun, Your Grace. When he died, my mother was taken in by her parents, my grandparents, Your Grace. Although they could feed and clothe her, they could not take me in as well, Your Grace. My grandfather took me into Grantham and gave me into Father Maegleas's care, Your Grace."

Colum-cille marveled at how difficult it seemed to be for these village priests to answer the simplest of questions.

"Do you know what happened to Father Maegleas after he left Grantham?"

"I thought he had gone to Flanders, Your Grace. That is where he told me he was going the last time we spoke, Your Grace. Since that time, I was informed by Earl Leofwine that Father Maegleas tried to kill Your Grace, Your Grace." Swaefred said this last apologetically, almost as if he had something to do with Maegleas's assassination attempt.

"Do you know what happened to Father Maegleas after he tried to kill me?"

Before Swaefred could answer, Bishop Lanfranc spoke, "He was murdered by the king who had no right to enact such a punishment without the Church's approval. The same case we are now examining with respect to Brother Beornred."

"The king was within his rights to execute Maegleas. He was a murderer and should not be protected against justice by the Church. Does not God tell us, in the simplest language, 'Thou shalt not kill'? He does not tell us that 'Thou shalt not kill unless thou art a priest.'" Edwy responded as if he had known what Lanfranc would say.

Edwy turned to Archbishop Colum-cille. "When the murderous Father Maegleas was executed, there was no outcry, from laity or clergy, secular or regular. His punishment established the king's right to deal with clergy who commit murder, whether in deed or in desire. Treason, regicide, is the same crime. Lesser crimes belong to the clergy to deal with as they will, defrocking those found guilty, and on occasion recommending further punishment. If Lanfranc's desires are granted, there is nought to stop clergymen from murdering without fear of consequences."

"Leave me. I wish to think over my decision."

The two village priests practically fell over each other trying to leave the archbishop's presence. Both Lanfranc and Edwy tried to continue arguing, neither desiring to let the other have the last word, nor being the first to exit the room. Colum-cille simply held up his hand, indicating that he would listen to no further arguments.

"I would rather hear testimony from the jury rather than arguments from the jurists."

Lanfranc and Edwy called for the jury to enter the room. Eight monks from Canterbury entered in the company of three Canterbrigian merchants. Once they had been introduced to the archbishop, each began, in turn, to describe Brother Beornred's character. Colum-cille was intrigued to discover how much their descriptions differed, neither monk nor merchant agreeing with any others of their status. Eventually, the jury finished giving their testimony and left the room. Colum-cille could tell they were as relieved as the Granthamite priests had been.

As the door closed, Edwy began to speak but Colum-cille waved him to silence.

"I must meditate on what I have heard. *Dei vobiscum.*"

When he was finally left alone, Colum-cille banked the fire in the fireplace. He rolled the carpet against one wall of the room and sat on the bare stone floor amidst the plushly furnished room. He waited while the last of the fire's heat escaped through the open windows, until he began to feel the chill autumnal air and the coolness of the stone beneath him.

Our Father, who art in heaven, guide me in this difficult decision which will affect generation upon generation of Thy Holy Church. I am but a humble hermit who wishes to worship Thy glory. Thou chose me to lead a Church, yet I am not suitable for such a task. Send Thy guidance to Thy humble servant. Show me Thy will.

His prayer to God said, Colum-cille sat in the room waiting for an answer.

AFTER HASTINGS

BOOK VI: WAR

1068. King Harold, with knowledge of the army's sailing, met the ships at Botulph's Town. The waves ran red with the invaders' blood as they tried to take the beach. The first ship beached when the sun was high in the sky and the battle raged until the moon shone over the water. Both armies fought until it was too dark to see.
—THE ANGLO-SAXON CHRONICLE

1068. In September, a strong wind sent by God drove the Magnus Feodus from Wissant to Botulph's Town, where the miles dei rushed on the English beaches like waves. They were met by the heretical usurper in whose ear the Devil whispered of the holy fleet's arrival. When the Christian soldiers set foot on English sand to free the land from its misguided leaders, the Pelagians, who call themselves Celts, launched an attack. As the day advanced, the heretics were forced from the beach, eventually fleeing the coast when the sun sank.
—CHRONICLE OF JEAN DE AVRANCHES

CHAPTER I

Hildebrand found his position insufferable. Although he had put together the *m*agnus feodus and led the battle against English heresy, Pope Alexander had not permitted him to travel with the army against the English. Instead of being near the battle, where he could get constant reports of their progress, he was forced to sit in a dank castle near Wissant, waiting for messengers who could be spared to cross the channel and deliver news several days, or weeks, out of date.

After the first reports were delivered to him, Hildebrand realized he would not really gain any useful knowledge and simply instructed messengers to continue to carry them to Rome. Rumors, brought him by the local fishermen, kept him as well informed as the official dispatches being sent to the continent by Heinrich and Philippe's armies.

The fisherman who stood in front of Hildebrand had, no doubt, put on his best clothing for his interview with the papal legate. Nevertheless, the horrible stench of dead fish he exuded filled the room. Hildebrand questioned the man from behind the dubious safety of a scented handkerchief.

"King Philippe has led his men to a small town near London. I think the name is West Minister."

"How do you know the king is near Westminster? I don't imagine you took your boat up the Thames?" Hildebrand had learned that he could not let the fishermen know his disdain for them. They had a strange peasant's pride and would dry up as a source of information if he let his feelings show. Nevertheless, he had to determine how accurate their accounts were.

The fisherman did not answer the question immediately. He had the look of a sinner coming to Confession, eager to announce his sins, yet afraid of the retribution.

"You may speak. Although a papal legate, I am also a priest. View me as you would your own confessor."

"I have sinned, my father," the fisherman began, as if Hildebrand had said some magic words, "There is a girl living in Dover in England with whom I have fallen in love. When I can, I visit Dover to see her."

The fisherman paused, as eloquent an admission of sin as Hildebrand had ever heard.

"And this girl, she told you about the army's location?"

"No, she wouldn't know anything about that, but her father, he knew where they were."

"This girl and her father, are they Pelagians?"

"No, Your Grace. They are good, decent Christians. Normans, even. Her father was telling me he planned to ride north to join Philippe's army."

Hildebrand was surprised. "Ride? Is this girl's father a knight?"

The fisherman laughed, "A knight? That's rich. If he was a knight, would he let me anywhere near his daughter, much less actually talk to me beyond, 'I'll have a herring.'? He's a tavernkeep. Not all Normans living in England are rich. When good King Edward ruled, many Normans went to England to make their fortune. Some were successful, others, like my girl's father, were not."

Having ascertained the accuracy of the fisherman's account, Hildebrand plotted King Philippe's position on a map he kept in his head. Although Philippe was making good progress, having nearly reached the capital, probably had reached it since the fisherman was in Dover, Emperor Heinrich's army was still boxed in between Harold and the beach at Botulph's Town.

If God smiled on the magnus feodus, and Hildebrand could not imagine any reason he would not, the war for England would soon be over. Harold would be killed or captured by Heinrich and Philippe would control London, which could then be given to William's oldest son, King Robert of England. Victory was assured.

Hildebrand once again turned his attention to the fisherman. "I thank you for your information. My major domo will see to your physical needs. Tell me, this Dover girl of yours, are you the first man she has known?"

"Yes, Your Grace."

"For your spiritual needs, you must renounce your Norman girl, eat only bread and water for the next year. In the year following this, you must fast for forty days and then abstain from both wine and meat until that year is over. Each week for the next two years, you must give alms to your Confessor. Think hard on the sin you have committed and repent and God shall have mercy upon your soul."

CHAPTER II

Philippe's march from the coast had been miraculously easy. Harold's entire army was engaged with Heinrich's assault on Mercia. Peasants fled or hid before the advancing French army. Normans, living in England since the reign of King Edward, joined Philippe's forces, afraid of losing their property if Harold was victorious over the Magnus Feodus.

Now, the walls of London stood in front of Philippe, a grim testament to the ancient city's might. Philippe found himself wishing he had found resistance during his march from the sea. As it was, he was still unblooded. The siege of London would be his first taste of combat. Théobald assured him it would be particularly inglorious and unromantic.

Philippe ordered his tent to be erected just out of bowshot from the wall. While his servants were building the royal residence, Philippe went looking for Gilles d'Argyre. As he hunted for the minstrel, Théobald maintained a constant barrage of strategy and tactics in his ear.

"As long as they have the river and the bridge to Southwark, they'll be able to stand against the siege until the Second Coming. There is little we can do about the river, but I recommend we destroy the bridge as soon as possible. We don't have enough men to lay siege to Southwark as well as London."

Philippe looked out at the Thames. The bridge stretched across the river, an impressive gray length of stone and wood. It would be a shame to destroy the bridge when it was London's only link across the river, especially since the city would soon be his. Nevertheless, Philippe realized Théobald was right.

"Jacques," Philippe called a minor baron from Dover, "I want you to take your men and build boats to go across the Thames. When you get to the other side of the river, make your way into Southwark. I want you to burn the bridge. If you can destroy any of the docks, wharves and piers, or boats, that would be even better."

"If your lordship would grant permission, my men and I could move around to the other side of London. We'll have to row upriver, but the journey will be shorter and we can land within Southwark. We won't have to fight our way into the city. They'll surely be on guard against an attack from the land."

Philippe gave his assent and Jacques vanished to gather the men and supplies he would need.

"Allowing him to move around London will add a day to his mission," Théobald admonished.

"Allowing him to move around London will also improve his chances for success. One more day of food and supplies won't hurt our cause too much. Besides, do we have our men positioned outside all the gates yet?"

"Not yet," Théobald conceded, "They'll be in position by the time the baron gets his boats built. We are capturing many messengers who are fleeing . . . "

Théobald's reports was interrupted by the blasts of several horns. The king turned his attention to the walls. The origination of the sound was obvious. The noon-time sun glinted off the brass trumpets and gold jewelry of a richly dressed party standing above the city gate. Philippe turned to the wall and began to walk, slowly as befit a king, toward the party. He was greeted en route by Frenchmen who were coming from the wall to inform him that the archbishop of London desired to parlay with him.

Philippe stopped outside of bow range and motioned Théobald forward. When his advisor stopped, Philippe could just barely hear him call out to the archbishop.

"*Philippus, rex francorum, dux Parisi*, greets William, *archiepiscopus Londinii*."

Théobald paused to hear a response from the wall. Although the wind carried the sound of a voice to Philippe, he was unable to hear any individual words.

"May his soul rest in peace in the Kingdom of God." Philippe found it disconcerting to hear expressions of condolence shouted across a battle field. There was no hint of sorrow in Théobald's voice.

"We will need time, until the middle of the afternoon on the morrow, to arrange a suitable spot. Five men may accompany the archbishop."

While the Frenchmen set up a tent to contain the negotiations between Philippe and the archbishop, Théobald began to prepare the king for his upcoming meeting. They had barely begun when Guillaume came, wheezing, to join them. Philippe had planned on leaving the ancient family retainer behind in France, but Guillaume had raised such a fuss, Philippe finally decided he could die in England if he so desired.

"It is important to remember that this new archbishop is heretical, possibly even more so than the Scot. The Scot knows no better than his infamous ways. The archbishop of London knowingly denounced the Roman Church."

"Do we know the man's name?"

"Yes. He is called Æthelric."

"Where does he come from?"

Théobald shrugged, but Guillaume had an answer for the king. "He is a cousin of some sort to King Harold. Back when Edward was king, Godwin proposed Æthelric's name as the archbishop of Canterbury. He was rejected and Robert of Jumièges was elected in his stead. That was just before Edward banished Godwin and his clan."

"He must be ancient."

"I suppose it depends on your point of view, although it seems to me he wasn't all that old at the time."

"I don't suppose you could name anyone who you would consider old. Tell me, what was it like when you ate with the apostles?"

The words were hardly out of his mouth when Guillaume slapped the king hard across the cheek, leaving the imprint of his hand emblazoned. It was an act which would have earned any other man death.

"Don't blaspheme! I may be old, but that doesn't mean I don't respect our Lord."

The three men walked in silence for a few moments before Théobald broke the silence.

"We really must decide what we are going to say in the negotiations with this holy man." Théobald put all his scorn into the description of the archbishop.

"We tell him we're here to take over London and that he should open the doors for us," the king replied, matter-of-factly.

"That is what we'll ask for, but it usually isn't that simple. It is customary to allow a grace period during which the inhabitants of the city, or at least the leaders, can decide whether to turn over the city peacefully or make the besiegers work for their entry. Frequently, enough time is given so the citizens have a hope of reinforcements arriving."

"Unless Harold can defeat Emperor Heinrich, there's no chance of reinforcements. My messengers indicate that Harold can't spare any of his men, certainly not his brother, Earl Aethelwine, or the Earl Sigeweard. How long are we to allow them to plot against us? A month? A year? Why bother with the entire endeavor?"

"I would suggest a period of three days might be in order. That will demonstrate that you have no expectation that they can receive aid. It also will remind them of the time Christ spent in the grave," Guillaume said.

"It is important the siege not last too long. It is already the last day of October. We are too near the end of campaigning season. We should have waited for the spring," Théobald had been pronouncing the same warning ever since Philippe's fleet had sailed for England.

As they spoke, they made a circuit of the camp, stopping occasionally to inspect the entrenchments the Frenchmen were laying. They continued to debate the course the negotiations would take. At one point, Philippe sent a footman to round up three noblemen to sit at the negotiations table with him.

Philippe entered the tent with Théobald and Guillaume. Three other Frenchmen were already sitting with Archbishop Æthelric and his companions. Before he sat down, Philippe indicated the men who had joined Æthelric.

The archbishop nodded to one of the men. He rose from his chair and addressed King Philippe, "His Grace greets your lordship. I am his humble servant, Brother Sibi. These other men are Airik the Mercer, Ealdorman Forspild, Ealdorman Lithsmann, Mathm of Kingsbury, and Ligulf, the *burgagend* of London." As Brother Sibi named each man, they rose to greet the king.

Philippe sat down without any further ceremony. He looked across the table at Æthelric. Even though Guillaume was older, the archbishop looked as if he were as old as Methusaleh.

Æthelric's visage was as wrinkled and craggy as the mountains which separated France from Iberia, his nose creating a massive pinnacle above the terrain of his face. Philippe assumed his hair was cut in the heretical fashion of the Celts, but what hair was left was just a few thin, wispy strands clinging to the back of his head.

Philippe felt a rush of excitement. He may have only been laying siege to a city instead of fighting a pitched battle, but this was his first negotiation during a war.

AFTER HASTINGS

"We have your city surrounded. You are under siege. If you will turn the city over to us within the next three days, we will not seek any reparations or inflict any punishments for our time or expenses."

Although Philippe had not expected his offer to be considered seriously, he was disappointed when, after Brother Sibi translated the offer into Anglo-Saxon, Æthelric greeted it with a raspy, cackling laugh.

After he had caught his breath, the archbishop spoke in his thick, guttural language. When he finished speaking, Brother Sibi made his comments intelligible.

"When London stands, England stands. When London falls, England falls. My cousin, King Harold, has entrusted the safety and well-being of this city, and through it the safety and well-being of this island, to us. We have pledged on the holy relics of Saint Erkenwald to carry out our charge.

Guillaume nudged Philippe and indicated the monk's translation was faithful. Before the meeting, they had decided to hide the fact that Guillaume could converse in their barbaric tongue.

Before Philippe could frame a response, one of the Frenchmen, the only man in the room of a common age with the king, said, "Although your loyalty is admirable, Archbishop, you'll regret your decision today when we are successful and I rule this island as king."

Philippe had not wanted Robert to attend the meeting. However, since he was supposed to be crowned king at Winchester after London fell, there was no way Philippe could restrict him from the meeting.

Brother Sibi was already dutifully translating Robert's outburst to Æthelric. When he finished, the Archbishop looked uncomprehendingly from Philippe to Robert.

"You have three days to decide if you will release the city of London to us."

Philippe rose and walked from the tent. Now, more than before, he wanted to find Gilles and relax with some music. He could sense his advisors following behind him, but he did not turn back to look at them.

"Robert!"

The Duke of Normandy's son and heir trotted forward on his stubby legs to run alongside the king.

"Yes, my lord?"

"Although you will, someday, be the king of this little island, you are currently merely the son of one of my vassals. Your attendance at negotiations is suffered because of your future position. It will not be suffered if you insist on interjecting your temper. If you must speak, I suggest you find good counsel."

Without looking at Robert of Normandy, Philippe could tell that William's heir was trying to hold back indignation. Although Robert would one day, probably soon, be King of England, for the time being he still needed Philippe's support. It hadn't taken Philippe long to learn when people stopped their tongues simply because he was the king. Only a few men, like Théobald and Guillaume, ever berated the king, and even they grew more cautious as the king became an adult. It would be interesting to see how they acted toward him now that he had been on a battlefield.

With a wave of his hand, Philippe indicated Robert should find a place to make himself useful. The boy stormed off, his short legs moving twice as quickly to cover the ground Philippe would have covered. With the Norman nuisance gone, Philippe resumed his aborted search for Gilles d'Argyre.

The time must have been right for him to listen to music. Whereas earlier Philippe had been unable to locate the minstrel in the camp, now, his business over, he practically tripped over d'Argyre as soon as he chose to look for him.

"Gilles, play me a song. The Song of Roland you've been putting together. I've heard bits and pieces. Surely, by now, you have enough to sing it to me in some semblance of order."

The minstrel looked saddened as he replied, "I have forsaken that *chanson*, my lord. No matter how much I tried to force the words, the meter and scansion would not work out in a manner with which I was happy."

AFTER HASTINGS

"You jest. That was certainly the most interesting and enjoyable piece I have ever heard you sing. I imagine minstrels will sing it for a thousand years."

"My lord is given to hyperbole, if I may be so bold. My story of Roland was nothing but a light ditty, never meant seriously. It was a failure. Instead, I have turned my humble talents to a dirge on the theme of our Lord's crucifixion and resurrection."

"Roland's betrayal and death struck you as too light a topic? Very well, sing me of our Lord."

Philippe sat on a nearby bench and Gilles took up a position in front of him and began to strum on his lyre.

"When Pontius ruled in Judaea
And Tiberius sat the throne
Our Lord in Heaven sent among us
His son, as man, to call our own."

As Gilles sang, Philippe could not but help think this dirge was nowhere near as beautiful as the earlier song Gilles has composed. Nevertheless, the king was able to enjoy the beauty it did have. Behind the minstrel towered the great wall of London, a wall the English avowed had stood since Caesar laid claim to the island. To the right, the River Thames flowed slowly past the city and camp, divided by the single stretch of bridge, its greys turned to black in the setting sun. Philippe ignored the sounds and smells of the military camp growing around him to concentrate on the beauty of the landscape and the sound of Gilles's voice.

A shout pulled his attention from Gilles and he looked toward the river. Bright orange and red flame leapt from the southern end of London's bridge. Philippe could make out the distant shadows of men racing around to douse the flames. If he listened carefully, he thought he could hear their voices, carried in an eerie echo across the broad river.

CHAPTER III

Brother Beornred knelt in the dark, dank solitude of his cell in York Castle. No light filtered into the small room and the only sound he could hear was the constant dripping of water in one of the cell's corners. Although a prisoner of the king, he was a mere monk and did not rank the apartments a nobleman would have been accorded.

"Why do the wicked enjoy long life, hale in old age, and great and powerful? They live to see their children settled, their kinsfolk and descendants flourishing; their families are secure and safe; the rod of God's justice does not reach them."

He had been reciting the books of Job and Lamentations almost continuously since Earl Leofwine had wrestled him to the ground at Senlac Fair. In their words he sought, and often found, succor and compassion. At other times, he could not but help wonder, as a latter day Job, what he had done to deserve the misery God had sent upon him.

The rhythmic dripping of the water was suddenly interrupted by sounds outside his cell door, indicative that the door was about to open. Beornred stood, confused. It seemed to be too early for another meal. He had not recited Lamentations enough times for them to feed him again.

When the door opened, the torches beyond it brightened the room unbearably and Beornred threw his arm in front of his eyes to ward off the light. He could tell that three shadows had entered the room, but had no idea of their identities. He imagined one was the gaoler who usually provided him with a bowl of porridge and a cup of water, but there was no way for him to tell.

One of the men spoke with a thick accent. It took Beornred a few moments to realize what the man had said.

"Yes, my lord," he replied, the safest answer he could think of.

"I'll see him upstairs. Clean him off first."

The speaker turned and left. Beornred got the impression that he disliked the cell more than anything else. The gaoler grabbed Beornred roughly by the arm and forced him out of the cell. Just as his eyes had adjusted to the dim light the door allowed in, Beornred was subjected to the brilliant flare of torches in the corridor outside his cell. He flinched away from the light and was roughly thrown forward by the gaoler, who led him through a narrow passage and up a set of winding stairs.

When they reached the top of the stairs, the gaoler made him stand in the center of the room and called for the other guard to get some water. When the man disappeared, the gaoler ordered Beornred to take his clothing off. The monk slowly undressed, aware of the gaoler's watchful eyes which only served to heighten his shame at being naked. Adam's words floated through Beornred's mind, "I heard the sound of You in the garden, and I was afraid because I was naked, so I hid." Beornred could feel his cheeks warming despite the cool November air. He tried to cover himself with his hands, but found that no matter how much he twisted an obscene amount of flesh was exposed to his captor.

The second man returned with a bucket of water. Without any prelude, he threw its contents at Beornred. The shock of the frigid water made Beornred forget his embarrassment at allowing other men to see his nudity. Instead he found himself shivering in the cold air, water dripping from his limbs and running down his chest. Despite his large size, he felt smaller than either of the men who were taking him to speak to the nobleman who had visited his cell so briefly.

His gaoler motioned for him to get dressed and Beornred gratefully pulled his coarse robe over his head. He could feel the scratchy wool absorb the water from his body. Although it offered comfort at first, it quickly cooled, hanging heavily, cold and damp on his shoulders. Although he found consolation in the protection the robe offered his naked body, the discomfort the robe inflicted was nearly as great. Nevertheless, Beornred knew he could withstand physical discomfort. It was common in the monastery at Canterbury. One of the few things both Archbishop Stigand and Bishop Lanfranc agreed upon was that mortification of the flesh could be suffered and would help its victim gain admittance to Heaven.

Beornred almost bumped into his gaoler when the man stopped in front of a narrow wooden door. The gaoler knocked on the door and stood aside. When a muffled voice called from inside, the gaoler opened the door and pushed Beornred into the room.

Before Beornred had even recovered from stumbling into the room, he heard the door close behind him. The room was small and sparsely furnished. A wooden bench was pushed up against one wall and a small desk stood next to the bench. On the wall opposite the bench was a small wooden crucifix. The Savior was looking toward heaven, His eyes pleading for mercy from His unseen Father, knowing, at the same time, that no mercy would come. He was dying for the sins of others.

For a moment, a strange thought passed through Beornred's head. Why would God inflict punishment and torture on His own Son when He was blameless? The monk quickly decided the question was not important. Quite possibly it was heretical. He would mention it at his next confession if he remembered.

Another monk stood contemplating the crucifix. Such was the power of the carving that Beornred had not even noticed the monk once his eyes alit on the cross. Not knowing who the monk was, Beornred held his tongue.

"It is certainly a handsome rood." Beornred recognized the accent as belonging to the man who had visited him in his cell. He hadn't been the nobleman Beornred had expected, instead merely a humble monk like himself.

"I like it. It makes me feel good."

"Yes, the sculptor managed to achieve both Our Savior's plea for leniency and a sense of hope in His face. It is a magnificent piece. Rarely have I seen such a well executed carving."

The foreign monk smiled as if he had made a joke, although Beornred had no idea what he said that might have been construed as humorous.

Instead of replying, Beornred smiled a little smile to indicate he understood the obscure joke.

"He was not only the Son of God and the Son of Man, but also the king of the Jews." The monk indicated the four letters above Christ's head. *INRI*. Jesus the Nazarene, King of the Jews.

"He was a good king. He tried to lead His people along the path of righteousness. Yet His people betrayed Him. They offered Him as sacrifice to the Romans."

"They shouldn't have done that," Beornred commented, "He was their king. Even if He was bad, which He couldn't be, they should not have killed Him."

The monk turned to look at Beornred. "A bad king should not be removed by his own subjects? Did not Rechab and Baanah slay Ishbosheth so the Israelites could live under the good rule of King David?"

Beornred tried to remember the part of the Bible the monk was talking about. He was not as familiar with the Old Testament since it was nowhere near as important as the parts that dealt with Christ. After much thought, though, he remembered David's response to the gift of Ishbosheth's head. "Did not David reply, 'when wicked men have killed a blameless man in bed in his own house! I will certainly avenge his blood on you and I will rid the earth of you.'"

The foreign monk looked at Beornred with wonder. "I was told you were an idiot," the man blurted. "Yet you quote scripture like a scholar."

"Is not the word of Our Lord the only thing worth knowing?"

"Tell me then, what does the Bible say about treason?"

At first, the only treason Beornred could think of were the obvious cases of Judas and Peter betraying Christ. He did not see how these cases could be linked to his own case. Thinking harder, he remembered an incident from the Old Testament.

"'As soon as Athaliah, mother of Ahaziah, saw that her son was dead, she set out to destroy all the royal line.'"

"And do you recall what happened to Athaliah?" the monk probed.

"When Athaliah ruled the kingdom for seven years she was killed by the priests for she was an abomination: a woman monarch."

"There are many reasons why Athaliah was executed. She was a traitor, an usurper, a woman ruler. But she was a traitor first."

"And our King Harold is a traitor, an usurper, a heretic and a fornicator."

The monk quickly crossed the room and slapped Beornred hard across the face, sending him sprawling on the floor.

"The king is not the one to be on trial. You are, Beornred, for making statements like that one. I can see you have no contrition or remorse in your soul. I am saddened that a man in holy orders can be so judgmental and unforgiving. You are to think about your transgressions. To focus your mind, I assign you penance of a *paternoster* for each day in a year, a genuflection for each day of the year, and a blow from a scourge for each day of the year. Each applied every day for a year. If this does not focus your mind, you must also repudiate food and drink for a single day each month. Remember, too, this penance shall do you no good if you do not truly repent of your words. It is not enough to stop slandering the king, you must realize the error of your ways in your mind and your soul as well."

The door opened and another monk entered the room. "Archbishop, forgive my interruption, but there is an urgent message from Archbishop Æthelric awaiting you in your chambers. You will want to see it."

"Return this man to his cell," Archbishop Colum-cille replied to the monk. As he left the room, the archbishop paused in the doorway, "Think on your repentance," he admonished Beornred.

Despite the archbishop's admonishment, Beornred could not renounce the words he had spoken. The monk he had just spoken to was the archbishop, but he opposed the pope. That meant that he should not be obeyed. Yet to disobey an archbishop would result in damnation. Beornred could feel devils running through his head, trying to force him to decide whether to obey the distant pope or the nearby archbishop. He was almost relieved when his gaoler closed the cell door behind him.

AFTER HASTINGS

He knelt in the dark cell.

"*Pater noster*," Beornred began, as much to foil the devils in his head as to carry out the penance imposed on him by Archbishop Colum-cille.

CHAPTER IV

Botulph's Town was burning.

The glow from the inferno could be seen for miles. Englishmen saw the glow as a disheartening omen, although part of war. Germans saw it as a favorable sign of future victory . . . an emulation of the light of Heaven.

Harold watched the flames from a frozen field, snow falling through the dark black clouds of smoke that blotted out the stars and the moon. He was close enough to the city to be able to read the letter a messenger had just delivered with no more light than the glow produced by the fires. Dangling from the rolled up letter was a wax disk, bearing the seal of Ligulf, the burgagend of London. Harold broke the leather thong which tied the scroll closed and unrolled it.

To Harold, King of the Angles and Saxons, Earl of Wessex, Conqueror of Wales and Ireland. Ligulf, Burgagend of the city of London, sends his greetings and hopes that your campaign in the north meets with better doom than the city of London.

The city has been surrounded by the men of Philippe of France and Robert, called by some Curthose, called by himself King of England. Yesterday, King Philippe and Pretender Robert, along with their advisors, met with Archbishop Æthelric, me, and a witan made up of good London burghers to ask us to relinquish the city. We denied their request and returned within the walls, which remain unbreached. That evening, the Frenchmen burned London's bridge at Southwark and other, smaller fires could be seen burning among the docks and piers of Southwark.

We shall defend London and hold out against the invaders as long as we can. Archbishop Æthelric holds mass and prays for the delivery of London. We require your assistance if we are to have any hope of surviving this siege.

I am sending this letter by a messenger who will row upriver late tonight in hopes of bypassing the besieging army with instructions to deliver it to your hands somewhere near Botulph's Town.

Written this All Saints' Day in the third year of the reign of King Harold of England.

Harold crumpled the letter and dropped it in the mud. He realized the camp was quiet, not a good sign. Godwin had always said, "Quiet men fear they are about to die. They are making peace with their Creator."

Harold feared his father was right, as he had so often been proven in the past. He began to wander among the men, something his father had often done on the eve of a battle. His boots left discernible footprints in the early snow covering the frozen mud in which his men camped. Scattered around the camp were small groups of men, mostly huddled around campfires. A few of the more industrious men had erected shelters to ward off the worst of the cold November wind sweeping in off the North Sea.

As he walked, Harold stopped often to offer words of encouragement to the men. He had made sure he carried a full meadskin when he started from his tent so he could offer the drink to soldiers and make himself seem more like a friend than a commander, another trick he had learned from Godwin.

Most of the conversations Harold heard were speculations about whether the next day's fighting would be any more successful than the previous day's. There was no hiding the fact that Harold was losing ground against the Germans. The burning of Botulph's Town was merely a reminder of that fact.

"Why should I care if Botulph's Town burns? I'm an Essexman. I should be protecting Ely." Unfortunately, this overheard comment was typical of what Harold had been hearing. The response was not.

"There's nothing needs protecting near Ely. All down there is swamp and all Heinrich's men are up here. Besides, if they beat us here, they'll go south, toward Ely. The more we fight up here, the less likely it is they'll reach Ely. Isn't it better to stop them here?"

Harold was impressed by the man's explanation and moved closer to where they huddled around a small fire. It was rare to find a man who understood what was happening during a battle, much rarer to find one who could grasp the bigger situation. When Harold saw the speaker, he was impressed in other ways. Even sitting, the man towered over his companion. Although his hair almost looked as if he wore a combination of Roman and Celtic tonsures, it was balanced by an unruly and ferocious-looking beard. Just by looking at him, Harold felt sorry for any man who faced him in battle.

"Good evening," Harold said as he entered the circle of light cast by their fire, "Can I offer you some mead?"

As the smaller man took Harold's skin, the king asked the men their names.

"This is Gregory of Abbenford and I am called Eric, Ivar's son."

"Gregory. That's a Frankish name, isn't it?"

The smaller man handed the skin to Eric and wiped his beard with the back of his hand. "My father came over from Normandy with King Edward. My mother is a Saxon from Abbenford. I was born and raised in Abbenford and I'm as much a Saxon as he is." Gregory pointed at Eric.

"And what is your story?"

Eric kept drinking for a few moments before passing the skin back to Harold. "Be better if that had been beer. I'm from the village of Ickleton. I farm a hide of land there, perhaps a little more. Because of my size, and because I can handle an axe, I tend to be put into just about every levy. Fought at Stamford Bridge. Started on the march to Senlac, but a wound I took at Stamford made me stop at Peterborough." Eric seemed almost apologetic, "And whose drink are we sharing?"

"Harold, son of Godwin."

Gregory looked blank for a moment, but Eric's reaction made the small man realize who was in their company.

"Lord. As always I am in your service." Even kneeling, the top of the big man's head nearly came to Harold's chin.

"You seem to have a good head on your shoulders. Who is lord of your land?"

"Modcraeft of Stortford."

"I've heard good things about your lord. He supported me when the peasants revolted near Colchester."

"That is true. I fought along his side when he went to the aid of Lord Thurstan."

Both men seemed to forget Gregory's presence as they spoke of the Colchester revolt. The small man left them to join a more friendly fire.

"I've heard little of the Colchester revolt. Only a brief account from Thurstan before Morkere began his rebellion in the North. Since then, my brother regales me with his great battles."

"It really wasn't much of a revolt, although it sounded bigger and worse before we came into contact with the rebels. Once we found them, we realized, rather quickly, that they had little leadership. A couple of minor barons who had fought with or against you and your father in the past. They really had no goals. Mostly, I think they figured there was a chance to steal their neighbor's land and maybe rob a church or two.

"Thurstan did a good job marshaling the men who fought with him. We attacked as an army, much like we did at Stamford Bridge. If the rebels had any real goals or knew what they were about, they might have been able to put up a fight. As it was, they broke at our first rush."

Eric's description of Colchester made Harold realize that he had been trying to lift his spirits since receiving the letter from *burgagend* Ligulf. Walking among depressed men may have been good for their morale, but it had only served to make Harold feel a greater sense of defeat. Meeting Eric and listening to his knowledge of warfare was what eventually gave Harold hope.

"I am glad Thurstan and Modcraeft can rely on men like you when the need arises. I only wish the need never arose within England or against my own subjects. Perhaps when this is over we can take the fight to the battlefields of the Empire and France."

As Harold turned to leave Eric, he tossed the skin to the big man. "Enjoy this. Tomorrow, perhaps, we enter into battle. I would like for you to bear my standard."

CHAPTER V

Heinrich watched Botulph's Town burn, its orange flames illuminating the night. He felt the mixed emotions he always felt when he went into battle. Although the city was a demonstration of his victorious forces, it was wasteful to destroy a city which could otherwise have been counted upon to pay taxes. Recently, Heinrich had begun to allow cities the option of sending money instead of men when there was a levy. It made sense. He needed both in order to wage war and now had ways to obtain either.

Rumors flew through the camp and Heinrich tried to ignore all of them. Most seemed to indicate that Harold was either dead or fled. Heinrich took that as a good sign, not because he believed them, but because of what they told him about his men. Had morale been low, there would have been more talk of Harold receiving reinforcements or another Moorish massacre, like the one which occurred at Roncesvalles.

In fact, rumor aside, Heinrich was afraid the Moors might continue to be victorious. If that happened, the men would begin to wonder if God had turned his back on Christendom. Many people still believed that the Antichrist would come soon, despite the fact that the millennium was more than half a century in the past.

Heinrich tried to put thoughts of the Moors out of his mind. They really had very little to do with the present situation. Harold was most likely somewhere near the town which burned. Heinrich's scouts would determine his exact whereabouts shortly. Within a day or two, the Imperial army would meet Harold's forces and finish the job which had begun on the coast.

Heinrich was so busy thinking he nearly bumped into a man standing in front of a fire. When the man realized who had brushed him he bowed his head and dropped to one knee in the mud.

"My lord."

"Rudolf. Get up. You can kneel to me all you want in my palaces and courts, but here you're just getting yourself muddy."

Rudolf rose slowly. Despite Heinrich's words, the emperor was known for his temper and the mercurial changes it exhibited. Once standing, the Duke waited for Heinrich to speak again.

"Somewhere out there, Harold the usurper lies quivering in the freezing mud and snow, wishing, I imagine, he had never deigned to take the throne which rightfully belonged to William the Bastard. Tomorrow, or perhaps the day after, I'll crush him.

"You'll crush him and return to the Empire. This has never been our fight. If I may be so bold to ask, why are we on this Godforsaken island?"

"Alexander is paying me well for this little expedition. You and I are mercenaries," Heinrich laughed, "More importantly, I place Alexander in my debt. When I next need to place a bishop or archbishop in a critical position, Alexander will remember that I retained England for Christ and he will not dispute my selection. Alexander's power will remain strong in England, but it will be weakened in the Empire."

CHAPTER VI

There were times, quite frequently, when Colum-cille sincerely regretted the decision which resulted in his accompanying Earl Morkere south from Scotland. If Harold had really re-instituted the Celtic Church as he had promised, Colum-cille did not think there would have been a problem. What Harold had done, however, was to create something new, a chimera combining features of the Celtic and Roman churches. Colum-cille worked to move this strange hybrid closer to its Celtic parent, but he had come to the realization during his first year as archbishop that he would never be entirely successful. Although monastic clergy was growing in size and importance throughout England, Colum-cille's own position as the archbishop of York demonstrated how firmly Rome, if not the pope, still held sway in England.

Colum-cille summoned a monk to join him. Although part of him enjoyed the summoning power his position gave him, he realized that enjoyment was a sin and resolved to do penance for it later.

The monk appeared, stylus and tablet in hand.

"I wish to send a general epistle to all the bishops in England.

"Harold, King of England, *et cetera*, Æthelric, Archbishop of London, *et cetera*, Lanfranc, Bishop of Canterbury, *et cetera*, *et alia*, Colum-cille, Archbishop of York, Primate of England, *et cetera*, sends greetings.

"One of our bishops, named Lanfranc who sits in residence at the ancient see of Canterbury, has accused the king of disregarding the ancient traditions of the Church by placing hands on and detaining the person of a monk, namely one Beornred of Canterbury, for a crime against the king's person.

"Lanfranc has made claim that it is the sole right of the Church to try cases in which a priest or monk has been accused of such criminous actions. The king has advanced his own claim that in instances of treason, the accused is bereft of the right to trial by clergy and should be defrocked to stand before the court of the king. Should the king's court determine innocence, the man should be reinstated in the clergy.

"I have thought long and hard on the issues raised and have consulted many learned men in trying to determine the proper course of action. Although Lanfranc's assertions are correct, they are correct only for the degenerate form of Christianity practiced in Rome. While the king's arguments are mostly correct, in them he places himself above the judgment of God in the heavens."

Colum-cille paused and took a large drink of wine from the goblet sitting on his table. The monk, who Colum-cille only now recognized as Brother Rihtdonde, used the archbishop's pause to catch up with what he had said. When Colum-cille noted that Rihtdonde had done so, he continued.

"In God's realm, there would be no question of clergymen committing such heinous acts as treason, however we live in what Augustine of Hippo called the Middle Ages, between His first coming and His return. Until He comes amongst us again, our world shall be less than perfect and clergymen may, on occasion, turn against the person of their rightful king.

"I hereby state and aver that when a clergyman is accused of the crime of treason, he shall be tried by a Church court, whatever form such court may take at the time of the accusation. Should such a court find the accused innocent, he shall be returned to his position and the incident shall plague him no more. If the accused is, in fact, judged by his superiors to have been guilty of the crime ascribed to him, he shall be defrocked of his position in the Church and the Church shall turn him over to the king's men for punishment, asking, at all times, that the mercy of the Lord be bestowed upon the guilty."

Colum-cille sat down. He was not particularly happy with his decision. In some ways he felt he was espousing the cause of the distant Roman Church which tried to force its way into all matters of religion. At the same time, he felt he was turning his back on fellow clergymen in order to appease Harold.

"Will there be anything else?" Brother Rihtdonde asked, his voice soft and full of awe.

"I need copies of that letter for each bishop in England, as well as the king. Please arrange for copies to be made in the scriptorium."

AFTER HASTINGS

Colum-cille watched as Rihtdonde took away the compomising letter which kept the English Church from the true Celtic path.

CHAPTER VII

"Don't let your men move until you hear the trumpeters sound their blast. It may seem like they are delaying, but I don't want us to move too early. The archers can begin loosing their arrows as soon as the Germans are in range, but don't let the infantry move until you hear my signal, no matter what happens."

When Aethelwine, Sigeweard Bearn, and Leofwine indicated their agreement, Harold dismissed them. The three men mounted their horses and rode off to join their troops, kicking up snow as they went. When they reached their part of the battlefield, they would send their horses to join the baggage train and fight on foot.

Harold waited until they were out of earshot before he spoke again.

"Are you sure about this?"

Eric shifted his grip on the pole he held. At the top of the staff was Harold's black raven standard, its wings stretched fully to an impressive man's height in breadth. Although bearing Harold's standard meant Eric would not be able to fight, it demonstrated the esteem in which the king held him already.

"I'm sure. I spoke to a few of the local men yesterday. Out there, at the base of the hill the Germans are standing on, is a river." Eric pointed at a slight depression in the snow. "It isn't too deep and it doesn't flow quickly, so it has frozen over, but it isn't so cold that the ice will be thick."

CHAPTER VIII

Sigeweard Bearn rode away from Harold in silence. Shortly before he stopped to join his thegns, he said, "I really hope the king knows what he is doing. It seems silly to allow the Germans to build up their momentum. Our men's morale is low enough as it is."

Without pausing to think about his answer, Aethelwine defended his friend, "He has something in mind, although what it is I haven't a clue. If you stay around Harold, you'll find that he frequently only lets one other person know any of his plans. It is possible Leofwine has some idea of what will happen."

"You seem exceptionally confident that we will survive the day and Harold will retain his throne."

"I have to maintain my faith, for without faith can I hope to win? Besides, although it may sound childish, he is my friend. I've been with him in exile in Eire. I've seen his return to England. He took his father's place and filled it well. He was elected king and fought off Harald Hardraada and William. He put down Morkere's revolt and has held off the pope for almost two years. I can't believe that God, whether the God the pope told us about or the God Colum-cille speaks of, would have allowed Harold to come so far and then permit him to lose his throne."

"I certainly hope you're right," Sigeweard Bearn said as he dismounted his horse and joined his men.

CHAPTER IX

Heinrich looked down the hill at the Saxon army stretched across the valley below him. He called for a cloak and a heavy woolen cape quickly descended around his shoulders. Despite his constant victories on this campaign, he was beginning to think it was a mistake to launch an attack on England in November.

"Rudolf, give me advice!"

Rudolf of Swabia hurried to Heinrich's side. "They won't attack uphill. That was the mistake made by William of Normandy. We can take our time and attack whenever we are ready."

"I hate waiting."

"They probably hate it more. The decision to attack is yours. No matter how long you wait, you'll know when the wait will end. They have no idea when we will come."

Heinrich watched the English banners hanging limply. There was no wind to cause their flutter. Standing beneath the banners, the Saxon warriors seemed motionless from this distance. From experience, Heinrich knew the shuffling and fidgeting which occurred when men awaited combat to decide their fates. If he was not careful, the same restlessness would affect his own men and they would lose their efficiency. He turned to look at Rudolf.

"We will wait."

CHAPTER X

"The day is nearly a quarter passed," Eric observed, "They should have attacked by now. These short days do not allow much time for fighting and the fires of Botulph's Town still blacken the sky."

Harold looked to where the Germans stood ready at the top of the hill. Although it was a little warmer than the day before, there should be no problem with the river ice breaking, if the Germans attacked today.

"They'll attack soon."

"No. Look, they're getting onto their horses. I guess they decided not to fight today." Eric raised the black raven banner Harold has asked him to hold, allowing all the Saxons to see it.

"They are about to attack. In Europe, they attack on horseback. Signal the archers to prepare."

CHAPTER XI

On the top of the hill, the Germans started to move. Flags waved to signal the warriors to move down the hill against the Saxons.

Seeing the army begin their approach, Sigeweard Bearn had a difficult time keeping his men from rushing to meet them. After waiting throughout a long night and a tense morning, the Saxons were ready for a fight. Sigeweard Bearn faced his men and shifted his grip on the long-handled Danish axe he wielded.

"Stay where you are! You'll have to fight your way through me before you can take a stab at the Germans on the hill! Let them come to us!"

Sigeweard Bearn was a large bear of a man, known for commanding the situation and ready to use force against his own men to ensure their obedience. Despite their desire to enter battle, none of his men dared break rank to face their lord.

CHAPTERS XII

Horses raced ahead of men down the long slope of the hill. In the vanguard, Heinrich set the pace, his standard bearer riding hard beside him. Far to his right, Rudolf of Swabia led the charge toward the Saxons' left flank, while Otto of Meissen would crash into the Saxon's right flank. Otto had been one of Heinrich's father's vassals and continued in his loyalty to Heinrich although the emperor suspected that Otto did not feel he lived up to his father's accomplishments. Heinrich was still relatively young, however, and would have the opportunity to prove himself to his father's retainer. More importantly, this war might allow him to break away from his mother's controlling hand.

The first Saxon arrows began to fall when Heinrich was about halfway down the hill, sticking into the ground ahead of him. The Saxon bows did not have the range to hit him, yet. Soon that would change.

Seeing that combat was about to be entered, Heinrich stood in his stirrups and waved his army forward.

CHAPTER XIII

When Leofwine called for the first hail of arrows, he knew the Germans were still out of range for the four foot bows his men carried. Nevertheless, starting the attack could mean drawing first blood against the Germans.

The first volley of arrows was sent into the air where they disappeared against the black smoke still emanating from the fires of Botulph's Town. Leofwine thought back to the monks' standard description from the chronicles: *the sky was black with arrows*. Today they could truthfully say the sky was black, although whether the cause was actually the arrows or the soot was anybody's guess.

On the fifth volley of arrows, Leofwine finally saw one of the Germans fall from his horse, pierced in the shoulder by the arrow.

CHAPTER XIV

Aethelwine couldn't help but think that Harold's strategy was strange. There was nothing, literally, the Saxons could accomplish by not attacking the oncoming wave of Germans. All Harold was doing was allowing the Germans to smash into the Saxon lines. Harold knew that a moving army hitting a standing army the way the Germans were about to do would cut through their enemy like a boat through water.

Aethelwine wasn't sure how long he could keep his men from rushing forward. During battle, the two natural reactions were to either rush toward your enemy or run away from your enemy. Standing still was not normal. Aethelwine had the feeling that the longer his men stood in one place, the harder it would be to get them to move forward.

When Leofwine's men began to loose arrows at the oncoming army, Aethelwine was relieved. He had managed to hold his men back, against his own better judgment, long enough for the battle to start. As Leofwine's third volley of arrows flew into the sky, Aethelwine signaled for his own men to begin to fire their arrows.

CHAPTER XV

The hail of arrows which had begun to fall on Rudolf of Swabia and his men were a nuisance, but not much more. Few of his men fell from their horses under the Saxon archers. Even when the arrows hit, they tended to glance off the mail worn by the Swabians.

Rudolf could tell that the attack actually was improving his men's morale. They had finally met the enemy, even if there had been no hand-to-hand combat yet. The Saxon attack, for all its ferocity, was proving ineffectual. Buoyed by their victories since reaching the English shore, and burning and looting the city which still burned after two days, the Swabians felt nearly invincible.

Although Rudolf usually expected the worst when he entered battle, the ease with which the Germans were going to destroy the Saxons made him wonder why William the Bastard had not been able to invade this country. All stories of the Norman made him sound invincible, almost akin to Charlemagne or the Saxon's own Arthur. The Saxons who beat William back two years ago had demonstrated that they were hardly more than boys who should be hiding behind their mothers' skirts.

Rudolf's shouts of encouragement to his men could easily be heard above the muted thunder of horsehooves on the snow-covered ground.

CHAPTER XVI

Harold knew the time had almost come. Soon, Heinrich would reach the river at the bottom of the hill and the Saxon forces would have to be released against the Germans, their distant cousins. If Harold won, he would still have to force the Frenchmen from his land, but he had done that before.

Harold had never known an England free of invaders. Although his father loved Cnut, the king who had raised Godwin from the masses was a Dane, not a Saxon. His two Danish sons also cared more for their distant land than they did for England. When Hardecnut had fallen over at a banquet, Harold had looked to Edward as a return to English sovereignty despite Godwin's warnings against the *aetheling*. In the end, Godwin had been proved right, as so often happened. Edward may have been born of King Aethelred, but he was no more English than his slut of a mother who married Cnut after Aethelred died.

The Battle of Botulph's Town, as Harold already thought of today's engagement, would decide whether England would exist as its own land or be replaced by some papal state.

"Look!" Eric shouted, clasping his free hand on Harold's shoulder to point out where the German army was hitting the base of the hill.

Without waiting to see the outcome, Harold told Eric to signal the English advance.

CHAPTER XVII

At the bottom of the hill, the snow seemed strange. Heinrich realized why and tried to stop his horse, but his speed was too great and he couldn't stop his horse from plunging onto the ice which covered the river winding its way along the base of the hill. Nor could he stop the rush of horses and men which followed him down into the freezing water beneath the thin layer of ice.

He wrestled to get his horse out the other side of the river, swinging his sword to help break the ice covering. Eventually he managed to get out of the river, but he could tell that too many men were stuck either in the river or on the far side, away from the Saxon army. Worse yet, those few Germans who were on his side of the river had no means of retreat.

CHAPTER XVIII

Seeing the Germans struggling in the frigid waters gave the Saxons heart they hadn't shown since their first attempt to repel the German landing parties a week earlier. Suddenly, victory seemed to be within their reach.

AFTER HASTINGS

With a shout, the Saxons rushed forward, often outpacing their leaders in the mad dash to be the first to shed German blood. Aethelwine found himself chasing after the men he was supposed to be leading, trying to regain his position at the front of the army to no avail. When he finally did reach the river's edge, he found an unparalleled scene of butchery, reminding him of nothing less than the bloodbath at Stamford Bridge. Within the first moments of battle, the river ran red with the blood of Germans caught in its icy grasp. Saxons stood on the shore dropping their swords and axes onto the Germans like farmers working their hoes.

The Germans could either try to defend themselves or struggle to get clear of the icy river they had fallen into. To make matters even better for the Saxons, more of the Germans continued in their rush down the slopes of the hill to fall on their comrades already in the river. Aethelwine wondered when they river would be so full a Saxon or German could simply walk across on the heads, bodies, and corpses of those already in the water without getting his feet wet.

Even as these thoughts filtered through his mind, Aethelwine began the thoughtless and methodical task of killing the near helpless Germans who lay foundering in the river. He did not like to think of the carnage of battle. Although he knew some men gloried in the blood they shed, he was not one of them.

CHAPTER XIX

Normally, Sigeweard Bearn enjoyed the feel of flesh giving way beneath his sword, the sound of a skull opening when he hit it with his axe. Today was different. He was not a warrior in battle. He was a butcher killing helpless lambs and cows. This was not a task to be set before a nobleman. It should be relegated to the thegns and ceorls who were more suited to the bloody work.

There was no glory in the reaping of souls he was doing. Only the repetitious lifting and falling of his arm as he cleaved another head and hacked another arm.

The aroma of blood filled his nostrils, as welcome today as ever. The smell of bread, giving him sustenance and filling his body with strength. Near the edge of the river, Sigeweard Bearn saw a German rise from the water, using his half frozen horse as if it were a stile.

Running toward the German nobleman, Sigeweard Bearn cried ownership, raising his axe to finally meet an opponent who could possibly fight back.

CHAPTER XX

Otto of Meissen fought his way clear of the water and stood for a moment on the solid shore. His horse stood, dead, in the water behind him, held erect by the force of ice and bodies it was wedged against. Before he even had a chance to catch his breath he heard a Saxon cry, "He's mine!" Looking in the direction of the yell, he saw a huge Saxon bearing down on him, his battle axe raised to deliver a blow.

Otto pulled his sword free of his scabbard and lifted it to catch the first strike of the axe. As he did so, he felt a shiver run through his body, not able to tell if it came from the shock of the blow or the cold air acting on the water which coated his body.

After the first blow, the Saxon dropped his axe to the snow. Otto tried to use the moment he had to his advantage, but another shiver ran through his body and weakened his swing. By the time he managed to bring his sword around at the Saxon, the man had pulled his own sword free and was stabbing at Otto's gut.

The big Saxon had a greater reach than Otto and was not suffering from the shivers which increasingly ran through his body. He tried to parry the Saxon's thrusts without even attempting a repost. He could tell he was outmatched and would be unable to kill or defeat this Saxon. Otto's best hope was to retreat from his fearsome opponent.

Even as he thought of retreat, he felt a burning sensation in his gut. He glanced down to see the Saxon's blade buried to the guard in his stomach. Looking up, Otto saw a grin on the man's face and heard his strangely accented voice.

"When you arrive in hell, tell your tormentor Sigeweard Bearn slew you."

CHAPTER XXI

Of the four Saxon armies which faced the Germans, only Harold's managed to maintain their shieldwall formation once they arrived at the river. They were opposing Heinrich's men, and the largest number of Germans who had actually managed to climb out of the river before the Saxons had arrived.

The formation simply put the Saxons into a position where they could easily use their roundshields to catch enemy blows and turn them aside while striking with their own short swords. Although the Germans had managed to gain the shore, few of them were in condition to put up a serious fight. The Saxon swords were in far more use than the Saxon shields.

Over the cries and screams of Germans dying on the shore and in the river, Harold could hear cries of "Harold" and "England" from his men. He had forbidden the cries of "Holy Cross" which had filled the air at Hastings. The Germans were too occupied with their dooms to even attempt a rally. Their cries, when intelligible, were for assistance from their fellows or from their God.

Harold searched through the bodies of both living and dead in an attempt to find Heinrich. If the German emperor had managed to gain the shore, Harold wanted to send him from England himself. Although the Saxons had come from lands now under Heinrich's control, Harold did not want to open the way for any more invasions.

CHAPTER XXII

Leofwine felt cheated in a strange sense. He had missed out on most of the fighting at Skipton, arriving in time to witness the end of the battle. The battle which raged around him now was hardly a battle. It was slaughter. Whenever Leofwine saw a German trying to emerge from the river, the man was cut down before he could gain solid ground.

He hated to join in with his men killing the defenseless Germans. He would almost rather help them from the river, with the stipulation that they leave England, never to return, but that would have made a bad example for the men he led.

Swinging his sword to decapitate one of the Germans, Leofwine's foot slipped on a piece of ice. Leofwine tried to catch himself as he fell, but he landed on his hand the wrong way and his sword flew into the snow where it buried itself. His wrist felt as if it were broken and he couldn't stop his slide into the icy water which held so many of his enemies.

Reaching for his knife with his left hand, Leofwine thought how ironic he had just been thinking of helping the Germans out of the water and now he was in a situation as bad as they were. Worse, actually, since if the Germans realized he was a Saxon they would be trying to kill him as well.

Leofwine tried to struggle up the river bank. He had fallen into a part of the river where the ice had mostly broken away, but the water was filled with the blue corpses of men already killed. Beneath his feet, it was impossible to tell whether he was stepping on mud or bodies. He really didn't want to know.

A sharp pain in his arm announced that one of his men had seen him and mistaken him for a German. Leofwine tried to shout for the man to stop and help him out of the water, but the thegn either couldn't hear the earl or thought he was a German. Moving in the water made it difficult for Leofwine to dodge the man's blows.

The next time the axe came down at him, Leofwine grabbed it on the shaft just below the blade, dropping his knife in the process. He tried to lift himself out of the water using the pole for support, but the thegn let go of the axe, causing Leofwine to drop back into the water further from the riverbank than he had started out.

The drag of the water made the axe useless as a means of attack, but Leofwine tried to hold onto it while he inched his way through the water to the river's edge. Around him were mostly dead and dying Germans. Although he could hear Germans moving in the distance, few near him were alive and still actively trying to get out of the river.

Drowning seemed to account for the majority of the German deaths where he was. Their bloated faces continuously pressed against him as he tried to make his way to the bank. The one good thing about being surrounded by dead Germans was that it meant fewer Saxons were in the area trying to kill him.

Leofwine suddenly realized that he had gotten turned around. He no longer knew which bank he wanted to head toward. In fact, he was having a difficult time determining which direction the banks of the river were and which way the river ran.

Leofwine continued to wade through the bodies, pushing them aside as if they were merely logs floating on the river instead of people who had been alive and breathing when the day began. His progress was slow, both because of the water and the bodies. More than anything else, Leofwine wanted to reach the shore so he could lie down and sleep.

He stumbled a couple of times on bodies and rocks, and had to work hard to break the surface again. Eventually, Leofwine crawled from the river onto the frozen earth, covered with the slush of trampled snow and bodies of men who had managed to get out of the water before they died.

Exhaustion overcame him and once clear of the water Leofwine closed his eyes and fell asleep among the dead Germans.

CHAPTER XXIII

Heinrich realized he had no choice. He had to sound retreat. His army had been destroyed around him. Worst of all, the Saxons were not the cause of his defeat. He had been defeated by winter. By cold.

Even as he was making his decision, he was fighting for his life. Saxons pressed around him tightly, each trying to strike the blow that would kill the German who had the temerity to make it across the deathtrap of a river and, worse yet, fight against them.

He fought without thinking. Lunge, parry, parry, thrust. Friedrich, his arms tutor, would be proud of him. Friedrich might be proud of him, but Otto would never show any respect to Heinrich after this fiasco. If Otto thought Heinrich unsuitable for following in his father's footsteps before, this massacre would kill any chance of gaining Otto's respect Heinrich may have had.

Heinrich felt his sword bite deeply into flesh and pulled hard to remove it. When the body in front of him fell away, he saw a pathway beyond the men who clustered around him. Opened miraculously by his sword's blade.

He stepped over the fallen man he had just slain and ran from the fighting. Although some of the Saxons gave chase, more of them concentrated on the battle that still raged around them.

AFTER HASTINGS

Once free of the battle, Heinrich tried to get some idea of what was happening. The river lay clogged with the bodies of his vassals. More were dying on the side of the river he was on. Up the hill, German archers were loosing arrows toward the Saxon position, hitting Saxon more often than German merely because the Saxons outnumbered the Germans.

Heinrich, himself, was bleeding from a score or more of wounds he had received. None of them seemed particularly deep, although a cut on his temple was bleeding in a steady stream. Despite the cold, he felt warm from his exertion in battle.

Near where he stood, he saw a trumpet lying on the ground where a herald had dropped it. Although dented, it would still work. Heinrich had seen servants blow trumpets at court all his life. It did not look too difficult to get a sound to emerge from the horn.

After repeated tries, he managed to get the horn to squeak. Nobody would ever mistake him for a trumpeter. He managed to make a noise close enough to his call for retreat that some of the Germans on the other side of river began to flee the site of carnage. Once a few men began to run, the dam broke and any Germans who could escape the English wrath fled for safety. Heinrich set off to the north, hoping to find a place to cross the river and regroup with his men before returning to Bavaria.

CHAPTER XXIV

When the horns sounded, Harold was not entirely sure what was happening. The fighting near him did not change much, although he noticed that fewer arrows fell among his men. There were still Germans to be slaughtered and his arm rose and fell, hacking and cleaving, accompanied by a burning sensation which gave him a clue as to how sore and stiff he would be after the battle.

If he survived. After the battle, he would have to arrange to have Leofwine or Aethelwine go after the remnants of the German army. The other he would take with him and Sigeweard Bearn south to relieve the siege at London. First a fight against the Northerners at the river, then a frantic ride south to beat the French. Stamford Bridge, Hastings, Botulph's Town, London. He was repeating the same events two years later.

Yet so much had changed between Hastings and Botulph's Town.

"The Germans are fleeing!"

A voice shouted nearly directly in Harold's ear. He looked over to see Eric, a huge smile on his face, had somehow managed to stay with him throughout the battle.

"On the other side of the river!" he shouted, "They're breaking and running!"

"Take prisoners!" Harold shouted, a cry which began to echo back and forth across the valley as more and more Saxons shouted it.

CHAPTER XXV

No sign had been found of Heinrich after the battle, although several of his barons had been found dead on the shore or in the water. Several other barons had been taken captive, the highest of whom was Duke Rudolf of Swabia. Harold's priests estimated that more than two thousand Germans had died.

In all, fewer than one hundred Saxons lay dead on the field at Botulph's Town. Nevertheless, Harold grieved, for Leofwine, his last brother, had been found a corpse on the banks of the river. Harold alone remained of Godwin's sons. Despite Aethelwine's presence, Harold was alone. He hated having to break the news to Gytha.

"Aethelwine, you must hound the remnants of the German army until there is not one German left on English soil. Sigeweard Bearn, you will join me as we ride to London. The French must be taught the same lesson we've taught the Germans.

CHAPTER XXVI

The glory of war continued to elude Philippe. While the Londoners sat in their warm homes in front of raging fires, Philippe, King of the Franks, sat in snow.

"I don't remember ever having a winter this cold. I almost believe this land is God-forsaken as the pope and Théobald claim," Guillaume rubbed his hands together near the fire. When the temperature dropped, Philippe had reluctantly tried to send Guillaume away from the siege, but the ancient advisor steadfastly refused to desert his king on the eve of battle.

"Your blood is thin. Perhaps you're just feeling the cold more than you used to," Philippe did not sound convinced.

"My blood may be thin, but I imagine yours is not. Yet you seem to be suffering the cold as much as I am."

Even as Guillaume made his observation, Philippe shivered. For all the luxury his tent afforded, it was still made of cloth, easily pierced by the winds whipping amongst the siege camp. Three fires blazed within its walls, yet their heat could only be felt within a short distance.

Exercising his royal prerogative, Philippe ignored Guillaume's comment. Théobald would be arriving soon and Philippe wanted to be ready to discuss the possibility of making something happen in the stalemate between the French and the English. He turned his attention to a plot of bare dirt which had an outline of the city's walls and the river sketched into it.

The problem, Philippe reflected again, was that the Londoners still had control of the river after nearly a month. They were able to ferry themselves back and forth to Southwark almost at will and bring in the supplies they needed. Whenever the Franks tried to dock at London's quays, they were repulsed by the Saxons.

In recent days, large blocks of ice had been seen floating in the river and the water had frozen solid along the banks. Philippe had some ideas about how he could use the ice and cold weather to his advantage, but wanted to hear Théobald's opinions before he put his plan into action.

"Guillaume," he called. Looking over at his advisor, he noticed that the old man had fallen asleep. Rather than wake him, he returned to his strategy. Guillaume would hear the plan when Théobald arrived.

The last time he had looked, the ice extended nearly five feet into the river, not exceptionally far, but it appeared to be solid. With care, men might be able to use the ice to make their way around the walls on both the north and the south. A carefully planned maneuver might permit one of the groups to enter the city and open the gates.

As he plotted the best way to get his men into the city, Philippe realized something was wrong. He couldn't recall ever having been with Guillaume when the old man was sleeping when his snores weren't loud enough to wake the dead. Moving over to him, Philippe realized that Guillaume was no longer breathing.

When Théobald arrived in the tent, he found the king slumped over Guillaume's lifeless body.

"Your majesty."

Théobald walked over to the king and tried to pull him from the old man's corpse. The king held on to Guillaume's body as if he had a deathgrip on him.

"We must discuss your plans for ending this siege and taking the city."

Philippe turned his head and looked at Théobald through the tears that coursed down his cheeks.

"Why?" he asked, defiance mixed with authority and grief in his voice.

It wasn't until this moment, when Philippe was acting his most childish, that Théobald realized that he had begun to think of the king as a man some time during the campaign. He was stunned by the realization but had to press forward prying Philippe away from his dead advisor.

"Guillaume had a long life. Extremely long. It is time that he was reunited with God. We'll call a priest to take care of his soul. However, Guillaume is in a better place than this. And warmer, I trust. The Saxons are still ensconced in London, waiting for us to drive them out."

As he spoke, Théobald moved to the door of the tent and motioned for one of Philippe's guards. When the man approached, Théobald quietly asked him for a priest. Philippe had allowed Théobald to take him a short distance from Guillaume's body, but continued to look back at him.

"I haven't seen a dead man since my father's funeral. It isn't the same. Henri was dressed in his most splendid robes and smelled of fennel and aniseed. There was no clue that he was anything but dead. Almost gloriously dead.

"Guillaume, though. I thought he was asleep until I realized he wasn't snoring. He doesn't smell like spices the way Henri did. He smells more like. . . incontinence." Philippe wrinkled his nose when he identified the aroma.

Théobald nodded invisibly behind Philippe's head. "Loosening of one's bowels is common when one dies. King Henri had been prepared by his physicians before he lay in state. As deaths go, Guillaume's was a peaceable and clean one."

While Théobald was speaking several priests arrived and began to administer extreme unction to the body. Théobald led Philippe away from the corpse and sat him down with the king's back to Guillaume.

"You said you had an idea of getting in to London," Théobald prompted.

Philippe sat in silence for a few moments, answering just as Théobald had given up hope for an answer.

"I have been defeated by London. It is time to return to Paris."

"Pardon! You can not return to France now. We are in the midst of battle. You will weaken the monarchy further and never be able to gain the respect of your barons and dukes."

"If I remain here, I will prove to my dukes and barons merely that at sixteen years of age I remain a tool of Pope Alexander and Count Baldwin. The one a man who claims divine inspiration, although it does not seem to be availing him any in England. The other a man who claims to be my vassal yet acts like my lord.

"I shall return to Paris and I shall demonstrate I am a king in my own right. Not merely a puppet who speaks the words Baldwin would have me speak. I know my position is not as exalted as I might wish. My barons rule their lands without a care for my decree, nothing has changed in the eight years since Henri's death, although Baldwin is stronger now than he was then."

As Philippe spoke, Théobald noticed a new level of authority in his voice. Another indication that he was a man, not a boy. Théobald would have to speak with Baldwin to find out what the count wanted to do next.

Without asking Théobald's permission or approval, Philippe called to one of the servants in the cluster near the tent's opening, "Tomorrow is a day of *pax dei*. Arrange for a meeting with Æthelric. He may bring only one advisor. Perhaps that Ligulf fellow. He seemed to be in charge of the citizenry."

Philippe looked at Guillaume's body, now surrounded by priests and physicians. When he turned back to look at Théobald, there was a fire of independence in his eyes.

"I will inform the archbishop of my decision to return to Paris and leave his city intact. Perhaps for the mere amount of one hundred pounds of gold. I'm sure he will agree to that."

CHAPTER XXVII

Even in the coldest winter, which England seemed to be experiencing, Svannehals loved the feel of the wind blowing through her long hair as she galloped along the open fields of the Cotswolds. It was something she had not been able to do enough in recent years. More importantly, it allowed her to leave the confines of Harold's court, wherever it happened to be located and the close-minded shrewish women who never forgave her the fact that she had caught the eye and heart of the king.

It had been nearly sixteen years since Svannehals had first met Harold, then only the second son of the most powerful earl in the kingdom. Godwin had already abandoned the laughable idea of Harold's entrance into the priesthood. His son, all his sons, would follow in his footsteps and become powerful barons. Of course, that was in the days before Godwin and his clan had been exiled to Ireland for opposing old King Edward.

Her eldest son, Godwin, had been born during that exile. Harold had not seen him until after he was able to return to England. Those days had been full of fear that her child would never get to see his father. Fear that he would be branded a bastard, unable to rise to any station of import. Of course, that was before William the Bastard had made a name for himself.

Now, those fears were in the distant past. Her son, one of her sons at any rate, would sit upon the throne of England. He would rule the island, both its people and its Church. Once she and Harold were married by the Scottish archbishop, their children would lose the taint of illegitimacy which had branded them for the last fifteen years.

Almost of equal import, the women of the court would serve her. They would no longer be able to look down on her, despite her lineage and relationship to the king.

Coming over a rise, the castle at Sarum came into view. Her ride, which had lasted for most of the morning was coming to an end. Even as her reddened cheeks stung with the pain of the cold, she enjoyed her final moments of freedom before returning to the walls of Sarum Castle even as she thought of how nice the fires of Sarum would feel to her chilled bones.

When she rode into the courtyard, she leapt from her horse and turned the animal over to one of the grooms. Now that she was on the verge of being queen, there was no reason for her to rub down the sweaty sides of her horse. That was the reason for having servants.

She entered the castle and walked through the narrow halls. Occasional thin windows permitted only the smallest amount of light into the dark passageways. Torch smoke filled the low ceilings and clung to her hair and clothes. Sarum was one of her least favorite places to stay. Nevertheless, Harold had ordered her to remain in the dingy castle while he was off fighting the Germans in the north.

"Sarum is far from where the Germans and French will be landing. If they manage to make it that far, chances are I'll no longer be king," he had explained before leading his army out of Winchester.

Knowing that her exile had been imposed for her own protection did not make Svannehals any more happy about it. Instead of being in one of her preferred castles, with people she liked, she was relegated to a drafty castle and the small-minded women who lived in Sarum.

The Great Hall of Sarum Castle had been taken over by those women, and although she had no desire to see them, that was the room Svannehals found herself in. The room had reasonably large windows and was well lit, permitting the women to continue with their embroidery. Svannehals recognized the tapestry they were working on as the piece commissioned by the traitor, Morkere. After his death, Leofwine had taken over the patronage of the project. Svannehals noted with glee that while some of the women were extending the story, still working on the battle at Senlac, others were pulling out threads to eradicate Morkere from his position of honor. More important were the women pulling the thread which had formed the images of the slut Harold had married to help solidify his claim to the throne.

AFTER HASTINGS

Trying to ignore their presence, Svannehals pulled a chair in front of the large hearth and warmed herself in front of the fire. She could feel the women looking up from their embroidery to stare at her, but she refused to give them the satisfaction of an acknowledgment.

Svannehals enjoyed the way the flames leapt at random, forming strange patterns. Long ago, some priest had told her that flames were the work of the devil, but she could not believe that anything so beautiful could have been created by the devil. She sat back in her chair, allowing the warmth of the fire to remove the chill from her body and motioned to a servant to bring her a goblet of mulled wine.

The warm liquid took the chill away from her insides as easily as the flames heated her flesh. She closed her eyes and tried to tune out the chattering of the women around her.

She recognized the nasel voice of Gunnhildr. There was nothing about the woman that Svannehals liked. Gunnhildr was an obese cow who had tried to undermine Svannehals since the day Harold was proclaimed king of the English. She would be among the first Svannehals had her revenge on when Harold made her queen. *Something suitable*, Svannehals thought, *to remind Gunnhildr of the time she took my etui shortly before I finished stitching the shirt I made for Harold and couldn't present it him on his birthday.*

Eventually, Gunnhildr stopped talking. The other women's voices flowed into each other, lulling Svannehals into a light sleep. Svannehals did not know how much time had passed before a servant approached her to tell her that a messenger had come from the king. She worked to tuck her hair back into place and she waited for the messenger to be brought into the Great Hall.

A young man was escorted into Svannehals's presence. Dirt was caked to his ragged clothing and he looked as if he had been through a bloody battle, although the cut on his cheek seemed as if it had almost healed.

When the man spoke, his voice came out in a harsh croak, hardly audible and certainly not understandable. Looking past him, Svannehals could see that the other women did not even notice the small man. For a moment, she felt a sort of sympathy for the man, a desire to like him in spite of the women working on their embroidery. A second look at the man made her realize how silly she was being.

He tried to speak again, his rasping voice torturing her ears. In annoyance, she gestured for some ale to be brought to the man. He drank the amber liquid like a dog, lapping at the goblet's bowl to get every drop as if he had been deprived of liquid for weeks. Svannehals watched his display of gluttony with distaste.

Letting out a long sigh, the man put the empty goblet on the table next to Svannehals's chair, a forlorn look on his face showing that he wanted more ale but could not bring himself to ask for it. Svannehals ignored the pleading expression.

Clearing his throat, he finally spoke, "I am come from King Harold at Peterborough, on his way to relieve the City of London from siege."

"He's riding toward London? Does that mean he defeated the Germans?"

"In a battle which the bards will sing of until the Second Coming," the man replied. "Ten thousand Germans attacked one thousand Saxons, yet the Saxons were victorious."

When he spoke of the battle, a fire blazed in the battered man's eyes, quickly to dim as he turned his thoughts from the glories of war.

"The king is safe, but his brother has fallen." The man spoke the message which had been entrusted to him with little emotion. Svannehals couldn't tell if it was because he didn't care or because the violence he had seen inured him to Leofwine's death.

The messenger continued without giving Svannehals a chance to sort out her feelings, "The king hopes to end the siege of London quickly and plans to hold his Christmas Court in Lincoln. He hopes the Lady Svannehals will join him at Lincoln Castle.

Svannehals's prayers had been answered. Not only would she be able to leave drafty old Sarum, but she would be able to go up to Lincoln, one of her favorite residences. The castle stood on the top of a hill, overlooking the countryside for miles, only a few steps from the cathedral.

She dismissed the messenger and quickly set into motion the plans which would move her court up to Lincoln. Her joy at leaving Sarum was only compounded by the consternation she knew the other women at the court would go through at news of their departure.

CHAPTER XXVIII

Hildebrand had been dreading the letter he knew Alexander would send him ever since he heard of Heinrich's defeat. He had been spending the time working on a new tract, *De obedientia regis*. Piled next to the vellum scroll on which he wrote, were literally dozens of other scrolls. He searched through them to find a copy of the *Vita Constantini*. Although the author claimed to be the great bishop Eusebius, Hildebrand had a feeling that it had been written much later. Eusebius' rhetorical style had been vastly different from the man who wrote the *vita*. He had just begun to unroll the vellum when there was a knock on the door.

Exasperated, he scanned through the headings on the scroll, trying quickly to find the passage he was looking for. The knock sounded again and Hildebrand barked out a harsh cry of "Enter!"

Pierre, one of the French servants he had been forced to hire, entered the room.

"*Pardon, sieur.*"

"In Latin, Petrus."

The servant began in his hesitating Latin, "Excuse me, lord, but the pope, he is here to see you."

Hildebrand stared at the idiot. Obviously the pope's messenger had finally arrived with the dreaded letter. Hildebrand could see no reason to put it off. His work on *De obedientia regis* was already interrupted.

"Send him up."

After Pierre disappeared, Hildebrand turned his attention back to the *Vita Constantini*. Constantine was an excellent source and inspiration for Hildebrand. He had proved himself a powerful king, yet was obedient to the wills of his religious advisors, at least the Christian ones who were the only ones who mattered. Hildebrand found the passage easily enough and began to transcribe it onto the vellum in a careful hand.

On the advice of Julian, the bishop of Tarsus, Constantine decided to leave Rome behind and move his capital to the small village of Byzantium, which he renamed for himself.

Hildebrand had just finished writing the passage when the door opened. He looked up to rebuke the presumptuous messenger and saw Pope Alexander standing in the portal.

"Your Grace. I had not expected the pleasure of your company." The words seemed stilted even to Hildebrand's own ears. He had never stood on formality with Alexander before, yet could not help himself.

Alexander walked into the room in silence. As he approached the table, Hildebrand could see his eyes skim the title tags which hung from the scrolls. After making his quick inventory of Hildebrand's desk, Alexander turned his back on the legate and walked to the fire, blazing on the hearth. He practically stuck his hands into the flames.

"Sometimes I think living a long life is a curse rather than a blessing. The cold gets into your bones and refuses to leave."

"Soon you will be back in Rome where the climate is more favorable than in France."

Alexander turned his back to the fire and Hildebrand could see anger in his features. "The temperature may be warmer in Rome, but the political climate will be as harsh as any winter the world has ever seen. I have to face the College of Cardinals who will want to know how my Holy Alliance could have been defeated so easily by the English. I'll have to deal with Heinrich, who feels I owe him something for his troubles even if he couldn't achieve victory. Instead of being able to point out that *he* saved

England for Christ, he'll rebuke me with having lost him hundreds or thousands of men on a fruitless expedition. Here in France, I have that *child*, Philippe, just waiting for me to give him a chance to press his desire to be an emperor, or worse, to join the heretic in England." Alexander spit into the fireplace.

"This is not the end of the battle. We must continue to fight against the English heresy until it is stamped out. It is a blemish on the face of Christendom," Hildebrand protested.

"Fight with what? The French? I might be able to persuade a couple of the dukes and barons to fight for me, but never the Normans or King Philippe. Heinrich would never submit to my will enough to risk even more men in battle against the English. The Normans in Sicilia are more likely to attack me in Rome than the distant English. There are no more warriors to fight for our cause."

Alexander had been pacing back and force across the room while he spoke to Hildebrand. As he finished speaking, he came to a rest in front of a small mirror and examined his face.

"Do you know what I see when I look at this reflection?" The pope's tone was suddenly casual, calm, pondering.

"The pope, I imagine, yourself."

"No. I see myself, but not the pope. I see Anselm of Baggio. A young priest at Lanfranc's school at Bec, hoping to make his way through this world helping people with their spiritual needs. This was long before I went to old Heinrich's, *pace requisivit*, court. Back then I had such great hopes and ambitions. Not for myself, ambition was never one of my sins, but for the world. Pride. That was my sin. I thought I could do some good. I think the happiest day in my life was when I was ordained at Milan, only thirteen years ago. I had my whole future to help people. By the time I was made bishop of Lucca two years later, I had already begun to discover that I could not make as much of a difference as I had hoped. Regret tinged the holiness of that day for me.

"I'm surprised that I can still see any sign of Anselm in this mirror. I thought he had died while I was a bishop. Taking the name 'Alexander,' I thought I had laid him to rest. Instead, I now find myself haunted by the ghost of that innocent and hopeful young boy. He's been trying to advise me for seven years, ever since you arranged my election to the pontificate. I should try to take advice from him, no matter how young he is."

Alexander fell silent and Hildebrand had no idea what to say so he allowed the silence to fill the room, almost tangibly. Eventually, Alexander moved away from the mirror, his back still toward Hildebrand.

"Sometimes I wonder if that young Anselm is actually the voice of God trying to give me guidance, may He have mercy on my soul for even considering that I might be worthy to hear His voice."

"I am sure that He speaks to you often, if not as a voice then in your dreams and inspirations."

"I wish I could feel as certain of that as you are. I wonder that He found me deserving to sit on the throne of saints Peter and Leo and Gregory."

"He has also permitted men such as Benedict Theophylact and Sergius *Buccaporci* to sit on the throne."

"You try to comfort me, but have I not done more damage to the papacy than those you mention? I lost England. *England*, Hildebrand. At night I lay in bed and hear Gregory the Great weep for his lost angels."

"Did not Leo lose Byzantium shortly before you were ordained? A much greater loss than England."

Alexander now turned to look at Hildebrand, fury once more burning on his face. "You take glee that one of my predecessors lost all those souls to hell! My crime is not slight compared to Leo's, it exacerbates his loss of Byzantium to the forces of the devil," Alexander crossed himself, "My crime is one in which you share. It was you who goaded me into continuing war against Harold."

"I find myself in need of a new ambassador. Archdeacon Lambert has not proved as useful in his position as I had hoped and I believe I have a post for which he is better suited. I would have you relieve him of his current duties."

Hildebrand had to think before he realized that Lambert was a papal legate serving in Constantinople.

"I beg you, Father, do not send me back to Constantinople. I will serve you and the Church anywhere else. I have been to Constantinople and find the place to my intense dislike."

"I need someone in Byzantium and you have experience there, no matter your opinions of the place. I have faith you will not allow them to intercede with your duties. Look upon this as an opportunity. Byzantium has already turned her back on true Christianity. You have lost England, perhaps He will permit you to redeem your soul and the Byzantines at the same time."

CHAPTER XXIX

Light filtered through the stained glass windows, painting the swirling motes of dust all the colors of the rainbow above the heads of the nuns sitting in their hard wooden pews. At the front of the nave, a priest knelt at a prie-dieu. In front of the priest, an enormous crucifix hung suspended by thin wires from the rafters.

Edith regarded the narrow stained glass windows, a rarity even here in France, they testified to the wealth of the nunnery to which Pope Alexander had sent her. She was not a nun by inclination or temperament, but found herself either unwilling or unable to refuse Alexander's command although she felt she could do more good somewhere else. The pope, she realized, simply wanted her out of the way.

Ignoring the Latin hocus pocus the priest was chanting, Edith thought back on her life since Harold had taken her away from Wales and Gruffydd. It seemed her lot in life to marry barbarians, first the obvious wildness of the Welsh prince and then the more cultured and hidden barbarity of Harold.

Looking back on her life with Harold, she should have realized that he would quickly tire of her and return to his slut, Svannehals. Even after she had married him, it was obvious that he would put her aside once her brother had died and Harold no longer had a reason for keeping her as his wife. His break from the Roman Church simply made his actions easier.

Edith couldn't lie to herself. Harold had not, in the end, put her aside, she had fled from her marriage. Despite all Harold's other crimes against God, she alone was guilty of deserting her marriage. Edith looked on her internment at the nunnery as an act of penance for her sin.

Surrounding her in this house of God were her sisters in nunnery. Most of whom, she imagined, held more deeply their belief in God. Instead of adding depth to her own belief, Edith found herself questioning her religion more now that she was in the nunnery. She had never considered herself evil or wanton, yet she was being punished for sins she did not remember committing. Her thoughts turned to Christ who asked God why He had forsaken His son and she wondered why He had forsaken her.

Edith was jolted from her introspection by the rest of the congregation rising to their feet. She belatedly joined them as the nuns began to shuffle forward to receive communion. The wafer seemed to stick in her throat and it was only the briefest sip of wine the priest permitted her that allowed her to dislodge the wafer. An evil omen.

She returned to her seat and endured the remainder of the Christmas Mass. In truth, life as a nun was not that much different than life as a queen.

After Mass was over, she would retreat to a common room to work. While monks frequently worked in the fields, nuns would sew and stitch and embroider. Exactly the activities which formed the bulk of Edith's occupation when she lived under Harold's room in England. Or Gruffydd's in Wales. Or her father's in Northumbria. All that really changed was to whom her obedience was. Father to husband to God. She had moved up the hierarchy and each step up the ladder had made her less and less powerful.

CHAPTER XXX

Harold sat alone in his chambers at Lincoln Castle. A solitary candle offered the room's only illumination. From outside, he could hear the joyful sounds rising from the courtyard. His friends and subjects were making merry in celebrating the Epiphany, which coincided with the anniversary of his own coronation. He thought back to the audience he held two long years earlier when he thought he was going to receive the pope's blessing. He would never have thought, at the time, that he would neither receive nor care about receiving Alexander's blessing.

In the wake of his victory over the Magnus Feodus, Harold already heard that Hildebrand had fallen out of papal favor. He was being sent back to his old post in Byzantium to try to arrange an end to the raids Harold's emissary had inspired. Harold vaguely recalled Hildebrand once saying how much he had hated Byzantium.

Carefully peeling the window covering back, he looked out over the revelry below. Eventually, he would make his appearance, dressed as one of the Magi who brought gifts to the Christ child. Somewhere below, he knew, Archbishops Colum-cille and Æthelric were dressed as the other wise men. The archbishop of London had initially protested against the mummery, which he called sacrilegious, but eventually came around to Colum-cille's urging, especially after Colum-cille hinted that Æthelric's reluctance hinted at popish inclinations.

Colum-cille was proving interesting. Had he been a baron, like Aethelwine, or even a thegn, like Eric, Harold could have become close friends with him. Instead, he was archbishop of York, and Harold's enemy. Or if not enemy, an antagonist.

Harold's musings were interrupted by a knock on the door. Before Harold could offer admittance, Aethelwine entered the room.

"I was just thinking I could like Colum-cille if I didn't have to get him to approve of my actions," Harold commented, as Aethelwine helped himself to a glass of ale. "I can't say I'm entirely happy with his solution to the dilemma with that Canterbury monk, but I suppose he did what he had to do. Of course, that just means I have to move on and try to get his approval for declaring my marriage to Edith null and permit me to marry Svannehals. Once that happens, we'll have to arrange for my sons to be legitimized."

Aethelwine laughed, "It sounds to me as if you have several year's worth of battles with Colum-cille alone."

Harold shook his head. "Battles with Colum-cille are not what worry me. I worry about the next attack by Alexander."

"Alexander does not have the men to attack you. Although Philippe won't follow your heretical ways, he will certainly stand against Alexander should the pope make any more moves against you. He has proven to have enough backbone for that."

"I know, and Heinrich lost too many men when the ice broke at Botulph's Town to think about waging a war that isn't defensive. The Christian kingdoms of Iberia are too busy fighting off the hornet's nest of Saracens you roused against them. I only wish the Byzantines had continued their attacks on Sicilia. A handful of raids before they returned to fighting amongst themselves and against the Saracens hardly does me any good."

"Their emperor, Romanus, was being attacked from the East by the Saracens. You could hardly expect him to fight your wars while neglecting his own. He wouldn't remain on his throne for very long."

"I would do the same in his place," Harold admitted, "but those damn Sicilians are really Normans. It hasn't been so long since they invaded Sicilia. I doubt they've sated their bloodlust."

Their conversation was interrupted by a knock on the door. Harold opened the door and was surprised to find a young page standing in front of him.

"Yes?"

"I bear a message for the king." The child held out a small scroll. Harold took the vellum and dismissed the boy who seemed grateful to be out of the royal presence. Moving next to the fire, he began to read, his voice hardly loud enough for Aethelwine to hear.

"To Harold . . . from Alexander . . . No soul is truly lost. . . . We would like to discuss. . . . Let us know if this is mutually. . . ."

When he finished reading the scroll, Harold dropped it onto a table.

"Pope Alexander wishes to discuss the salvation of my soul and the souls of all other Saxons who have been led down the path of iniquity under my care. Now that he is beaten he is willing to permit me my throne if I submit to him."

"Submission to him would help redeem your soul . . . if it is truly in jeopardy."

Harold gave his friend a withering look, "I do not believe my soul to be in jeopardy, although I suppose that may be the devil's corrupting influence. If it will make you happy, I will seek spiritual advice in the matter."

Harold leaned into the hall and called for a servant. The page who had brought the letter from the pope was still in the corridor and hurried back at the king's summons.

"Do you know who Archbishop Æthelric is? He is dressed much as I am, but he is wrinkled and gnarled like an ancient tree. Bring him to me." As the boy was about to leave, Harold added, as an afterthought, "And bring my sons, Godwin and Edmund."

The boy took off at a run to find the Archbishop and Harold turned to Aethelwine, "I am doing this because you asked it of me. I do not for an instant believe my soul imperiled. Had He not wanted me to achieve victory over the Romans, He would have not allowed the ice to break beneath the Germans."

"Yet He might merely have been trying to teach you something, desirous of your return to the Church of Rome."

"If such be the case, I can hardly go against His will. If He wants me a Roman, I will place my soul in the care of the Roman Church. If He does not desire me to do so, I shall remain a Celt. I do not see Byzantium falling and she has been broken from Rome since my father's time."

"Do not heathens and Saracens invade Byzantium even as we speak?"

"And is it not true that the Byzantines fight them back? Perhaps if their new emperor, Romanus Diogenes, were captured or killed by the Saracens I could take your worries more seriously, but that's not likely to happen."

A knock on the door heralded the arrival of Edmund and Archbishop Æthelric. When they entered, Harold offered them some of the wine but refused to tell them why he had summoned them until they were joined by Godwin.

Harold made small talk while he waited for his oldest son to arrive. When the door opened, Colum-cille stood in the opening instead of Godwin. Although Harold was not entirely sure if he wanted the archbishop of York present, he invited him into the room.

Godwin eventually joined his father, his general disarray and grin on his face hinted that he had been sporting with a serving girl.

"I received a letter today. An Epiphany epistle if you like, since Pope Alexander seems to enjoy having me receive his letters on this day, which asks for reconciliation between the English and the Romans. My intention, when I first saw the letter, was to ask my cousin, Ulfyctel, his opinion of the matter. But while I was waiting, I decided to take my own council.

"I will not abdicate my throne or my power. Alexander is not in a position to try to force the issue."

Harold indicated the two archbishops.

AFTER HASTINGS

"We three magi are come to announce a miraculous birth. No, a rebirth. The Celtic Church is well and truly alive in England. Rome shall have no more power over us.

"Before those assembled in this room, I announce that I would have Godwin as my heir upon my death, may it be many years off."

Godwin's smile got even bigger when he heard his father's news.

"I would also like to announce a marriage and predict the offspring. Edmund, last year I worked toward your marriage to Arnketil's daughter. As you know, that is not going to happen. Instead, you shall marry into the House of Christ and become a priest. Don't be sad. You'll make a good priest. Eventually, you'll make a good archbishop. Perhaps of York, perhaps of Canterbury. Most likely, the decision will be your brother's.

"Both of you should remember that an arrow alone is weak. Many arrows together are strong. You must support each other in everything you do.

"Now, I feel the need for some entertainment."

Printed in Poland
by Amazon Fulfillment
Poland Sp. z o.o., Wrocław